Sneaker *Wave*

Sneaker *Wave*

by

Jeff Beamish

OOLICHAN BOOKS
FERNIE, BRITISH COLUMBIA, CANADA
2013

Library and Archives Canada Cataloguing in Publication

Beamish, Jeff, 1960-
Sneaker wave / Jeff Beamish.

ISBN 978-0-88982-278-8

I. Title.

PS8603.E3523S64 2011 C813'.6 C2011-905739-5

We gratefully acknowledge the financial support of the Canada Council for the Arts, the British Columbia Arts Council through the BC Ministry of Tourism, Culture, and the Arts, and the Government of Canada through the Canada Book Fund, for our publishing activities.

Published by
Oolichan Books
P.O. Box 2278
Fernie, British Columbia
Canada V0B 1M0

www.oolichan.com

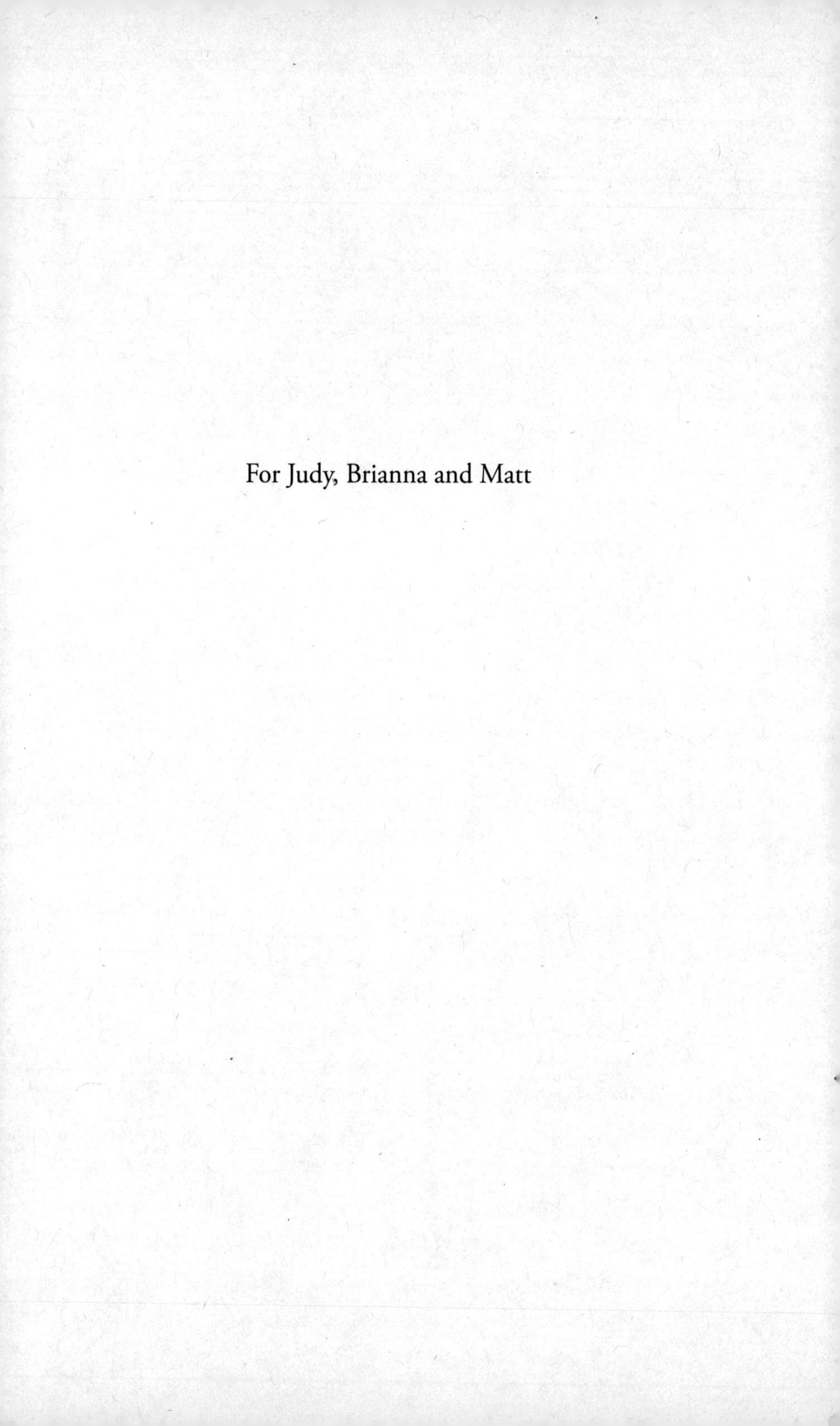

For Judy, Brianna and Matt

Author's Note:

This is a work of fiction. The town of Deception Pass is fictional, as are the characters and incidents in this story.

1

The boy detects a movement behind the television and looks up to see his father's impassive eyes squinting back at him through the living room window. Making no attempt to conceal himself, the man studies his son. With his jacket sleeve, he wipes away the small patch of fog left by his breath. Then he turns abruptly and leaves.

In this briefest of acts the boy senses something passing from his father to him. An invitation perhaps, the boy thinks, rising to his feet. He frowns, remembering, and sits.

Don't be a fool, he tells himself. Don't always be so quick to believe the slightest glance from your father means the end of whatever has choked your home into silence.

The boy's bony arms fold his knees into his chest as he wills himself not to indulge, not again, though before he realizes it he's at the front door, where he sees his father break into a run down the gravel driveway and out onto the street, his feet surprisingly quick in his rubber sandals. The boy doesn't pause to change out of his pajama bottoms or even to slip shoes on over his stocking feet.

On the dew-wet road he spots his father a half-block away running as effortlessly as he can with his thin limbs and their gangly Tin Man-like gait. The boy bursts into a sprint until he's close enough to hear his father's labored grunts and the snap of his sandals against the pavement. And this is how they continue – the man never glancing back as he keeps to the center of the road, the boy hugging the sidewalk about fifty feet to the rear, careful not to fall under his father's shadow. To those they pass, each gives the appearance of being alone – like two distant planets whose orbits are only connected by gravitational pull.

They run past the boy's school, his shuttered classroom, and turn onto the two-lane highway, where his father slides over to the gravel shoulder and falls into the comfortable stride of a jogger embracing a languid Sunday morning in the Pacific Northwest. The boy ignores his own sore feet, his burning throat, and focuses on how it's not much farther to the bridge, the one that leaps spectacularly from cliff-top to cliff-top across Deception Pass, the swirling channel of seawater that also gives its name to both the bridge and their town. Once they reach the bridge, the boy's sure they'll stop and take in the view, maybe squint through the low cloud towards the San Juan Islands in the distance, then continue across to the state park on the other side. Up until last year, each week they would wander the maze of trails carved through the park's thick Douglas firs and cedars until his father would turn to him and say, "What if I pretended to be lost; could you lead us home?"

The boy now smiles as he recalls the half-dozen times he directed the two of them through the rainforest while perched upon his father's shoulders, his feet swinging freely.

Up ahead his father reaches the bridge, which is teeming with weekend tourists taking in the dramatic drop to the channel below. At mid-span, the boy searches his father's movements for a sign he'll finally stop and motion him to catch up and join him in this longed-for awakening. Instead his father veers sharply right, charges at the low metal railing and dives over it head-first, disappearing from sight.

A man cradling a camera screams. A woman rushes to the handrail, looks down and pulls away violently, like something disturbing threatens to attach itself to her. The boy ignores them, like they're part of some parallel event, and creeps forward. When he reaches the railing, he stares down at the water churning below the bridge; all he sees is a circular ripple spiraling relentlessly outward like it will never stop.

"Does anyone see my dad?" he shouts.

The boy starts to pull himself up onto the railing so he can get a better look and perhaps spot his father surface and swim to shore. From behind, a woman ensnares him in her arms. He can smell cocoa butter on her skin, can hear her breathing unevenly. She doesn't speak, just squeezes him, and the boy doesn't struggle.

If a person were to ask if that boy was me, I might shrug or offer an equivocal response, not because such duplicity would so easily find a home in this recounting, but because at times I truly doubt being there. I do know it took three days for my father's shattered body to turn up, the current taking it out into the strait and down the coast toward Fort Ebey, where a beachcomber came across it. But did I really follow him out on to the bridge, watch him leap to his death, feel the comforting touch of a stranger? Or did I simply invent my role in his last moments, trying to force upon him one final connection that I desperately longed for, one tangible slice of camaraderie that had escaped us both in his final months?

These questions didn't surface in me immediately; such doubt took months to emerge. So when the police took my statement later that day, I didn't hesitate in telling them I had been on the bridge and that my father slipped and fell by accident. It was a claim driven mostly by the embarrassment of his suicide – and one that would become sadly ironic a dozen or so years later, when I claimed a second, unrelated tragedy I witnessed was also a mere accident.

Just like the first time, no one would believe me.

2

I waited for Sarah around the corner from her home, my hands stuffed in my pockets, my back resting against the trunk of my mother's faded brown Dodge, which like me stood out like an intruder on these streets dominated by BMWs and Lexuses, in this neighborhood inhabited by stock brokers and fortunate entrepreneurs.

Across the street a man in white tennis shorts ripped at a sap-soaked cedar hedge with an electric trimmer. Too stingy, I thought, to hire the cheap Mexican laborers that had drifted north to our town on the heels of the tranquility-seeking Californians, whose increasing presence saw seaside cottages replaced with rambling mansions and the local bowling alley converted into a mini-mall packed with art galleries and coffee shops where legit locals would go broke just lingering.

I waited, ignoring anxious glances from the hedge-trimmer, and from a grey-haired couple with tanned athletic legs and a black standard poodle that sniffed in my direction as they passed. I had lived here in Deception Pass for all of my seventeen years, and I knew these people saw me for what they thought I was: the son of a second-generation blue-collar man whose big-wheeled truck hugged the curb each afternoon outside one of five local taverns, those dark places with few windows, and even fewer outward glances. Or maybe they just saw me as trouble, especially if they'd heard about the mess I'd helped heap on Sarah two and a half weeks earlier during our screwed-up Memorial Day weekend trip to a small lake in the shadow of Mount Baker.

Either way, it was their problem, not mine.

As I turned to look back up the street toward Sarah's house, she was almost upon me, approaching quickly in cotton sweatpants and an old torn T-shirt a couple of sizes too big. She kissed me on the lips and said loud enough for anyone in earshot to hear, "So let's get the fuck out of here, Brady."

We left the car and walked the mile or so down the winding streets toward the tiny beachside commercial area. She noticed me staring at her, or, more exactly, her hair, which was tied in the back into two tight pigtails.

"I got bored," she said.

I smiled. "I hope people don't see us together and wonder if I've been successfully trolling the school playgrounds for twelve-year-olds."

"Wouldn't be the worst thing said about you lately."

"Don't you start too."

"Besides," she said, cupping her hands over her breasts, "I think I still look a little older than twelve. And I suspect you still find me appealing enough."

I laughed but said nothing. She had no idea. Pigtails or no pigtails, her beauty was like a sharp knife to my throat, one she wielded carelessly, almost with disinterest.

When we reached the beach, we climbed up onto the boardwalk which ran the length of the half-dozen older buildings that were crammed with small restaurants and gift shops. While the main, gentrified part of the downtown area had relocated a few miles inland, each of these old beach buildings retained its original moss-covered roof and faded cedar siding. Each went through a cycle of being mildewed and bleached by the winter rains and hot summer sun. Each survived as it stood because its owner refused to sell, perhaps waiting for serious money to be offered by a resort chain or condominium developer. Each kept its charm, and in some cases a decades-old menu, which for Sarah and I meant white clam chowder, sourdough bread and hot chocolate, in large and inexpensive servings.

In between sips and slurps, she elaborated on what I already knew, or suspected, about the fallout from our failed weekend trip: Her father's partially successful efforts to hobble her by trying to force her to stay home when not in school and only to see friends not named Brady. When she defied him and met up with me, the fights grew particularly nasty. He'd threatened to toss her out on the street, and when she called his bluff, he instead vowed to cut off the cash he'd set aside for her to attend the dental program at Western Washington University. Sarah hadn't completely caved in to this threat, but had backed down enough that lately I had hardly seen her. His real triumph, though, was convincing our school principal that I posed such a great threat to Sarah that she could only attend our high school graduation dinner/dance – which had been held last weekend – if she went as the date of some prick named Phillip Turnbull – the son of a respectable family friend.

Beneath our table, I slid a foot out of its flip-flop and ran it over her feet and shins, feeling the large scabs that still covered the cuts and scrapes from our misadventure. I sat back and watched her lips move tirelessly, pleased by how much I'd missed her.

We left the restaurant and ambled down to the beach, our backs warmed by the early June sun. We clamored over the rocks and around driftwood and logs deposited by winter storms, then slipped off our flip-flops and walked barefoot on the damp grey sand exposed by low tide. When we reached the ocean we let the rippling waves wash over the tops of our feet.

"So when will this shit stop?" I asked. "When will I no longer have to wait for you around the corner?"

Sarah picked up a smooth stone and with a sharp snap of her wrist skipped it across the water. She watched it touch the surface three or four times and laughed. "That corner thing I did for you," she said. "So you wouldn't have to lay eyes on him. I'm sure he knows who I'm with right now."

"So he's finally backing off," I muttered.

She threw another stone. "I wouldn't say that. He talked to his lawyer last week about trying to get a restraining order against you. Same as the last time; no legal grounds."

I considered this and shook my head.

"As for today, well, I think he's still basking in the glory of his grad night victory. He won't give up."

We walked further along the deserted beach, inching further out into the waves, which licked at our pant legs.

"So what did you think of Phillip Turnbull?" I asked.

She rolled her eyes. "What do you really want to ask me?"

"That's it. Just about Phillip Turnbull. No one else."

She stared at me, and when she didn't immediately respond, I added: "You seemed to like him."

She kicked a small spray of water in my direction.

"What I mean, well, you seemed to enjoy dancing with him."

"You want to ask me something, ask. You have since we got home from that fucked-up weekend, so go ahead…"

Sarah suddenly screamed as a large wave snuck in and crashed across our legs, soaking my pants and knocking her onto her back. I reached for her but she was gone, the force of the wave sweeping her away. I ran after her and when I reached her side she was rising to her feet, the wave retreating, her clothes dripping wet, a low laughter rising from her chest.

"You okay?" I asked.

She caught her breath and then smiled. "See, that's what we get for standing here arguing."

She pulled off her T-shirt and shook herself free of her sweatpants, and threw them to me. She turned, her wet underwear clinging to her skin, and walked out into the ocean until the water reached her shoulders. She began swimming, twisting smoothly into the deeper water. "You can join me, you know."

I stepped back toward the beach and dropped her clothes onto the sand, and then kicked off my flip-flops and began removing my sweatshirt. I threw them aside and started to undo my pants, but Sarah was already swimming for shore. I watched her draw closer, and couldn't help thinking that, given time, she could turn almost any mishap to her favor.

She emerged shivering, and rushed to my side, likely unaware that I regretted being too slow to join her. She hugged me tightly, her wet body leaving marks on my dry clothes.

I wrapped my arms around her, pretending to offer her protection from the wind, but really just clinging to the warmth of her body, wishing I could hang on forever. She pulled away suddenly, too soon, like she often did, without any apparent reason, as if she longed for change as much as anything else. She shook the water from her hair and began wringing it from her clothes.

"Better get you home before you freeze."

She nodded.

"You believe that theory that every seventh wave is the biggest?" I asked as she pulled her wet clothing back on. "Maybe that was the seventh."

She shook her head. "I've heard that's bull. That there's no pattern to the sea; not like that anyway. The waves are random, unpredictable, and you never know when a sneaker wave like that will wash in."

I shook my head. "I still think there's a pattern."

"God, Brady. Can't you just agree that sometimes shit happens, for no reason? It just happens."

As we walked back, she wrapped her arms tightly around my ribs. Her presence, which to me usually felt so painfully fleeting, carried a solid, fixed weight. I tried to revel in this, but soon became stuck on her words about shit happening: Were they meant to convey some cryptic message about some past transgression, or did they carry no hidden meaning at all, which suggested I was now swimming in paranoia about her, stupid fuck that I was?

Sarah shivered, and we quickened our pace, ignoring the expansive sea and its hidden danger.

Ten days later Sarah's father received a phone call that, at the time, I guiltily joked to myself was a 'stroke' of good fortune, at least for a suddenly sex-deprived teenager. Sadly for him, Sarah's uncle – her father's brother – had suffered a stroke while playing touch football in a Wednesday night after-work league. He was in hospital, two thousand miles away in Texas. Sarah's dad quickly began booking a flight to Houston the next morning for himself, his wife, Diane, Sarah and Sarah's younger brother, Dan. Then he remembered one small detail. Sarah had two final exams the next day and another on Friday. So he booked her on a Saturday afternoon flight. She was to study on the flight down, stay Saturday and Sunday and fly home that night, studying again, for her last two exams on Monday.

After her first exam on the Thursday, Sarah dropped by my locker. Her smile gave way to a more pensive expression as she told me about her uncle and her family's sudden departure for the airport that morning. Then she invited me over for dinner that night, just me and her.

"I know exactly what you need," she said when she opened the door that night, leading me up the stairs. She walked right past her room and straight into her parents' room, and pushed me onto their bed.

"In here?" I half protested.

"Yes."

Sarah parted the sheets on the king-size bed with a flick of her long wrist and laughed as she started undressing. Soon she sat upright on my lap with her legs curled behind my back, the most she was ever willing to submit.

Later, when we began getting dressed, I pointed to the sheets. "You are going to wash those, right?"

She started making the bed, pausing just once to glance up at me like I was stupid for not understanding the sheets would remain unwashed, or perhaps stupid for not asking the one question she knew I so badly wanted to ask.

As we said goodnight outside her front door, she grabbed my hand and pulled me onto the front lawn, her bare feet leading us out onto the heavy dew. She nodded at the decaying cottage next door that we could just make out through the trees.

"That place finally gets torn down next week? My Dad's pretty happy. He talked to his friend who owns the construction company. They're subdividing the lot and building two 4,500 square foot homes."

I nodded. "Guess your dad would be happy. Those partiers who lived there – they didn't exactly fit in with the rest of the neighborhood. No BMW, just a shitty old pickup."

"My dad's friend stripped everything of value from the house, appliances and stuff, and the rest of the garbage will get bulldozed into a pile along with the wrecked house and trucked to the dump. Goodbye scumbags, hello higher property values."

I nodded, then Sarah tugged on my belt, an absent-minded gesture I suspected belied what really went through her mind. "So I was thinking," she said. "You know how we got screwed out of a proper grad party together? That Phillip Turnbull crap and then home early. Well, I was looking around over there. That shithole's still got a big old deck out back, some furniture we could haul outside, even running water, until Monday at least. I thought of hosting a small party right here tomorrow night – small 'cause I fly out Saturday – but anyway, then I thought, why not next door? We can wreck what we want, not clean up a thing. Not even bother the neighbors too much, because that place is almost in the middle of a forest. We could run an extension cord from here, so we got power."

I grinned. "Sounds like you've given this some thought."

She shrugged.

"If so, have you thought about this? Whether Luke and Sam are invited."

It was a question I'd asked a dozen or so times in the months I'd known her. What about Luke and Sam? Sarah never outright rejected them, not like her girlfriends did. But she never really embraced them either, and who could blame her. And now, after the shit they'd caused on the Memorial Day weekend, I waited for her to fall to the ground laughing, because it was an outrageously funny request. At least I could tell them I tried.

Instead she gave me a surprised look. "Of course they're invited."

She turned away and walked back up the front walkway, her wet feet leaving footprints on the light-colored tile. As she moved, I thought about how I should have anticipated this – how I should have grasped the depth of what had changed over that weekend. I didn't though – at least not quickly enough.

Sarah called out, "Later, babe." She turned and closed the door before I had time to speak, before I could see what was coming.

I'd known Luke for four years, ever since he had thrust himself into my life, like a noose around my neck, or maybe his. I still owed him, not so much for what he'd done for me when we first met, but for what he'd given up. Sam had arrived in town two years later, and Luke and I liked to tell him we kept him around only because he often passed for twenty-one, the legal age to buy beer in Washington State. He had a face that was prematurely aged by a receding hairline and the first hint of a wrinkle between his eyes. The truth, though, was that Sam's scheming stupidity ruled our lives more than we liked to admit.

As I walked home from Sarah's, my mind slipped back to the various calamities that ensued after Sam's arrival. One in particular would never dull in clarity, which was fine, because, after more than one year had passed, I could finally look back on it and smile. Even if that smile was tinged with regret.

On a cool April night, we had lurched away from our seaside town, Sam loosely gripping the faded Ford Escort's steering wheel as he plunged in and out of breaches in rush-hour traffic, stomping alternately on the brake and gas so we nearly tumbled from our seats, the three of us swearing and laughing. Luke, steadying himself with one hand on the dashboard, shouted in sharp bursts, his voice strangely hopeful: Did you see that car we cut off, that bitch behind the wheel, or, hey guys, how did I do back in town? So how did I do? In the backseat I fought for space with two children's car seats and a diaper bag bursting at the zipper with God knows what. I considered tossing out that shit, shedding any reminder it brought, but worried my buddies would see this as an admission of guilt, not as a way of making space. So instead I joked and hollered and grinned like I wasn't bothered by anything; pretended I wasn't looking up and down the highway for hints we'd gone too far. We crossed underneath Interstate 5's six concrete lanes, ignoring the echoing hum of congestion. Tires-screeching, we veered onto a side street where traffic thinned to nothing, and suddenly we were unleashed, shooting along a series of deserted farm roads, Sam negotiating the twists and turns like he'd driven the route hundreds of times, or simply felt at ease being terminally lost. Either way I was comforted to see someone move without hesitation, without a hint of fear.

Familiar breezes spiced with salt and seaweed slowly dissolved, leaving us with inland air steeped with car exhaust and the heavy stink of manure, a sickly sweet smell, a constant reminder that on that evening everything had changed. Luke raged on about the eleven one-dollar bills and the handful of coins he'd discovered in the car's ashtray; how it was enough to buy burgers and three thirty-two-ounce sodas at the Jack in the Box on the way home. I just wanted to ask this: On the way home from what?

Sam pulled onto a wide gravel lane, and Luke noticed it first, the sign proclaiming, City of Sedro Woolley Garbage Dump. He turned to Sam.

"Relax, dude," Sam told him. "You gotta have some faith."

Sam followed the road toward the mounds of garbage that rose up neatly, wondrously, before a backdrop of thick green cedars. We approached a chain-link gate blocking the road, and Sam didn't slow down, or even hit the gas to take a run at it. Instead he crashed straight through it like it didn't exist, not even flinching as the gate came apart at the hinges and bounced noisily off the car's roof.

"You guys know my neighbor, the state wildlife guy who likes to listen to that '80s punk music like it's some hot shit?" Sam asked. "Well, I got to talking to him, and he told me something in confidence."

Luke looked back at me and grinned, like, sure, we knew.

"Well," Sam continued, "seems this dump's been overrun by black bears. No fence the city's built has managed to keep them out. Seven or eight of them snuck across the border from Canada, from their homes in the Rocky Mountains."

"It's the Coast Mountains just north," I corrected him.

"Anyway," he said, "they're bringing some serious problems, presenting a substantial danger to people and all, so the state's sending a team in here tomorrow to tranquilize them. Gonna relocate the whole works."

I nodded. "So tonight's the last chance to see them."

Sam laughed. "No. Tonight's the last chance to perform a public service."

Before I could ask what he meant, Sam slowed and, just like that, we spotted our first bear fifty or so feet away, sitting comfortably on its hind legs as it foraged through a green garbage bag with paws more nimble than I imagined possible. Even in the dying light we easily picked out another, and a third, and a fourth. Sam skidded to a stop.

"They's so cool," Luke whispered. "Never seen one in the wild before."

Sam smiled. "Told you. Enjoy the sight for a moment, then we gotta get to work before it's dark."

He reached under his seat, grinning at our puzzled expressions, and pulled out a knapsack, dumping its contents to reveal a stack of fireworks he'd no doubt bought on the Swinomish Indian Reserve. "A couple of Black Bombs and

Screechers placed at the feet of the lead bear, and just picture it, we'll have an incredible stampede. They'll hightail their asses back to Canada, and we'll save the State a whole pile of work. And have one huge shitload of fun to boot."

Luke looked at the bears and back at Sam. "They're bears, not horses or wildebeests or some shit like that. They don't stampede. And how would you know the lead bear? Even if there was such a thing."

"Only one way to find out, my friend."

Sam scooped up the fireworks and climbed out of the car, his knapsack in one hand, a lighter in the other. He didn't look back to see if we'd follow – he knew at least I would.

"You comin'?" I asked Luke, hesitating.

He stared out at the bears, unusually pensive, his dark eyes partly obscured behind long black hair. "You surprised by how fast I got me this car tonight?" he asked.

I shook my head, an honest answer. "So…" I said, and when he remained silent, I shrugged and leapt out and began jogging toward Sam, who in the distance was grappling with his lighter.

Halfway to Sam I stopped suddenly, almost defiantly, and stared off into the encroaching darkness. I glanced back at the car, then ahead to Sam, and thought about the distance I'd at that moment put between myself and my friends, and about how it was something I should do more often. It wouldn't be easy. People sometimes talked about the three of us like we were one person, or at least three souls inhabiting one seriously flawed body. But while Luke and Sam were comfortable with this characterization, I wasn't. We were far less alike than everyone thought, and if they couldn't see it, well, to hell with them.

I had considered telling Luke and Sam that night that I was losing interest in some of the reckless shit we did, maybe explaining how we were one rolled car away from never seeing our high school graduation in another year. Once I had made my point, I could begin making myself scarce. I pondered this idea, felt it gaining momentum, gathering depth, and I embraced it with an urgency that surprised me.

Up ahead, Sam had finally won control of his lighter, and the fireworks began. He lobbed a short black device at the bear, and it exploded with a loud pop. The animal stood, confused, and Sam followed up with a ten-shot Roman candle, the last three or four flaming balls striking the bear's chest. The whine of a Screecher finally sent it into retreat, and Sam screamed, "Run you fucker," before moving on to his next target.

After he had dispatched a second bear into the wilderness with another noisy volley, I turned back to the car to see if Luke had moved to join us. He sat frozen, his eyes focused on Sam, and I knew what he thought, even if no one else did, because when it came to Luke they just didn't get it.

I did though, and for a rare moment I felt I could start to make sense of the rest of it, of everything else. Inadvertently my hands flew up and began nervously pointing – Luke, Sam, then back at me – like they were beginning to unlock some equation. "What the fuck?" I whispered to myself, and stuffed them back into my pockets, alarmed by my body's initiative.

My feet moved forward seemingly on their own, panicked, and I wanted to scream out to Luke and Sam that they were in danger. My hands flew up again, and this time I let them because with the strange sequence of motion came a calm, one broken only by Sam's scream, a sound so distant that part of me wondered if the noise was real.

"Run," he shouted, and he tore past me, a large bear bounding toward us, like a twilight shadow sprung to life.

I hesitated, sure the surge of doom I had just felt was

distant, not immediate. Seconds later I too burst into a run, not so much because I was frightened by the sound of the bear's paws clicking across the gravel road, but because I was worried my friends might drive off without me. I joined Sam at the car as he yanked on the door and found it locked. "Luke," he screamed, pounding on the window, "open the door. Quick."

Luke didn't move, just smiled coldly and pointed at the bear, which was covering the last forty feet to the car in a sprint. This ugly mess of matted fur and pointed teeth had somehow shed its awkward lumbering stride and had transformed itself into a streamlined beauty, fast, powerful, and – I finally realized – lethal.

"Luke," I screamed, retreating behind the car with Sam.

The bear came straight at the Escort, veering slightly to the driver's side and toward the back where I cowered with Sam. We scrambled along the passenger side, almost tripping over each other as we raced to the car's front, trying to keep metal and glass between us and the beast, now close enough to reveal tan coloring on its muzzle and what I swore was anger in its eyes.

It hesitated before charging around the car. Sam and I lunged away, swearing at Luke as we ran, pounding our fists on the side windows, fearing we'd slip and fall and be eviscerated.

Sam suddenly broke away from the car and raced down the road we had driven in on, and I expected the bear to pursue him, the one with the fireworks, the one who had started all this. Instead the animal stayed with me as Sam disappeared into the night, and I was too busy running for my life to recognize the burst of insight that should have accompanied the bear's choice.

We looped around the car once more, like in a life-and-death game of musical chairs. I pleaded for the bear to lose interest, but who knew how many times it had been tormented by people as it fought to eke out an existence on garbage and crap.

The bear stopped, grunted twice and rose on its hind legs, like it was contemplating climbing over the car to reach me. That was when I saw two more creeping out of the garbage, stealth-like in the dusk, deployed by some hidden force of nature. I pounded at the Ford's side window with my fists until the glass cracked and finally shattered, as did the skin around my knuckles, leaving bloody streaks on the window. Before I could plunge my hand inside, I was forced away from the car by my pursuer, as if he was herding me in the direction of the other bears.

I was pleading with Luke, tears mixing with the sweat on my face, when above my head something exploded with a resonating thud, sending red, green and blue sparks swirling down around me. Seconds later a second firework erupted, followed by a third, all of them a chemical cacophony but also a sign that Sam hadn't deserted me and was singeing his hands to put each shot perfectly on target.

Four more deafening bangs followed in succession, suffusing the sky above the car with a delight of colors and leaving the night bursting with so many shooting stars, albeit fake ones, that even a perennial loser would feel hope. Inside the car Luke pressed his face against the window. Eyes wide and child-like, he stared up at the bright shower that engulfed us and smiled, not noticing the bears retreating into the night nor the flashing blue and red lights from a single police car that pulled up behind us.

For not the last time in my life, I forgave him, helplessly.

As Luke, Sam and I walked to Sarah's I thought about how this party was one of the few pleasure-driven ideas in my Grade 12 year not given a breach birth by Sam. And that, I thought, had to be a good thing, didn't it?

Sarah answered her door with a hammer in her hand.

"A Luke-control instrument?" Sam asked.

"No. It would take more than a hammer to stop him," Sarah said. "This is the key to the place next door."

Luke grabbed it from her hand. "Show me the way. I'll do the honors."

Three whacks of the hammer knocked the knob off the back door, and we were inside.

Luke wandered to the wall where it looked like the kitchen table once sat. Without saying a word, he lifted his foot and kicked a hole in it.

"Luke," I warned him.

"This place is getting ripped down anyway. Am I wrong? So who gets hurt if we begin the process tonight."

I looked at Sarah, and she just laughed.

"I'm gonna like this," he said, putting his foot through the wall in another spot.

We carried two, heavy, stain-steeped sofas out to the patio, plus seven or eight chairs. Then, in a rare moment of inspiration, Sam brought out a couple of scratched end-tables and two garish lamps. We followed his lead with whatever furniture remained, and in no time we had transformed the deck into an outdoor living room – albeit a shabby one. Sam hooked an MP3 player, speakers and the lamps to an extension cord, and ran it back to Sarah's, while Luke struggled with three ice-laden coolers. Sarah popped open a beer and surveyed our work, a pleased expression on her face.

An hour later people began arriving, and with them emerged the one flaw in our brilliant set-up. Some weren't invited. Okay, most weren't invited. But we lacked a door to slam in their face, or a private property line to point to, so suddenly everyone was welcome, and it seemed everyone began showing up, nearly half of them female, much to Luke and Sam's delight.

I soon felt strangely like an unknown guest, not a host.

"So who did you invite, Brady?" Sarah asked as more people arrived, spilling off the deck into the house and out into the yard.

"Not all these people. Just Sam and Luke, and two other guys and their girlfriends. How about you?"

"Maybe a dozen people or so."

Sarah looked at Luke and Sam and laughed. "I won't ask them how many they asked."

I heard a familiar voice rise above the crowd, "I like it – very Bohemian," and turned to see Phillip Turnbull and three of his friends arrive. I wasn't impressed. Nothing could have pissed me off more. It felt like something Sarah's old man might have organized.

"Hi, Sarah," Phillip said with a smile, a bag full of booze and mix tucked under his arm.

"Least they brought their own drinks," Sarah said to me after they'd gone by.

"You know," I said to her, "if this is too much, if you've got a bad feeling about this, I can go back to your house and call the cops. Just say I'm a neighbor complaining, and I bet they'd disperse everyone."

She took a sip from a plastic glass of rum and Coke, and I wondered which Sarah would answer.

"So why wreck the party?" she exclaimed before she turned and was gone.

Luke idled up to me. "You see that dweeb Phillip Turnbull?"

"I noticed him."

"Might be looking to pick up where he left off at the grad party. I can kick his ass out of here if you like."

"Don't worry about it, Luke."

Sam was suddenly beside us. "You still going on about Phillip Turnbull, Luke. Forget him. He's harmless enough. The one Brady should be worried about is Nick Harris."

"Why?" I asked.

"Just look at him talking to Sarah."

From where we stood on the deck, we could see Nick leaning far too close to Sarah, saying something we couldn't hear. Whatever it was, she found it funny.

"You know, Brady," Sam said, "Nick's already got two steady girlfriends he's screwing regularly, and a third one he sees on the side. Think he might want one more."

And who could blame him. Sarah looked stunning. As I sipped my beer I wondered which was the most pertinent question: How did I get her in the first place, or how much longer could I hang onto her?

I stood on my own and watched Sarah and Nick. Her eyes, always so direct and piercing with me, frequently looked down as the two of them talked, a shy smile forming on her lips each time. I imagined at those moments he said something flattering, something seductive. I moved to where I could no longer see them.

This is the truth about how we are judged in high school: While we are given letter grades to mark our academic progress, just as important but never recorded on paper is our social standing, a twisted measure of our worth that we carry with us every moment. Simply, you are either revered or reviled, or you slip into a third group, the vast invisible and ordinary crowd in between. The rules are simple. Once your peers judge you – and they do, very quickly – it takes something remarkable to change your status, though it can be done.

I moved through school in the shadows of the invisible crowd, while Luke firmly planted himself with those to be reviled, and Sam defied all logic by taking a tenuous spot in all three categories.

Sarah, who oddly cared the least about any of this shit, had without effort emerged as someone to be revered, as were most of her female friends, excluding Cynthia, the sweetest of all, whose thick body elicited insults like Dyke, Lesbo, Chunky. But you are who you hang with, and just being around Sarah gave us all a boost in status, especially Cynthia and me.

Before Sarah arrived I had never cared about my status, and was content to live beneath the radar, out of the sight of humiliation. That is, until the Thursday morning after my first date with her, when she caught up to me just outside the school's parking lot. She called out my name, and I felt immediate delight in that and the way she quickened her stride to catch up to me. She looped her arm around mine, and I could see the look of admiration, of jealousy, from other students, and I liked it, as pathetic as that sounds.

On our date I'd taken her to a movie in Oak Harbor, a sappy romantic comedy where the wooden characters tossed around cutesy lines we'd soon forget. When we walked from the theater into the October-night mist, I looked over at her and asked, "So what now?"

I started to offer a quick suggestion but she stopped walking and said, "I guess you want to fuck."

As I grappled for a response, any response, she added, "Isn't that what you guys always like to do? To fuck?"

"Umm…I was going to suggest we drive out to the naval air force base on the edge of town – only ten minutes from here – and I could show you the fighter jets taking off and landing."

She nodded. "So we'd fuck out there in the darkness in the car? In your mother's car?"

I shrugged. "I just thought…the planes, F/A-18 Hornets,

are kind of cool if you haven't seen them before. If you're new to town. I suppose we could, you know, talk while we wait or something. There's like nineteen squadrons at the base, and they aren't on any schedule you can figure out, so you've got to wait for the fighters."

We started walking again, and she studied me before turning her gaze forward. She seemed to be processing my words, searching for some kind of subtext that even I didn't think really existed.

"I'd like that," she said, the edge mostly gone from her voice. "Watch the planes and talk."

I nodded, and suddenly found myself trying to suppress a grin at some wicked words that rolled across my mind, taunting me to spit them out.

"What?" she asked.

I contemplated not answering, before saying, "Does that mean we're not going to fuck?"

Sarah laughed so hard she almost folded herself in half, and even I, in what would become the least thoughtful year of my life, realized that this was what she needed the most right then.

In time I found I could read her moods and I extended that first night into a pretty incredible run, maybe based on the sheer luck of saying and doing the right thing that night, maybe on the basis of something else I'd never know.

So what do you do when someone tries to usurp such good fortune, tries to put you back down? Do you step aside and calmly tell yourself you weren't worthy of such serendipity in the first place? Or do you do whatever it takes to hold on? I guzzled down some more beer and wondered how Nick Harris's face would look if it met a baseball bat head on, or how his well-tuned body would move after being struck down by my mother's car.

As the night lurched forward, the dozen beer I'd brought

quickly disappeared from the cooler, and I suspected I'd pounded back all but a couple of them. The individual voices in the house and on the deck became a blur of noise, a ringing in my ear. The music blared and would be turned down again by Cynthia or someone else only to blare again. The spilled drinks on the deck stuck to my feet, the overpowering smell of beer, liquor and weed made me nauseous. Someone puked against a cedar tree in the back yard. People laughed, shouted, screamed.

At one point Luke and Sam pushed me over to where Sarah stood. A huge grin consumed Luke's face, and his hands massaged a paper bag. "We've been looking for you two," he said. "Got a presentation to make."

"Oh, really," Sarah said.

"We do," Sam laughed. "Me and Luke got you a graduation gift."

"You're gonna love this," Luke mumbled, reaching into the bag, producing a small bottle and handing it to Sarah. "Happy graduation, Sarah."

She looked at it puzzled, and began reading the label.

"The product is called Sweet Release," Sam shouted to anyone in earshot. "You give it to your boyfriend, or boyfriends, and it makes their semen taste sweeter. This particular flavor is wild apple."

A few people laughed, and Luke and Sam pored over Sarah's expression. "C'mon Sarah, at least blush or something," Sam said.

"What's to blush about," she said. "What a great gift. Especially with me going off to college and all."

I slipped away unnoticed, and moved around the front of the house where cars lined the street. I sat on the front steps and watched the dark clouds race quickly beneath the night sky.

By 12:30, more people had arrived, and the party

appeared to be drifting in two competing directions. On the deck, dozens of teens danced and laughed in what I suspect was the version of the party Sarah had envisioned. Inside the house a more sporadic beat ensued as Luke and a crowd of others punched holes in the walls, pried up floorboards, and smashed bathroom mirrors and fixtures. They broke anything that looked breakable, like they hated the house. Two groups, and me unsure I belonged in either one.

One guy I didn't recognize ran from the house and made a beeline directly for a pile of discarded lumber in the yard. He picked up a four-by-four post. Screaming, he charged back at the door but at the last moment veered to his right and threw the timber through a bedroom window. A spray of broken glass glistened in the light from the room. Some cheered, some looked on in amazement. Sarah simply nodded. Inside, a group turned the post into a battering ram, trying to create their own doors where only walls had existed.

As I watched – wondering how long it would take for the police to be called – Cynthia jerked me away to dance. I struggled to match the beat of the hip-hop sound, and she laughed, as if she thought my awkward movements were some deliberate mockery of the song.

Suddenly Sarah was there, dancing with us, then she moved on to someone else. Bodies crashed and throbbed. So did my head.

I clumsily hugged Cynthia and retreated to the deck's rotting edge, where I watched Sarah move with the grace and confidence of someone who knows the world will give her whatever she asks for. Someone who's discovered a secret and is now unstoppable. She danced with everyone around her, Phillip Turnbull and Nick Harris included.

The sound of smashing and banging from inside the house rose above the music, and that's probably why I didn't hear his voice.

He tugged sharply on my shirt to get my attention.

When I turned around, I almost laughed when I saw him. He stood there in slippers and a plaid housecoat, as if he'd gone downstairs to let the cat in and had taken a wrong turn. I started to ask him if he was sleepwalking, then he cut me off.

"Get Sarah Roberts here, right now."

"Who are you?"

"The neighbor you're keeping awake. Now get her."

"This isn't her party. I'm not even sure she's here."

But Sarah had already seen him, and stood at my side. "Mr. Opal," she said.

"Come with me," he yelled above the music.

Sarah began to say something, but stopped when she saw she couldn't be heard. Luke and Sam suddenly staggered over.

Luke looked at our latest guest and did laugh out loud. "You wanna drink or blaze, dude?" he asked.

The neighbor looked at Luke long and hard, then turned back to Sarah. He motioned with his finger for her to follow, and started through the trees towards her house.

Sarah looked at me and rolled her eyes, but followed him. Luke looked at me and Sam, then slid one finger across his neck in a cutting motion. I nodded.

The three of us followed them into the darkness, and not one of us returned.

At least not as we'd left.

When I sat down years later to write down what transpired in Sarah's house, these were the first words that spilled across the page: "I never saw what engulfed us in the next few moments. Never heard its roar, felt its shake or smelled the foul sediment it churned in its wash. Never sensed, until it was too late, the death and loss it carried."

It was dreck – purple prose screaming for a lighter touch – but worse than that, it was a lie. It would come to me as

I slowly reworked those three short sentences that I had to be blind, stupid, or both, not to have seen it coming, not to have seen *something* coming. No, the true surprises that would blindside me and everyone else were all still to come, one by one, in the years that followed that night.

I didn't witness how those remaining at the party learned what happened in Sarah's garage, though that doesn't matter: I trust the version told to me by others over what my own dulled eyes had seen. To those back at the abandoned house, Sarah re-emerged in a breathless sprint to the deck. She pulled the plug on the MP3 player and closed her eyes for a moment as she grappled for composure.

"Everyone's got to go," she yelled. "The police are coming..."

Then a pause.

"There's been an accident."

3

The minutes following Tom Opal's accident and Sarah's run for help passed in a blur of moving bodies. A small group of people left the party and rushed to the garage, staring, whispering and pacing in a way that suggested genuine concern for the man who lay unconscious on the garage floor. A second wave of partiers followed them, ambling in with excited yells of "look at that poor fucker" and "that's so sick, man." One of them, whose name escaped me, attempted some basic CPR. "There's a faint pulse," he said. After several minutes he turned away, shook his head and stood silently with the rest of us waiting for the ambulance. More than half the party-goers turned and left within a minute of getting a look inside the garage, clearly anticipating the trouble bearing down on us.

I stood outside the garage at the side of the house, my back leaning into the stucco wall for support. "Hurry up," I whispered to the distant ambulance. I didn't notice Brittany's arrival.

"Brady," she coaxed, "what happened?"

I couldn't look at her face. Her wide mouth seemed like a provocation when I needed to imagine myself in control. I shook my head and waited for her to leave.

She repeated her question, and I turned my back on her.

"What do you want, bitch?" Luke demanded, attempting to stand face to face with her, to appear imposing, even though she was taller.

"I want to know what happened." Her voice bordered on hysterical.

"None of your fucken business."

"Like hell it isn't."

"Like Sarah said, someone had an accident." Luke's voice was cold, nearly menacing.

"Well, you guys would know. I saw you follow him over here."

Luke's mouth opened but emitted no sound. His hands tightened. Finally he said, "I don't answer to you."

Brittany turned and left, and Luke looked at me. I think we both knew we hadn't heard the last of her.

In the distance, a siren drew closer, its wail cutting in and out of the wind. Moments later it stopped outside and I mustered all my courage to walk around front to the driveway and to the double-wide front garage door, which was now lifting up, the chain of its opener making a slow chugging sound.

As the paramedics hurried inside, I wondered if Tom Opal might actually be alive. I, too, had detected a faint pulse when I checked his wrist and neck right after it happened. But it belied everything else I sensed when I leaned over him. He had grown cold in my hands and his eyes had rolled back, as if a shroud had enveloped him.

I couldn't help but watch the paramedics as they went to work efficiently, checking Tom Opal's pulse, airway and pupils, stabilizing his head and neck, covering his face with an oxygen mask and finally placing a collar on his neck. They began stripping away his housecoat, looking for God only knows what.

"What happened?" one of them asked.

"He fell...on his head," Sarah said.

They glanced at each other but said nothing.

They stood, whispered back and forth, and one of them disappeared to the ambulance and returned a short time later with a backboard, which they slid carefully underneath Tom Opal's body. As they carried him out, they didn't answer when Sarah asked if he'd be alright.

"Stay here," one said to Sarah. "The police are on their way."

Then they were gone, leaving us alone in the garage. By now, the noise of car engines pervaded the neighborhood as a final wave of partiers left.

"Watch the door – I'm closing it," Sarah yelled, and Luke and Sam and I stepped out of the garage and on to the driveway as the door lowered. Sarah and a few of her girlfriends went the other way, into her house. I looked back at the house, and thought about how I wasn't given enough time to make a choice.

Almost immediately a police car pulled up, its silent unhurried arrival contrasting with the ambulance's departure. A single officer, thick and slow-moving, got out. "Where's the owner of the house?" he asked.

We pointed to the front door. I felt Luke at my side, felt his breath in my ear, and as the cop walked by I debated this: Why did Luke suspect I'd be the first to fold – because he knew I possessed an inherent weakness or because he believed I had a propensity for doing the right thing? Luke placed an arm on my shoulder and whispered my name. I shivered. The cop opened the front door, and I wanted to yell out, to tell him what had happened, I swear to God, but that wasn't part of the deal. He disappeared inside, Sarah shutting the door behind him.

Our code of silence began.

If you had told me then how long it would last, I would have laughed. I would have thought you were crazy. Then again, I always seemed to underestimate what my friends were capable of doing.

More police cars arrived and more cops went inside. Two came out and took our names, and told us not to leave, not just yet. Neighbors slowly emerged from their houses, drawn by flashes of light, burst of sirens or the whiff of tragedy.

When I saw her, I knew immediately who she was. Unlike the other neighbors who stood on the road or their front yards keeping their distance, she ran up the driveway on her bare feet toward two cops. A tangle of dark hair covered her eyes.

"My husband," she said, "he came over here earlier."

"What's your husband's name?" one cop asked.

She sobbed at the question.

It took another twenty minutes before police began treating Sarah's house as a crime scene. For her part, Sarah had done exactly what the four of us had agreed, recounting the so-called accident in a sincere and straightforward manner. She told the senior officer that the four of us accompanied Mr. Opal to her property to speak, away from the noise. Sarah entered the garage first through the unlocked side door, walked down the three steps, followed by Mr. Opal, Luke, Sam and me. But he'd lost his balance – Sarah suggested he caught the toe of a slipper on a step – and fell forward, striking his head on the metal base of an exercise bike. He was out cold.

But something troubled the cops. They'd called the hospital, to see if Mr. Opal had regained consciousness. He hadn't, I overheard one say. In fact, his condition was grave, something we'd all feared from the moment it happened but still found difficult to believe. The cops huddled together in the garage, their faces showing nothing as they talked.

They told Sarah they wanted to investigate the accident some more. Two cops went to the vacant house next door and came back telling their colleagues they should take a look. Then we were asked who was hosting the party, and we explained, as if this justified what they had seen, that the house next door was already wrecked and abandoned and about to be torn down.

The teens who remained at Sarah's – those ten or so too loyal or stupid to leave – were assembled in her living room and interviewed one at a time, by various cops in various empty rooms. Sam, Luke and I sat on the front step, awaiting our turn, while Sarah and a cop went to the phone in the kitchen for another unpleasant task – phoning her parents.

Sam popped open a ginger ale he'd grabbed from the fridge. I almost jumped at the sound.

Two hours ago I would have been horrified at the suggestion Sarah's dad would find out about the party. Now what he thought or felt suddenly seemed unimportant.

"They're suspicious," Sam said suddenly.

"Who?" I asked.

"The cops. Who do you think?"

We sat in silence until a voice behind us asked, "Which one of you is Brady Joseph?"

We all turned around to see a cop in a brown suit standing at the door. His pants showed too much sock, his thinning hair did a poor job of covering the top of his scalp, his chin disappeared far too quickly into his neck, all of which gave the impression of a country hick. I hadn't seen him arrive, and got the feeling he'd been called in from home.

"I'm Detective Morrison," he said, as if this was supposed to mean something.

I struggled to my feet, finding it difficult to find my balance. "I'm Brady."

He studied me, and said, "Come with me." I followed him into the house and into Sarah's parents' bedroom.

"So, Brady...," he said, rubbing his large forehead. "Tell me what happened."

I wish I could say how torn I felt at this moment. How my first impulse was to do the right thing. Instead I launched into our story, almost effortlessly.

When I finished, Detective Morrison nodded and scribbled into a small notepad. His hands were steady, and it struck me in an odd way they seemed to be the only solid thing in the house.

He smiled at me, and said, "Too bad the party got ruined, huh?"

I stared at him in disbelief, and realized, even in my drunken state, he'd thrown out this supposed passing comment to gauge my reaction, perhaps to see if I possessed an ounce of decency or if I'd agree that, yes, the party's early end was the night's main tragedy.

"You know," he pressed on, "there's just one thing I'd like to clear up. I heard Luke was really ticked to have the party interrupted. Made some threat against Mr. Opal before you left the party."

I must have looked puzzled.

"Maybe made this sign," Detective Morrison said, running his thumb across his throat in a slitting motion.

"Oh, that," I said, suddenly alarmed. "That was Luke saying Sarah was in trouble. Because her dad was sure to find out she was at the party with me and my friends. Her dad isn't too fond of some of us. That's all."

"So you're saying it wasn't directed at Mr. Opal?"

"God, no."

He thought about this for a moment, his face revealing nothing, before finally moving to the door.

"Your friend, Luke. Bit of a hothead isn't he? Got a juvenile record for assault, uttering threats, a few other things. And, of course, auto theft, like you and that Simpson kid."

I nodded.

"How long have you been friends for?"

I shrugged. "Since Grade 8. Luke and his dad followed Luke's step-brother, Paul, to town when Paul got posted to the naval airforce base on Whidbey Island."

He nodded. "So what else can you tell me about Luke?"

"What do you mean?"

"Anything about him. Just curious what kind of person he is."

I shook my head, annoyed. What did this cop expect? That I'd detail how Luke had amazed me from the start. Like how he had, without a single lesson, without being old enough even to apply for a license, somehow learned to drive a car, or more to the point, how to steal one, knowing to avoid the models with factory-installed immobilizers because they'd cut the gasoline flow before you got half a block, that's if you could start the car at all. Luke had always pretty much picked things up on his own, sometimes out of boredom, or anger, but mostly out of necessity. Not just learning how to cook for himself, but how to shoplift the ingredients.

"He's a guy, just like the rest of us," I said finally.

The detective put his hand on the doorknob and studied me carefully. "I'm sure when Mr. Opal regains consciousness he'll be able to corroborate everything you've told me. Of course, if he's got a different version of what happened, well, then if someone's not telling the truth, well, he'd be in a mess of trouble. You know what I'm saying."

"Why are you telling me that?"

He nodded. "Nice meeting you, Brady. I know we'll be talking again."

He closed the door softly, and I swore I saw it buckle in its frame. I gripped the Roberts' dresser to steady myself and closed my eyes.

In the hall, Detective Morrison passed me again, this time followed by Luke, whose eyes searched mine, found nothing, then looked away. The two of them disappeared into Sarah's brother's room.

The house had fallen eerily quiet. No music, no laughter, just hushed whispers. I heard Cynthia's voice from the kitchen, and peeked around the corner to see her and Brittany talking with Sarah at the table. I watched Sarah for no more than fifteen seconds, afraid of being seen, and I knew she couldn't change in that short time – grow older, heavier, more composed, right before my eyes – but she did.

I retreated to the shadows, where I waited, for what I don't know. Eventually, Detective Morrison walked by and told me I could go home. We could all go home. But we were to stay out of the garage, because they weren't done in there yet.

Luke suddenly stood next to me. "Where's Sam?" I asked.

Luke shrugged. "Left right after he was questioned. So did most others."

He followed me to the kitchen. The three girls looked up, their faces frozen in a look I'd soon see far too often.

"What can we do, Sarah?" I asked.

As soon as I spoke I regretted my choice of words. As she looked at me, then Luke, I wondered if she'd laugh hysterically or say something like, "Haven't you done enough already?"

Instead, she simply said, "Go home."

Not an order, not an acerbic put-down. Just a statement.

I wanted to go put my arms around her, tell her everything would be okay. Something inside told me this would be the right thing to do. But like so many times before, I ignored the message.

"Goodnight," I said, and left.

At the door, Luke placed his hand on my back. "I'll walk you home, buddy."

He opened the front door, but instead of walking out, we stepped in. Into a space that stretched out forever; so large none of us could ever escape it.

4

On the Memorial Day weekend, three weeks before Sarah's disastrous party, Sam pulled off the highway into a run-down gas station, as arranged, and we quickly spotted the four girls gathered around a picnic table in a rest stop-like area past the pumps. We parked next to the Lexus that Brittany acted like she owned, even if it was her father's. Sam nudged Luke and nodded toward the girls – I assumed specifically Chantel – before making some crude motion with his tongue. Luke shrieked with anticipation.

All I could do was laugh. Not just at them, but at everything, especially the familiarity of our route, which had taken us alongside withering fields of tulips on Highway 20, through Burlington's teetering downtown and even directly past the road to the garbage dump. So much had changed in the year since our arrest for auto theft, since our incarceration in a juvenile detention centre. And so much hadn't.

Take the car. Sam liked to boast that he worked hard to buy the 1973 Ford Mustang. He had, of course, even if most of the work involved selling B.C. bud to our classmates. But at least it wasn't stolen. And then there was this trip, a Memorial Day weekend camping foray – something Sam announced began the two-week countdown to our high school graduation party. Or put another way, another lame-ass excursion into some stupid shit. The only difference was this time we wouldn't be alone.

The girls had chosen as our meeting spot this shitty town with the not-exactly endearing name of Concrete, which today rested in its usual catatonic state.

"Hey, ladies," Sam hollered as we approached, his voice tinged with so much hope I almost had to look away.

They stared at us, expressions fatigued, and said nothing. Finally Chantel stepped forward, wearing long earrings, cream-colored capris, pricy suede sandals and scoops of unnecessary makeup. Sam was right; she was hot. But her outfit was not exactly practical for camping. I looked at her once more, my mind summing it all up in a paradox: Expensive but worthless.

She folded her arms across her chest and ventured, "The deal was we'd meet at six. It's almost seven. Care to explain?"

"Traffic's a bitch, you know the story," Sam replied.

"Uh huh," nodded Brittany, no longer looking at us.

We waited, our feet shifting, until Cynthia turned to Sarah and asked, "You sure about this, girl? About you going with the three of them, 'cause there's lots of room with us."

"Not too late to change your mind," Chantel agreed.

Sarah studied me seriously for a moment, before flashing a quick grin, like a glimpse of upper thigh beneath a skirt that left you wondering if you really saw it. She got up, walked around the table and kissed me hard, as if to answer Cynthia's question.

Then she reached back and slipped the lid off a steaming coffee.

"Car's full of beer; Sam got hisself five 24-packs of Bud," Luke said, smiling proudly. "Why would you drink that?"

"I'm not," she said. "Brady is. And then he's driving."

Luke and Sam laughed out loud.

"I don't want coffee," I protested.

"Tough shit," she said.

"I've only had a couple of beers."

She raised an eyebrow.

"C'mon, mix it up with her, Brady," Sam cajoled.

"Hey buddy, looks like you've become her bitch," Luke chipped in.

I shrugged and took the cup from her.

A smile formed on Sam's face. "Let's hope Sarah doesn't decide she wants you to wipe her ass, Brady."

Luke laughed so hard he spat loose a gob of drool that hung off his face until he quickly wiped it away with his sleeve.

"That's so gross," Chantel said. She stood quickly, and Cynthia and Brittany both followed her into the gas station's store, all three of them looking back at us with an expression that left me puzzled. Not disgust, but something deeper. It came to me suddenly that whatever it was, it was survival-driven – some instinct that screamed for them to grab Sarah and get her away from Luke, maybe from me and Sam too. I stared at the three of them, a pang of envy rising.

I pumped gas while Luke leaned against the Mustang and Sam droned on about how the '73 Mach 1 Fastback was the last kick-ass Mustang model, making it incredibly sought-after. I started to tell him that that might have been so if the car hadn't been ruined by rust and neglect, and then a polite voice interrupted.

"Excuse me, sir. You finished with that squeegee?"

For a moment Luke just stared at the kid who looked to be about sixteen. I'm not sure what threw Luke off more: The teen's perfectly fitted, blue pinstriped suit, or the fact he'd called Luke sir.

Luke handed him the squeegee and, when the kid

was gone, leaned toward me and Sam and shook his head. "What a tool."

"Look," Sam said, "there's another one of them." And there was, a second teen, this one with hair falling below his collar, in contrast to the first guy whose head was shaved nearly clean, but still neatly dressed in a suit.

They both went inside and paid for their gas, and shot looks at Chantel, Brittany and Cynthia, who lingered inside the store. Then the pair ambled out with cans of soda, eventually wandering over to where Sarah still sat. They ignored her at first, then the short-haired kid turned and said something to her.

"Shit," Sam said with mock awe, "wonder if they're Jehovahs like my crazy parents. Might be trying to save Sarah's soul."

"Or maybe they's just some spoiled rich little pricks," Luke replied. "Think they can do whatever."

The kid placed his foot on the bench across from Sarah and leaned forward in conversation.

"I wish we were close enough to hear," Sam said. "Might be hilarious."

We watched them for less than a minute, which was all it took for a look of annoyance to sweep across Sarah's face. She finally motioned for the teens to leave. Just like everything she did, it was a direct move – a wave of the hand as if to dismiss a servant.

They didn't move.

"Should we bail her out, guys?" Luke asked.

"I'd kind of like to see her kick the shit out of the both of them," Sam laughed.

"She's okay," I said.

Sarah's mouth became more animated, as if half the words she uttered started with the letter F.

"Guys," Luke said.

"She's okay," I repeated, suddenly a little unsure.

Now the teen spoke with force too, almost loud enough for us to pick up his words.

"C'mon," Luke said starting to walk. As we neared, I picked up just one word the guy uttered: "Bitch."

The pair didn't see Luke coming until he was about ten feet away, then they turned and stepped back from the table.

"You trash want something?" Luke said.

The short-haired kid raised his hands, as if he were caught in a stick-up, and moved back. "We don't want any trouble. We were just talking."

Luke moved straight at him. "I heard what you called her."

The long-haired kid started to take a step toward Luke but saw me and Sam approaching as well and he too backed away. They moved around us toward the gas station's pumps. The short-haired kid turned suddenly as they retreated, "Speaking of trash, what the four of you doing here? On your way to a hillbilly convention or something?"

Luke later swore what happened next wasn't premeditated. Who really knew? He grabbed the coffee cup from my hand and took off across the parking lot.

They saw him coming, and with the flick of a remote unlocked the doors of a Ford Expedition and climbed inside. Its engine started, but before the short-haired kid got it in gear, Luke raised his foot and slammed the sole of his boot across the door.

Sam and I were now halfway across the parking lot. Sarah yelled, "Let them go."

The SUV's window rolled down. "If there's a dent you're dead, you fucken piece of shit," the kid snarled at Luke, the veins in his forehead bulging.

No way could the kid have prepared himself for what happened next. I'd seen it before, or at least something like it, so I knew how Luke could move without thought or hesitation, without his eyes betraying him. Before I could call out or grab his arm, he emptied the cup of hot coffee onto the driver, the same way you'd spew out a vile insult or throw a sucker punch.

The kid screamed and writhed, the coffee washing over his lower face, neck and upper chest. Maybe Luke had enough pity not to go for his eyes; maybe his aim was just off. The kid brushed his face and neck with his hands, like his own touch would make it better, then reached down and pulled up his suit jacket and held it tightly against his reddened flesh. I started to reach in to help – don't ask me how – and he interpreted my move as another attack. He slammed the SUV into gear and pounded on the gas pedal, the vehicle barely missing Sarah and her girlfriends, who'd come running over. We watched their vehicle tear onto the highway and out of sight, its screeching tires resounding in our heads.

It was several seconds before anyone spoke.

Sarah turned to Luke, her words slow, angry. "I know you think you were trying to help me..."

"Just standin' up for you."

"I don't need that kind of help. What is wrong with you?"

"You're welcome, Sarah."

I put my hand on Luke's shoulder. "You should have just let him go."

Luke knocked my hand away. "I did that because you did nothing, like always."

Brittany stepped forward. "What happened?"

"I did nothing because they were leaving," I told him.

Luke shook his head. "If you'd just stood up..."

"Shut up, Luke," Sarah screamed, and they glared at each other until Brittany asked, "Are you finally gonna come with us, Sarah? Or maybe you want to be the next one to share a cell with these losers."

"Damn right I'm coming with you."

"Wait a minute," Sam objected. "Don't let this spoil the weekend."

She stared at him, lips curled. "That's a rip. Scalded flesh can do that. And by the way, Sam, Brady's coming with us."

She turned to her friends. "That okay?"

"Do we have a choice?" Brittany asked.

Sarah ignored her, and her three friends grudgingly nodded or gave tepid approval with a shrug, while their eyes pressed down upon me like I was shit fouling the heel of their best shoes.

"Screw that," Sam said. "Brady, you don't want to go with them, do you? You want to go with us, like we planned. Remember, we didn't start this."

"Brady..." Luke pressured.

My chest tightened.

"C'mon, Brady," Sarah said, "grab your things."

I wish I could say that, in hindsight, this moment somehow stood out for what it really was. That the decision I faced had correctly presented itself as momentous. Instead, the opposite was true. It masqueraded as just another mundane choice, one in an infinite number we face each day.

I wish too I had recognized the opportunity presenting itself. A perfectly valid excuse to bow out of whatever else Luke and Sam had in store for us, not just that weekend but in the months to come. In other words, a fresh start away from them, something I had strangely hungered for when I stood alone in a garbage dump awash in bears.

None of this came to me when I looked at Luke, his wild eyes hinting at some future trouble, and then at Sam, who rocked gently from side to side like the beer he'd pounded down would forever hold sway over him. Worse than that, when I turned back to Sarah, her impatient stare, her arms folded across a bright rose-colored tank top, I saw little more than an object of my desire, someone I wanted to laugh with and touch this weekend, not someone who needed my protection.

So this is how I succumbed to my shallowest of thoughts, my most primitive feelings. How my mind, my anger, fixated on Sarah's friends, those bitches, who continued to glare at me like I didn't belong, like they were dismayed I didn't understand that some gulfs were too deep to be transcended.

When my words came out they were mostly directed at Sarah's girlfriends and barely suppressed a crippling fuck you. "We should stick to our original plan, and Sarah should come with me and the guys, at least for tonight."

"You think so," she said. "Chosen to be loyal to your friends, such as they are. But why would you think I'd even consider going with you three after all the shit that just happened?"

"Because. It's probably the wrong thing to do, but it might continue to be an interesting weekend." I told her.

Her girlfriends shook their heads in disgust, giving me a small smear of satisfaction. Luke nodded in approval and Sam offered a simple, "He's so right."

"Let's go, Sarah," Cynthia said turning back to their car. "The three of them, they're so retarded."

Sarah didn't move. Her eyes widened, and she said, "It might be interesting. That's the best you can do?"

I nodded. She crept close, her eyes searching mine for confirmation of what she already knew: That I understood her more than all of her friends, that I saw what everyone else missed. And she knew, of course, I had just deployed this insight to manipulate her like a drug dealer would an addict.

But now she grinned, she grinned, and I had her.

All I needed to do was forget that she deserved better.

5

When I arrived home from Sarah's party, I fell into bed and struggled for hours to expunge Tom Opal from my head, only to find he'd seep back in the moment it took to inhale, the small jagged fragments of memory quickly reassembling themselves into something monstrous. He persisted even in the half sleep I finally settled for, before that too slipped away and I realized I lay hopelessly wide awake. Out of bed I stumbled and turned bleary-eyed to the blood-red numbers on my digital clock – 9:03. I fumbled on sweatpants and a T-shirt and trudged downstairs, my legs stiff for the first time I could remember, my head aching, my ears ringing from last night's music and alcohol or both. At the worn-out bottom step, I paused. Inadvertently my hand flew up, like it had that night at the garbage dump, and began pointing, first straight ahead to the front door, then to the garage door on my right, then to the living room's wide entrance on my left, and finally to the short ground-floor hallway that led back to the kitchen.

I motioned again to each of the four portals, and repeated the movements a third time, then a fourth, giving each entrance-way a number. Front door 1, garage door 2, and so on. My hand continued the sequence another half-dozen or so times, for reasons I didn't understand.

My fingers pointed one more time at the front door, and stopped there. Images began swimming through my mind, out of order at first, until they too fell into sequence: A boy tottering in the driveway outside his home, listening to the sounds of the upstairs shower running and his mother's voice spitting out a country tune, though sounding more to him like she was coughing up water and cheap shampoo. This noise tumbling through the open bathroom window was confirmation she somehow hadn't heard the crash he felt sure by now would have brought the whole neighborhood to see what a complete screw-up he was and would always be.

He tore past the part-shed, part-greenhouse she'd built one weekend instead of taking him on a camping trip with his Grade 5 class, the trip that everyone went on but him, and that's why he'd called her a bitch, and she'd slapped his face, the first and only time she'd struck him. The shed/greenhouse, whatever, now lay on its side, glass shattered, the burgeoning marijuana crop mostly crushed and partly uprooted, though she'd surely harvest and smoke the damaged plants for medicinal reasons and all that shit. He could barely believe the old car that had sat in the driveway forever had rolled forward only ten feet and struck with enough momentum to topple the structure, because she was no carpenter, only someone with a twisted sense of determination.

As he ran past the damage, he tried not to listen for the sound of their cat, Mr. Orange, another victim of circumstance, who lay crushed but still alive and whimpering under the wreckage, his warm nap place slowly becoming a coffin. The boy knew he had to hurry.

He threw open the front door, and then stopped to

shut it quietly behind him. He rushed to the stairs, looked up them and turned into the living room. He had made his choice; he had chosen this seemingly mundane portal. The living room door. So all that was left to do was quickly remove his shoes and stuff them under the sofa, before taking a seat, flipping on the television with the remote and striking a relaxed pose that suggested he'd been there all morning, never venturing outside into a world where, in time, everything became uncoupled.

From upstairs he heard the metallic screech of the shower door being opened, and the noise prompted a rush of panic inside him. What if she figured out he'd slid the old car out of gear and panicked when it began rolling forward? What if she finally came to realize he was too much trouble? He knew these thoughts would do him no good, and managed to blot them out. He stared blankly at the television and waited, not even daring to wonder what his decision to sneak back inside and forsake the damn cat revealed about him.

The moment felt strangely vivid, like it was etching itself upon him. The sodden smell of rot rising from the house's partially flooded crawlspace. The sound of his mother moving through some far-off space in their small house, conflicted as always, possibly avoiding him and whatever sad reminder he carried, possibly seeking him out with lonely desperation. She called his name, and he nearly jumped.

"Brady. Where are you?"

"Brady."

My name resonated once more, but now the woman's voice, my mother's, carried the weight of many more years. And it emanated from the kitchen, where I imagined she sat with a cigarette and coffee. "What are you doing out there? Come and tell me about your party last night."

My hand rolled into action again, but this time more earnestly. Front door, garage door, living room entrance, hallway, kitchen. One, two, three, four, five. Each of them a choice.

"Be right there, Mom," I shouted, and went to the phone in the living room, where I called the hospital and learned Tom Opal was still in critical condition. I felt unsure if this was good news or not.

In the kitchen I grabbed a glass of water without looking at my mother, gulped it down, and sat across from her at the table.

Now forty-two, my mom, who wore a lime-green housecoat as she hunched over the morning paper, looked closer to fifty in the harsh sunlight. As she had left for work yesterday afternoon, her hair neatly brushed and face covered in make-up, she passed for someone closer to thirty.

"I heard you come down the stairs a couple of minutes ago, but you just stopped. Sit down, I've got something to tell you."

"Something happened last night," I blurted out. "At Sarah's party."

"What?" she asked, her worried face, I assumed, more a reaction to my expression than my words.

I looked down at the badly stained kitchen table. "Mr. Opal, Sarah's neighbor, he came over to quiet things down. But he had a fall in Sarah's garage....He's in the hospital, I think in a coma."

"Oh my God," she said. "Mr. Opal. Yes, I know him. Came in for the odd drink. Works in Albertsons doesn't he?"

I shrugged.

"That's terrible," she said. "How did it happen?"

"I told you. He fell in the garage."

"Well, how? People don't just fall and seriously injure themselves."

I stared at her in disbelief. "Apparently they do, Mom."

She took a deep sip of her coffee, followed by a drag on her cigarette. "Did anyone see it happen?"

"Yeah. We'd gone to the garage to talk to him. Away from the music. Me and Sarah and Luke and Sam. As we entered the garage he lost his balance on the steps and fell forward. I don't know how a fall can do that to you, but it did."

"Oh my God."

"Would you quit saying that, Mom."

"What?"

"That, oh my God. It's freaking me out."

She looked puzzled, but nodded.

"Is Sarah okay?"

"Mom, Sarah didn't fall. Of course she's okay."

"That's not what I meant, Brady. What a terrible thing to have happen in your home. And oh my God, the four of you witnessing it."

I sighed. "Saw it, heard it. His head sounded like a pumpkin cracking when you drop it on the road."

"How horrible. Are Sarah's parents and brother coming home?"

"I guess."

"She's gonna be in trouble with her dad, isn't she? She wasn't supposed to have a big party, was she?"

"She didn't technically have it. It was at the vacant house next door, on the huge deck in the backyard. It wasn't a big party....Well, it wasn't supposed to be, but a bunch of people showed up and it got noisy."

"Poor Sarah."

"Would you quit saying that," I yelled. "She's okay. It's Mr. Opal who's not."

My mom looked stunned by the anger in my voice. Truth is, her relationship with Sarah annoyed me, though I wasn't sure exactly why. I hadn't been surprised they showed true affection for each other. After all, my mom's easy to talk to and easier to like, as long as you don't have to live with her. But what had surprised me was the way they confided in one another, at the kitchen table or out on our tiny back patio. My mom with her personal stories of failed relationships, bad decisions, wasted potential, each one, I'm sure, intended to provide Sarah with an example of how not to live her life. Sarah with her talk about her dreams, her plans, all of it steeped in so much honesty that it sent me running because who am I to hear her innermost thoughts? And talk of sex. Sometimes they shared a joint – that alone made me cringe – while they discussed my mom's sexual conquests, and I wondered if, in my absence, Sarah chipped in details of our encounters.

"I know it's upsetting," Mom said.

I shrugged and studied the table again. "That's not all. The police came. They're suspicious. They seem to think Luke did something to hurt Mr. Opal."

"Oh," she said.

"They don't seem convinced it was an accident."

"How come?"

"I don't know. You'd have to ask them."

My mom went to the counter and poured herself more coffee. I studied her when she returned to the table, noticing the bags under her eyes. They seemed to stay with her longer each morning, sometimes still hanging in when she left for work in the afternoon.

"You out late last night, Mom?"

"Got home before you did. Why didn't you come talk to me when you came in?"

"I didn't want to wake you."

"You should when you're upset like this."

"I'm not upset."

"Could have fooled me."

"Maybe I didn't want to wake you because I didn't know if you'd be alone in there. It being a weekend night."

She bristled, stubbed her cigarette out, and lit another one. "That's not fair, Brady."

"Hey, you asked why I didn't wake you. I'm just answering."

"Well your answer's not fair. I haven't had someone over like that for quite some time."

"Right, at least a couple of weeks."

Anger flashed in her eyes, and she started to speak and stopped. "I don't have to justify what I do. I've been single for most of the last seventeen years, and I've brought back only a handful of guys to my room at night, or on weekends, or however the fuck you put it."

"Long as it's not one of my teachers again."

"I'm going to ignore that."

"Of course, at least you came home on those nights," I said, quickly getting up and going to the sink, where I ran another glass of cold water and gulped it down, keeping my back to her.

"Brady," she said, "is there something you want to tell me?"

Her trace of cognition caught me off guard, though only for a second. I turned to face her, keeping the distance of the kitchen between us because, well, distance was what I was accustomed to. "Seventeen years, mom, and you're just getting around to asking me that now."

Her face froze in horror, either because she realized what I was getting at, or because she had figured out that what had happened to Mr. Opal was no accident.

"Yeah, Mom, there is something I want to tell you."

She stubbed out her cigarette, her hand twitching.

"Remember when your greenhouse shed collapsed and

killed Mr. Orange? It was me. I knocked the old car out of gear."

She smiled, looking relieved. "Brady." Her voice was soft, like bare feet on sharp stones. "You think I didn't know that? I was pissed, sure, but you forgive people you love, and besides, I didn't want another huge fight – you were always so hard on me."

"I was always so…I gotta go, Mom."

I left the kitchen, forgetting she had said she wanted to tell me something.

I showered and fried some sausages, but wasn't hungry. About eleven I began pacing back and forth by the telephone. Finally I picked it up and dialed Sarah's cell phone number, and held my breath.

"Hello." Mr. Roberts' harsh voice.

"Hello," he repeated.

"Mr. Roberts. It's Brady."

In the second before he hung up I heard him mutter a single word: "fucker."

For two hours I wandered around town, through the downtown area bustling with shoppers and the occasional tourist, past the small hospital (did it contain a morgue, I wondered), down along the beach, up past the expensive homes. I stopped two blocks from Sarah's place and tried to work up the courage to go knock on her door. All I could envision, though, was her father opening it.

Ever since my first date with Sarah, I had become an object she expertly deployed to antagonize him, so much so that I sometimes felt that was my sole purpose in her life. When I picked her up the first night we went out, her father had asked me my name, and once we'd left he Googled it and the name of our high school, quickly stumbling upon some student gossip website and some blogs and Facebook entries that detailed the basics of my auto theft arrest with Luke and Sam a half-year earlier. It was mostly all there: How we had caught a break and only had to serve six weeks in the summer followed by twelve straight weekends once school began, all of it in a "cozy" juvenile detention centre, not an adult facility. And how the state prosecutor believed, but couldn't prove, we'd stolen a dozen or so cars before that, all of which had the shit run out of them and had been dumped somewhere. The website also heaped plenty of other crap on us, such as some of Luke's prior arrests, tales of our penchant for selling and using drugs, whatever.

When I had dropped Sarah back at home her dad was waiting. He brought me inside for a drink – I thought a soda but he offered me beer, which I declined – and told us both what he'd found on the Internet. He had finished his scotch, and violently shook the ice in his glass while waiting for us to respond.

"So what," Sarah shrugged at last.

He rattled his ice once more. "Haven't we been through this before?"

She turned to me. "I'll walk you to the door," she said, and I wondered what I wasn't being told. I also wondered why I hadn't seen this coming.

"So that's it?" I asked at the door, sure she'd given in to her father's wishes.

She smiled, wrapping her hands around my arm, her eyes round. "So what are you doing tomorrow night?"

What followed over the ensuing months wasn't always pleasant, especially with Sarah flaunting our relationship at every opportunity. I could only imagine the fights that ensued at her house on the nights she returned home and said she'd been out with me. She would tell me her father's animosity wasn't as bad as I thought, that, really, everything was cool. Then she'd flash a wicked grin.

And all that was back in the relatively carefree days, before I helped nearly get Sarah killed on the Memorial Day weekend and before I helped leave a nearly dead man in her garage.

I ran all this through my mind once more, and turned for home.

When I walked in the door, Mom appeared from the kitchen, looking, well, clean, maybe even fresh. As though she'd scrubbed away the night before and our bitter conversation that morning.

"I'm cooking lasagna for dinner," she said, smiling, waiting for a response, like it was some momentous occasion we'd be eating a meal together. When she didn't get one, she continued, "Then I was hoping you'd go out with me tonight to see a movie."

"A movie?"

"Yes, how about it? Unless you've already got plans with the second prettiest girl in town."

"Her dad won't even take a message for her."

"Time will change that. So, what do you say?"

"I dunno."

"C'mon, it'll cheer you up."

"I don't need cheering up."

"Okay. It will take your mind off things."

I shrugged, hoping she'd keep insisting.

"That a yes."

"I guess."

The Deception Pass movie theater had only one screen, but if you liked the movie it happened to be playing, it saved you a trip to Oak Harbor or Anacortes, our more prosperous neighbors to the south and north. That night, as Mom and I headed out on the town, the movie being offered was a romantic comedy, which I was prepared to embrace as a welcome distraction, no matter how lame.

We bought our tickets and stood in the small line outside on the sidewalk, waiting for the early show to let out. The smell of garlic from a popular Italian restaurant across the street filled the air. Mom grabbed my arm, and pulled me close. "Smells better than what I made for dinner, huh?"

I smiled. "No it doesn't."

She squeezed my arm and looked into my eyes. I found it difficult to meet her gaze. "Oh, Brady. You know, if I had met a guy anything like you in the past fifteen or so years, I would have married him on the spot."

I looked back at her and this time she looked away, her lips tightening.

"Hey Brady," said a couple of guys from school as they walked by. "Killer party last night," one said. They laughed, and were gone.

"What charming friends you have, Brady," Mom said.

Then another voice greeted us, this one from a woman in her late thirties approaching from across the street. "Kathy? Thought that was you."

"Amanda, what a surprise." My mom grabbed my arm, "Oh, this is my son Brady. Brady, Amanda."

"Nice to meet you," the woman said. Short but athletic-looking, she carried a bag of groceries, which she moved into her left hand so she could shake my hand.

"Brady. Kathy's told me so much about you."

I looked to the front of the line, awkwardly hoping it would begin moving.

"Brady, I've told you about Amanda before," Mom said. "She's the one I sometimes go walking with."

I searched my memory and could recall hearing her name several times, but never meeting her. I nodded.

"You'll have to excuse Brady. He's a little out of sorts. There was an accident at a party last night at his girlfriend's house."

Amanda nodded. "I heard. Tom Opal. Amy, a friend of mine, works in the Albertsons. A reporter from the *Lookout* came by to interview her. They're doing a front page story for tomorrow's edition."

I wanted to run, just tear up the road into the darkness, not sure what I found most disturbing: That almost the entire town already knew about Tom Opal's injury or that the few who didn't would read about it in tomorrow's newspaper.

Amanda must have seen the alarm on my face. "Oh Brady, you must feel terrible about what happened…it being at your girlfriend's house. It's just one of those tragic, unfortunate things."

"He's doing just fine," my mom said. "He doesn't let things bother him too much; he's my rock."

Amanda seemed to ignore Mom, and without speaking she stepped up, placed her arms around me and squeezed hard. I felt my body turn rigid, and then slowly relax, my muscles succumbing to her firm arms, my objections melting in the sweet fragrance of her hair and neck. Tears built quickly in my eyes, leaving me feeling alarmed, ashamed. I closed my eyes hard and tried to hide my face so no one would see.

My sleep improved only slightly that night, and I awoke exhausted. I pounded down the stairs, finding myself stopping on the bottom one. Without thinking, I pushed my right hand forward and pointed. Front door, garage door, living room and kitchen. I did it three more times, counting as I went. In the coming years, no matter where I lived or where I slept, it would be a morning ritual I'd repeat in some way, only vaguely aware I was doing it.

Today, my choice was obvious. I went to the front door and grabbed the Sunday edition of the *Deception Pass Lookout.* My heart skipped when I saw on the front page a black and white photo of Tom Opal, wearing his Albertsons uniform. Above it was a headline, "Popular local man in coma after accident." I went back inside and sat down in the living room. The story said:

Tom Opal, a life-long Deception Pass resident, suffered a serious head injury Saturday when he fell while making a noise complaint at a neighbor's house on Bayshore Drive.

Mr. Opal, 44, is unconscious and is listed in critical condition at Deception Pass Hospital. News of his condition shocked many who know him as meat manager at Albertsons for the past seven years and as the past-president of Deception Pass Little League.

Deception Pass police detective Tom Morrison said Mr. Opal lost consciousness when he fell forward onto the cement floor in a neighbor's garage about 12:30 a.m.

Det. Morrison said Mr. Opal had gone to the backyard of a vacant house across the street to complain about noise from a party. There, he spotted the 17-year-old daughter of another neighbor, local doctor Ian Roberts, and accompanied her next door to her home's garage to speak away from the noise.

Det. Morrison said Mr. Opal apparently tripped walking down three steps and struck his head. Present were Mr. Roberts' daughter and three other teens.

"It appears to be one of those sad, tragic events," Det. Morrison said. "The teens said he fell suddenly and struck his head on the base of an exercise bike.

"I wish I could say his prognosis is good, but doctors are unsure."

Det. Morrison said police are investigating the circumstances around the accident.

"It's routine," he said. "But anytime you have a large number of people partying and someone gets badly hurt, there is cause for investigation."

Dr. Roman Termal said Mr. Opal suffered a rare injury to an artery during the fall, which snapped his head back.

The damage to the artery, which runs from the spine to the back of the brain, led to clotting in the artery and swelling in the brain, Dr. Termal said.

Though Mr. Opal also suffered a skull fracture and some bruising of the brain from the fall, it is the injury to the artery, caused by snapping back of the head, that is troublesome, he said.

Allanis Hogart, who worked with Mr. Opal for the past five years, said staff at Albertsons were devastated when they heard Saturday morning about the accident.

Ms. Hogart had opened the store at 8 a.m. when family friend David Leman arrived to inform staff of the accident.

"As soon as I saw David's face I knew something was wrong," Ms. Hogart said. "All of us are hoping and praying he pulls through."

Staff immediately set up a condolences card next to an arrangement of flowers inside the store. "By noon," Hogart said, "the card was full. So I grabbed another off the shelf and it wasn't long before that one was full, then another and another. By 5 p.m. we had eight cards to deliver to Mrs. Opal and her family."

Mr. Hogart said Mr. Opal's wife Eunice, and daughter Kerry, 6, and son, Josh, 8, are taking the news as expected.

"They're crushed. Just crushed. But Eunice is a strong woman."

The story went on to detail Opal's involvement in Little

League, to offer accounts of his sense of humor. But only a dozen or so words stuck in my mind: *Det. Morrison said police are investigating the circumstances around the accident.*

An hour later Sarah phoned, the sound of her voice strangely comforting.

"Sarah. I tried to call yesterday. Your dad...."

"Gonna take care of that."

"Can I see you today?"

"Listen. You work today, right? So meet me tonight about eleven at that little playground around the corner from my house. You know the one?"

"Sure. About eleven."

"Either way I'll be there."

"What do you mean either way?"

Our town's lone full-service gas station, my part-time employer for the last year and a half, was located on Main Street at the north end of town. Unlike the stations on the highway between Anacortes and Oak Harbor, it drew the majority of our town's local customers, something that didn't escape me as I arrived for an eight-hour shift of pumping gas. I thought of the newspaper article identifying Sarah and three teens as being present at Mr. Opal's unfortunate "accident." In some ways it would have been better if the story had identified me – that way every second customer, or what seemed like it, might not have asked if I was there. "Hey, Brady," they'd say, "heard about Mr. Opal. It's terrible." Then they'd pause. "Were you at the party?" I'd nod, and wait for it. "Did you see what happened?" Some didn't ask, maybe feeling they didn't know me well enough. Some of those who did ask poked and prodded for the inside story, for some piece of information not available in the paper, for something they could tell their families over dinner or friends over a beer. A couple, I felt, regarded me with suspicion, casting doubt over the events as outlined in the newspaper. "How could someone fall?" their expressions said. "How?"

In the early afternoon, Luke and Sam walked by while I filled up an SUV. They both nodded and said nothing, going into the service station's small food store. Their routine usually consisted of each buying a Pepsi, making them paying customers, then hanging around chatting with me for the next half hour or so. Lucy Stall, the officious college student who patrolled behind the counter inside, hated their presence, and once told me it would cost me my job if they got caught stealing anything. Through the glass window I saw the cold stare she gave them today. She had pressed me at the start of my shift for details of the "accident," asking me twice if Luke was in the garage when it happened, her inference obvious. "Why don't you ask him yourself," I'd said. "I'm sure he'll be by today." Luke and Sam paid for sodas, and emerged to take seats on the outside bench. I collected $75 from the SUV's owner, rang it up before a silent Lucy, then went out and stood beside them.

"You been paid a visit today by that cop?" Luke asked, dispensing with small-talk.

"No."

"Well you will. He's already talked to Sam. Bet you'll be next."

"What does he want?"

"The truth," Sam said. "Least that's what he told me. Seems Mr. Opal was covered with some pretty heavy bruises around his abdomen. That's the cop's word – abdomen. Anyway, he wanted to know where he got 'em. I told him to ask Mrs. Opal. Like how the fuck would we know, right?"

I took a deep breath.

"Has he talked to you, Luke?"

Luke's hands began to move rapidly over the bottle, twisting the cap on and off. "Not actually talked. Seems like he hopes to get what he wants from the three of you. You two and Sarah."

"Well he won't," Sam said. "We've already told him what happened, right guys. That's it."

We waited in silence as Tyler, another gas jockey, walked back inside, counting twenties, after fueling an RV.

"But that prick did come by my place," Luke said. "He had a search warrant. Didn't say nothing. Looked through my room, took some clothes and boots."

"What?" I asked.

"Stuff I had on that night, at Sarah's."

"Fuck," I whispered.

Luke laughed. "So when he was leaving, I yelled, 'Good luck, you fuckers, but you won't find anything. And I want that stuff back or some compensation.' They looked pissed."

"How's Opal?" I asked. "You guys heard anything?"

"Still in a coma, the cop told me. Told me it doesn't look good."

"That's bullshit," Luke said. "He's just trying to make us feel desperate. Bet Opal recovers, then it'll be his word against ours, and there are four of us. That's assuming he'd even be able to remember what happened after getting his brain rattled."

"And if he doesn't recover?" I said.

"Then it will be our word against no one."

A pickup truck cruised in to the far set of pumps, and I jogged out to it, relieved to leave my friends. The truck's tinted windows obscured my view of its lone passenger, but as the driver's side window dropped I found myself face to face with Detective Morrison. "Good afternoon, Brady. I see you're having a chat with your friends."

I froze for a second, lost for words, my face reddening.

"Fill'er up with regular," he said.

I grabbed the nozzle and started the gasoline flowing, and picked up the squeegee. "Windows are fine," Morrison said as he leaned against the outside of the driver's door.

I nodded, returned the squeegee and stood by the nozzle in silence, scanning the road for another customer.

"What's Luke got to say for himself today?" he asked.

"What?"

"Just wondered what Luke was saying. Saw you talking."

"Why?"

"Oh, I don't know. He looked a little animated."

"Well, that's Luke."

He nodded. "So I've heard. Listen, I was wondering if you've given any thought to what I said the other night. About anything else you want to tell me. Anything that might have slipped your mind."

"I told you everything."

"No doubt your friend Sam told you I asked him about the bruises on Mr. Opal. Doctor says they're fresh. Mrs. Opal said he didn't have them when he ventured over to the Roberts place."

"She must be mistaken."

"Really?"

The nozzle clicked and I jerked it free and slammed it back onto the pump. "Seven dollars. Looks like you had a pretty full tank to begin with."

He didn't make a move for his wallet.

"Sorry to be the bearer of bad news," he said. "Ever heard of epidural hematoma? Serious swelling of the brain caused by damage to an artery. Mr. Opal's just hanging on. Chance he could die."

"So I heard."

"And if he dies, well, that doesn't mean this is over. It

just means the stakes are much higher. As high as they can get, if you understand?"

"Seven dollars."

He smiled. "Hate to see you get dragged down by all this. Or your girlfriend, Sarah. She's a nice girl."

"Seven dollars."

He pulled out his wallet, counted out seven ones and gave me one last look. "This thing burns a lot of gas. Suspect I'll be seeing you again. Soon."

I wanted to tell him to make sure he had an empty tank next time, but I watched him pull out, in silence, and turned back to the bench where Luke and Sam had sat. It was empty.

I twirled gently on a swing in the playground near Sarah's house, listening to the pounding roar of the surf in the distance. In the houses around me lights dimmed one by one and darkness crept closer, only held at bay by the odd streetlight. While I waited, a damp mist drifted overhead, and I felt myself melting nicely into the black landscape.

After about ten minutes, I saw a shadow move across the road underneath a streetlight, and I knew it was her. She drew near without even searching for me, almost like she could see in the dark, and I saw she wore a light-colored hooded sweatshirt, with the hood up, obscuring her head. I'm not exactly sure why, but something about the hood's pathetic stealth-look struck me as funny.

"Glad to see you smiling again, Brady," Sarah said as she took the swing next to me and slid her arms around my ribs.

"You got out okay?" I asked. "Shit I can just imagine your dad, getting the call in Texas in the middle of the night, and having to fly back home and…"

"He knows I'm here."

Her words startled me. "Really?"

"Let's just say we've reached an understanding. He doesn't treat me like a child prisoner, and I don't find another place to live." She pulled away from me, dangling gently for a moment by the swing's thick chain, then she spun around so she could face me. "I gave him his one day of bitching. And he took it, and started in again this morning."

She slid a leg in between mine and planted both feet on the ground. "So, after I talked to you I packed my stuff in a suitcase and said goodbye."

"You what?"

"You gotta know by now, Brady, I'm not gonna eat shit. So they stopped me, and I told them I'm an adult and they'll treat me like one or I'm gone, just like that. They know I've saved some money, and I've got some places to stay, so anyway, the fucker backed down. Asked me to stay, said he'd lay off, that we'd work together on this."

"What if they called your bluff?"

"I wasn't bluffing. I would have left, and that's a fact. Might have even called Kathy for a place to stay, or one of the girls."

"Glad it worked out."

"It worked out 'cause I took a risk. Because I made it work."

Her gaze felt a little too direct, a little too accusing. "Did you hear anything more about Tom Opal?" I asked.

"Yeah, I did. My dad went to see him early this afternoon. After our little talk."

"And?"

"He came home and was awfully quiet. Don't know if it was because of our agreement or because of what he saw at the hospital. Only said Opal's in bad shape. That was all."

"Oh."

We sat in the awesome quiet of the night, before she said, "He also told me that if this wasn't an accident, if someone really had hurt Tom Opal, then the other three had a responsibility to come clean, to protect themselves."

"Funny," I said, "how everyone is suddenly suspicious."

"I know, and speaking of that, later today the cop came by. That Morrison guy."

I nodded.

"Talked to my dad alone for fifteen minutes on the back deck, before coming into the living room. I was studying. Told me about bruises on Mr. Opal. How he didn't have them before. Wanted to know how he got them."

"I know. I heard all that too."

"Then he told me I don't have to be scared of Luke."

I sighed.

We spun in silence, our thoughts twisting like our bodies. I said, "We should listen to that detective and your dad. Come clean before all four of us are deep in shit."

Even in the darkness I saw surprise on her face. "We've told them our story, that's all we have to do. Nothing more. It's simple. We do nothing, and time makes everything okay."

"I don't think it's that simple."

"It is," she said, annoyance rising in her voice.

"You think this is the right thing, but it's not. Once you leave the house in daylight you'll see. You'll get the looks. Don't think we're fooling anyone. This is about more than staying out of jail. It's about…"

"Shut up, Brady."

"What?"

"I said 'Shut up.' That's all you gotta do, just shut up, and this will pass."

"You know, you've got the most to lose here," I told her.

"You don't know shit. We've all got plenty to lose."

"What if he dies?"

"Then he dies."

"Nice," I told her.

"I know it's terrible, Brady, but we can't make him better. Don't forget, it was just one of those freak things. Just a weird accident."

"Only it was not an accident."

"Yes, it was."

"He didn't fall on his own," I reminded her. "He was thrown down. There's a big difference."

"Yeah, and nine hundred and ninety-nine times out of a thousand when that happens the person gets back up. It was no one's fault. None of us wanted him to get hurt or killed. But people sometimes get killed playing sports, or falling off a curb. It was a risk he took approaching us so aggressively."

"Just keep telling yourself that."

"Fuck you, Brady," she said shivering, no longer concealing a coldness that spilled out. "Just deal with it."

"I can't."

"No you can, because this is the thing you haven't figured out. The reality of what happened in my garage is whatever we make it. Whatever the four of us say, that becomes true. It's that simple. Don't forget, the four of us went through something much worse than this. My god, Brady, only two weeks ago. On the Memorial Day weekend. And how did we get through that?"

"That wasn't worse," I told her. "This is."

She turned away, her face disappearing behind her hood, and said: "I could strangle you right now."

"I've got to go to the police."

It felt great finally to say those words, which all weekend had lay at the base of my throat choking me.

Sarah turned to me, and I wanted to tell her to take the hood off. That such a child-like piece of clothing was at odds with her face, which carried so much weight, so much anger. "Friends stick together. That's what they do.

They don't ruin each other's lives, especially when there's no reason for it."

I looked away.

"Tell me, Brady. Tell me you'll keep quiet."

"I can't promise that."

I felt her hands clutch my jacket below my throat and begin shaking me, like the bullies I so feared entering high school. "Tell me, Brady."

"I can't."

She released me and stood up. "God help you if you talk."

I saw a single tear sliding down her cheek. Just one, belying her hard stare.

6

In silence, we drove up the road toward the sprawling Mount Baker National Forest, where the mountain's snow-capped peak absorbed the day's final sunlight. Shannon and Baker lakes huddled below in the shadows. Traffic thinned to the occasional car full of teenagers. Just like us, they were probably going to a Memorial Day weekend party somewhere off in the wilderness, on the shore of the two lakes.

Soon Sarah's friends would arrive at their destination, a private campground near Shannon Lake where they would have a designated site, showers and some order in their weekend. Tomorrow, Chantel's uncle would show up with his speedboat, water skis and tubes for a day of fun.

The four of us, on the other hand, would select a spot off the road that hadn't been grabbed by someone else. If we were lucky, the forest service would have plunked down an outhouse within walking distance. The only running water would be streams pouring into the lake. Our recreational opportunities would be limited, although maybe not for Sarah. I suspected she would borrow Sam's car and spend at least part of tomorrow on the boat with her girlfriends, never once admitting to them that Sam, Luke and I weren't quite as interesting as I had suggested.

The road turned from pavement to gravel, and dipped and climbed around Baker Lake's edge, past the occasional campfire and groups of partiers shouting over blaring music. On a home-made sign someone had scrawled the words "Raymond's Stag" and drawn a crooked arrow in the direction of a short side-road.

"Where do you guys want to camp?" I asked.

"Further ahead," Sam said, "away from these clowns."

Sarah laughed. "Do you think they're any worse than the three of you?"

A pickup truck, its bed filled with teens drinking beer and clinging to the sides for life, swerved past us, traveling in the opposite direction. We saw more fires, more parties, two police cars, and one teenager fall down drunk against a tree by the side of the road, his friends laughing as he turned and vomited.

We crossed a single-lane bridge, and the road narrowed to one lane. For the next five minutes we saw no one.

"How much further does this road go?" I asked.

"Don't know," Luke said. "Anywhere along here would be good."

"Right there," Sam said pointing into a semi-flat area beside the lake and several large cedars.

I pulled off the road, and we got out. Though we could see the stone remains of an old campfire, it looked like no one had used this spot this season. Other evidence of past parties had been swept up by Park's people or had been swept away by the elements.

Sarah turned on a battery-operated lantern as I wrestled with her tent. Once I had it in place, she ducked inside and quickly arranged mattresses, sleeping bags and our knapsacks full of clothes. While Luke and Sam floundered with their tent, I helped Sarah gather some kindling from the base of the cedars. Then we grabbed the firewood Sam had loaded in his trunk that afternoon. By the time the fire was lit, Luke and Sam finally had their tent set up, and the four of us gathered around the flames on lawn chairs we'd wedged into the trunk beside the beer.

As darkness fell, the lake gradually transformed itself into a pool of black except for a small luminous patch where the quarter moon reflected off the water's surface. Only the occasional car passed, and even the distant screams of partiers dwindled as the wind shifted, leaving us to listen to Luke's usual incessant ramblings, illustrated by his rapid and expressive hand motions.

We talked, laughed and drank, the mood, I'm sure, still somewhat subdued by what had happened at the gas station. In time Sarah squeezed my shoulder and whispered, "Let's go for a walk, Brady."

I'd met Sarah seven months earlier when our physical education teacher dispatched me to the school gym to help the girls' wrestling team put away some mats. Inside two girls rolled in a tangle of arms and legs on a blue mat, one of them fairly husky, the other smaller, quicker and on top, her blond hair spilling from her headgear. I grabbed one of several dozen mats that covered the floor, but stopped at the sound of giggling followed by the blonde girl's, "That the best you can do, bitch?" As I moved in closer, the bigger girl flipped the blonde off, almost too easily, and rolled on top of her back, wrapping her arms across the blonde's ribs. "Look who's in control now," the larger girl cooed into the blonde's ear, hesitating for just a moment before emphatically adding the word, "Bitch," which elicited more laughter.

The heavier girl noticed me first, a sudden jerk of her

head my way followed by two angry eyes. Her chubby cheeks red, she climbed off the blonde and rose to her feet.

"We were just...," she started to say, then stopped and crossed her arms. "What are you doing standing there gawking like that?"

"Do you know where these go?" I asked pointing to the mats. "I'm supposed to be helping put them away."

"You get off watching us or something?"

I could feel my body tightening.

The blonde stepped forward, and I braced for another earful. Instead she revealed no emotion, and simply pointed. "Right there. The mats go into those doors under the stage. I'll help you. Cynthia's got to get to class."

The blonde worked in silence, never once asking me about my clandestine entrance, and more surprisingly, not spewing out a rush of meaningless but cool-sounding put-downs. She didn't seem to care about the sweat-streaked makeup on her face or that the unforgiving singlet she wore made her body look slightly masculine. It struck me that, unlike many other Grade 12 girls, she didn't resemble some garish Christmas ornament, decorative and flashy in appearance, but hollow on the inside. And oh so fragile.

As we completed our task, she looked at me only twice more. The first time I think I managed to turn away before she saw me clumsily stealing more than a quick glance at her lean body. The second time I wasn't so quick in averting my gaze, and when she saw my eyes upon her she stopped suddenly, rested her back against the stage and studied me. Her eyes flashed something dark, turbulent, just for a moment, but she said nothing, like her closed lips suppressed all kinds of terrible thoughts, and maybe not just about me.

She never told me the things I'd later learn: How her family had moved to Deception Pass from Seattle over the summer after her father decided to set up his medical practice in town. How much she despised moving. How a large reason for the move was her parents' hatred for her group of friends.

After I watched her stuff the last mat under the stage, she turned to me and said, "We're done."

I expected her to disappear quickly to the showers, but instead she paused. I searched for a clever line, something she'd always associate with me, but drew a blank.

I met her again two weeks later while I walked a neighbor's black lab in the hills near the Deception Pass Bridge. I didn't hear her footsteps behind me, just her voice.

"Hey, mat buddy."

I turned to see her break stride, a large Golden Retriever at her side. She panted slightly, her forehead damp with perspiration, her legs long and bare and her large feet tucked inside expensive New Balance running shoes. It was the first time I'd seen her not wearing a singlet, and her beauty struck me like a hard kick. "Oh my God," I whispered, before asking, "So you remember me?"

She laughed, a rare show of emotion. "The guy Cynthia figures must be a voyeur."

I wanted to tell her I was only human. Instead I asked, "Where you running to?"

She studied me for a moment, like I'd just asked her something too personal. "Down around Bluff Road, to the beach beneath the bridge. Then back home. Need to train for the track team at school." She grinned. "Need to get out of my fucken house before I'm driven insane."

"See you got company," I said, pointing to the dog sitting obediently at her side.

"Roper," she laughed. "Nearly forgot he was there. My dad's gone to alarming lengths to train him. He doesn't need a leash, I just need to remember the commands. So where are you walking your dog to?"

"Oh, Mikey? He's the neighbors'. I'm just doing them a favor. But I usually go down to the bridge and back."

She nodded once more. "Well, mat buddy, gotta keep movin'." She turned and was on her way before I thought of anything else lame to say.

As she rounded a corner and began disappearing from sight, Roper at her side, I pulled sharply at Mikey's leash and began jogging, then running, yelling for the damn old dog to keep up.

My one advantage over her was living here all my life. I knew my way around. While she moved along the road that looped through the expensive homes beside the ocean bluff, I headed straight toward the beach, stumbling off the road and down one of dozens of informal and unmarked trails that locals had blazed between houses. I struggled to keep from tripping over Mikey or scratching my face on low branches. The trail dropped steeply, and I lost my balance on the wet leaves more than once, but stayed on my feet and kept moving. I broke through the trees onto the beach, my body turning damp.

"C'mon, boy."

We ran along the rocks at the edge of the shoreline, leaping over the odd log. In the distance, at the end of the road that wound down to the beach in the shadow of the bridge, I could see the small parking lot, which was likely where she would appear.

Mikey and I reached the parking lot and began walking. I plunked myself down on a log and waited, the only sound the traffic on the bridge above and Mikey's labored breathing.

I watched the ocean water race silently through the narrow channel, twisting dangerously out to sea on the same route that had carried my father's body.

A minute or so later she appeared, her run becoming a walk as she reached the beach. She didn't notice me, her gaze instead fixed across the channel toward the state park. Then a surprised look spread across her face, one so sudden I wanted to turn around to see if the channel's water had miraculously parted.

"How did you beat me here?" she yelled, approaching.

I tried to sound cool. "Took the shortcut."

She sat down beside me. "You ran didn't you?"

"No."

"Listen, no shortcut would get you here before me. You had to run."

"Why would I do that?" But as soon as I said those words, I wished I had bit my tongue.

She leaned close, her eyes large and achingly clear.

"Okay. I ran."

She grinned, placed both of her hands on my shoulder and rested her chin on top. I could hear her chest rising and falling, could feel her sharp knees prodding at my legs.

"Cynthia's right. You are some kind of sex offender, aren't you?"

"No, I…"

"Then why did you run here?" she asked.

When I still didn't answer, she added: "This is where you're supposed to say something, you know, like, 'So I could track you down and rip your flesh into a bloody mess with my bare hands.' Or maybe just, 'So I could ask you out.'"

Her words both startled and disarmed me. "I guess that's it. The second one."

Before I realized I'd done it, I reached my right arm around her shoulder in an embrace. Her mouth flew open in a wide grin that bared her teeth, and she leaned forward and kissed me with salty lips. "That's your answer."

She stood and jogged back up the hill toward her expensive neighborhood, not once looking back, not pausing to give me her name or phone number.

☙

Luke and Sam shouted some stupid abuse as Sarah and I left the campfire for our walk.

"Just let me grab a flashlight," I told her.

"No," she said. "Let's explore the darkness."

I stared into the blackness that infused everything except the small area around the campfire. I started to object, to say there was almost no moon tonight, that we could fall off a cliff or something, but cut myself off, sure she wouldn't be dissuaded. "This is crazy," I laughed.

We made our way to the gravel road, and Sarah pulled me to the right, away from the other parties, onto the one stretch of road we hadn't yet traveled. We stumbled along, using as a guide the gap in the treetops that revealed a sky teeming with stars. More than once we wandered off the road and nearly tumbled into a ditch or the thick undergrowth. Eventually, we learned to listen to our footsteps, for the sound of gravel turning to dirt, a sure sign we'd lost our way. In time, too, I felt my jaw loosen, my muscles relax, and almost told Sarah she'd been right about the walk, about her instincts.

"I'm sorry," I told her.

"For the scalded kid…?"

"For convincing you to come after that."

"Wouldn't exactly say you convinced me."

"So why did you come?"

She stopped walking. "It was more than what you think. Not just because you know me so well. It was more like, well, I guess I liked your effort."

In the distance, the sound of running water rose, and we slowed to an even more cautious pace, until the trees fell away and the sliver of moon illuminated a one-lane bridge traversing a wide, fast creek.

We literally felt our way onto the bridge, detecting the smell of freshly-cut cedar. The deck planks had likely been replaced recently. At the short span's center, the water roared underneath.

Sarah kicked her sandals off, and balanced her feet on one of the four-by-four beams nailed to each side of the bridge deck, a pathetically short guardrail. She lifted her heels and slightly leaned her body over the raging water below, her focus shifting to someplace or something I didn't understand. She leaned back and looked at me suddenly. "What?"

"Just trying to decide whether you were about to fall to your death."

"You say the sweetest things," she said. "That's why I keep you around."

I stepped up beside her and gazed out over the noisy darkness. "Oh, so that's why. I've always wondered, because you could have any guy you want."

"Maybe I do have any guy I want," she said, leaning close.

"I could take that two ways, you know."

She shoved me gently.

We walked back in silence but when we could see the light of our campfire in the distance, I asked her once more, "So what is it about me then?"

"What?"

"You know, why do you keep me around; what is it you see in me?"

She studied me for a moment, my persistence no doubt puzzling. Then she laughed. "C'mon. I'll show you."

We bid goodnight to Luke and Sam, and reveled in our warmth, in a flourish of anxious hands, lips, hips. Then we lay together, sticky, content. I slid my tongue down her neck, in between her breasts, and finally down inside her belly button. She laughed. I turned my head on its side, and rested it on her belly, and she stroked my hair with both hands. We stayed that way for several minutes, and I felt myself nodding off.

"I love you," she told me for the first time, surprising me with words I'd never expected her to say, with an emotion I sometimes doubted she could feel.

I tried not to hesitate. "I love you too."

We pulled our underwear and shirts back on, and I slid my hands over her ribs, and drew her close, expecting her to squirm free, to find a more comfortable position that left her just out of my reach. But she didn't, and her breathing deepened into sleep. I lay still, thinking about her confession of love, wondering if it was genuine or something she bestowed on me to calm my insecurities. In time, before I finally nodded off, I wondered why I made everything so difficult.

I'll never be sure what woke me – a not-so-distant noise or a crushing feeling of something terribly wrong. Or maybe I simply sensed my inexplicable good fortune coming to an end. I heard a car door slam, then another, then another. Voices. What were Sam and Luke up to? I lifted my head and through the tent's thin walls I saw a flashlight beam cut through the night.

"What's happening," Sarah whispered, half asleep.

"I don't know. It's kinda strange."

The light disappeared, silence blanketed the night once more, and Sarah's breathing deepened as she drifted back asleep.

I lay in anticipation, of what I didn't know, so when the zipper on our tent's door exploded upwards, I sat bolt upright. "Sam, Luke," I yelled.

Arms reached into the tent, tearing at our sleeping bags and legs. Sarah sat up too, and then disappeared violently, pulled screaming from our warm, safe womb.

A hand pulled on my foot, and I kicked it away and threw myself out the opening into the darkness.

Two or three sets of legs greeted me. I tried to struggle to my feet, but our attackers kicked me hard in the ribs.

"Stay down," a voice ordered.

"What the fuck do you want?" Sarah screamed. I crawled to her voice, blinded by the flashlight beams, and when I reached her she clung tightly to me as we lay on the cold ground.

"You try to run or get up and you'll be sorry." The same angry voice. I suddenly knew what this was about.

As my eyes slowly became accustomed to the dark, I guessed there were at least six men, maybe more. Two stood over me and Sarah, and the rest attacked Luke and Sam, who swore at the shapes pulling them out of their tent.

Grunts and groans filled the air. "You fuckers, stop kicking me," Sam screamed, his voice trailing off.

"Well, stay down," a voice told him.

Luke tried to rise, getting kicked, flailing, spewing out a string of vicious threats.

One of the men shone a flashlight on Luke's dazed face. "Is this the piece of shit that did it?"

"That's him," came a voice from the darkness. I didn't have to see a face to know it was the short-haired kid from the gas station.

The man with the flashlight walked up to Luke and spat on him. "You scum. I just spent five hours in the emergency ward with my brother. Second-degree burns. A possibility of scarring. Fucked up my cousin's wedding reception. All because of you."

Luke wobbled on his knees.

"Leave him alone," Sarah screamed. "It was a fair fight. Your brother lost."

"Shut up, bitch," the man yelled back. "We're not

interested in the rest of you. Just him. Just setting things straight."

Someone turned on Sam's electric lamp. In the fresh light I could see four men in their late teens or early twenties, plus the two kids from the gas station. One of the men brandished a tire iron. Another who hovered over me and Sarah wielded a baseball bat, his eyes poring over Sarah's shivering and barely covered body.

"Here's how we'll set things right," said the man in control. "A fair fight, between this piece of garbage and my brother. Not like the last time they met."

"Luke can hardly stand up," Sarah shot back. "Tell your brother to come back later."

The man turned to Sarah. "I've heard enough out of you."

"You're awfully brave when you got all this help," she spat back.

Sarah tried to stand, and the man with the bat reached over and shoved her down. She sprang to her feet again, and the man raised the bat for a second time, as though he were going to strike her, but instead used his free hand to wrestle her back down. I stumbled to my feet, absorbing a punch from the other guy standing over us. The man holding Sarah saw me coming, and with one arm swung the bat at my head in a short stroke. I raised my left forearm to protect my face and felt a surge of pain radiate out from a point near my elbow, before my entire arm went dead. I threw a punch with my right hand, and before I knew it found myself wrestled back to the ground by the man who had stood behind me.

"Leave him alone," Sarah screamed, scratching at the face of the man who lay on my back.

The man in charge turned away from Luke and Sam, as did the guy with the tire iron. "Stop, Sarah, you're making it worse," I yelled.

Bodies and hands grappled around Sarah until she was thrown down and slapped hard on the face, the sound echoing into the night.

"Let them go, or you're dead."

Everyone turned to see Luke standing with an axe in his hand, his body still tottering, as though at any moment he would crumple to the ground and pass out.

The guy with the tire iron stepped toward Luke. "You're gonna get the worst of it, you little shit."

"Let them go," Luke repeated.

The tire iron man took another step toward Luke, and Luke drew the axe back with a speed that belied his drunken state, leaned forward and swung hard at the guy's head.

The axe traveled in a blur and I thought for a second I would see and hear a head split apart like the firewood we'd hacked into pieces hours ago. But Luke's target snapped his head back several inches, and the axe blade whistled by.

We exhaled.

"Holy fuck, he just tried to kill me." The guy with the tire iron staggered back in disbelief.

Luke stepped forward, cutting the axe through the air with one swoosh after another. The weight on my back was gone. The men holding Sarah pulled her back with them, the heels of her bare feet dragging on the ground. Luke moved straight at them, and they dropped her and she quickly jumped to her feet and ran behind Luke.

The man in charge ripped the baseball bat away from his buddy. "There's six of us. We can take this one guy. He can barely stand."

I scrambled to my feet and ran to Sarah. Suddenly Sam was beside us. "I've got the keys, let's get out of here," he said.

"Luke," I called. "To the car. Let's go."

Luke stood there, and for a moment I had the haunting

feeling he wanted to fight, to go down swinging in a bloody last stand.

The six attackers began spreading out around him. I lunged forward, grabbed the back of Luke's shirt and tugged, carefully, like you would the collar of a vicious dog. "Let's go."

Behind me I heard Sam's car start, followed by Sarah's voice: "C'mon."

Then I heard the slightly panicked order of the man in charge. "Get the gun. Get the gun."

Luke stumbled past me toward the car, his silhouette slipping through the car's headlights, an eerie shadow. I jumped through an open door right behind him. Sam punched the gas pedal, and we lurched forward onto the gravel road.

"You're going the wrong way," Sarah screamed from the front. "The way out's the other way."

"It was blocked – didn't you see," Sam yelled back.

Sam struggled to keep his clunker on the winding gravel road, his agility and reflexes smothered in beer and weed. The road dipped down to the lake, and the car's two right tires caught the edge of the water. Sam wrestled the steering wheel left and we continued on.

"This way's a dead end," I told him. "Where are we going?"

"Away from them," he hollered back.

Sarah took a quick glance over my head and out the rear window. "I see headlights moving. They're following us."

Sarah's panic spread to Sam, who accelerated. I glanced at Luke, who simply stared straight ahead, his jaw slack, his eyes half shut.

We rounded a bend and the car's headlights illuminated the narrow wooden bridge that Sarah and I had walked to hours before. Sam slammed on the gas pedal, like the bridge was nothing more than a straight-away to gain speed.

Halfway across the left tires caught the wooden beam that served as a railing. As we braced ourselves to plunge over the edge, Sam yanked the wheel to the right, for a split second putting the car back on course. Then we struck the rail on the right, bounced and became airborne. Everyone except Luke grabbed hold of something.

Our car's right front corner awkwardly tucked itself down, and we struck the water with the passenger side windows and the roof. From the bridge, I suspect everything looked so clear: Sam's car upside down in about five feet of water, the strong current spinning it and bumping it downstream from rock to rock.

But inside the car, confusion reigned. I landed in the front seat, my body rattled by the impact, by the icy water that quickly engulfed us. Panicked, disoriented, I didn't know down from up or where my friends were.

I pushed myself out through a window, and in a second, my head broke through the surface. Sarah was beside me, struggling to catch her breath. We heard Sam's voice, barely, above the creek's gentle roar, calling for Luke.

The current swept us downstream from the car, which rattled slowly through the water, its four tires and chassis bobbing in and out of sight.

Sam swam against the current, fighting to reach the Mustang, trying to find Luke. I followed, at first walking and stumbling slowly along the uneven rock-covered creek bottom, my head barely out of the water, then finding it easier to swim.

Then I heard Sarah's voice; she'd spotted Luke, who had drifted past us in the darkness, out into the lake. He coughed and gagged until Sam reached him and helped him keep his head out of the water. Sarah and I joined them.

I scanned the shoreline, looking for the shortest route back to land, and that's when I saw a handful of people standing on the bridge, silhouetted by three sets of headlights. A single rifle shot rang out, and Sarah moaned in disbelief. A second shot was fired, only this time we heard the bullet splash in the water about thirty feet away.

We flailed back into the lake's deeper water, away from the shore, thinking we could disappear into the darkness, and in doing so we saw something offering more cover than the thin black of night. A huge boulder protruded from the water, and we struggled against the current to reach it, placing its mass between us and the shore. A bullet bounced off the other side of the rock, followed by a second and a third. We clung to the rock, embracing the protection it offered from our attackers. My emotions hopelessly ebbed and flowed: Panic, hope, anger, guilt.

We took stock of our injuries: the bleeding gash on Sam's forehead, Sarah's aching ribs, the coldness permeating us all. We stared at Luke, who looked drunk, dazed. Then we heard it, a barely-audible groan, low and continuous.

"Say something, Luke," Sarah urged, but he stared straight ahead, his lips quivering as they released the steady moan. She shook him and his head jerked.

"My legs don't feel right," he finally whispered, before resuming his relentless moaning.

Sarah pressed – "Are they cold or hurt?" – and he nodded, and we knew we had to get out of the water before he froze; before we all froze.

Sam suggested swimming across the lake to the far bank, though we all knew it was too far, and then he suggested swimming to shore up the road from our attackers. I wasn't quite listening, just thinking how we were so screwed, so I barely heard Sarah's arguments, that they'd shoot us on the way or simply drive about two hundred more feet and be right on top of us again, with the gun.

"They're not trying to shoot us," Sam said. "They had plenty of chances to do that before we got behind this rock; they just want to torment us. Besides, you got a better idea?"

Sarah shook her head, she didn't have a better plan, other than to stay put until our attackers tired of their game and finally left, which, put another way, meant we would continue shivering and inching helplessly towards hypothermia.

In time, Sam pulled himself out of the water and partly onto the rock, and lay shivering, weakly nodding when I asked him if it was warmer up there. I was so focused on Sam that I didn't see Luke suddenly lunge to life, grappling for my shoulders.

"Why didn't you just help her, Brady?" he moaned.

"Let go of me, Luke."

His face was no longer blank, but twisted.

"Why, Brady? Why don't you ever help your friends?"

I let go of the rock, grabbed his arms and pushed him away. "Why do you have to ruin everything, all the time?" I yelled, watching him struggle with the water, like he'd forgotten how to swim.

"I asked you," he gasped, "why don't you help your friends?"

He tried to swim back to the rock, but I blocked him with my body and pushed him again. His right hand came up, not in a swim stroke but in a punch, so slow that I watched stunned as it rose from the water and grew bigger before striking my mouth.

I flew at him and forced his head under water. He fought back, arms flailing, his body smaller and weaker than mine. I shoved at the side of his head with one hand and at his chest with the other, and using my feet against the rock as leverage, I dunked him, trying to drown his words.

"Brady," Sarah screamed. Her hands, cold and clumsy, pulled my head back, her traitorous fingers pressing in on my eyes. The bitch, I thought. Then I heard a loud splash and felt another set of hands, Sam's, wrenching at my arm until I released Luke.

I turned and looked at them, and saw their dismay. I spat out water, and returned silently to the rock, where the three of them joined me, one by one, gasping. We hung on once more, shivering, trapped, ignoring the tug of an icy current leading nowhere we wanted to go.

Sam spoke first. "What we have to do…is help each other. Forget all this other shit. Take turns. One at a time. On our side of the rock. Just out of sight, cause those fuckers are still firing from time to time."

We all nodded, even Luke.

"Sarah should go first," he suggested.

"I won't argue," she agreed.

I welcomed the distraction as we pushed Sarah, dripping wet, onto a slippery ledge cut into the rock. She lay horizontally on one hip, her back to us, her wet bra and panties clinging to her body. There was nothing for her to hang on to, so Sam placed his hands on the small of her back, almost tenderly, and I rested mine in between her shoulder blades. Luke tried to support her feet, though I realized he might just have been trying to hold on, trying to keep his own head out of the water.

And we stuck to this simple pattern, three of us in the water, one mercifully out, ignoring the laughter from shore and the occasional bullet bouncing off the rock or tearing into the water nearby.

Luke took the next turn, and before it ended I heard the rapturous squawks and calls of newly roused birds and saw the first creep of dawn's light.

When I scrambled onto the rock, I soon felt the touch of several sets of hands in more of a nurturing embrace than the cold business-like clasp I had expected. The icy palms and stiff fingers on my back soon radiated warmth where they pressed against my flesh, the most beautiful touch I could recall, one steeped in sacrifice. This warmth quickly built into a heat so deep I was sure I could draw from it later, even if I were to slip unnoticed from our rock and slide down to the lake's stone-covered bottom.

A realist might dismiss what I felt in those minutes as little more than the onset of hypothermia, perhaps coupled with the slight relief from being removed from the worst of the cold.

I knew otherwise. That's why when we eventually heard the hum of an approaching car followed by a voice from shore shouting, "Have a good walk home, losers," I felt a strange rush of disappointment that I would not get my second turn on the rock, a second touch from those life-infusing hands.

Sarah, who was back on the rock, peeked over the top.

"They're leaving. All three vehicles. Backing off the bridge and going. I see someone else coming...in a truck."

She slid into the water. "Let's get to shore."

We joined her, swimming side by side, Sam helping Luke, none of us turning back for a last look at the rock we so surely believed we'd forever left behind.

7

The months that led up to and followed graduation should have been the summer of Sarah; her orange bikini at the beach in the state park, her knees and elbows pushing into me as we moved easily through the early evening on the winding streets between our homes, the dusk sky still alight with endless possibility. Instead it was the summer of our arrests. And, of course, the suspicion that the four of us knew more about Tom Opal's condition than we had admitted.

On the morning after my playground meeting with Sarah, the newspaper did not carry a story about Tom Opal's condition, so I wouldn't find out until later that he would undergo surgery that day to remove the clot and bring down the swelling in his brain. It did, however, offer a short story on page A3 that caught my eye. It said:

A suspicious fire last night destroyed a drive-thru espresso building that had become an institution with Deception Pass coffee lovers.

Whelan's Espresso Drive-Thru on F Street burned to the ground about 10:20 p.m. Deception Pass fire chief Garth MacMillan said it appears an accelerant was used in the blaze, which he described as "likely arson."

The drive-thru, an eight-foot by eight-foot wooden structure, was closed at the time and no one was hurt.

Fire investigators were expected to return to the scene this morning.

The drive-thru is the second one owned by the Whelan family of Concrete, Wash. to be destroyed by fire in the past week. On Wednesday, the Whelan-owned drive-thru in Anacortes was gutted by a fire that investigators have said was arson. No one was hurt in that blaze, which also happened in the evening when the drive-thru was closed.

I tossed the paper aside, grinning with a satisfaction I knew should have sickened me. Once again I was sure the redoubtable, the loathsome, the sinister Luke Newell had done his research. He knew who had taken those shots that had pinned us down at the lake.

On the first school day after the disastrous party, I planned my arrival to coincide with the ringing of the first bell. No hanging around the halls waiting for my exam to begin while dozens of students stared and asked me about Friday night. I quietly took a seat in the cafeteria, where I'd write my algebra exam with more than one hundred other students, and scanned the room, seeing a few faces looking back at me. Sam and Luke weren't there – they'd embarked on a much less academically inclined path through high school. Neither was Sarah, who'd taken her algebra exam last week with a different set of students. Chantel was there, though, and when our eyes met she studied me for a moment before looking away as though she hadn't seen me at all.

When the exams were handed out, I dug in, not wanting to be distracted. I'd later tell myself I would have breezed through it if I hadn't been interrupted, but I wasn't sure I really believed that. That's because the harder I tried to concentrate, the more my mind began to wander and the more the time flew by. So for a split second I welcomed the announcement on the public address system that offered a real diversion from the jumble of numbers before me. The vice-principal's voice, direct and brief, called Sarah Roberts, Brady Joseph, Luke Newell and Sam Simpson to the office. I stood up startled, suddenly unsure if I was really supposed to leave my exam, especially with the clock ticking down. My math teacher nodded at me, and I left, aware of the many eyes watching me.

When I drew near the office I saw two uniformed police officers, and swallowed hard. My first instinct: They were here about the espresso building fires.

Mr. Edwards, our principal, stood nervously at the door to his office. He signaled me inside, where Sarah and Sam squirmed uncomfortably on a bench. Luke walked in behind me, and the two of us sat down too. As the four of us searched each others' faces for a sign someone knew what was happening, Detective Morrison walked in. He looked at Luke.

"Luke Newell, I'm arresting you for assault in the first degree."

Two officers stood Luke up and handcuffed him, setting off a string of the foulest swear words.

Then Detective Morrison turned to the three of us. "Brady Joseph, Sam Simpson and Sarah Roberts, I'm charging each of the three of you with one count of criminal conspiracy."

Three more cops appeared, gesturing for us to stand. I did so, stunned, my mind somehow numbing itself. They handcuffed us, read us our rights from a small scrap of paper and marched us out of the office, out the front door I had tried so hard to avoid earlier that morning, and down the steps to where three patrol cars, likely most of the small force's fleet, were parked.

An hour later, in the cramped Deception Pass jail, I realized our very public arrest had not been without purpose. Detective Morrison had, in effect, enlisted the help of the entire town, making sure everyone heard about our alleged code of silence and giving them all an opportunity to treat us with the appropriate disdain. Assuming we got bail, we would no doubt find it difficult to slip back into our old lives unnoticed and unchallenged. We would become the talk of the town – living, breathing, walking pariahs – with nowhere to turn, until one of us cracked.

None of this really had begun to sink in as I was led from the patrol car through the back door of the police station and past a female clerk who gave me a look exuding disappointment, not derision. From that moment, the police kept the four of us apart. Each of us was fingerprinted and promised a chance to call our parents or an attorney, but we never got a chance to speak to each other. Sam, Luke and I were taken to the three cells in the basement; Sarah, I learned later, was kept upstairs in a meeting room, even though there was a designated cell for women. Unlike Luke and Sam, who both had the company of drunks sleeping off a Sunday night bender, my cell was empty. The only "furnishings" were a soiled mattress and a toilet with a steel seat. I sat on the floor against the back wall – sickened by the smell of piss emanating from the mattress – and tried to gather my thoughts.

Twelve hours had passed since Sarah and I had met at the park, but her presence lingered. I still felt her fingers on my shirt as she ordered me to shut up. She hated bullshit, but how would she characterize our code of silence, or as the cops called it, our criminal conspiracy?

I searched back to our time in the icy water only a couple of weeks ago, and sensed we'd all learned a little too much about our combined strength – and, in the hours that followed, about the workings of the world. As events collapsed in on each of us, I realized these were lessons that nothing good would come from now.

Just after 1 p.m., Detective Morrison appeared with a turkey sandwich wrapped in cellophane and a Coke. He entered my cell and placed the meal on my cot. "You've got a 3 p.m. arraignment and bail hearing in the town courthouse," he said. "Your mother's got a lawyer you can chat with just before that."

I nodded, thinking about how my call home had shaken her, likely sending her straight to the bedroom nightstand, where she kept her marijuana stash. For once I couldn't blame her.

Morrison stood and stared at me, before saying, "Don't look so powerless. Don't be a victim. You can just say the word and it will be over for you. Everything set straight."

I looked down at the dirty floor, refusing to acknowledge he was right. "I know you're guessing," I told him. "You don't really know what happened. You just think you do."

"We'll get more evidence," he said. "We always do."

He turned and continued on toward Sam's cell, where I heard him use the same words, the same pitch.

An hour later I was led to a conference room to meet with my attorney. Charles Higgins shook my hand, and said, "Good to see you again, Brady."

The first time I'd met him was after my arrest for auto theft a year ago, and I'd been instantly impressed by his business-like appearance, his calm confidence. Maybe my mother wasn't a total screw-up after all, I'd told myself in those first few moments.

"I've known your mother, professionally, for the last eight to ten years," he'd said. "I'm the town's best DUI lawyer. Get a lot of business from the bar your mother works in."

"DUI?"

"Driving under the influence," he'd said. "Drunk driving. Got a great acquittal record."

I'd stifled a scream, but he'd done okay on that one. Of course, the stakes were much higher this time.

One at a time, a single court bailiff walked each of the four of us across the street to the Deception Pass Courthouse. Once inside we were kept apart. Mr. Higgins told me Luke would appear first, followed by Sam, Sarah and me. The charges would be read, a further court date set and our lawyers would seek bail. I sat hunched over in a chair, my heart racing, my mind unfocused. In and out of my head popped an image of Tom Opal in his housecoat.

When the bailiff called my name I stood quickly and followed him into the town's lone courtroom. I spotted my mother in the gallery, sitting apart from another dozen or so people. I was told to stand next to Mr. Higgins and face the judge, who still had not looked up.

She finally did, her face long and tanned, in contrast to her grey hair. "Brady Joseph, you've been charged with one count of criminal conspiracy. Do you understand this?"

I nodded.

"We are here to discuss bail and set a date for your next court appearance. Do you understand this?"

I nodded again.

And so began my second foray into court, a five-minute appearance at which the judge, my lawyer and the state prosecutor were the only ones to speak. The conversation moved in a triangle between the three, my head following. Every word, every move sounded preordained, except for the prosecutor's final demand: He wanted as a condition of my bail that I not be allowed to contact Luke, Sam or Sarah. This prompted protests from Mr. Higgins and admonishment from the judge that they'd already settled this. She would place no such condition on my bail, she said.

When we were done, my lawyer turned to my mom and smiled, like it had been him who'd won my release. In reality, even Luke had won bail with the help of a public defender, though the arrangements with a bail bondsman in the following hours had nearly collapsed. We were free, literally, though not figuratively.

Outside the court my mom took my hand as we walked to the car with Mr. Higgins.

"I've got to go back to the office, but you should know this Kathy. The case against your son is very weak. It's really nothing more than intimidation. They want that Newell kid and they're using the other three to try to get to him. We just gotta hold our ground."

I waited for her to suggest that maybe I should just tell the truth. Instead she nodded her agreement, and we drove off.

Driving home she barely spoke a word, which made me think about her reaction to my auto theft arrest. As in this instance, she hadn't screamed at me, scolded me or even given me a disapproving look. She'd just gone about the business of dealing with the justice system, like it was all there was left to do.

I walked to Luke's, a pre-Second World War bungalow seemingly held together by the moss on the roof and the green mold on the outside walls. I knocked and no one answered. As I walked around back, I heard a strange sound, a half-shout, half-groan that I immediately knew came from Luke.

"Aaarggghh. I'll kill that bitch," he yelled to Sam as I walked into the back yard.

The two of them turned to me with startled expressions, then relaxed.

"Hey, dude" Sam said. "Just got here myself. We were about to come looking for you."

"Who are you talking about?"

"What do you mean?" Luke asked.

"I heard you. Something about killing that bitch. Who?"

"You didn't hear shit," Luke said.

I turned to Sam, who stretched out on the bottom of the steps as Luke raged. "Brittany," he said softly. "The girl got this whole thing rolling. Went to the police with her suspicions. Our friend here is a little disappointed with her."

"I swear. I'll shit-kick her if I see her."

"Why blame her?" I asked Luke. "It's not her fault, the trouble we're in."

"Yes, it is. If she..."

"The cops would have figured it out anyway."

"Like fuck they would," Luke said.

"Luke, Brady's probably right you know," Sam said. "Besides, Brittany can't hurt us. She doesn't know anything, so just forget her. Fixate on somethin' else."

"You guys seen Sarah?" I asked, trying to change the subject.

Luke nodded, his foot scraping at some grass growing up from a crack in the back sidewalk. "Saw her leave court, with her parents and a lawyer."

"Did you get a good lawyer?" I asked Luke quickly.

He shrugged, pacing the shattered cement patio. "State appointed somebody. Seems alright."

"Your dad couldn't afford a lawyer?"

Luke laughed. "The old fuck doesn't know. He's not around. I didn't get through to my stepbrother until later. He helped with bail. Two fucken grand. Now he's out looking for Dad. You wouldn't believe how pissed Paul's sounding about what a great inconvenience this is for him."

"So your Dad might not know?" I asked.

"That's right. Let him read 'bout it in the newspaper tomorrow. Of course the old fuck can barely read."

"The newspaper?" I asked.

"Yeah," Sam said. "Didn't you see the reporter from *The Lookout* there in court, scribbling away in a notepad?"

"Shit, no," I answered.

"We're big news," Luke said.

I groaned. "Guys…" I said, my cautious tone betraying my thoughts.

"Don't say it, Brady," Luke snapped.

"Just listen."

"Don't fucken say it," Luke said standing up.

I stepped closer to him, wrongly thinking a forward move would disarm him. "Just listen, Luke, how bad could it be if we came clean? Tell 'em he started it and…"

Luke pushed me hard with both hands, and I stumbled back.

Sam stepped in between us. "You're both a couple of stupid shits. Park your asses."

Neither of us moved.

"Park 'em," Sam repeated, taking his spot on the stairs.

I stepped back and leaned against a decaying cherry tree. Luke sat himself angrily near Sam, who suddenly laughed.

We both looked at him like he was crazy.

"Nobody's asked me about my lawyer," he said after a short silence. "My parents surprised me and got one. Guess the JW sometimes need help defending the church's monstrous financial interests in court or something. Anyway, this guy's good, expensive shoes, that's how you tell, and he seems to anticipate everything before it happens. And he's friends with Sarah's lawyer. Well, not her real lawyer. The one hired to get her out on bail today 'cause the real one from Seattle, the really good one, couldn't get over on the ferry fast enough. Anyhow, he's like, talkative with Sarah's guy, and he said something interesting."

Sam paused for dramatic effect, prompting Luke to yell, "Just spit it the fuck out."

"Chill, buddy. My lawyer says the cops, the prosecution, the state, whatever you want to call them, they've got no case against Luke. Like no real evidence. Remember the clothes and boots they took from you? Nothing there, no matching strands of material or shit from Opal's body, none of Opal's DNA on it. Sure they're suspicious as all hell, mainly because of the other bruises which the doctors say involved some kind of blows to his body at about the same time he hit his head. And that the neighborhood was full of crazy teenagers. But they can prove nothing. Not unless one of us talks. And you know what? My lawyer says if none of us says a single word they don't have a case against Luke, just like we suspected. And if they don't have a case against Luke, they definitely don't have a criminal conspiracy."

Sam laughed again.

"So my lawyer and Sarah's lawyer, they made it clear enough what we should do. That is, do nothing, say nothing to nobody, 'cause they say this will never go to trial. Before the next court appearance, when the prosecutor has to start detailing his case, they'll fold. They say we will never see the inside of that court again. Never. Not in our lives, if we play our cards right. That's not all, either."

Luke grabbed Sam and began shaking him playfully. "Don't stop. First time in my life I want you to keep talking, you crazy motherfucker."

Sam continued, words spilling through a huge grin. "I hear the judge today, that woman, she wasn't pleased any of us was even charged. Didn't as much say it, but my lawyer watched Luke, Sarah and me go before her, and says he could tell she was somewhat pissed. Doesn't like the court to be used to pressure people to talk. Doesn't like games. Sarah's lawyer, you know he asked for the case to be dismissed? Judge almost did it too, I'm told. Said she will if there isn't a stronger case by next month when we're set to go back."

"I love it," Luke said, slapping Sam on the back. "Did you get that Brady?"

I nodded.

"So can you do this, Brady?" Luke asked, his face serious again. "Can you just keep your mouth shut?"

I didn't move.

"Brady," Luke said, standing up, brushing the paint chips off his jeans, but not moving forward.

Finally, I told him this: "I can keep quiet, but that doesn't make it right."

Luke sat back down. "Whole lot of things not right, are they? But you can't always change 'em."

The next morning *The Lookout* carried the following front page headline over the yearbook photos of the four of us: "Local teens charged with secret attack"

The story said:

Four Deception Pass teens were arrested Monday for allegedly attacking a local 44-year-old man whose critical injuries were first thought to stem from an accidental fall.

The four Grade 12 students at Deception Pass High School appeared in court Monday after police said investigators determined the head injuries suffered by Tom Opal at a neighbor's house were the result of a beating.

Luke Newell has been charged with assault in the first degree. Sarah Roberts, Brady Joseph and Sam Simpson were charged with criminal conspiracy. The four, all aged 17, were released on bail and will return to court July 5.

Deception Pass police detective Tom Morrison said the four teens had claimed Mr. Opal fell and struck his head early

Saturday while complaining about a noisy graduation party at a vacant house on Bayshore Drive.

The four had accompanied Mr. Opal next door to the Roberts house to talk away from the loud music. They were the only ones inside the Roberts garage with Mr. Opal when the incident took place about 12:30 a.m. Mr. Opal is still unconscious at Deception Pass Hospital.

Morrison said police, with the help of doctors, have determined Mr. Opal suffered other injuries similar to those of a beating, not a fall.

He said police believe the four teens struck a code of silence immediately after the alleged attack and quickly began insisting Mr. Opal tripped walking down three steps and struck his head on the metal base of an exercise bike.

Mr. Opal, the meat manager at Albertsons and a former past president of Deception Pass Little League, underwent surgery Monday to remove a clot causing swelling in his brain. Doctors say it's too early to tell if the surgery worked. Mr. Opal is on a ventilator to help him breathe.

Friends and family of Mr. Opal sat in court Monday afternoon while the charges were read against the four teens.

Prosecutor Dan Evans said the state will show that Luke Newell attacked Mr. Opal and the other three teens conspired to keep the attack secret. Evans also described the attack as "somewhat premeditated."

Attorney Karl Jordan, who represented Miss Roberts, asked Judge Bernice Hogan to dismiss the charges against his client because of a lack of evidence.

Though Judge Hogan ruled against the request, she warned the prosecution it would need a stronger case by the next court hearing.

Eunice Opal, Mr. Opal's wife, did not attend Monday's hearing, but praised the police for bringing charges against the teens, who were arrested Monday morning at the high school.

"While we pray for Tom to recover, it's good to know the police are busy bringing these kids to justice," she said.

The charge of assault in the first degree covers incidents in which great bodily harm has been inflicted on someone. It carries a sentence of five to twenty years in jail.

At 8:30 the following morning, a school secretary phoned to tell me I could finish my exams if I "presented" myself at the school at 10:30 that morning. What about my friends, I asked, thinking mostly about Sarah, who would need the make-up exams to ensure a smooth entry into Western Washington University. Just worry about yourself, she told me, before hanging up.

I stood at the counter in the school office for five minutes, the secretaries all ignoring me, before one of our two vice-principals emerged and signaled for me to follow him. We walked the empty hallway in silence, something that suited me fine. And then the bell rang, and the halls quickly filled with the Grade 8 to 11 students who were completing their last day, plus any Grade 12s who had one remaining exam or were emptying out their lockers and saying their good-byes. Students stared at me, a few shooting me with disapproving glances, but many more giving me a look of admiration that, thank God, still elicited a feeling of sickness in me.

We entered an empty classroom, and the vice-principal placed my partly completed algebra exam on a desk. "You've got seventy-three minutes left," he told me. "I'll return, I'll take the completed exam, then I'll give you a five-minute bathroom break. Then I'll give you the English exam. This door will be locked, and you are to talk to no one while writing your test. For the English exam you'll have the full ninety minutes to complete it, and then you'll go home. You'll get your marks in the mail. I don't want to see you here ever again. Any questions?"

I shook my head.

At the door, he paused and said to no one: "You know, I'm one of the few people in this town who did NOT like Mr. Opal. He politicized Little League. Was a know-it-all to the nth degree. Was a talker, not a listener, and it's the listeners who learn and really contribute something to this world."

He opened the door and turned back to me.

"But you know what?" he said. "He still deserves to be treated with respect, just like everyone else. What's the point of teaching kids about algebra and English when after twelve years of school they still know absolutely nothing about common decency?"

Later, after countless wrong answers, I assembled my locker's contents – the last vestige of my final year in school – shoved it all into my backpack and left the locker door wide open, just like I'd been told.

A cleaning crew – six chatty middle-aged men brandishing brooms, buckets, mops and various cleaners – ambled past me and into the cafeteria, the next room to be closed down for the summer. I watched the door swing shut behind them, and stood picturing them scrubbing and cleaning away the residue of so many lives. The school's halls now exuded an eerie silence as the remaining students counted out the year's final minutes in classrooms already stripped bare for the summer. I started toward the open front door, where a harsh light poured in and flooded the empty hallway, almost in anticipation of the headlong surge to follow the final bell. My steps, at first long and strong, slowed, then stopped.

I readjusted my backpack so it no longer dug uncomfortably into my shoulders and then turned around.

I slipped alone out the back door, by no means for the last time.

8

The hours after we staggered from the icy lake were spent in a small hospital in Concrete waiting for the effects of hypothermia to abate and for justice to be dispensed. Shaking hypothermia would prove to be the easier of the two, though by no means easy. Luke had it worst – perhaps he had been the drunkest and in the weakest condition to combat the cold. He had also badly strained both his knees in the crash and bruised a kidney, though we'd later jokingly blame the beer for that particular internal discomfort. But the cuts and bruises we all acquired in our plunge into darkness went almost unnoticed in our struggle to get warm; to battle the coldness that seemed to inch out from our cores.

After individual examinations, the doctor, a man whose name I forgot as soon as I heard it, placed each of us in a bed in the tiny emergency ward and ordered the nurse to see we were covered with blankets and hot water bottles. He addressed the four of us at once, telling us we were all experiencing mild to moderate hypothermia, and that we must warm our cores, something that would involve hours of lying back and relaxing. Don't rub your legs and arms, or you'll make things worse, he told us, and don't exert yourselves or put any strain on your cardiovascular systems.

So we lay there as ordered, submitting to the occasional rectal thermometer and each giving a statement to a young cop the doctor summoned after hearing our story.

When the cop left, we lay mostly in silence, too tired to talk, not yet willing to call home like he'd told us to do. Luke, however, struggled to rest. Every few minutes he'd shout out a swear word or two, more out of anger than pain I suspected.

"Listen, Luke," Sam finally said, "you're driving us all crazy with that swearing shit, so I'm gonna show you something."

Luke grimaced. "What?"

"Finding your chi. Also known as your *qigong*."

"Your what?" Sarah asked.

"Your chi. It's your life-force. Your inner peace. You learn about it in ancient Asian religions, now popular in tai chi, you know, that slow-moving martial arts shit."

"That's great," Sarah laughed. "So your parents are crazy Jehovah's Witnesses and you're converting yourself to Buddhism."

Sam shrugged. "Be skeptical all you want. But I want you all to try it. It will help relax you and remind you you're still very warm and alive after our little ordeal."

Luke quickly stuffed a hand below his hospital gown and felt around his crotch. "I can't find it. My chi has shrunk down to nothing."

We laughed, wonderful laughter, but Sam persisted. "Okay. Lay flat on your backs, relax, bring your fingers together but not quite touching. Focus on your breathing, calm, then switch your focus to your fingers. In time you'll feel the electricity hopping from one hand to another. Sort of a tingling. That's your life-force. Embrace it. It will bring you peace."

I tried it, unconvinced by what I felt between my

fingers. So I watched Sarah and Luke, certain that if their hands could conjure heat in an icy lake, they could easily find warmth now. And I was right.

Sarah hollered that she could feel it. "That's so cool."

Luke surprised us the most, first by trying it – then by being stunned by the results. "My fucken fingers are on fire. They're fucken on fire. I can feel it in my hands, too."

Sam nodded to himself and lay back on his bed satisfied, while Luke continued to hold his fingers close, still swearing but now in amazement.

About noon, a man walked into the hospital's emergency ward and in a quiet but clear voice, one sounding a little tired, said: "Hi kids. I'm police chief Walter Regan."

He led us back into the hospital until we reached a small boardroom, and he pointed inside as if he were welcoming guests. The four of us took seats around a long table, with Chief Regan taking a fifth spot at the head of the table. He had us introduce ourselves, and then told us we were recovering fine and would be released later that day.

"We're recovering fine and all," Sam said, "but we almost died out there."

Chief Regan didn't acknowledge the comment. "Based on what you told Officer Francis about your attackers stating they were in this very hospital last night, and that you had ruined a wedding reception, the suspects were quickly identified. Rod Whelan is the older brother of Jason Whelan, the kid you scalded. I've reviewed your statements and I've already taken statements from the two of them, plus the two friends they said were there."

"But there were more than four of them," Sarah said. "At least six."

"Four is what they told me, and all four statements are consistent in that," the chief said.

Sarah, who was curled up in a ball on a swivel chair with her chin resting on her knees, looked at me, then back at Chief Regan. "So two of them will get off scot-free."

Chief Regan studied her. "Sounds like you're making an assumption."

"What do you mean?" Sarah asked.

"I'll get to that. I want the four of you to listen carefully."

He went on to recount fairly accurately the incident at the gas station, then continued: "The two Whelan brothers, Dan Jensen and one of Rod Whelan's friends then sought you out. Jensen had taken a good look at the old car you'd been gassing up. The boys had never seen you before and figured you were on the way to the camping area north of town like so many who come through here each spring with high school graduation parties on their mind. They traveled up the highway and onto the gravel road until they saw your car parked alongside the lake. They grabbed a tire iron and a baseball bat and confronted you early this morning."

He paused. "How am I doing?"

"So far fine," Sarah said.

"They called you out of your tents, identified Luke Newell, and challenged him to a fight."

"They didn't call us out of our tents," Sarah said bitterly. "They dragged us out, kicked us, punched us, even hit us with the baseball bat."

"Well there is our first discrepancy on the events. I'll continue. Rod Whelan says at this point Mr. Newell ran and grabbed an axe and swung it at the fourth member of their party, Don James, just missing his head by inches."

"If I'd tried to hit him, he'd be dead," Luke said coldly.

"So you agree you swung the axe. Okay. At this point the four of you retreated to your vehicle and tore out of the area northbound."

"They had the way back to town blocked by their cars," Sarah said.

"Then, at a wooden bridge several hundred yards further north you drove off the bridge and into the creek, and were swept into the lake."

"You forgot the part about them shooting at us for an hour or so while we clung to a rock in the water," I told him.

Chief Regan's face was expressionless. "That's where your versions of events disagree again, kids. They said they had no gun and fired no shots."

"Bullshit," Sam yelled.

The four of us twisted in our seats, in disbelief, in raw anger.

"In fact, they said they left immediately after you drove away, and didn't see your accident, otherwise they would have helped."

"This is so fucked up," Sarah said.

"You don't believe them, do you?" I asked, my voice suddenly small.

"Doesn't really matter what I believe," Chief Regan said. "It's what can be proven in a court of law. There are no independent witnesses. It's your word against theirs. To top it off, they're from around here. The Whelan family has lived here for generations. They own a large sawmill that employs a good number of people, plus a chain of drive-thru espresso bars throughout this county and several nearby ones. They've got a damn good lawyer too – I just spent the last half-hour up against him. And I can tell you, none of them would be convicted on what you got. Their stories are absolutely consistent, and I ask you this, who do you think the court would believe, these local folk, or you, some kids who came to town looking for trouble?"

I glanced over at Sam, who looked lost at what we were being told, and then at Luke, who had laid his hands out before him, fingers slightly apart, searching for his chi once more.

Sarah unfolded her body, and asked: "Why would we have stayed in the water and exposed ourselves to hypothermia if they hadn't been there shooting at us? What would have possibly kept us in the water for so long?"

Chief Regan turned in his chair, facing Sarah. His face and hands tightened, but when he spoke his words were calm, measured. "That's a very good question, why would you? I spoke to the doctor. He confirmed he thinks you were in the water well over an hour. I admit, I don't believe you would have stayed in the lake for the heck of it. Something kept you there. But my suspicions aren't enough to make a case."

"Why not just charge them?" Sarah asked. "Let the court decide who's right."

"How old are you young lady?"

Sarah bristled at the question. "I'm seventeen. You already know that."

"Well I've been a cop for twice that long, and here's one thing I've learned. If you want to go up against the most powerful person in town, you make sure your case is rock solid. Or you walk away."

"That's bullshit," Sarah said.

Chief Regan continued. "And here's one more thing. If I was to lay charges, it wouldn't just be against the Whelans and their friends. I'd also be charging Luke Newell with assault. He's already admitted to scalding Mr. Whelan. And that incident precipitated this entire mess. Let me tell you something else. If you both lived in this town, shared its streets, its shops and schools, I expect I would have to charge you both, just to keep peace, just to show you there are consequences to your actions. I'd get a conviction against you Mr. Newell, but as I said, I think the Whelans would walk away. But here's the thing…"

He leaned forward toward Sarah, like he was alone in the room with her. "You don't live here. You don't have to get along with the Whelans. You can leave, and not come back. And you can take home this lesson: Be careful who you pick your fights with."

Luke groaned, his forehead wrinkled in concentration, his fingers in the chi position but shaking, almost violently, like they'd never find peace. Regan looked at him, clearly puzzled.

Sarah leaned forward toward Regan. "No. Fuck that. That's not the lesson we'll be taking home. It's this: If you keep your story straight and stick together, and you can afford a good, slimy lawyer, you can get away with just about anything."

Chief Regan sat back in his chair. "If that's what you've learned, fine. You can always lay a civil suit against the Whelans." He turned back to Sarah. "Your daddy's a doctor, I'm sure he can afford a good, slimy lawyer too."

Sarah's forehead crinkled.

"Yes, I spoke to your father an hour ago. My deputy asked you four to phone home, but you ignored him. So you forced me to do it. Your father sounded a whole lot surprised to hear you were in the company of these three fine gentlemen."

For the first time since crawling out of the lake, I felt warm.

"I also spoke to Brady Joesph's mother and Sam Simpson's mother. Didn't find anyone home at your house Mr. Newell, which was too bad, but I'm still trying. None of them were very happy when they heard about your confrontation. Your dad's on his way, Miss Roberts. Mr. Joseph and Mr. Simpson, you are to call home as soon as we leave this room."

Chief Regan stood. "I suggest when your families come

to get you that you pick up your camping gear and the rest of your clothes and head home. And about your car Mr. Simpson, I think we're gonna have to wait a few weeks until the spring runoff abates before we can get a tow truck's hook on it. Even then, an old Mustang…I think it'll be headed for the wrecker."

He paused at the door. "Any questions?"

Luke's whole body now shook, the reverberations rising up from his fingers. He slapped both hands down hard on the table.

"Here's one. You always been a chickenshit?" Luke asked.

"I'm gonna let that one slide," Chief Regan said. "You're tired and cranky, and I'm giving you that one free shot. But no more."

"The only thing I bet you let slide," Luke said, "is that Whelan guy's dick up your ass."

I gasped out loud. Sarah groaned. Sam covered his eyes.

Chief Regan closed the door and walked around the table to Luke. By the time he reached him his cheeks were red. He didn't hesitate – just cuffed Luke hard on the face and tipped Luke and his chair back onto the floor. Regan looked at the three of us. "None of you make so much as a move. Just stay in your chairs."

He turned back to Luke, who was scrambling to his feet. "If you think I'm such a coward, when you get back up I want you to say it again, this time right to my face."

Regan backed away, keeping an eye on Sam and me as he moved. We watched Luke rise as the large cop clenched his fists.

Sam leaned forward. "Luke, it's not worth going to jail for. Or getting the shit beaten out of you."

Luke's eyes shifted wildly as he stood and faced Regan, but he made no move. After what seemed like forever, he shrugged. "There's always tomorrow, or the next day, to set things right."

Regan glared at Luke for a moment and left without another word. Luke grabbed a glass vase and hurled it at the wall. It shattered, a mix of glass, water and dying flowers cascading to the floor. He turned to Sam. "That chi thing is a pile of shit."

We returned to the emergency ward, and took turns on Sarah's cell phone. I called my mom and told her I had survived and to hold off selling my shit to cover her bar tab. She didn't laugh. Sam phoned home to enlist a ride from his uptight brother, Tom, who only agreed to drive up for forty dollars in gas money, even though he'd surely burn less than fifteen. Sarah called Chantel's cell phone, and when no one answered, left a detailed message about what had happened and how we were all okay but wouldn't be joining them. Luke chose to make no call, which got me wondering if he was really living at home these days, or if he'd gravitated to one of his other haunts. For once I almost envied him.

Sarah dialed the number of her dad's cell phone. Before she hit send, she laughed, though with a trace of apprehension. "This should be good." She placed the phone to her ear and spoke almost immediately, like someone on the other end had picked up the phone before it even rang.

Her face showed little emotion as she talked and listened, like it was just any old conversation. She nodded a couple of times impassively, before snapping the cell phone shut and turning to me. "He and Mom are already on the way. And by the way he's pissed at everyone. The cops, me, you."

We waited on our beds in silence, until I said to no one in particular, "You know Sarah's dad has a special whistle... not one of those things that a referee has, but a special way of whistling to get the kids to come. He calls it the family whistle."

Sarah turned to me annoyed. "Why are you bringing that up now?"

"I don't know. Guess I've always thought it was weird. That you guys would be in like a crowded mall or something, and if he couldn't see you he'd start whistling and you and your brother would hear him and follow the sound. I dunno…"

Sarah folded her arms and stared at me. Luke and Sam smiled, like they'd forgotten how much they still hurt.

"Brady, is it like the way you'd whistle for a dog or something?" Luke asked.

I glanced at Sarah, who seemed to be daring me to answer.

I hesitated. "Sort of."

"Are you trying to piss me off?" she asked.

"I don't know why I brought it up. Must have a head injury or something."

"If you don't, you're gonna, real soon."

Less than an hour later in the waiting room, we did hear a whistle, in loud short bursts, but coming from Luke. As Sarah reached up to smack him he pointed to the emergency ward's glass door.

Dr. Ian Roberts burst through, followed by Sarah's mother, Diane. He stopped just inside the door and, without saying a word, stared at his daughter. His eyes moved quickly to me, then Sam and finally Luke. There was no emotion, just like when he examined someone's hemorrhoids I suspected.

He turned and breezed over to the nurses' station, where he consulted with the nurse, and finally returned to Sarah. "You're very fortunate," he said, "you know that?"

"No shit, Dad" she said, rolling her eyes.

Dr. Roberts turned to face Sam and Luke. "Who's coming for you two? Your parents? The sheriff?"

"My brother's coming for the three of us," Sam replied.

"No he's not," Dr. Roberts said. "He's coming for the two of you. Brady's coming with us."

I looked at Luke and Sam, my eyes screaming for help.

"We need Brady," Luke said. "To…help us get our camping stuff."

"You two can handle that." Dr. Roberts turned to me. "Let's go, Brady."

I wanted to argue – to tell him I would make my own decisions. Instead I reluctantly waved good-bye to Luke and Sam and slowly accompanied the Roberts family to their Mercedes, wondering how, as with so many things, I failed to see this coming.

In the car, I waited for the doctor to explode, and when he didn't I immediately wondered what perverse plans he'd conjured up to punish me for so badly endangering his daughter.

"Tell me about the run in with those Wheelan guys," he said when we'd swung onto the highway.

Sarah slowly launched herself into the story, starting from the confrontation at the Exxon station.

Her old man listened carefully for once in his life, only responding with an occasional grunt.

By the time we'd reached the outskirts of Sedro Woolley, Sarah had finished her story and her dad appeared to be processing what she said, as if preparing to give a diagnosis. Suddenly his head began moving from side to side, as if he was scanning the businesses that lined Highway 20. All of us, even Diane, watched him closely, intrigued.

"Figures a crappy little town would only have crappy little restaurants," he said.

"Dad, you're not thinking of stopping for something to eat are you?" Sarah asked.

Dr. Roberts turned suddenly into the parking lot of a take-out hamburger joint. "I'm sure the food is unbelievably greasy, but I like the seating arrangements."

I looked at the collection of vacant outdoor picnic tables.

"We'll freeze out there, Dad," Sarah said.

"It's 75 degrees out. Besides, if you're cold take your blankets."

"We'll look stupid."

"Wouldn't be the first time. Besides, who gives a shit."

Sarah grabbed the door handle in anger, but her dad stopped her with two words.

"Not yet," he said, turning in his seat so he faced Sarah, who sat directly behind him.

"So now I want to know the first half of the story. How you came to be at the gas station with Brady and those two other little fuckers, and in Brady's tent later that night. I want to know why you lied to me and your mother. Why you told us you were going away with your girlfriends?"

"Why did I lie?" Sarah asked. "Out of kindness to you. To keep you from getting all worked up."

"You mean because you knew I wouldn't let you go otherwise," he said.

"Like you could stop me."

"I told her to lie," I said suddenly. "She wanted to tell you that me and my buddies were camping nearby and she'd be meeting up with us for part of the weekend. I thought it would be better not to mention it, given how you feel about me."

Dr. Roberts stared at me sphinx-like for an uncomfortably long time. "Nice to hear you're so thoughtful when it comes to me, but I didn't ask you to speak. I don't need two of you feeding me shit."

Suddenly a door opened and Sarah climbed out of the car. "Speaking of eating shit, I thought you said we were stopping for lunch here, Dad," she said before slamming the door.

Dr. Roberts ordered for all of us at the take-out window after announcing the hamburger and bottled water were the only menu items worth consuming.

"Let's find a seat," Diane said, pulling Sarah away from her father and counseling her with advice like, "Don't provoke him anymore, dear. He's angry enough."

Sarah chose a table in the sun, and I sat with her and her mom, wishing we'd never stopped here or I'd never climbed into Sam's old Mustang about this time the day before.

Sarah suddenly asked, "What's he doing now?"

Diane looked. "I think he's adding the condiments."

"How does he know what Brady wants?"

"He knows. Don't sound so angry. He's trying to be helpful. Besides, it's just condiments."

I went over and helped Dr. Roberts carry the food and drinks back, and that's when he told me, "Brady, you and I are sitting at another table, just the guys."

"Dad," Sarah protested. "Enough already. Now's not the time, so back the fuck off."

He looked at her sharply. "So you nearly get killed, and you're lecturing me. You're a scream."

I picked up my meal and followed him, eager to keep him from altogether snapping. We sat out of earshot of Sarah and Diane, and began eating. I prepared myself to ride out his barrage, cursing myself for not simply telling him to go fuck himself. Seems I'd left that up to Sarah. Several minutes later, he wiped the corners of his mouth and barreled his eyes down upon me. "So, I've been telling you to stay away from my daughter and you've been defying me at every opportunity."

I shrugged. "Well, it's Sarah's choice…"

"So you're blaming her for everything?"

"No, I uh…"

"So is it just sex or something more?" he demanded. "In other words, do you have feelings for her, or do you just like screwing her and pissing me off?"

I grappled with how to answer that, whether to answer that. But he moved on again.

"You know, I'm asking you these questions, but they don't matter. There is only one question I want you to answer. It's this: After demonstrating you and your friends are fucken menaces, are you finally prepared to do what I asked weeks ago, the right thing, and get the fuck out of my daughter's life?"

A fair question, I thought, and the only one I was not going to answer. But almost before I realized it, I did: "No."

Dr. Roberts closed his eyes for a moment, and when he reopened them he had changed.

"I appreciate your being honest," he said, pleasant words that belied the ferocity with which he spoke them. "So if we're being honest, and I knew it would come to this, do you know about my daughter's first lover?"

I should have told him to fuck himself.

"She was thirteen. Did you know that? Some punk with long hair over his face. Could never see his eyes, but I knew what he was up to. Knew he was the first. Did she tell you that?"

I shook my head. "No. But even a fool can see what you're trying to do."

"The floodgates had opened. Little shits started hanging around my place all the time, all wanting a piece of her, of her flesh. She did nothing to discourage it. Nothing. When she was fourteen, two college guys. A year later some guy who worked construction. When I found out I stepped in, but usually she broke it off. None of them lasted for long. She'd just gravitate toward another, then another. Lose interest, same way you probably did after your new kitten grew into a cat. She never seemed too discerning either. She grew tired of the horny jock on the football team just as fast as the stonehead in the pants falling down around his ass. I suspect she screwed them all, you know that? Then she dumped them."

"Good for her. But I've heard enough."

He turned and looked back at Sarah and Diane, then leaned forward towards me.

"You wanna hear what cinched my decision to leave Seattle. To buy a practice half the size and half as profitable? You wanna hear?"

"No. I don't."

"You'll like this one. You think you know her. Listen to this. I got home one night, and my driveway was full of cars. Nowhere for me to park. So I was pissed, and I went inside and I heard a bunch of guys hollering, cheering, like they were watching a football game, but they weren't."

I stood up. "You're a liar."

Sarah stood too, and Diane tugged on her arm and mouthed something like, "Let them finish."

We were finished, but he was still talking, that fucker was still going on, and before I could get away he said, "Not a football game, a gang-bang. They were all taking turns screwing her. I could hear her groaning and shouting encouragement, my own daughter, and I went upstairs to her bedroom, and two of them were hanging around outside her door, including this black guy who already had his pants off 'cause he's next and he's anxious, and I could see his black ass and his aroused pecker and I shouted out when I got to the top of the stairs, and he saw me, and he swore, not like, oh-shit-I'm-busted, but more like, oh-shit-now-I-won't get-my-turn-with-that-slut."

I stepped over the picnic table's wooden seat, and leaned forward. "Liar."

"You ask her," he snapped back. "You ask her right now."

I walked away, toward Sarah and her mother. Sarah saw something in my face, something that chilled her, and she twisted her mouth up and snarled at her dad, "What did you say to him?"

I kept walking to their car, not able to get away from her perfectly screwy parents fast enough, though a drive back to town with them was still to be inflicted upon me, unless I decided to walk, or maybe and perhaps mercifully lie down in the path of an approaching truck.

Sarah was at my side. "What did he say, Brady? What did he say?"

Dr. Roberts ambled past, giving himself a satisfied nod, and got into his car, and I blindly followed his lead once more, hating myself more than ever, but unable to help it.

Thankfully, the last half of the drive home from our disastrous camping trip passed silently. Sarah, perhaps chilled once more from our outdoor stop, encased herself tightly in a layer of blankets and leaned her head against my shoulder. The car sped smoothly along the highway, and her breathing slowed and she soon drifted off leaning against me. I wanted to pull her closer, to feel her undeniable warmth, partly just to spite that prick in the front seat, yet she remained strangely and impossibly distant behind the thick layer of cloth.

Those two stark eyes in the rearview mirror – they both knew the damage they'd done.

9

When I heard my mother's laugh rising from somewhere inside the house, I almost stopped mid-step in the driveway and turned back. Already the day shaped up to be a shitty one, and the last thing I needed now was to arrive home and find my mother entertaining one of her inquisitive friends who would be full of questions about how I was doing after my arrest, like they really gave a shit about me. Likely they were more interested in feasting off gossip and innuendo related to Tom Opal's misfortune.

My first day out of high school had begun with an 8 a.m. phone call from Mr. Reynolds, the manager at the service station where I worked, telling me he was giving me at least a week off, "without pay, of course, starting today, until things blow over." I was tempted to ask him what things he was alluding to. So I'd ventured out into the surprising morning heat and walked up to Luke's house where I learned my friends had not bothered to write their final make-up exams and didn't give a shit if they finished high school or not, because Tom Ferrence, the local drug dealer who supplied them with what they smoked and occasionally sold, had approached them with some "opportunities."

"You don't want to get involved with that guy," I told them. "He's trouble."

Luke grunted. "He's trouble. What about us? Besides, today was the first time that prick ever treated me with any respect."

"He's got a business plan for us, Brady my friend," Sam said. "You know we've occasionally been selling some of our stuff to the rich kids, our classmates, the ones who don't mind paying our inflated prices in exchange for the honor of doing business with us instead of hardened criminals like Tom? Well, Tom thinks he can give us some new opportunities."

Nothing I said could dissuade them, so I left, wondering if I should look for another summer job, make plans for college or resign myself to making twenty-five dollar drug deals alongside Luke and Sam.

Arriving back at home, I now wanted nothing to do with whatever loser was visiting my mother. That is, until I slipped inside the front door, wandered out back and found my mother smoking a fat one with Sarah on our cramped back patio.

"Hi Brady," Sarah said, passing the joint back to my Mom and standing up to hug me. Her body pressed against mine, and I blushed when I saw my Mom staring with a big stupid smile.

"Pull up a chair, Brady," Mom said.

"What are you two talking about?" I asked, wishing the question hadn't sounded so defensive.

"You," Sarah said.

I looked at her, perhaps a little too hard.

"Oh lighten up, Brady," Mom said.

After an awkward silence, I asked, "So your dad let you out?"

Sarah rolled her eyes. "I'm not a dog, to be let out and in like that."

"Sorry, I mean..."

"Let's not talk about him," she bristled.

"Fine," I muttered.

"It warms my heart to see you two together like this," Mom said.

"That was almost funny, Mom," I said, meaning it.

My mother took a final drag from her joint before getting up. "I've got to go shopping. See you in a couple of hours."

Sarah smiled at her. "Bye, Kathy."

The two of us sat in silence until I heard my Mom's car start. I began to speak and Sarah interrupted. "Brady. I don't want to talk about it, other than to tell you to keep doing what you're doing. That's all."

"And what am I doing?" I asked.

"The right thing," she said.

"No, I'm not. None of us are. Let's not kid..."

"Brady," she said standing. "Follow me."

I did, into the kitchen, where she tugged me against her and kissed me.

"What I have in mind doesn't involve talking," she said.

"But my mom could come home," I protested.

Sarah laughed. "She's given us until two."

Maybe my face gave off a baffled look that my mother was somehow involved in this, I don't know. Sarah reached up and touched my lips with her fingers, like she hoped to wipe clear my expression.

I looked down, past her breasts poking at my ribs and focused on the smooth white skin that disappeared below the thick belt wrapped around her low-cut jeans. I slipped my fingers over this flesh steeped in possibilities and wondered why I argued.

Upstairs in my already-cooking room, my small bed soon became a mess of slippery limbs, matted hair and sweat-soaked sheets. Finally, as my clock – the now ridiculous action hero model I'd received for my twelfth birthday – flipped onto 1:30, Sarah let me catch my breath. I laughed out loud and kicked aside the tangle of sheets still wrapped around my feet. We turned on our sides facing each other, and Sarah used a single finger to remove a bead of sweat from my nose and place it on her tongue.

"You love that, what we just did?"

"No shit," I said.

"Do you love *that* or love me?" she asked.

"Well, both."

She smiled, and said, "You've never said it first, that's all."

She suddenly reached across me to her small purse, which she'd placed on my night-table when we'd come upstairs. She fumbled inside, and pulled out a small digital camera.

"What's that?" I asked as she straddled my belly and aimed the camera at my face.

"What do you think," she said snapping off one shot of me, then holding the camera out at arm's length and shooting one of herself, before putting the camera back in her purse.

"I know what it is, but why did you do that?"

She grinned. "Freezing that look in your eyes. I don't often see it. Freezing the look in mine too."

"You're so weird," I said, laughing

I reached around the small of her damp back, and pulled her closer, and watched as her face suddenly grew serious. "This is what it feels like to have your own place in the world, not to have to do it rushed on the family room carpet, like a couple of animals, when mom and dad are out. Do you see the difference? Do you see what it can be like?"

I nodded.

"Do you?" Her face still serious.

"Yes."

She kissed me, climbed out of bed and began slipping her clothes back on against the wet resistance of her flesh, something I found almost as breath-taking as when she took them off.

I looked at my clock and made a mock protest: "But we still have another twenty minutes."

"Later, babe," she said.

She looked around the room once more. "You know your boss hasn't just given you the week off. He's really fired you."

"He told me it was just for the week."

She sat down on the bed next to me. "You should go out this afternoon and look for another job."

I shrugged.

She surveyed the room one more time, then said, "You know, things are going to have to change if we want to stay together. My dad won't let me continue to live at home and see you. Not forever. He'll start to reassert himself."

I shrugged, knowing she was right.

She looked back at me. "So if you want to keep seeing me, I'm going to have to live somewhere else. Just think about that."

She kissed me, and I started to climb out of bed. She placed her hand on my chest. "Just think about it."

When my mom got home I was sitting out on the back deck, and she hollered out, "Brady, you want a cola?"

"Yes," I yelled back.

A few minutes later, after she'd put the frozen groceries away, she came out with a warm can of cola and a glass filled with ice and sat down across from me.

I glanced at the can before opening it, something Mom noticed.

"Yes, it's Albertsons brand, not Coke."

"I didn't say anything."

"No but you looked. This was half the price, so tough."

"So you went to Albertsons?"

"I always do."

"Okay."

We sat in silence, and she said, "You want to ask what happened, so go ahead, don't just sit there in silence."

"Okay," I said, irritated. "What was the reaction to you in Albertsons? Did the clerks form a lynch mob when they saw you?"

"Well, funny you should ask. Yes, these clerks who joke and gossip with me every Wednesday were suddenly quiet. Rude even. Couldn't hide their fucking contempt. The one that checked our groceries out, she wouldn't even say hello or goodbye. Treated me like shit. Maybe I'll have to start shopping somewhere else. Or maybe I'll just keep shopping there, just to piss them off."

"Sorry I asked."

"Well, you did ask."

I guzzled back some of my cola, which had begun to cool.

My mom's face suddenly lightened, "I guess it was a nice surprise seeing Sarah...up close and personal like that."

"Mom..."

"I'm surprised she's not still here."

"Well she had to leave."

"Okay."

We sat in silence again, until she said, "So what are your plans for the summer?"

"What do you care?"

"Fuck off, Brady."

I'm sure I blanched at those words. "You can't talk..."

"Yes I can talk like that and I will. I asked you a serious question and you can at least have the decency to answer it."

"I don't know what I'll do this summer, alright."

"I think you should look for another job."

"Fine."

"And I think you should consider asking Sarah to come live with us."

I nearly choked on my bargain-brand soda. "I should what?"

She lit up a cigarette before saying, "You want to keep seeing her, that's what you're going to have to do. I told her she could come live here if things didn't improve at home."

"Mom…"

"Well don't be falling off your chair to thank me. My god, what teenage boy wouldn't love a girl like that coming to live with him? Give your head a shake. I even told her she could move into your room. None of this spare room shit. You're an adult now, in theory anyway."

"So if you say I'm an adult, why did you call me a teenage boy?"

"When."

"Just now. You said, 'what teenage boy.'"

"I did not. And quit changing the subject."

"So this is what you and Sarah were talking about before I got here? The two of you sat out here, smoking up, planning my life for me."

"Thanks for the fucking gratitude."

"Hey, listen…"

"No you listen. Did you even notice Sarah's eyes?" I started to tell her I did, but she continued. "Well I noticed them, and I asked her why her pupils are so huge. It has something to do with the prescription her dad has given her to calm her down. He said she was getting too hysterical, but I think he's drugging her to keep her under his control."

"Before you invited her to live here, you should have asked me first. To see what I wanted."

Mom looked at me hard. "I don't think you know what you want. Because if you're hesitating at an offer like this you're even more confused than I thought."

I shook my head at her. "You ever think that living here wouldn't be the best thing for Sarah? You ever think of that, Mom?"

"Of course I…"

"Like shit. You ever think that maybe living with me isn't what she needs. That it would fuck things up with her family for a long time. Screw up her university plans, because they don't offer a scholarship for the dental program she's going into and she needs her parents to pay for things. She doesn't have a job. And how would it look with this criminal conspiracy before the courts, and she moves in here. Did you think about any of this, because after all, you're an adult too?"

I waited for a raucous response. Instead, she took a drag on her cigarette, and said, "She loves you. You love her. You should be together. There's nothing complicated about that."

I rolled my eyes for effect, and then realized the move looked lame.

"You do love her, don't you, Brady?"

The question startled me.

"Brady…?" A touch of alarm now leaked from Mom's voice. "Brady…? You've told her you love her."

"How do you know that?"

"Cause I know. So you tell me now, you love her, right?"

I sighed in exasperation. "I think I do, but I don't really know."

Mom buried her face in her hands. When she looked back up, her eyes were lost. "Brady. If you don't love her, if your feelings are uncertain, you better tell her. If there's no real future, and you only enjoy screwing her, don't lead her on. Don't do it."

"I'm not leading anyone on, and can you please just back off."

Mom sucked on her cigarette, and stared out into the dark corners of our yard. The birds chirped, she noisily inhaled and exhaled, and I shook the ice in my glass until it reminded me of Sarah's father.

The first days of summer drifted by in a way that seemed, well, not exactly right, but not quite wrong either. My Mom talked to a bar customer who owned a gas station in Anacortes, and he gave me a summer job. Presumably I was a bit more presentable to the public one town over. Luke and Sam seemed to have plenty of money, so I was certain they'd stepped-up their dealing in spite of my best advice. And, like me, Sarah also found a job in Anacortes, as a waitress at the Country Kitchen, a restaurant owned by one of her dad's patients. It seemed that while Luke was regarded as a ruthless criminal and Sam and I as two louts too stupid to turn on him, Sarah was viewed in a slightly different light. Our town saw her, I decided after careful consideration, as an honest and caring girl who fell in with the wrong crowd; as someone bullied and threatened into silence; as someone scared for her safety and that of her fine family. She would not be totally ostracized, though she would not be completely embraced either.

As for me, I did my best to ignore the whispers, the cold stares, even the occasional confrontation with people who said things like, "You should be ashamed of yourself," or, "You little creep." The worst of the public's reaction was the day an elderly lady who walked with a stoop followed me for about two blocks downtown all the time shouting obscenities, forcing me to quicken my pace to a near run to lose her. The funniest was when a little girl in a lineup at the 7-Eleven looked at me and proclaimed loudly to her embarrassed mom, "Isn't that one of those little bastards?"

Some mornings before she started her shift, Sarah would drop by my house, giving us some time alone to sustain our relationship. I never raised the issue of her moving out of her parents' place – and moving in with us – and she didn't either, at least not directly. One day, as we sat on the back patio watching huge white clouds race overhead in the hours before a rainstorm, she turned to me and said: "You ever feel like you're standing still, while everything else rushes forward?"

I shrugged and looked away, trying my best to come across as just another obtuse guy confused by all abstract concepts, bedeviled by anything that couldn't be grasped in his hands, such as a cold beer.

One day Sarah told me her dad's medical practice, which he'd purchased from a popular retiring doctor, had begun foundering because of what he called "the fallout from the incident." He said it would be months before he really knew how bad it would be, but estimated he'd lost about one-third of his patients. And this was sick – I almost felt happy to hear it.

Tom Opal continued to languish in the hospital, though I only heard snippets of information about his condition, sometimes from sources as unreliable as Mom, who heard all the best and worst rumors in the course of her workday. I must admit I spent far too many hours thinking about him and fantasizing he'd recover and things would return to normal, if there really was such a thing.

Our July 5 court date crept closer and Mr. Higgins said it was hard to mount a defense against a case that didn't appear to exist. You can't battle a ghost, he remarked. So don't worry, this will all be over soon, he advised. In a way he was dead wrong, but in a more immediate way he was right.

On July 2, just as I headed out the door for work, Higgins called to say the state prosecutor had just informed him the charges against the four of us were being dropped. A lack of evidence, he chortled. My mom hovered closer and closer to me as I talked on the phone.

"You mean, that's it," I asked Mr. Higgins. "It's over."

"Yes," he answered. "Unless the prosecutor or the police suddenly get some new evidence. I don't think that will be happening, will it Mr. Joseph?"

Mom ripped the phone from my hand to confirm what she thought she overheard.

"Yes," she screamed into the phone, laughing and pulling me close for a hug.

"I told you I got a good lawyer," she said after hanging up the phone.

"Mom. The State had no case."

She hugged me again, and I felt my spine straighten.

"What's wrong," she asked.

"Well, there's still Mr. Opal."

"I know," she said. "But assuming he actually remembers what happened when he comes out of the coma, it's still his word against yours, and he's suffered a head injury."

I sighed. "Mom, that's not what I meant."

The next day *The Lookout* did carry another "Page one" story, this time without our photographs. It said:

Charges against four teens accused in an attack that left a popular 44-year-old Deception Pass man in hospital with a critical head injury were dropped Wednesday by the state prosecutor.

Prosecutor Dan Evans said the state lacked evidence to proceed with the charges against the teens, who were accused of beating Tom Opal when he checked on a noisy house party June 19. Police have said the four entered into a conspiracy of silence immediately after the attack, which shocked and saddened those who knew Mr. Opal.

"We'd hoped we'd have more people come forward with information, but it didn't happen," Evans said.

Asked if he believed Mr. Opal was beaten or simply fell like the teens claim, Mr. Evans refused to answer: "I'll only say we will continue to work with police on this case."

Luke Newell had been charged with assault in the first degree. Sarah Roberts, Brady Joseph and Sam Simpson had been charged with criminal conspiracy. The four, all aged 17, were to have returned to court July 5.

The teens had claimed Mr. Opal tripped and fell down three steps, striking his head, while complaining about a noisy graduation party on Bayshore Drive. The teens and Mr. Opal had gone alone to the garage in the Roberts house about 12:30 a.m. to talk away from the loud music coming from the vacant house next door.

Mr. Opal remains unconscious at Deception Pass Hospital.

In spite of the teens' claim, police, with the help of doctors, determined Mr. Opal suffered other injuries similar to those of a beating, not a fall.

When the teens first appeared in court last month, Evans said the state would show Luke Newell attacked Mr. Opal and the other three teens conspired to keep the attack secret. Evans also described the attack as "somewhat premeditated."

Attorney Karl Jordan, who represented Miss Roberts, said the four teens should never have been charged in the first place.

"The fall was a tragedy, to be sure, but it was clearly an accident," he said. "All the police have done is try to create four more victims."

Dr. Ian Roberts, Sarah Roberts' father, said he is considering legal action against the Deception Pass Police Department for "recklessly trying to destroy the reputation of four teenagers.

"It saddens and upsets me that the police would try to find

fault in what was clearly an unfortunate event," Dr. Roberts said Wednesday. "I think the prosecution's decision today means all parties can focus on the condition and recovery of Mr. Opal and begin to move forward with their lives."

But the decision to drop all charges angered Mr. Opal's wife Eunice. "I can't believe it," she said. "The police and doctors made it clear that Tom suffered injuries that were not related to a fall. All I want to know is this: Is there one decent person who can come forward and give my family justice?"

Mr. Opal, the meat manager at Albertsons and a former past president of Deception Pass Little League, underwent surgery last month to remove a clot causing swelling in his brain. He remains on a ventilator to help him breathe.

Two days after the charges were dropped, Detective Morrison cruised into the gas station while I worked the late shift behind the cash register. I watched him pre-pay with a credit card at the pump and fill up his truck. I wondered if he knew it was me running the station. Instead of leaving he came inside, grabbed a chocolate bar and turned to me.

"How's the new job?" he said without a hint of surprise.

"Same as the old one," I said taking his money.

He studied me, and for a split second I wondered if this really was one of those awkward and unfortunate chance meetings.

Then he said, "Guess you and your friends are pretty happy about how things turned out. Even hear your girlfriend's father is talking about suing the police department."

I shrugged.

"Well. I want to talk to you, but not so much as a cop working a case…well, it's hard to explain, but I don't want to question you. Just tell you a few things."

"So tell me," I said, trying not to sound the slightest bit interested.

"Not here. Not while you're working."

"I'm not off until midnight."

"That's fine. You want to meet somewhere in Deception Pass?"

I felt my eyes narrow as I considered his request. "This some kind of trick?"

"No. Just want to tell you something that's obviously important. Also, what's the word...interesting? Okay, not an overly creative sales job on my part. But you don't have to say a word. Just listen."

I nodded. "Okay. But it wouldn't really do me a lot of good to be seen with you anywhere, not with me trying to put all this behind me."

"I understand. You name the place and I'll be there."

I thought for a moment, settling briefly on the pettiness I felt over his decision to toss us in jail, then moving on to my recurring fears he could so easily trip me up. "So anywhere?"

"Yes."

"You got a pen and paper – and a flashlight?"

Just past midnight I sat on a moss-covered picnic table surrounded by blackness, wondering if the detective would materialize at my chosen meeting place, assuming he could actually find it. I'd picked the most isolated destination I knew of in Deception Pass – a heavily-treed corner of Whiteside Park where years ago Luke and I had discovered a small clearing at the end of a deer trail.

We had stumbled upon the trail while searching for the base of the largest tree in the park, the one holding a giant eagle's nest, the one Luke swore must be a redwood, even though we didn't get many of those this far north. We'd pushed through the dark undergrowth and were resting on a fallen tree when a deer and two fawns thumped past, and we gave chase. We soon realized we were on a trail they'd beaten down over time, and we emerged in what eventually became our clearing, our oasis of light, warmth and life. The deer were gone, but Luke reached down and scooped into his palm a handful of dark pellets they'd left behind, and shouted, "Holy shit, they're still warm."

Of course, that was before we used my Mom's garden shears to widen the path, before word spread of our great hide-out and it was overrun by other teens, never again a deer, and before the cedars and firs reached out and blocked the sun, and our clearing became something less.

Day by day it had become somewhere to drink beer and smoke up without being seen. We'd even followed through on a stroke of brilliance by Luke and hauled in a picnic table from an area in the park about two hundred yards or so away. The table, where I now waited, had seen all kinds of parties over the years, and not just by Luke and Sam and me. Luke claimed he lost his virginity on top of it with a Grade 10 girl who saw him for several more weeks before finally finding him to be too much. We'd introduced a handful of other teens to our secret spot, and they did the same with some of their friends. That's how it became an all-too popular hangout with local teens, and we began feeling unwelcome in our home away from home.

Tonight all was quiet though, and I wondered what I would have done if it had been full of underage partiers. While I pondered this point I saw a flashlight beam cut through the brush, and I called out, "Keep coming. You're on the right track."

In time, the detective cautiously emerged from the underbrush and shone his light on me and carefully around the clearing, almost like he suspected a trap. How vulnerable he must have felt, coming alone in the middle of the night to the turf of teens he'd suspected of a horrible crime, teens that no doubt harbored a serious grudge against him.

"I'm alone," I called out, but he continued to stab his light into the darkness around me. Finally he set the flashlight on the table between us and sat down.

"Could you have picked a more deserted place?" he said, a hint of annoyance in his voice.

"Nope," I told him grinning.

"I didn't think so. So where'd the picnic table come from?"

I thought about not answering before telling him, "We dragged it in here a couple of years ago."

He chuckled. "Some would call it stealing, though if I was a judge I'd rule it wasn't. The picnic table never left the park. Just got relocated, that's all."

"What did you want to talk about," I said abruptly, stiffening my body and reminding myself, Don't react to him in any way.

"Two things. I better talk fast before the flashlight runs out. It was hard enough getting in here even with your directions and my light. Hate to try to leave in total darkness." He sighed. "I got a visit from the police chief from the town of Concrete. Fellow named Walter Regan. Believe you met him several weeks back when you had a run in with some locals."

"Okay," I said, swallowing hard.

"Well, the chief was calling about a couple of arson fires, one in Deception Pass, the other in Anacortes." I glanced up at Detective Morrison's face – it took on an eerie shape with the only source of light coming from below – and saw he studied me carefully as he paused. "Both were espresso huts owned by a man named Whelan. You know where I'm going with this. You had a run-in with the younger Whelans. The chief put two and two together and made an assumption, then a telephone call to me."

"He's gotta be about the most useless, fucken cop..."

"Hold on there. No one's accusing the four of you of anything, but you can't blame someone for making the connection."

I looked at him. "So you gonna charge us for another crime we didn't commit?"

"Would you let me finish before going off like that."

"Sure, finish."

The detective shook his head. "Sometimes cops talk. Not a big deal. He just told me about what had happened out there by the lake and that the four of you had a motive – revenge...in any event, your names came up in the arson investigation. We got to talking about what had happened, and how he felt he'd let you down by not going after the Whelans. It also became clear he didn't know what had happened here with Tom Opal. Anyway, I put the phone down and said to myself, 'Holy shit.'"

His swearing startled me. "What do you mean, 'Holy shit'?"

"Holy shit, as in, I get it. It all makes sense. I can see why the four of you have so little respect for the law, why you think that getting your story straight and sticking to it can overcome everything. Because that's what happened to you in Concrete with the Whelans and their friends. They rehearsed their story, stuck to it, and you know the rest. You learned a shitty lesson the hard way, and now you're putting to work what you learned."

I stared into the darkness, doing my best to show him nothing. "Another assumption," I told him. "You like coming up with these theories, don't you?"

"And had I known what had happened to the four of you in Concrete, I would have done things differently with the Opal case. I wouldn't have charged any of you. Shit. I would have known you couldn't be pressured or scared into turning on each other just because of some legal heat. In the end, charging you meant I couldn't question you anymore. So I couldn't reason with you, and keep appealing to your conscience, to your decency. And that would have been my best strategy, knowing what happened in Concrete. So I concede, I screwed up. I used the wrong approach, and everyone is paying for it to some degree."

Don't react, I reminded myself again. "So why are you telling me all this?"

He sighed, and I wondered if he was inherently unhappy at home when big cases went unsolved.

"Because, it's never too late to appeal to someone's decency."

"You can appeal all you want. Tom Opal fell. End of story."

"You know I don't believe it. I can't prove it – at least not right now – but I don't believe it. In fact, you and I both know that I've figured it out."

"No, you think you've figured it out. I know you haven't. Remember, I was there."

"If it's any consolation, if I'd been the cop in Concrete, I would have charged your attackers. I wouldn't have done the expedient thing. That often blows up in your face – or in someone else's."

"I gotta get home. Are we done?"

"You can leave anytime you want. We're just here shooting the breeze. I wouldn't want your mom to worry."

"She won't be worried. She's still at work."

"That's right. Works at that little bar downtown. Nice woman."

"If you say so."

He laughed, then fell silent, before finally saying: "I

hear you lost your dad when you were young. That you even saw it…"

"Yeah, I know," I said, my voice suddenly dripping with anger. "Poor me. And, you know, if I had a dad he would have straightened me out long ago, and none of this would have happened." I stood up. "Sorry. That's enough bullshit for one night."

"But there is one more thing I'd like to say, if you'll listen. Remember, there were two."

I hovered in front of him, debating whether to leave. Already I'd exposed too much, both by my words and expressions, and at each moment risked showing him more. Still, I was curious. I shrugged and sat back down.

"I know, you think I'm using the dad thing to press your buttons, but I'm not."

Now he stood. "I was just trying to lead into the second point. That maybe it would be a good thing right now to have another shoulder to lean on at home. Because this thing isn't quite over yet. It's Mr. Opal. He's slipping away. No easy way to say this. He'll be dead by the end of the week."

I sat calmly without emotion, eyes steady, fingers crossed on my lap, hoping he'd wonder if I failed to react because I'd already figured out Tom Opal was doomed or because I was just another heartless fuck that the world didn't need.

"I thought you'd want to know this before you read it in the newspaper or something," he said.

Now Morrison hovered over me, his eyes piercing, waiting for me to speak or do something other than stare away in silence. He had ventured far into the darkness brandishing cutting words he so clearly hoped would penetrate with the precision of a surgical instrument. Now he sought a sign he'd found his target.

We remained motionless for what seemed like forever,

and I'm sure he had no idea how hard his message tore at me, how it had already laid bare something he felt so sure existed, something we both wanted exposed.

"That's the two points, but there really were three," he continued. "The third one is this: I know one of the four of you will cave in, in time. I suspect it will be you. If not you maybe your girlfriend. But someone will. You'll come to see me, in my office, and you'll tell the whole story. And here's the thing. I know you're going to do this in time, but it would be a hell of a lot easier on everyone – everyone, you included – if you did it sooner rather than later."

He picked up his flashlight and disappeared into the bush, not seeing what he'd left lying in plain view, not just flayed, but eviscerated. I thought of calling out to him, ending it right then, but he was gone. So in the blackness I sat alone, vulnerable, the forest rustling around me. I waited, not to heal or even to scab over – because some things never mend – but to feel whole enough to stand and make my way home.

10

The next day I ran – not figuratively, like I'd done so often, but literally – out onto my street, the pavement smooth under my cheap runners, the morning air warm in my lungs, each breath deep and strong. Past the small aging homes, along the rocky beach and then onto the winding two-lane highway and across the bridge teeming with tourists taking in the dramatic view. The waters rushed past below, blue and shiny, as effortless as my steps. My attention shifted to the cars cruising slowly by, and I quickened my pace, driven by the sense I could outrun them, the near certainty I could tear across the island until I ran out of road, then turn around and sprint home.

Machine-like, my heart pumped oxygen and life to my limbs, propelling me into the state park, under the expansive branches of the greenest cedars imaginable and through the campground. The smell of bacon and campfires filled the air. Tents were zipped and unzipped, kids laughed, a baby cried. On I went, past the small sea-side lake where a handful of people splashed in the shallow water, past the public washroom, its sides somehow untouched by graffiti, then into a slow loop back onto the highway toward home.

Two blocks from my house, I slowed to a walk and

marveled at how this mass of skin and muscle and bone could do whatever I asked of it. Then the incongruity struck. How physically, I might never be stronger, but emotionally, I might still be years from my prime. How I'd been given a body but not the sense to use it. That my heart – not the one pounding healthily in my chest, but the figurative one – remained my least developed component, my weak link, something incapable of leading. A heart that didn't understand how to love the girl of my dreams and that couldn't find a way to forgive a mother for the most common of mistakes. A heart that lacked the courage to admit I did something wrong. And worse, one without the capacity to suffer enough to want to make things right.

So this is what I did when Tom Opal died two days later: Nothing. I felt a tinge of regret for my actions and silence. But I did nothing.

Tom Opal's funeral service was set for the largest church on the edge of town on the afternoon of July 17. From all accounts, he never climbed out of the coma that followed his fall, and I heard he was weakened by the surgery to repair the clotted artery that had caused the swelling in his brain. He languished for days, his vital signs fading, until his wife agreed to take him off life support, fearing he was suffering through a fight that had all but ended. His wife chose the largest church in town, not because she and Tom had worshipped there but because the service was expected to draw a good percentage of the population.

In the days leading up to the funeral, the hostility toward the four of us reached a nasty peak, though I must admit I detected great confusion over what people believed transpired in the Roberts' garage. Many expressed their feelings in words like "killers," "scumbags" and the like. Luke, of course, had it the worst, and on the day after Opal's death he invoked what he called a zero-tolerance policy – he decided he'd deck anyone who gave him grief. He hadn't realized most of the name-callers would be female, and he refused to hit women, who he would only swear back at, usually ineffectively. Most of the men who dared yell anything at Luke did so from passing cars, with one exception. Three of Tom's co-workers did confront Luke outside a convenience store in a loud exchange, but the police arrived before any punches were thrown, though Luke claimed to have backed the trio almost into the store with his clenched fists alone. While this ugliness burned a place in most memories, it was the more ambiguous moments that left a mark on me. The eyes searching me for a hint of truth. The people who wanted to hate me, who wanted to scream at me or spit in my face, but couldn't, because they just didn't know. I felt a strange sympathy for them, the way they were so lost.

The Lookout carried a front page article on Tom Opal's death. I didn't read it.

Four days before the funeral, Sarah had phoned. "We've got to talk right away," she said.

"When are you coming over?" I'd asked.

"No. Let's have a change of scenery. Meet me under the bridge, you know, where you first asked me out. In half an hour."

I searched for the same log I'd sat on months ago when I'd raced along the beach with Mikey in my lame attempt to surprise Sarah while she jogged. The log had disappeared, probably swept away by a high tide or storm. I found another one close to the spot and waited, my eyes drifting to a pair of kayakers fighting the channel's current, their paddles spinning rapidly as they inched forward.

Sarah had approached from the road with her arms folded in front of her chest, her face tight, and sat down, close, like the first time she joined me on this beach. She made no move to touch me. She'd slipped off her flip-flops and absently used her big toe to dislodge smooth, wet stones from the rocky ground.

I placed my arm around her. "What's wrong?"

"Nothing's wrong. Other than Western Washington suddenly booting me out of university."

"What?"

"Budget cuts they say. They had to trim back on the dental program. So I'm out."

"They can't do that. Not after accepting you."

"That's what my dad said. Even got a lawyer involved. But it didn't make any difference. I'm out for September. Told me I could reapply for the following year."

"What about other universities, like in Seattle or something…"

"They're all full now, Brady. Don't you think we've thought of all this?"

"I guess…"

"The thing is, Brady, that someone got to Western Washington. Some fucker here in town with some pull screwed this up for me. Called up to that shithole in Bellingham and said, 'You can't let that Roberts girl in. You know what she did?'"

"I don't think…"

"Of course that's what happened, Brady. Use your head, or are you still waiting for the call back from the first gas station you worked at? You know, the one that gave you a week off after Mr. Opal's unfortunate accident."

Now I kicked at the rocks under my feet, wishing I could find comforting words that didn't sound so lame.

"So what are you going to do?"

"I dunno." She stood suddenly. "Well, that's not true. I do know. That's why I wanted to see you."

I stood and tried to take her hand, but she stepped back and said, "No, I just want you to listen carefully. Cause I can't keep living like this. Getting booted out of university before I start. Sneaking around your house. None of this is working."

"So..."

"So I think it's time we changed this. You and I. It's time we took control. That we moved in together. And not here, not in this town, but somewhere else. Like Seattle. We'll go there and get jobs, and get a place together, and clear our fucken heads and figure out where we want to go, what we want to do. Start moving forward again."

I had stared at her as I waited for the right response to pop into my head. Nothing came. I tried searching deeper, and found myself bereft.

"So..." she said.

"This is kinda sudden."

"No it's not, Brady. This is where we've been headed all along, from the moment Mr. Opal fell."

"He didn't fall, he..."

"This shouldn't be a hard decision."

"It's a big decision. Leaving everyone. We have no money to speak of, and..."

"That's why I'm not rushing you. Take a week. Longer if you need it. But I need an answer."

"What if...what if – and I'm not saying this would be my answer – but what if I said no. What would happen then?"

She reached forward and kissed me, a slow painful gesture that only half hit my lips, and I knew the answer, and suddenly wondered why I always asked for everything to be spelled out.

I caught up to Sam as I wound my way deep inside

Whiteside Park on our familiar trail choked by a thick summer growth of branches and foliage, like a clogged artery.

"Funny meeting you here," he said, pushing aside a fir tree branch, continuing on in silence.

When the two of us reached our clearing we were greeted by Luke, who sat sipping a Mountain Dew on our crumbling picnic table, right where Detective Morrison had rested. The three of us exchanged small talk – about the town's half-deserted streets, the cool wind off the ocean today – until Sarah arrived about five minutes later.

"Had a hard time slipping out," she said in a slightly breathless voice. "My mom tried to convince me to stay home until well after the funeral."

We all nodded, once again soaking in her presence, her scent.

"Good meeting time, huh?" Luke said finally, looking at his watch, the one he'd shoplifted from Walgreen's two years ago. "Opal's funeral started fifteen minutes ago. Everyone who hates us is together somewhere else."

"You are so brilliant, dude," Sam said laughing. "So what's on your mind?"

Luke spun the pop bottle in his hand, around and around. He grimaced, then tried to speak slowly, though the words sailed out almost faster than we could comprehend. "You guys have done great. We all have. I knew we could stick together, pull this off, just like we've done. There's no looking back now. Not really. Except...I don't know, Brady has second thoughts, if you can call 'em that, cause he never really agreed in the first place, though he went along. Sam. He's done okay for hisself." Luke smiled. "I think this whole thing has even made him some kind of minor celebrity, and he's gotten laid a couple times 'cause of it. And Sarah, well this hasn't been great for her, but she's never complained. Probably never will either."

Luke paused, but only for a second.

"But, I don't know. Well, I just wanted to say that if anyone has second thoughts, doesn't think they can hold it together, and I'm not just talking for a couple of months more, I mean, well, forever, you know, they should speak up now, 'cause wouldn't it just suck to have someone cave in down the road. I'm talking years later, you know, after everyone has taken the heat for so long."

We looked at Luke, then at each other, Sarah sitting on the picnic table, her shoulders unusually hunched, Sam standing next to me, wearing the same satisfied grin as always, seemingly untouched by anything, and me, of course, my hands stuffed down in my pants pockets, my mouth tightly shut.

No one spoke, and I'm sure none of us had expected Luke to emerge from his black and white world to hint at an option other than our constant silence, our continued deception. In the rhythmic rise and fall of our support for him, this moment represented a low, a momentary trough. I swore I could hear the creak of the trees shifting their weight in the wind as we waited for someone to say something, anything.

But in a world filled with so much confusion and so many things that were never what they seemed, I was sure of one thing: There were instances when one word, even one expression or gesture, sent your life spinning off in all sorts of directions. This was one of those, and it would become a moment that would haunt me more than just for that night in the garage, because, let's face it, Tom Opal's death wasn't so much a calculated and character-revealing event as an inadvertent and unfortunate one. However, what happened next involved much careful consideration, hours of not so much weighing right and wrong but contemplating this outcome and that outcome.

I felt that because I'd never know whether Luke's offer was a sincere invitation for three of us to clear our names or a simple ploy to help forever cement our deception. What I do know is that I was prepared for almost anything he might say, so when I finally spoke my words were skillfully chosen.

"It would be murder now, wouldn't it?" I offered. "Now that Tom Opal's dead, it would have to be a murder charge, or at least manslaughter."

Sam nodded. "Would have to be at least manslaughter. You bet."

Sarah sat up straight. "You'd be talking about some fairly serious time in jail." She shrugged. "And since they have no evidence other than what we've given them, that would be bullshit."

Luke grinned. "It would be bullshit."

And so it went.

As we left the clearing to go our separate ways, Sarah slid an arm around me. Sam and Luke, both walking ahead, looked back and smiled. "You two gonna duck back into the bushes for a quickie?" Sam asked.

"Isn't your right hand calling you?" Sarah shot back.

For a moment it felt like old times, until Sarah whispered, "Have you given what I said any more thought?"

"Of course," I told her.

"So…"

"I had a week or more to decide, didn't I?" I said.

Sarah simply nodded, squeezed my hand and went off alone.

When I got home my mom sat in the living room, like a parent waiting up for a teenager pushing the bounds of his nightly curfew. Of course, in my house there was never a curfew and rarely ever anyone waiting up to see if I made it home.

"Brady," she called as I tried to rush up the stairs with only a curt hello.

"What, Mom?"

"Can you come in here? Remember I said Amanda was coming over. Now we want to talk to you." I leaned over the railing and saw Amanda sitting in my favorite chair, by the living room window.

"Can it wait, Mom?"

"No. Let's talk right now, just for a minute."

I sighed. "Okay," I said leaning against the door to the room. "Let's talk, just for a minute."

"C'mon, Brady. Sit down." She tried to make her voice sound tender, relaxed. Instead it sounded strangely awkward, emitting, for the first time I could remember, a trace of self-consciousness.

I sat on the arm of the love seat just inside the door, my body bristling.

"Thanks, Brady." My mom looked at Amanda, who smiled back warmly.

"Well, Brady. With all that's been happening in your life…I just want to…to give you some good news."

"You win the lottery or something, Mom?"

She laughed softly. "In a way, Brady. Yes. The biggest lottery ever. I've fallen in love. Deeply in love."

"Oh, God, not again. With who this time?" But then I knew. Before my words filled the air, I already knew.

My mom looked nervously at Amanda, then back at me, but before she could speak, I was out of my chair, a finger pointing at her in short accusing jabs.

"Don't say it, Mom. Don't you dare say it."

"I'm in love with Amanda," she said calmly. "And she's in love with me."

"That's bullshit. It's not right."

"It is right, Brady. I thought you of all people would understand. All these years leading up to this, they weren't right. Did you ever wonder why I could never really fall deeply in love with someone? Why I…"

"Cause you hate things like commitment. Cause you hate responsibility. I don't know, maybe just cause you like variety when it comes to screwing."

She flew out of her seat. "Don't you talk to me like that," she screamed.

"Maybe I should go, Kathy," Amanda said, sliding forward in the chair. "Give you and Brady some time to talk it through. I know, Brady, it's all a shock, such a big shock." She started to stand.

"No, please, everyone sit down," Mom said, suddenly plunking herself onto the couch. "Let's just talk."

Amanda took her seat too, but I remained standing.

"Listen, Mom," I said, my palms raised toward her. "You can have your little fling with Amanda, just like you've had with God knows how many guys, but I don't want to hear about it. I don't want to know about all the disgusting and disturbing shit you do. Just leave me out of it. And do me a favor, Mom, don't advertise it all over town – you're already enough of an embarrassment."

I waited for her to charge forward, to grab me and belt me, because that at least would bring the conversation to an end.

But she took a deep breath, and said, unable to conceal the bitterness in her voice: "No, Brady. That's not the way it will be. You see, Amanda's moving in with me, with us. We're tired of keeping our relationship a secret. You could say we're coming out."

"Don't do this, Mom. Haven't you humiliated me enough already for the past seventeen years?"

"Listen, Brady," Amanda said. "There's nothing humiliating about two people being in love. About a house built on love, a family built on love."

I turned to her, and I swear to God, I tried to stop the words, but I couldn't. "You know, Amanda, you can talk about love and family and shit like that all you want, but what you bring into this house is an abomination. Just more sickness. The last thing we need is another freak show. Specially the one we'll have when my mom tires of aging queers and goes back to her old tricks, so to speak, and your whole fucken sick relationship falls to pieces."

The room fell quiet, and I could hear my breathing, shallow and fast. I waited for Amanda's face to ball up in tears as she bolted from the house, never to return, though I knew I was rarely that lucky.

But I didn't expect her to sigh and look at me with large luminous eyes, and simply say, without a trace of defensiveness in her voice: "I'm sorry you feel that way, Brady. But I know you'll change with time."

I needed forceful words, clever and convincing arguments, but all that came to mind were the vilest swear words I'd ever heard, so I clenched my fists and fought for a trace of composure as I waved the conversation to a close.

"Don't do this, Brady," my mother said. "I didn't raise you to be like this."

I started laughing. It was a sad, mocking sound, and she knew what I was implying.

She turned to Amanda. "He thinks I didn't raise him at all. That I was way too lenient every time he got into trouble. But when a boy sees his father fall to his death, when a boy doesn't understand that his dad had a common mental illness, schizophrenia, and that's why he disconnected from the entire family, and that it was nobody's fault that…"

"Enough, Mom," I said, my voice more angry. "This doesn't concern her."

"But it does, Brady. If Amanda's going to be part…"

"She's part of nothing," I screamed, and then I was gone, out into a town filing out of a lengthy funeral service, a town, at least temporarily, engulfed in grief, in hatred toward four teens. I walked up to Luke's house, ignoring the few stares I attracted from faceless shapes in passing cars, and stood before the dilapidated structure that seemed to decay before my eyes, though I knew the process had been a long and painful one. Okay. So if my home was a nuthouse, well, Luke's was an insidiously sickening house of horror. I laughed out loud, alarmed for a second that someone would hear me. Then I laughed again, more discreetly. How pathetic that I only managed to find comfort in someone else's life being more screwed up than mine.

Three days later, Amanda moved in while I was at work. I can imagine the strain my very existence foisted upon their twisted relationship – Amanda suggesting they give me more time, my mother saying 'screw it, let's grab your stuff.' My Mom won out – she usually does, wearing her opponents down with the constant force of a blunt object. She later told me the move took about five hours but would have been cut to two if I'd been around to help. But she was quick to point out that they knew I wouldn't offer my services, so they went ahead with the move on a day I worked, without so much as telling me.

Late that morning – while almost every room of our house slowly became transformed with new furniture, pictures and various other things Amanda had accumulated over thirty something years of life – Sarah pulled into the gas station and motioned me outside.

I slid into the passenger seat and she leaned over and

rested her forehead against mine, and for a second I would have gone anywhere she asked.

"I'm coming over for dinner tonight," she said. "And I've got a surprise for you."

"I don't know if I can take another surprise," I said.

"Oh, c'mon. Cheer up. This is a good one. You'll see."

"Well it can only be better than the one my mom pulled on me the other day. Brace yourself, okay. My mom's..."

"Gay. I know about her and Amanda," she said. "I've known for weeks."

"You what?"

"She told me. I think it's great. I'm really proud of her for having the courage to listen to her heart."

"You know this won't last. It will come to another famous crashing halt, and the whole town will have another reason to laugh at us."

She looked at me carefully, and glanced at the pickup truck that pulled up to the pump behind us. "I know you don't realize this, Brady, but love is a hard thing to find. You got to seize it if you get the chance."

About an hour before quitting time, Mom called the gas station and broke the news they'd gone ahead and moved Amanda in. I didn't reply, except to say I already knew of her plan to have Sarah over for dinner. "Great" she said, sounding truly excited. "Amanda and I are already making something for the four of us."

When I got home, I slipped in quietly and headed straight to the shower, trying to ignore the changes to our home – the paintings on once-bare walls, the furniture crammed into every available corner.

Sarah arrived while I was in the shower and I found the three of them in the kitchen – Sarah chopping carrots, Amanda scrubbing away at built up grime in the sink, Mom just watching, her jaw moving up and down rapidly. Sarah leaned back and kissed me, and Mom and Amanda both chuckled like schoolgirls.

"Isn't this great," my mom cooed.

"What?" I asked.

"You know. Everything."

As I retreated to the living room, Sarah yelled, "Brady, put on the Channel 11 news. At 6 o'clock we can see my surprise."

I stopped suddenly, gasping like I'd been kicked in the chest. "What?"

"My surprise," she said. "It's on the news."

"What do you mean it's on the news?" I asked, returning to the kitchen.

"You'll see."

While the roast cooked in the oven and vegetables simmered on the stove, the four of us crowded around the television's slightly fuzzy picture.

We heard the familiar Channel 11 News jingle, and then three stories were teased by the female anchor: A deadly fire in Bremerton, more layoffs at the Boeing plant, and, "Startling new revelations about the alleged teenage cover-up in the death of a popular Deception Pass resident."

As the anchor woman began with details of the deadly fire, I turned in horror to Sarah, crowded next to me on the love seat.

"Don't look so alarmed," she said. "The striking new revelations, or whatever, she said, they're good, just hold on."

"I can't wait. You gotta tell me."

She leaned into me and pointed at the television. "Oh, look at that nasty house fire."

I sat, barely breathing, ignoring glances from Mom and Amanda, until finally, the anchor woman said this: "In the north-west town of Deception Pass, funeral services were held yesterday for a popular forty-four-year-old resident whose troubling death has divided the town and left a cloud over four local teens. The police say Tom Opal died of complications from head injuries after being attacked by teens while he tried to break up a noisy party. The teens, all high school seniors at the time, say Mr. Opal fell. And they argue they're being targeted by a justice system bent on assigning blame. But Channel 11 News has some shocking new evidence. And it may help put to rest the mystery that has haunted the town in the shadow of the historic Deception Pass Bridge. Pam Matsusami has this report."

I glanced over at Sarah as images of her house flashed across the screen. She smiled at me for a second, and said, "Just watch."

And I did, awed by the various faces and places on the screen, transfixed by the clichéd words of the reporter's voice-over as she talked about the night of the party, our story that Opal fell, the police suspicions, the charges laid against us and then dropped. She continued: "And in this town the debate raged. Tom Opal was a loving husband, father of two, former little league president and popular manager at a local supermarket. So when he died one week ago, the pitch of the debate turned nearly hysterical."

A drug-loving classmate of Sam's appeared on screen, and said, "The problem is the cops. Anytime something bad happens in this town, it's, you know, the same thing, it had to be a teen, right? That's what they think. Tom Opal fell, those four are innocent. It's persecution."

Then a female clerk at Albertsons, "The whole town knows what happened. Those teens killed him. Then they covered it up. Now none of them has the decency to come forward, and since they were the only ones in the room, it's a hard case for police to prove."

And, Eunice Opal. "Yes, I believe police arrested the right people. The evidence shows Tom didn't fall, he was attacked. It's not easy living here, knowing they're roaming the town free, maybe even laughing out loud about how they got away with it. But I believe justice will prevail."

Then back to the reporter: "But Channel 11 News has done the one thing that police weren't able to do. Give one of the teens a lie detector test. And the results are shocking."

I gasped, loud enough I'm sure for Mom and Amanda to hear, when the next footage showed Sarah submitting herself to a polygraph test.

"You didn't," I whispered.

She smiled and nodded. "I sure did. Just watch."

The reporter continued, "Hank Edwards has for fifteen years administered polygraph tests for the major Pacific Northwest police departments and the Washington State Patrol. We hired him and his equipment to ask Sarah Roberts five questions, and the results showed she told the truth for each one. Is your name Sarah Roberts? Yes. Do you live on Bayshore Drive? Yes. Did you attend a party at a vacant house next door on June 19? Yes. Did Luke Newell attack Tom Opal in your garage that night? No. Did Tom Opal accidentally fall and strike his head? Yes."

My Mom burst out of her chair and screamed "Yes." Amanda smiled with delight. Sarah laughed. She just laughed.

Finally, Detective Morrison appeared on screen, asked to comment on the results. "They're interesting, but don't mean much. None of the teens would take a polygraph through the Deception Pass Police Department – their lawyers flat out refused. It's curious Miss Roberts would take one now, when we can't control the questions asked."

The news coverage ended with footage of Sarah walking along her street, and switched to Tom Opal's funeral, and the reporter's last voice-over. "Only the four teens know for sure what happened that tragic night, but the polygraph strongly suggests they're telling the truth. While that doesn't make Tom Opal's death any easier to swallow, it may prevent four more people from being engulfed by a lingering tragedy."

Mom rushed over, tears welling in her eyes, and hugged Sarah. "That proves it," she said. "That proves he fell."

Then she laughed at Amanda. "Maybe this means we can shop at Albertsons again."

The phone rang, and I knew who it would be.

"Brady," said Sam after I answered. "Put her on. I know she's there; she told us to watch the news."

I could hear Luke shouting Sarah's name in the background as I passed the phone over. Sarah giggled, Amanda said something about the roast burning before she and Mom disappeared, and the television news blared on.

When Sarah finally put the phone down, she smiled at me and said: "Well?"

"How did you do it?" I asked. "I know, the questions were selective. That part I understand. But the one about Opal's fall being an accident."

"It's not that surprising," she said, her voice dropping to a whisper. "He did fall, though he had a little help. And it was an accident. No one meant for it to happen. So the answer was yes. It was the truth. It really was. You know there are companies that help people pass polygraph tests. I found two in Seattle, but you know what? I didn't need them in the end. I knew I didn't need them."

"But what if you'd faltered, even slightly? It would have shown up on the test, and where would we be now. It was awfully risky."

She got up and turned off the television, then leaned over me, her hand brushing underneath my chin. "Anything worth having involves a risk."

❧

As the four of us gathered around the dining room table, I tried to remember the last meal I had eaten there, but couldn't. Mom brandished Amanda's digital camera, and asked us to gather together behind the food for a "family photo." I cringed as she set the self-timer and scooted back around the table to join us. As the flash exploded, I wondered if the camera was capable of exposing multiple charades.

We began with small talk, large glasses of cheap wine and moderate servings of dry, overcooked roast, and limp, tasteless vegetables. "I almost forgot," Mom blurted. "A toast. To new beginnings."

Then the conversation drifted to plans for me and Sarah. Sarah twisted a soggy piece of cauliflower with her fork, and I knew that while she'd shared so much with my mom over the last few months, she hadn't mentioned her ultimatum.

"Funny you should talk about the future," Sarah said, not looking up. "I've made some plans, now that I've been rejected from Western Washington."

She smiled at Mom and Amanda. "I'm going to Seattle. Not forever, but long enough to get things back on track." She paused. "And I've asked Brady to come with me."

Various emotions flashed across Mom's face – apprehension about losing her only son to the world, perhaps fear of being alone (until, I suspect, she remembered she now had Amanda). Then a smile formed, and she said, "Good for you. Amanda and I will do whatever we can to help you two. Find you a place. Give you enough money to get on your feet. You know, you can even borrow my car for awhile. We have Amanda's, and…"

"Mom," I interrupted, "I haven't decided if I'm going yet."

The room fell silent, and I sensed Sarah bristling in the chair beside me.

"If it's too big of a step for you, Brady," Mom said, "you two can always live here together. Amanda and I would love that, wouldn't we?"

"Yes," Amanda said simply, like she had any fucken say.

"Thanks, Kathy, for that offer again, but...I think I need to get out of this town. Let peoples' memory of Mr. Opal fade. And now because of the polygraph test, I wouldn't feel like I was running away. More like chasing new opportunities."

As Sarah talked, I noticed my mom staring at me, probably recalling our earlier conversation when I revealed my love for Sarah was, well, less than rock solid. Now I regretted opening my mouth.

"You know, Brady, your job at the gas station definitely isn't enough to keep you here," Mom said. "You could get something better in Seattle. Lots more opportunities there, you know."

"I've tried telling him that," Sarah replied. "He's just not sure what he wants...if he wants me, is what I mean to say."

I listened to her voice for a hint of sadness, or regret or any other emotion. But this is all I heard – words carefully crafted to elicit enough pathos for me to finally give in and agree to go. Not cold, but definitely calculated.

I began shoveling food into my mouth, trying to rush along this nightmare of a meal. I gulped down large mouthfuls of wine, watching my mom dispense advice to Sarah like she was qualified to tell other people how to live. The conversation shifted back to small talk, jokes, meaningless chatter that suggested all was well in the world.

Eventually Mom slipped into the kitchen and re-emerged with a plate of brownies she'd thrown together, literally I'm sure, for dessert – "See, Brady, I really can cook" – and the meal lingered on.

That's when my stomach began tightening. Almost

unnoticeably at first, then building quickly. An internal alarm bell going off, a prompting from my unconscious, a sense of danger so strong I had to forcibly slow my breathing.

I could recall only feeling one such thing before, six years ago when I was eleven. Back when my mom had fallen into the habit of staying for drinks after work each night, because finally I was old enough to stay home alone. She'd removed the empty propane tank from our backyard barbecue, and got it filled on the way to work. It rattled around in the trunk of her car on the way home, the valve being knocked slightly open. She had parked in the garage, and gone upstairs to bed.

Later I had wakened in a sweat, with an overwhelming feeling in my gut that something was wrong. I couldn't smell the propane, which by now had drifted through much of the house, moving toward the furnace where it would surely ignite on the pilot light in a deadly blast.

I had stumbled from bed, driven only by a hunch that danger was upon us. I had shaken Mom awake, and she had told me not to worry, that she was home now.

"No, Mom," I screamed. "Something's wrong."

She, too, had staggered from bed, humoring me, turning on lights as she wandered. She was the first to smell the propane. She had raced downstairs, suddenly infused with panic, and hit the button on the garage door opener, then grabbed her car keys so she could open the trunk and close the tank's valve. The firefighters who later came said they thought the house was mere seconds from exploding.

Now, the same intuition that protected us that night had come alive, sending me disconcerting – no terrifying – flashes of alarm.

Around the table I looked, moving from face to face, searching for a sign of who was in danger, and from what.

Was it Mom and Amanda, and their relationship?

Sarah, and her increasing duplicity? Me, and my resignation to accept, and promote, Tom Opal's death as an accident? Or was it all of us?

Away from the table I moved, ignoring the startled stares. Through the kitchen, down the hallway, toward the front door. Stop. My hands flew up, pointing quickly. Front door, garage, living room. Did one lead to safety, or destruction?

Sarah appeared at my side and grabbed my hands, her eyes wide. "What are you doing, Brady?" she demanded. "What's wrong?"

"I don't know," I told her, for once honest.

11

On the seventh day after Sarah's sea-side ultimatum, I hovered near the living room phone, working various scenarios through, before finally dialing her number. The phone rang and rang before Sarah finally picked it up, breathless.

"Sarah."

"Brady. I was in the shower."

"I know. I mean, I guess you…can we meet somewhere and talk?"

"Look," she said. "I've gotta work lunch and dinner today – more than 11 hours – someone's sick, and what time is it now, 10:10. I leave for work in another fifteen minutes, so if you got anything to say, say it now."

"I didn't know that, about you working. I thought we could meet for lunch…why don't we meet, after work?"

She paused. "Why can't you tell me on the phone, right now, whatever you've got to say?"

"It's better we meet."

My words elicited a silence that stung. Finally she said, "What's so hard about a yes or no?"

I didn't know what to say. "It's more complicated than that."

"No it's not."

"So can we talk, in person?"

"What was wrong with yesterday, or the day before?" she demanded. "Why haven't you called me since you got all weird at dinner? I left three messages for you."

"I know…I was just trying to get things worked out in my head."

She sighed. "You know the park above the middle school in Anacortes? Meet me on the bench overlooking the tennis courts, 9:30 tonight."

"Sure."

"And, Brady."

"Yes."

There was silence, and then she hung up.

Upstairs in my room I yanked open my nightstand drawer and pulled out an envelope, my name scrawled on its front in red pen. I'd found it on the nightstand a half-hour after Sarah had left following dinner. Inside were the two photographs she'd snapped after we'd made love on that sticky afternoon in my room. That now seemed like ages ago.

Sarah's attempt to freeze that moment had worked perfectly. The 4x6 photo of me captured a single bead of sweat trapped in my eyelash and a strangely crooked grin on my face. Sarah's snapshot of herself, taken by her own outstretched arms, came back a hint out-of-focus and under-exposed, softening her features to an even more intense level of beauty and giving her skin an angelic glow. I swore the image held so much allure you'd study it and wonder, over and over, how you could not deeply love and desire this person.

But, in all honesty, that beautiful, almost heavenly image of Sarah was not the one etched most strongly in my mind. The one I saw when I closed my eyes at night, when I tried to fantasize about her seductive features, when I tried to lose myself in her occasional tenderness, was a different Sarah. It was the one who was first at Tom Opal's side on the night he "fell." It was the one who first realized the seriousness of his injuries. Who screamed at me to stop when I started to leave the room to call an ambulance. Who put all of us, and our freedom and reputations, above Tom Opal's desperate medical needs, without hesitation, without doubt. Who struggled to find his pulse, and turned to us, her eyes, clear and clinical, and said, "Okay. We'd better get our stories straight, 'cause I've got a shitty feeling about this."

That was the Sarah I couldn't shake from my mind, no matter how hard I tried. She came in powerful flashes, her chilling determination, her cunning strength.

And here was the thing: How could you fault Sarah for having instincts that first looked out for her friends, for those she cared about? But then, how could you love her without qualification? How could you love her enough?

I didn't know.

That was not what made me hesitate, though. That was not what finally made up my mind.

I bestowed one last long look upon the two photos before tucking them away in the envelope and burying them in my nightstand drawer.

That night, as I neared Anacortes from the south-east in Amanda's car, something odd struck me about the town. It wasn't until I pulled on to the main commercial strip a couple of minutes later that I realized the entire area had been engulfed by a blackout. No streetlights, no traffic lights, no bright glow emanated from homes and shops, other than the occasional one running off an emergency generator. All I could see was the beams of my headlights, and others, cutting through the eerie blackness.

I turned up the hill stretching above town and minutes later pulled up behind the school, next to the dark field that on any other summer night would be illuminated by tennis court lights. I got out and looked inside Sarah's car, parked along the curb in front of mine. Empty. I turned into the blackness and carefully made my way along the steep slope.

"Hey, Brady." I heard her voice, and wondered how she knew the footsteps were mine.

"Over here," she said. "Watch out for the drop-off into the tennis courts. Quite a fall, don't you know."

I stumbled toward her and took a seat on the bench beside the shape lit only by the moonlight and distant lights of the oil refinery across the bay, which had somehow avoided the blackout.

"You're early," I said.

"No power at the restaurant," she said. "Got sent home just before nine."

"What caused the blackout? Did you hear?"

"Don't know, but it's beautiful," she said. "The whole town plunged into darkness."

I looked down at the car headlights crawling along, and the large gobs of blackness consuming the downtown, industrial area, marinas and the residential neighborhoods.

"Kind of creepy," I said. "Dangerous too. No traffic lights. I wonder if the hospital has power, or if the 9-1-1 dispatch is even working…"

"Stop it, Brady," she said, her voice impassive, "just stop it."

"So," I said.

'So."

I heard her body shift on the bench, away from the darkness stretching out before us, toward me. I picked up the smell of grease on her uniform, a rare shallowness in her breath.

"You at least owe me an explanation," she said.

"An explanation?"

"About why you won't come. About why it's over for us."

"Here's the thing. I don't think you should go either," I told her. "I think you should stay here. Give things more time. Maybe next year you'll get accepted into university, and then..."

She sighed. "That's not what I asked you. I knew you'd say something like this, Brady. Try to talk me out of it. Try to find some way of leaving everything in limbo. But I'm going. So the question is, are you coming with me? Are you ready to take the next step?"

I took a deep breath and forced out the word. "No."

She turned and looked out over the darkness, like she couldn't stand the sight of me any longer.

"You always act like it's me, like it's me who's so detached," she said. "Then after all we've been through the past few weeks, after everything, you do this. Just dump me like I mean nothing..."

"It's not like that."

"Do you really even love me?"

"You know the answer."

"Then why are you doing this? Why?"

I knew I couldn't tell her. Not right now.

"Brady?"

So instead I used abstract words that encased the sharp edges of what I really needed to convey. "Well, it's just that this next step as you call it...it's just that it doesn't feel right."

"Doesn't feel right," she said slowly. "Funny. You never said that while you were screwing me."

Her words hung in the air, a cold wind I wanted to shield myself from. "Sarah, don't..."

She stood up. Her voice resigned, bereft. "I'll make this easy for you, Brady. It's now or never. I'm going to my car and leaving. If you come after me, or if you don't, I'll have my answer. I'll have all my answers."

Moments later, I heard her car door open and close. I sat frozen on the bench, and remained that way even when I heard her car start up and slowly pull away. Soon I picked up its headlights as they pierced the night. My eyes followed them down the hill onto the main street, then along for another mile toward the road to Deception Pass. Eventually her headlights melted into a rush of traffic, and I lost her.

I pulled off my shirt and threw it down beside my towel, flicked off my flip-flops and tip-toed across the stone-covered shore of the state park beach. At the ocean's edge I paused, only for a moment, to squint out at the miles of whitecaps whipped up by the strong westerly wind charging in between the San Juans and Olympic Peninsula. I sprinted forward into the surf, trying to ignore the cold sting of the water on my feet and legs, and plunged in, head-first, alone.

I surfaced, short of breath, and waded out further, bracing my feet in the sand as each successive wave struck. When the water reached my chest, I turned toward shore and waited. A split second before a large wave arrived, I dove forward, swimming as hard as I could, feeling its monstrous force catch my body like a piece of driftwood and propel me toward the beach. The wave rose, and then culminated in a final thunderous end, depositing me in a heap near shore.

I staggered to my feet, and charged back into the surf, noticing a numbness rising up through my body. I body-surfed three more waves, then settled past the break, my breathing slower and deeper, my skin feeling thicker and stronger. It was comforting to remind myself how quickly my body could adapt.

At first I rode only the mid-sized waves, then caught some of the larger ones, until one slammed me hard into the beach, knocking the wind from me and bruising my wrist. As I struggled to my feet a second wave broke across my back, and I again went down, my pale body thrown onto the shore, salt water swirling in my mouth and nose, making me cough and gasp.

Up on one knee, I looked down the beach, and saw I was alone. I knew what would happen if a rip tide pulled me out, or if a strong wave knocked me unconscious against the shore?

If it all turned bad, here right now or somewhere else in the days or months to come, at least I would go down alone, without dragging with me an unfortunate person trying to help.

The simplicity of this insight reassured me, and back out I ventured into the breaking surf, some innate sense now helping me select the right-sized waves.

In time I pushed my way past the break, and swam out further, until I bobbed in water well over my head and felt the growing tug of a current beneath my feet. In the distance, the waves massed one-by-one, gathering their strength, preparing for their assault on the shore.

12

The house where Sam and Luke told me to meet them sat near the highway on a dead-end street, in a section of town rumored to be the future home of a big box shopping center. For now, the half-dozen or so small bungalows looked like victims of some infectious disease – abandoned cars littered overgrown front lawns, moss encased decaying roofs, peeled paint framed dirty windows. It was like they waited for a wrecking crew, for their owners to give a shit, for something to happen. I checked the address, looked at my watch, then headed up a cracked driveway, wishing I'd worn a sweatshirt or a jacket to shield me from the late September dampness.

I banged on the door, and peered in a small window. From inside Sam's voice stirred, then the door rattled open, its bottom scraping against the doorjamb.

Sam handed me a beer. "Step into Deception Pass's finest party room."

I stared at the beer in my hand. "It's 10:30 in the morning."

"Perfect," Sam said, signaling me to follow him inside.

"So this is your place?" I asked. "That's the surprise?"

"Part of it," Luke said, suddenly emerging. "So whatd'ya think?"

I looked around and what I saw was: A dingy kitchen teeming with empty beer cans and dirty dishes, a living room with lime green carpets, orange drapes, overflowing ashtrays and a stack of porno magazines, a moldy smell emanating from who knows where. And the dust — you could almost see it in the air, even without a beam of sun to give it shape. I'd never really noticed dust, not until Amanda moved in two months ago and went to work, mildly horrified by my mom's aversion to cleaning. The first time Amanda went through our place with a white cloth she revealed thick layers of dust on almost every stationary object, and smiled, "Good thing you two are allergic to dusting, and not dust."

I nodded to Luke and Sam. "Bet the girls are flocking to this place."

"Try to hide your sarcasm," Sam told me, steering me through the kitchen and into a room that appeared to be a garage converted into a family room. "Will you look at that fucker. The mother of all sound systems, connected wirelessly to our computer and big screen TV."

On top of a ratty shag carpet sat the most expensive system I'd seen outside any store.

"That's sweet," I told him. "Bet the TV and sound system are worth more than the entire house. So what's all this costing?"

"What do you care?" Sam said.

"Well, did you both get jobs, or win the lottery?"

Luke walked to the stereo and turned on the local rock station, then stood far too close to me.

"I think this place might be bugged," he half shouted over the music. "You know, under surveillance."

I looked at Sam. "What's he talking about?"

Sam laughed. "Paranoia maybe. Or maybe not. You tell him Luke."

Luke disappeared into the kitchen, came back with three

more beers, even though I hadn't finished the first one, and motioned to us to sit down on a sofa. Only, he didn't sit. He stood, and began pacing the room as he talked, apparently using his feet to collect his thoughts.

"I think the cops are watching us," he began, talking over the music. "You know, Morrison. Bugging the phone, pointing eavesdropping devices at the house. Shit like that."

"Why would you think that?" I asked

"You know Tom Ferrence," Luke said, his hands flying, "sells us, you know, our stuff. Well one day at a party he introduced us to a friend of his, who introduced us to another friend. Well one day a guy came by who knew that guy, you follow, and offered us a chance to make some real money. Not just dealing a little pot here and there, but helping run some of the shit across the border from Canada. Picking it up on a farm road near the border late at night. Several garbage bags of B.C. bud. Be risky, but be worth $20,000. Can you imagine? $20,000. The stuff we could do with that money. "

"You weren't stupid enough to…"

"Just listen, Brady," Luke said. "This guy, name's Stu Maust, kept coming to us with the deal. You know, we tried to check him out. Ferrence didn't know him personally, but knew of him. People thought he was okay – pulled off a couple of deals, though information on them was sketchy. Anyway, we were considering it, you know, when one day he said the people he worked for were nervous about us. Worried we'd go to the cops or maybe try to rip them off. They wanted information about us. Wanted to know that we were players like them."

Luke charged the stereo, making my heart race, and turned its volume a little higher, then continued pacing. "So, we told Maust, like, you know, we've been dealing for a year or two and never ripped anyone off or gone to the cops. Then he said this was the big time. The start of some serious money. And the guys he worked for wanted some assurances. Wanted some collateral. So Maust says to me and Sam, 'They want to know about the guy you killed at that party. Want to know what kind of shit you laid on him. Look, they wanna know you're serious, and that you're stand-up guys who'll do some shit, then keep quiet about it.'"

"Shit. You didn't say anything, I hope," I said.

Luke squeezed his beer can and gave me a disappointed look. "You don't get it, do you, Brady? This guy Maust. He's gotta be an undercover cop. Trying to trick us into a confession."

"No. They wouldn't do that."

"Shit, Brady," Sam said, "for such a smart guy, you sure are stupid. Course he's an undercover cop. We tried to check him out some more, but no one knew exactly where he lived. Then people started clamming up. Fuck. Ferrence, he was suspicious too. Told us to stay away from Maust."

"So what did you say to this guy?"

Luke laughed. "That was sweet. Next time we met, I told him we knew he was a cop. Demanded he take his fucken shirt off, cause I knew he was wired. He wouldn't do it. I stepped up, like I was gonna rip it off, and the chicken shit patted his jacket, you know, like he was letting us know he was packing a gun. He backed off, and told us we blew our chance. I told him to blow himself. Haven't seen him again."

"That was fucken incredible," Sam said. "Detective Morrison listening somewhere, probably shitting himself. Couldn't believe he was outsmarted again by us, a couple of drop-outs."

While I processed this, Sam said, "But that's not all, Brady. Seems the cops are after us for something else."

"What?"

"Someone's been lighting espresso drive-thrus on fire. All of them owned by the Whelan family."

"I know, one here in our town, one in Anacortes," I said.

Sam laughed. "And one in Sedro Woolley and one in Burlington. Then even another fire at the rebuilt one in Anacortes."

We both looked at Luke, whose face remained blank, until a small grin formed. "What? But I'll tell you something, Brady. I go out at night, and now I'm being followed. They think I'm setting the fires."

"He's right," Sam said. "The other night we drove down to the convenience store, and Luke said, 'Like, watch, we're gonna be followed,' and sure enough, a ghost car is there, in the distance, following us. We drove in circles and so did it, always just in sight. Our buddy, that paranoid prick was right."

"So did you?" I asked Luke.

"What?"

"You know. The fires?"

He gave me a long look, and said, "You forget why we got the music playing?"

"So anyway," Sam said changing the subject, "me and my partner here have found some other business opportunities. Much more profitable than selling weed. Specially when we think our nocturnal movements are being monitored."

"I'm almost afraid to ask," I said.

"Come with us," Sam said, "to the back shed."

I followed him out across the calf-high grass, to a large wooden building. Luke opened the padlock on the door, and I followed him into the darkness. The lone window was covered in cardboard, so even when Luke pulled the chain on a single light bulb, it remained dark in the room. Sam slammed the door shut behind us, then turned on a ghetto blaster.

"Do we have to talk over that thing too?" I said, annoyed.

Luke just shook his head. "We can talk over it or go to jail."

I sighed. "What is it?"

"See, you can't tell, can you? Our new source of income. Our meth lab."

"Your what?"

"We're not writing it down for you, Brady," Sam said, "you're gonna have to listen. Crank, ice, meth, crystal... Crystal methamphetamine. We cook it here."

"Far more profitable than selling pot," Luke said. "Ferrence showed us. Take about fifty bucks in ingredients – all legal stuff. You know, ephedrine, some of the shit found in Sudafed. Then you cook it in with some paint thinners and household cleaners and red phosphorous, you know stuff from matches. If it's pure enough, you've got yourself several thousand dollars worth of product."

I glanced around the room for obvious signs of what they were doing, and Sam said. "You won't find beakers and all that shit. All we need is a blender, coffee filters and Pyrex pan, as well as the ingredients. We got it all. Now we just got to cook it up and get it to our dealer. You see, we're the supplier now. Far less risky. Also means we don't have to deal with all those meth addicts. They're even more unpredictable than Luke."

Back in the house, Luke offered me another beer. I refused, and he stuffed it in my shirt pocket.

"I don't know anything about making that shit," I told him, "but I do hear it's dangerous. Highly flammable. What do you do with all the byproduct?"

Luke signaled for me to be quiet with a cutting motion across the neck, one that brought back terrible memories, and he turned the stereo back on. I felt a headache building.

I turned the stereo down, and said, "I gotta go."

"Bullshit," Sam said. "You don't have to work today. Open that beer, let's get caught up."

I hovered near the door, before finally sitting down.

Sam said, "You're working, like six days a week or something your Mom was saying. You should work smart, not hard."

Luke gave Sam the same signal to watch what he was saying.

"Oh, relax, Luke. I'm just telling Brady all those hours at seven bucks each is a tough way to get rich."

"Well, I gotta. I'm trying to save up for school."

"For what?" Luke laughed, launching himself forward on the couch.

I regretted opening my mouth.

"C'mon, tell us," Sam said.

"Well, it's not really school. It's a training course. Ten weeks. Five days a week, followed by a volunteer placement. Costs $3,000 for the course, and I can't be working while taking it, so I need to save up some cash, and…"

"Brady," Sam yelled. "What is it? What are you training to be?"

I smiled. "A firefighter."

Luke and Sam each sat back, processing my words. "A firefighter," Sam finally said. "Very noble. Very responsible. You sure they want you?"

I laughed. Responsible was a word Amanda used when she learned of my career interest. I sat at the kitchen table one day in late August, reading over the training academy's newspaper advertisement. It billed itself as the only qualified training program for most Washington fire departments. It only offered two ten-week sessions per year, one starting October 15, the next March 18. I ran the numbers through my head while eating breakfast – $3,000, with me earning seven dollars per hour or about $280 per week, minus my current expenses. Could I have enough cash in time to enroll for March? Was there a waiting list? Did I meet all the physical and mental requirements?

Suddenly I had felt Amanda's presence behind me, like she was reading over my shoulder. In fact she was. "Brady," she said, "are you interested in training to be a firefighter?" I quickly folded up the newspaper, and shrugged. She sat down across from me. "You know, my brother's a firefighter in Bellingham. I could arrange for you to visit the fire hall and he could show you around, talk about the job."

I shrugged, then got up and poured some juice.

"So are you interested?" she asked.

"I suppose," I said taking a long sip.

Two weeks later I took Amanda's car up to Bellingham, where I met her brother Roman. He introduced me around the fire hall, to a guy called Johnny, who was the captain of that shift, and to two more firefighters on duty with him. On the way up I told myself not to let slip to his colleagues the relationship my mom shared with his sister. But Roman introduced me as his sister's partner's son. No one winced.

Roman showed me around the lime-green truck, followed by various pieces of rescue and first-aid equipment. But what caught my interest the most was not the hundreds of feet of hose or the jaws of life – instead, it was the fire hall's living quarters. Four beds in the same room, a small living area and a large kitchen, where preparing the daily meal on a rotating basis emerged, at least in my mind, as the most unifying and pleasing of all the mundane tasks the crew would perform in their twelve hours together each day.

I liked the bad jokes they tossed around, all the teasing they shared, in the hours before they'd be called out to help a stranger. So uncomplicated.

As I drove home that night I was still impressed by the invitation to watch the team quickly dispense with a late summer brush fire, and with their invitation to share with them a huge meal of home-made pasta. When I walked in the door, Amanda sat reading in the living room. She smiled, the whites of her eyes solid. "So what did you think?"

I nodded in approval. "Thanks."

"Are you interested in the training session?"

"Yes," I said. "I'm already saving my money."

"Brady," she said, stopping me as I moved toward the stairs.

"You know, if you wanted to start the course in October, I could lend you the $3,000," she said, obviously having read the advertisement and given it some thought. "Interest free. You could start paying me back, when you get your first job."

I stood stunned by her offer, by her direct kindness, and wondered how I had come to hate such a person.

"So, Brady," Sam now said. "Like I was saying, you gotta start working smart. Specially if you need to raise $3,000." He looked at Luke. "You know what I'm saying buddy."

Luke shook his head, and said, "I know what you're saying, but let's not go there."

"Why not?" Sam asked

"Let's not go there."

"What are you two talking about?" I asked.

"I'm suggesting we cut you in," Sam said, "and our friend here is resisting."

Luke threw his empty beer can at Sam, turned toward me, and said, "We need someone to drive the product from here. After it's made, you know, to a couple of dealers in Mount Vernon. It shouldn't be either Sam or me, 'cause the cops are watching us, maybe even tailing us. So we need someone else to drive, but..."

"Go ahead and say it, Luke," Sam said.

"But it shouldn't be you, Brady."

"I don't want to do it anyway," I said defensively.

"It shouldn't be you, Brady," Luke continued, ignoring what I'd said, "because you're a total fuckup."

He spewed out the words like they'd sat in his stomach for weeks, making him sick.

"Thanks, buddy," I said.

He crept into my space, way too close, his eyes angry, his hands anxious, and said, "It's true, Brady, you fuck everything up. Why did you do that to Sarah? All she's ever done is try to help you."

His hands flew up and pushed hard against my chest. "Why?" he yelled.

"Forget it, Luke," Sam said, pulling at Luke's arm. "It's done now."

Luke shook Sam's hand loose, and spat out, "I want to know, Brady. Why?"

"I gotta go," I told him, pushing past him toward the door.

I glanced back before I left the room and saw Luke's rage dissipate into slumped shoulders and a defeated grimace.

Sam caught me at the front door and leaned close. "Don't worry about him. Listen, Wednesday night, two drops in Mount Vernon, you'd make $2,500. That's a huge cut. But we gotta know by tomorrow night, because if you can't do it, we're gonna try to find someone else. Luke is really paranoid about one of us doing the drop. With good reason."

"I'm not interested," I told him.

"Will you at least think about it?" Sam said.

I shrugged, and left.

Later that day I called the fire training academy, and was told they had three spaces left for the October session, but they needed the money by Friday. Also – as I wasn't being sponsored by a local fire department – I had to pass a physical test and an entrance exam. The woman on the phone asked me my height, my weight, if I could run one and a half miles in thirteen minutes or less, and how many push-ups I could do before stopping. So can you make it by Friday, she asked?

I wished I knew the moment I gave in. Was it when I began dismissing the insanity of doing something bad to get somewhere good? Or was it when I simply convinced myself that I wouldn't get caught? All I can say for sure was I spent the rest of the day telling myself I wouldn't capitulate, then stopped by Luke and Sam's place late that night and told them I was in.

Sam smiled and slapped me on the shoulder, and said, "Smart man."

Luke gave me a harsh look, and said, "You better not fuck this up, too."

On Wednesday, I worked the day shift at the gas station, then went to Mom's work and borrowed her car, promising I'd have it back to her long before midnight.

"Don't be late," she stressed, passing me her keys at the bar's back door. "You know I don't hang around here past quitting time any more, I come straight home."

I looked at her coldly but said nothing.

Outside Luke and Sam's place I heard music and laughter, just like I knew I would. They'd invited a few people over to help make my coming and going that night less suspicious.

At the door I was greeted by a woman who looked to be in her late teens, early twenties. She sweated like she'd been dancing, and leaned against the busted up screen door sizing me up.

"A friend of Sam's or Paul's?" she asked, her big eyes trying hard to focus on my face.

"You mean Luke," I told her.

"Hey, Luke," she said. "My name's Carla."

"Never mind," I said brushing past her.

Luke met me in the hallway, and I followed him past a handful of people I didn't recognize in the kitchen. They all looked a few years older than us, and my first impression told me they'd never leave a party as long as there were drugs and booze in plentiful supply.

Luke stopped in the laundry room by the back door, looked quickly at his watch, then out the window, then around the room at his guests. Even he rarely got this wound up. "So everything's fine?" he asked.

I nodded.

"Just have a beer, and in a half-hour we'll take you to the shed and get you ready," he said.

Sam appeared, looking too relaxed. "Brady. I'll introduce you around."

It turned out Sam didn't know the names of everyone in his house. When we got to Carla, the girl I'd met at the door, she told Sam we were already good friends, and added, "It's pretty good shit for two beginners."

I grabbed a beer from the fridge, and spent the next ten minutes trying to pin down Sam alone, to find out what Carla had meant. "I thought you were selling this stuff, not throwing it around at parties in your own house?"

"What do you care what we do with it. Besides, these losers are great guinea pigs for us. Helped us perfect our technique."

In the shed, Luke turned on the ghetto blaster and, to the best of his ability, detailed the two drop locations and who I'd be meeting, the times, the amount of cash I'd be receiving, and some general words of caution.

He asked me three times if I'd understood it all then looked at Sam. "He can't do this. No way."

"Luke," I said, "what's your problem anyway?"

Before he could answer, Sam reached into a cupboard and pulled out two packages wrapped in newspaper.

"Doesn't seem like much," I said.

"Potent shit. One pound each package," Sam said. "Going price in Washington State is about ten grand a pound. We're selling each one for six, you know, to establish ourselves."

They carefully duct-taped the packages to the sides of my body, then helped me pull my jacket back on. Luke studied me carefully, and said, "He looks wider than when he came in here."

Sam laughed. "Of course he does. He's packing one helluva party, couple of pounds of one."

Luke lifted a corner of the cardboard covering the window and peeked out.

"Is the coast clear?" Sam asked in a mock voice of concern.

Luke looked at me. "Last chance to back out?"

"I'm fine."

"And if you get caught..."

"I know. I keep quiet." I paused. "Just like always."

I mostly took the backroads to Mount Vernon, veering off Highway 20 just past La Conner and zipping by empty fields that in the spring would be filled with the colors of tulips. Halfway there I pulled over, killed the engine and sat in silence as darkness dropped from the sky. The odd truck rumbled past, shaking my mother's car. The occasional set of car headlights appeared, either in my rear-view mirror or dirty front windshield, then quickly flew by.

From the moment I'd left Sam and Luke's, I'd watched

for any sign I'd been followed, but saw none. At Luke's request I now listened for the sound of a police helicopter overhead, but heard none. I studied my watch. Eighteen minutes to the first meeting, which was only a ten-minute drive away. So I waited.

This would be the moment, I had told myself earlier in the day, when a sickening regret would wash over me. When I would be engulfed by second thoughts about what I was trafficking, about not trying to talk my friends out of it, about the strangers I was dooming, especially after that afternoon reading in the newspaper about Washington State's Attorney General's characterization of meth dealers as "the scum of the earth." Instead I looked at my watch once more, and determined I felt nothing but a tinge of fear – and not for my friends' safety, but for my own. They didn't seem to matter. None of them did.

When I reached the drop point – a darkened parking lot on the western outskirts of Mount Vernon – I immediately spotted the car, an old souped-up Chev. It sat alone in the gravel parking lot, seemingly resonating a single question to anyone passing by: What am I doing here? I pulled up alongside, killed my engine. After checking to see both packages were still in place, I got out of Mom's car and into the dealer's.

"Are you a cop?" the man asked as I sat down.

"No," I said, puzzled by the question, repulsed by the smell of cigarette smoke.

"No. You're too young, aren't you? Let's see the stuff."

I pulled out one packet and handed it to him. He took it, his eyes studying me for a moment from underneath a Yankees cap. He looked to be in his early twenties, a few years older than me, dozens of deals wiser. He turned on a small flashlight, placed it in his mouth and illuminated the package, which he sliced open with a penknife. He examined the crystals, and slid the entire package into a large plastic bag that he suddenly produced.

He turned to me. "So how many deals have you done?"

I didn't answer.

"Well, probably enough to know that six is too much. You saw how clouded those crystals were. I can't get top dollar when the ice's not pure. Neither can you."

He waited.

"Six was the deal."

"Well I'm giving you four. That's plenty for this second-grade poisonous shit you and your friends made."

I tried to conjure up some kind of reply, unsure if the product sucked or if this guy sensed he could rip me off. But I did know one thing – a smaller cut meant I'd come up short with the training academy. That I was taking a great risk for no reason.

"Guess we don't have a deal," I said, surprised by my own conviction. "So give me the stuff back."

He studied me for a moment, and grinned. "Guess we don't. Here's your shit."

I took it and got out, but before I could close the door, he called, "Wait. Get in."

I sat back down.

He produced an envelope from underneath his seat and handed it to me, taking the package back in return. "Here's six. Count it in your own car."

I didn't look at the money until I reached a mall parking lot in Burlington, about ten minutes to the north. Six thousand, as promised. I had five minutes before the next deal, which was to take place in the parking area outside the mall's movie theater. This time I pulled into the designated meeting place early, and waited. An SUV parked in the row in front of me suddenly turned its lights on and crept forward, stopping in the empty stall beside me. We studied each other, me and the other driver, before I got out and walked around to the passenger side and got in.

I looked at him, a man in his late thirties with thinning hair, and asked, "Are you a cop?"

"No. Are you?"

"No."

"Well, glad we got that settled," he said. "Let's see."

I produced the final package, and he opened it in the light of the parking lot, while I scanned the area.

In time, he reached into his jacket and pulled out an envelope. "Works for me."

He gave me the money, and I got out, glad to be free of the crystal meth.

As I walked around the SUV to Mom's car, I shook in the night's dampness. It was like the chill you get late at night watching a horror movie at home, when you suddenly feel you're not alone. This was the moment when I expected the police to materialize. To pop out of any of a dozen nearby vehicles. To end my careless foray, to finally bring me to justice. If not for one crime, then another.

I grabbed the car's handle and expected to hear a cop's voice, to see two or three ghost car's roar up. I froze, fingers on the cold handle. But nothing happened.

The next morning I dropped the cash off at Luke and Sam's, where they counted it into four unequal piles, one for each of them, one for me and a fourth for Tom Ferrence, who had set the whole thing up.

Luke handed me the cash. "Glad you can do something right," he said.

"Thanks, guys. I gotta go. It's a long drive to North Bend."

"So you're really gonna go do it," Sam said, "take that money and pay for your spot in firefighter school, or whatever they call it? Lot of other ways to spend it. Plus you could make more right here with us."

"Thanks, but no thanks."

"It's a three bedroom house, you know," Sam said. "Give that some thought too."

I nodded, and turned toward the door.

"Saw Sarah last week," Luke said suddenly.

I stopped. "Good for you."

"She was with Nick Harris. I hear he's screwing her good."

"Nice, Luke," I said. "Nice."

"Just thought you'd wanna know," he said, each word sounding increasingly heavy, like water turning to ice. "Everything she did for you, and look how you repay her, you stupid fuck."

He suddenly rushed me, his eyes wild, the way I'd seen them so often in our early high school years, when he picked up three assault charges, when he cared little if he got hurt. But before he reached me Sam intercepted him and threw him to the floor, pinning him with his larger body.

"Let me up, Sam," Luke screamed.

"Get out of here, Brady," Sam yelled. "Been building for weeks, this has."

"Let me up, Sam, or you'll be fucken sorry."

"Go, Brady, go."

I stood there stunned, money in my hand, my instincts telling me to stay and talk this through, Sam nodding vigorously toward the door.

"Just go, okay, Brady," Sam repeated, and I did.

Two days before I left for North Bend, I too saw Sarah, for the first time since our breakup. She had gone to Seattle, and stayed five weeks with a girl she befriended there in Grade 11. Sarah moved into her friend's place, a one-bedroom apartment in the city's north end near Green Lake, and found work at one of the myriad of trendy coffee shops on the old highway out of town. But she quickly found Seattle expensive, and, according to Luke and Sam, saw little chance of getting ahead financially and of soon sleeping somewhere other than her girlfriend's sagging sofa. She tried to give the impression that for her the whole thing just didn't feel right, though I think the real reason she returned home, to the relief of her mom and dad, was a little more complicated than that.

Could it have been she felt a tug, not just of the heart, but of a bond formed in an icy lake with three friends, then sealed in her parents' garage?

When she returned home, she made immediate contact with Luke and Sam and began seeing Nick Harris. I don't know what I found the most disheartening: That she was likely giving her body, such a wonderful offering, to someone else, or that she was sharing her feelings, her desires, possibly her secrets, with that same person, and that he really didn't give a shit what she felt, though he was clever enough never to let on.

Weeks before I bumped into her at the coffee counter at the Deception Pass 7-Eleven, I had envisioned such a chance encounter dozens of times, polishing the scene in my mind so carefully that it had become almost as palpable as a real memory. In my imaginary meeting, we would pass on the street, and she would smile at me softly, a subtle acknowledgment that she now understood the nobleness that had underlined my earlier betrayal and that she had come to learn that life without me offered endless opportunity. She would pause before walking past me steadily, not closing the door on some future friendship.

In reality, our meeting in the convenience store was a more mundane encounter. I believed I spotted her first, face down, fingers carefully mixing her usual three sugars and one cream into a large coffee at a counter near the back of the store. I studied her for a moment, and thought about leaving, just slipping out the door, before I finally approached. We stood four feet away, although the gulf between us felt greater.

"Hi, Brady," she said without looking up, and I nearly jumped.

Her head rose and her eyes locked onto mine, studying me. Her fingers continued stirring, her eyes searching, ignoring the quiet hello I mumbled. Finally she snapped a lid on her coffee and moved to the cashier, no wasted effort, just the sureness that was always Sarah. She left the store without looking back. And I so much wanted to ask her what she'd seen.

Amanda and my mom drove me to North Bend, both of them taking the day off work so they could drop me off and continue down to Seattle for sightseeing and dinner. The night before I'd packed the trunk of Amanda's car with my sleeping bag and pillow, two pairs of dark blue pants I'd bought the week before at the Wal-Mart in Oak Harbor, three light blue shirts, eight pairs of underwear and socks, six T-shirts, most of them white, a pair of steel-toed boots, one pair of jeans and one pair of sweatpants, a breathing apparatus and spare cylinder that Amanda borrowed from her brother, my toothbrush and toothpaste, antiperspirant, a pile of training manuals, and a list of courses, which included names like Apparatus Training, Fire and Structural Integrity and Live Fire I, II and III. I'd also packed a razor and shaving cream, two items that prompted Amanda to grab my smooth face and laugh, "Why shave? I've never seen a single whisker here."

Then her face grew serious, and she said, "We're gonna miss not having a man around the house." I briefly considered asking her why two lesbians needed a man around in the first place, and grunted as I retreated from her gaze.

"Do you have enough spending money," Mom asked, still no doubt puzzled by how I'd raised the $3,000. When I'd told her I would be attending the October session and didn't need a loan, I saw her trying to work my hourly rate into $3,000, trying to come out with the number of hours I would have had to work. She finally gave up.

We left at 6:30 a.m., meaning we rose that morning at 5:30, the earliest I can ever recall Mom getting out of bed. As Amanda steered her car out of town and toward Interstate-5, the three of us talked in scattered bursts, sleepy and gentle, no accusations, no regret, reminding me of the softness in Sarah's voice after we made love, when her guard relaxed to reveal, I'm sure, the most tender patch of her existence. We drove on, toward Snoqualmie Mountain, which would soon be blanketed with fresh snow, and I quickly forgot about my friends.

13

In the New Year, my days and nights fell into a comfortable rhythm. If I worked the day shift, I'd rise early, disappear into a hot shower and then ride my motorcycle twenty-five minutes south to the Oak Harbor Fire Hall. I never sped, always keeping my underpowered Honda to less than forty miles an hour, just the right pace to observe the daily changes taking place around me. The shifting tide under the big bridge. Cedars rocking gently in the first breaths of an approaching storm. The fighter jets exploding into the air at a hint of trouble overseas. Wildflowers suddenly appearing along the roadside in a first burst of color, a sure sign of an unstoppable rebirth. I'd put in my twelve-hour shift at the fire hall as the fourth man on the four-man crew working four days on, four days off, through a program called the volunteer paid on-call career incentive. While I was only paid a small sum, when we got called out, those occasional heart-stopping moments when the bell rang and we raced to some usually minor disaster, I knew how fortunate I was to have landed a position that allowed me to gain experience as a firefighter. To add to my luck, I got the position by forfeit, thanks to someone else backing out Dec. 27, just five days before the job began.

When I worked a stretch of nights, I'd shower right after dinner, then go to the fire hall, where the crew slipped into a night-time routine of equipment maintenance, an hour of television and finally bed, our sleep dependent on what calls, if any, interrupted it. We responded not just to fires, but to all the calls for paramedics – car accidents, heart attacks, industrial mishaps. Some nights we'd sleep until morning, amazed by our good fortune, and then I'd slowly make my way home, to another hot shower, to Mom and Amanda trying to draw me into friendly breakfast conversation. I soon became comfortable with this predictability.

I took all the first-aid courses I could, some of them offered through the fire department's own training center. I volunteered for the local search and rescue team, called out occasionally when a hiker went missing or when a disoriented senior wandered away from a nursing home.

I occasionally socialized with my colleagues, slowly creeping into their world. The day before a stretch of four work days, three of us would go grocery shopping at the Safeway, meeting at 11 a.m., starting in the produce section and ending in the bakery. We'd all three navigate our purchases through the check-out, then race each other two blocks down the road to Harbor Views Tavern, where we'd wash down a greasy burger with draught beer. The waitresses never asked me if I was twenty-one. Guess they thought if you're old enough to save someone's house, or business, or life, you're old enough to drink beer.

At home, I watched for cracks to start forming around my mom's relationship with Amanda. A smile cut short, an unkind word, an indifference in the air. Anything. I watched for her to stay late after work, or miss a long morning walk together. It hadn't happened yet, but given her history the flavor of the day only remained appealing for so long. Turning her back on all the men in the world took willpower and commitment, and, well, that just wasn't Mom. That much I thought I knew.

I learned more important things too, from courses, from the men around me, from making mistakes, the latter being the lessons that resonated the loudest. I knew all about mistakes, as though they were my area of expertise, not unlike treating head injuries or working the pumper truck was for others. In time, I began embracing my errors, not as something to bury away in disgrace, or to deny, but something to turn in my favor; to take something away from.

In time I learned the answers to my most troubling question. For my first four months working in Oak Harbor, I found myself studying the men, trying to determine if they knew I'd made headlines for some alleged infamous act. At times, I managed to convince myself that everyone knew, but had dismissed the allegations, just like the state prosecutor had, based on Sarah's lie detector test, or perhaps based on the many hours they had spent in my company. At other times, I felt certain they had heard nothing, and when – not if – they did, I'd surely know it by the disdain they'd show. Most days, though, I was on cruise control. I just didn't know. But then, in early May, as the one year anniversary of the accident approached, this annoying internal debate finally got put to rest. Deputy Chief Ray Lewis called me into his office, folded his huge hands in front of him and said: "So I heard about the trouble you and your friends had at a party. Last year. Guy named Tom Opal died."

I felt grief and embarrassment wash across my face. Although I knew this would come, the shock of it still left me gasping for a response. "I…uh…"

"Listen," he said. "I know you've sorta been cleared, and I know a lawsuit has been filed by one of the fathers against the cops. And I know you work hard here, and the guys like you, like the way you soak everything in. But you gotta know this. Your history will filter down. The guys will find out. So you should tell them first. Sit them down, and tell 'em what happened, what the situation is, so we don't have some crazy rumors starting. Understand?"

I nodded, already fumbling in my mind for an easy way to broach it.

"One more thing," he told me. "Know where I heard about this?"

I shook my head.

"Chief Walinski in Deception Pass. You've sent him a resume or two trying to get on there."

"Yes," I said, recalling my decision to put my name forward, not so much as a sincere request for a job, but more like a stubborn assertion of a right I figured I possessed as a citizen of Deception Pass.

"He called me asking about you. You know they have three guys retiring next year?"

"I didn't know that."

"Well they do. He thought it took balls to apply, given what happened and all. He liked your directness. He wants me to keep an eye on your progress here."

While I learned the many intricacies of my new job, I also learned broader and more abstract lessons that year, the most memorable being about time. For starters, friendships don't die in a split second. It only seems like that. They fade and lapse, like a water-starved tree slowly losing its leaves until all that remains is a bare, exposed trunk and thin branches outstretched to the skies in lonely desperation.

"So, Brady," Sam said. "It's been a long time."

"It has…I mean, you've grown," I said, nodding at his bulging arms and shoulders.

He laughed, then flexed. "Oh, that. I've been working

out for the last few months. Lifting weights, and shit. You noticed the difference?"

"You kidding. You never used to have any muscles..."

"Thanks. I think. How's the new job?"

"Good, though it's mostly a volunteer position. Don't make a lot."

He shrugged. "Beats pumping gas, and there are not too many big scores presenting themselves these days."

I smiled, looking around his messy place for any outward signs of change, of reform. All I noticed was clutter, and the smell of stale beer. But some changes had forced themselves inside during my absence.

While I had been taking my course in North Bend, Luke and Sam's dangerous but lucrative business had been shut down. The police got themselves a search warrant, and one Tuesday morning paid the two of them a visit. The warrant made vague references to a suspected marijuana grow-op, and gave the six officers the right to search the house and shed. The tip came from an anonymous source and complaints about "noxious odors emanating from the property." Sam later told me they did have a small stash of pot and crystal meth in the house that he quickly flushed when he saw the cops at the door. The cops moved quickly to the shed, where they were no doubt disappointed not to find a harvest of weed. But here's the thing. One of the officers had once been involved in taking down a crystal meth lab, and he looked at the dozens of boxes of matches, the frying pan and the coffee filters, and knew what was happening. Still, they didn't find the ice. Not even the sludge, which Sam had dumped into a nearby storm drain after cooking up the last batch. The cops searched the house from top to bottom. What followed was a series of conversations between the cops and their superiors, where, one can assume, someone made the decision not to proceed with charges for operating a meth lab. I think they were worried about the possibility of a second shaky charge against Sam and Luke being tossed out, especially with Dr. Roberts' lawsuit threat still hanging in the air.

But even Luke and Sam realized they'd been lucky. The police had come close to stumbling onto a sizable crystal meth score, one that could have put Luke and Sam away for years. Luke's paranoia exploded. Since that day they had been living on what they made off the last deal. Now they sat back and watched their recently found popularity with the druggies quickly plunge.

Sam studied me, like he was arranging his thoughts, and this immediately struck me as strange. He'd never before really worried about anything he said.

"So. I want to talk to you about Sarah," he finally said.

"What about her?"

He hesitated again, and I felt flushed with annoyance.

"Well, I wanted to ask you. You haven't seen her much lately. I know you're busy with your new job, so I thought you must be wondering how she's doing. You do think of her from time to time, don't you?"

"From time to time, yes."

"So. She's doing pretty well. You know, me and Luke have stayed in touch with her. She's working at that restaurant in Anacortes again. You know that?"

I shrugged. "I think I heard it somewhere."

"I think she's pretty happy."

"Good. Is she still trying to go to dental school?"

"Maybe. Opportunities abound. She's just trying to decide which one to grab."

I nodded, somewhat skeptical.

"So, you gotta level with me," he said. "Do you still have, you know, feelings for her?"

I fidgeted, trying to decide if I wanted to answer. Finally, I said, "It's been months, we've both moved on."

"Okay, so you're saying…"

"Where are you going with this? It's creeping me out to hear you talking about such abstract things as people's feelings."

"So, you want to see her happy, right?"

"Yes," I said, impatiently.

"So," he continued. "And you want me to be happy, too, right?"

And that seemed to be all he had to say.

I also discovered this about time: It takes three minutes and twenty seconds to drive, at the speed limit, from my house to the city cemetery, as long as you make the traffic light at Colfax and Pender streets. If you miss the light, add another twenty seconds. The average heart beats seventy-two times per minute, slightly more than one beat per second. It takes just one second for your life to change forever.

All of this means nothing, and everything. It just depends on how it comes together.

On the one year anniversary of Tom Opal's death, I drove to the cemetery where he was buried. I missed the traffic light at Colfax and Pender, and waited, my heart pounding, my head wondering why I was doing this. I'd never stepped foot in the cemetery before. I knew that only one road led into it, but didn't know the road looped around in a kidney shape and fed back out into the entrance road near the main gate. When I passed through the gate, the clock in Mom's car read 11:18. I slowed to a crawl, casting my eye over rows of headstones, some set in the ground, others towering above graves in the form of heavy cement crosses, their exteriors a dull gray-black against the backdrop of the thick green grass. As I progressed, the gravestones became smaller and less garish, many of them with freshly-cut flowers, and I realized I was sliding forward in time to the more recent graves.

Then I looked up and saw her, messy long blond bangs and sad eyes unmistakable, her two distracted children in the back. She stood by her van in disbelief and watched me slowly pass, no doubt wondering how I could spoil this moment too, how I could haunt her at a graveyard, of all places. I wanted to look away, to slam my foot on the gas, but, just like watching a car crash, I couldn't take my eyes off her.

Two minutes later, and I would have missed her altogether. Two minutes earlier and I might have seen her sobbing uncontrollably over her husband's grave, her kids not knowing where to look while they wondered if their father's body really rotted in the ground below their feet. Had I witnessed such a thing, who knows what I would have done. Maybe stopped the car, crept up to her and, before I realized it, told her everything, as if it would somehow help. Or maybe I would have tucked my head down and driven by unnoticed.

But, of course, I had been noticed, and all I could do was continue on the loop that wound past an empty green field that would also be teaming with bodies one day. As the road hooked back, I saw her van backing up and lurching to a stop in the middle of the road by the main gate, at the exact spot the circle came together. She had me trapped.

I stopped and calmly waited, and when she didn't move, I shut off the engine. I stared at her but was unable to make out her expression through her van's open window, a hundred or so yards away. She sat frozen, as lifeless as her husband. Her children growing restless, maybe alarmed, in the backseat.

All I could hear was my own breath, deep and strained, and as I listened to it, I felt something shift abruptly inside me. I felt anger and defiance rise up, maybe like an animal backed into a corner by a predator. I thought about this –

about how I had become the hunted, the pursued, in the months after Tom Opal's death. About how I now felt an urge to drive up to Mrs. Opal and tell her to suck it up, Princess, because she didn't know shit; because her husband's death was no one's fault, just a fucked-up accident, and she needed to realize this for the good of us all. It made sense – the sudden hostility I felt toward her – because it was a simple defense mechanism to fend off an aggressor, and not another sign of some sick character flaw within me.

I cursed out loud. You asked for it, bitch. Prepare for an earful. I started the car, and when I looked back up she was pulling away.

The clock read 11:25. Less than seven minutes for a person's entire perspective to change.

In the next year, I lived in the shadows and on the edges of Deception Pass, spending the majority of my time in Oak Harbor, where I shopped, hung out with firefighter friends, got my hair cut and my teeth cleaned, some days only returning home to sleep. I saw Luke and Sam a handful of times, and Sarah only twice. Sam would invite me over so the four of us could get together, like old times. I always declined. One day he stopped by the house to invite me to a party the three of them were planning. When I said I couldn't make it Sam's voice turned serious, and he said, "Sure it's not, you know, because of me and Sarah? That maybe you're not okay with it yet?"

"Yeah, I'm sure."

Time crept by, another Christmas, another year volunteering with the Oak Harbor Fire Department, another stupid anniversary for Mom and Amanda (this one a ridiculous eighteen months, as if anyone ever celebrated such a thing).

On Super Bowl Sunday, on my way to a party at the fire

hall, I stopped by Albertsons for some soda and cola. Yes, that Albertsons. I wore my uniform because I'd be working that night after the game. If anyone noticed it was me, they didn't let on. No one hollered or spat at me. In fact, the cashier, a liquid-eyed girl about my age, engulfed me with a warm smile that stayed with me long after I'd left.

The two times I saw Sarah she wasn't with Sam and Luke and she didn't see me. Once, she and her mom were crossing the street downtown, walking silently to some unknown destination. The other time she was driving along a road that seemed far off any route that made sense in our previous life together. I tried not to think about where she could be headed, in this new life of hers.

At Easter, my mom insisted on barbecuing a huge turkey for Good Friday dinner for the three of us. I stared down at the huge bird as it spun slowly on the rotisserie, and remarked, "Why did you get such a big bird? We'll be eating turkey for a month."

"Well, take some to your friends at the fire hall," she said. "I know they love their food. You'll be a hero at dinner time."

"Why are you trying to barbecue it anyway? Wouldn't it be easier in the oven?"

"Stop trying to pick a fight," she said.

"I'm not."

"Yes, you are."

I turned to go back into the house, and she said, "You miss her, don't you?"

"Who?"

"You know who. Sarah."

"What are you talking about?"

"You miss Sarah," she said emphatically. "You bury yourself in your work and with your firefighter buddies, but I don't think you can get her out of your mind."

"Give it up, Mom. It's been more than a year and a half. It's over."

"Maybe, but it doesn't mean you don't miss her."

"Good-bye, Mom," I said sliding open the door.

"You still love her, don't you?" she yelled.

"What?"

"You remember once telling me you weren't completely sure you loved her. Well, I think you've figured out that you do, only now it's a little late. That you did the wrong thing in breaking up with her."

"You know, Mom. You can go fuck yourself." I stepped back inside and slammed the sliding door behind me so hard it shook the house.

Amanda appeared from the front hall, her face puzzled by the loud bang, and I walked past her and up the stairs, ignoring her queries, consumed by a rage that screamed, BREAK SOMETHING.

That fucken bitch, I spat as I entered my room and slammed that door too. I knocked a lamp over and kicked the wall beside my bed with my bare heel, caving in the plaster. That bitch, I repeated in a muffled voice that sounded like a dog barking. She thinks she suddenly knows everything about love. But she knows shit, because she doesn't realize that sometimes you have to do the wrong thing for the good of someone you care about.

And one last thing about time. Funny how you mark it. I used Tom Opal's death as my marker. Life before his death. Life after. Like he was Jesus Christ, and not just another flawed person like me.

It was nearing the second anniversary of his death when I finally saw Luke, Sam and Sarah together, in one place, for the first time since we had met at the picnic table hidden away in a forested park.

It was 11:30 p.m. on the Saturday of the Memorial Day long weekend, and just in case I needed another shitty anniversary to celebrate, it was two years since the four of us spent an early morning trapped in an icy lake. I was driving through downtown Deception Pass with Matt Bellows, another on-call Oak Harbor firefighter looking for a full-time job, and two girls, one of them his terminally chatty girlfriend Jessica and Jessica's friend, Hillary. We'd finished dinner and a couple of jugs of light beer at a pizza place down the road, and they were dropping me off at home, our thirst and hunger satisfied, our stomachs sore from hours of laughter. While I felt an aversion to Hillary's frequent use of the word "I" when she spoke, it was hard not to find her attractive, especially when her wide smile revealed a diamond piercing on her tongue. We sat together in the back seat of Matt's aging Ford SUV, the radio blasting out an eclectic mix of songs from his iPod, Hillary pressing close to me as she did a somewhat funny impersonation of her boss's heavy Greek accent as he bellowed orders in the bakery where she worked. That was when I saw Luke and Sam, who appeared out of nowhere on the sidewalk and darted quickly through the heavy spring rain and disappeared into the town's seediest drinking hole, the Loose Tooth Tavern.

I watched the door close behind them, then retraced their steps to the laundromat next door, where I saw Sarah peering blankly out the front window into the darkness, her face illuminated by the fluorescent lights. We missed the traffic light, and rolled to a stop directly across the street from Sarah, the four of us invisible to her through Matt's tinted windows. I stole glances at her as I struggled to keep up with the conversation in the car and fought to maintain some semblance of eye contact with Hillary.

"Look," Jessica said suddenly, pointing at Sarah, whose black T-shirt helped her stand out from the laundromat's shocking white interior and whose life had been caught up in a far different current from mine. "Laundry on a Saturday night. Sucks to be her."

As Matt jerked the car forward, I took one last look at Sarah's frozen image, and turned away with the same detachment a pedestrian used when stepping over a junkie sprawled out across the sidewalk.

14

For most Deception Pass residents, Mullins Hall held some special memory. Almost every person had attended at least one dance or party there, spilling beer on the linoleum floor inside or stomping out cigarettes on the large wooden deck that caught the moisture-laden offshore breezes. Probably half the town's married couples had held their wedding reception at the hall, and in doing so were photographed out back in the rose garden, the sky and ocean's stark blue a dramatic backdrop. For more than sixty years the hall had seen a cast of thousands stagger drunk, consummate business deals, fall in love, fall out of love, do things they'd never forget.

It would hold several bitter-sweet memories for me, though I didn't know it yet as I pulled into the dusty gravel parking lot in the humid, late-August heat for the Deception Pass Fire Department's retirement party.

Deputy Chief Lewis had been right about the retirements in my home town. Three of them. He'd been right about something else: My chance at landing one of the jobs. I was interviewed twice by Chief Keith Walinski, who told me these were the most sought-after job-for-life positions in town. I didn't expect I had much of a chance, because no matter how hard I worked in Oak Harbor and how well they thought I could do the job, I doubted the Deception Pass Fire Department could stomach having someone with so much baggage. Chief Walinski proved me wrong when he called me in a third time and told me I got the job. I longed to know who had pushed for me. Had Walinski really liked what he'd seen in me? Had Lewis or someone else aggressively gone to bat for me? Or did I owe my thanks to Sarah, whose lie detector test had at least created reasonable doubt?

Tonight the retiring firefighters, local boys in their fifties, would be honored, or more accurately roasted, right before the introduction of the three new recruits, me and two out-of-towners. Then the band would take the stage, and we'd all get drunk. I'd heard that over three hundred and fifty tickets had been sold, a testament to the theory our town's firefighters threw the best parties.

As the sun dipped toward the sea, Chief Walinski stood on a picnic table outside, beer in hand, and whistled. Then, perfectly synchronized, the fire truck in the parking lot fired off its siren. Most of the crowd suddenly emerged and gathered on the deck, in the rose garden and anywhere they could find in sight of the chief.

"Got some business to take care of tonight," he said and my stomach tightened.

Truth is, this night scared the hell out of me. Panic had washed over me two weeks ago when I heard I'd be publicly introduced. What if people booed or swore? What if someone shouted, "Murderer?" If I'd learned nothing else – about loyalty, friendship, common decency, or loving someone else – I'd learned this: Some things are out of your control.

But when it came time for my introduction, my name was greeted only by applause, subdued at first but it quickly built, followed by shouts of encouragement. Had everyone forgotten, or forgiven, or were they just too drunk to give a shit? Or maybe they were hiding their hostility where I hid my guilt, below the surface, tucked away in a neat place where it could rot.

"Let's party," the Chief screamed suddenly, and in seconds the band played, and Mullins Hall shook to life.

Brittany's appearance came about fifteen minutes later, after a half dozen people – my boss from the first gas station I'd worked at, my Grade 11 home room teacher, one of my mom's former friends, a few high school acquaintances – had wandered over and offered sincere-sounding congratulations.

She stood before me tall and lean, her face angular but eyes round and soft, all unchanged from two years ago when I saw her last outside Sarah's house as she pressed me about Tom Opal.

"Been a long time, Brittany," I said.

"It has," she said.

We looked at each other awkwardly, and when I was about to excuse myself, she finally began to speak, politely filling me in about spending the last two years at dental school at Western Washington, passing the state exam and getting a job working for her father as a dental hygienist. Friendly conversation, no doubt belying what she really wanted to say.

I thought of ways of excusing myself so that she wouldn't get that chance.

"I'm here with a girlfriend," she said looking past me into the hall. "She doesn't know anyone, so I'm trying to keep an eye on her."

"I'll let you get back to her."

"But I want to tell you something," she said a little too suddenly. "If you've got a few minutes."

"I don't, not right now."

"It's important."

"I bet it is," I said. I turned and began walking away.

"It's something you've got to hear," she yelled over the sound of the band.

I stopped and turned back to her, barely noticing that she seemed to teeter, like one stern word, one nasty look, would send her to the ground.

"You've got nothing I want to hear."

"I do," she whispered through the crowd that swirled and staggered around and in between us.

I stepped forward and grabbed her arm a little too hard and led her out to the rose garden where we were somewhat alone.

"Okay. Now say what I know you and half the people here want to say, and then leave, so I can enjoy my night," I told her.

She didn't appear surprised by my anger. "I want to say sorry," she said.

"Sorry?"

"For what I did two years ago," she said.

"I don't understand."

"That night at Sarah's. I told the police about my suspicions, soon as they arrived. I told them I thought Luke had hurt Mr. Opal, that he'd set out to hurt him and did so."

"So?"

"And you know where it all led. To the investigation, to you four being arrested, based almost solely on my suspicions. I guess it also led to what happened to Sarah, getting kicked out of Western Washington, the trouble with her dad, the way everyone looked at her and the rest of you. Even after the four of you were cleared, how it…well, even just a minute ago, how you suspect it still lingers."

I almost laughed. "You think you caused all of that to happen?"

"I know I did."

"It would have happened anyway, even if you hadn't said a single word. The police would have formed their own suspicions. Might have taken another five minutes longer, that's all."

"If all that's true, why do you look at me like you hate me?"

I looked down, away from her. "I don't hate you. I'm just…I'm just trying to move on."

She nodded, and I gave her a half smile and began to move away

"You know," she called after me. "In spite of what you think, my going to the police would have been bad enough, but it's not all I did."

I stopped. "What do you mean?"

"God, Brady, there's so much more."

I looked at her, unsure I wanted to hear.

"Do you know why I went to the police?"

"Like I said, 'cause it was the right thing to do."

"Don't be so sure," she said, fighting back tears. "The whole time I was talking to them, I had one thought in mind. How this would get the three of you out of Sarah's life."

She placed her hand on her forehead and suddenly began to sob. "How I thought the three of you weren't good enough for Sarah, and this was my chance…"

I shrugged. "Can't say I necessarily blame you for that."

"No, there's more. Before you start to feel sorry for how pathetic I am, there's more. You know, when Sarah told me Mr. Opal fell, gave me her word no one hurt him, and when the charges were dropped, when Sarah passed the lie detector test, when all those things happened, you would think I'd have the decency to go to her and tell her what I did. To apologize. To try to be friends again. But I didn't.

And when September came I went off to college and turned my back on her."

Now she began sobbing uncontrollably, her body wracked with guilt she didn't deserve, with guilt I wished I could feel so profusely. I stood and watched her cry into her hands, as the band played, people danced and sang and laughed without noticing her. I searched for the words to comfort her, to let her know her suspicions were justified, and I located them quickly, easily, and, of course, tucked them away unsaid. Suddenly she stumbled forward and wrapped her arms around me. I kept my hands at my side, unsure, until they reached up seemingly on their own and encircled her.

When her friend finally found her, Brittany was still consumed by an embrace I found both agonizing and uplifting. Agonizing because I'd refused to accept the great heaviness she felt through no fault of her own. Uplifting because I had found it somewhere in my heart to shoulder a tiny piece of her burden with my comforting arms. That small act had brought me a warmth I hadn't felt for months.

"Brittany." The voice made us both jump.

"Carmel." Brittany didn't immediately let go of me, only laughed and wiped her eyes.

"I just wanted to see if you're okay, but it looks like you're doing just fine." Then her friend noticed the tears, and looked at me alarmed, like I was the cause. "What happened?"

"I'm okay." Brittany took her friend's hand. "Just reliving some old times. Carmel, this is Brady. Brady, Carmel is the friend I mentioned."

I would like to say I could describe every detail of that first encounter, but truth be told Brittany's confession and its prospect of widening guilt had rattled my beer-dulled senses. I barely noticed Carmel's beauty, barely heard the ensuing small talk. She told me she and Brittany met at Western Washington University, became friends and both got jobs in town as dental hygienists, thanks to Brittany's dad and his contacts. Then she asked me if I liked to dance, and I jolted from a daze, lied, and said yes.

"Me too, but so far it's been gray-haired firefighters who keep stepping on my toes and spraying me with beer as they talk. One of them even brought his half-full beer cup along with him."

The band was playing a rare slow song, which had nearly emptied the dance floor.

"I love this one," Carmel told me. I finally took her hint and her hand and we drifted inside the hall onto the mostly deserted floor. A few more couples joined us, but it felt like we were alone. We moved easily, swirled clumsily.

Carmel laughed. "I'm not sure you're any less drunk than the rest of the firefighters. But you're not stepping on my toes quite as much."

"That's because this is a slow song. Wait until the first fast one."

She smiled. "That a threat?"

The song ended and the band picked up its pace. Suddenly we were in a crush of spinning bodies, and Carmel laughed as we collided with strangers in a chaotic scramble to the beat. More and more people tried to pile onto the dance floor, grinding us to a near stop.

For one of those rare moments in my life, I followed my instincts, pulling Carmel close and dancing through the crowd, past Brittany and others congregated around the dance floor and out the door onto the deck, under the stars.

A half dozen couples followed. Carmel clung close, grinned, then whispered, "Good move."

During those first two songs I elicited a few more details

about her: She grew up in Crescent City, California, picked Western Washington University because she had family living nearby – her dad's brother and wife – and now lived with Brittany and Brittany's family until the two of them got on their feet financially.

We danced three more songs, all of them fast, and while I followed my body's lead, my mind suddenly intruded to tell me what I must do next. I moved my mouth down to her ear and whispered, "Can I kiss you?"

I could see she loved the question, but she asked, "So what's your hurry?"

I felt my face turn serious for a moment, and I said, "Because I have a feeling I won't get a second chance after you talk with Brittany again."

"Why? What will she say? Are you such a big Romeo you think she's going to warn me to stay away?"

"I wish it was that simple."

"Are you an ex-boyfriend of Brittany's? Is that it?"

"Far from it."

She reached forward with her mouth and kissed me on the lips, slow and soft. This time I followed her lead. She rested her head on my shoulder, and we ignored the song's fast beat.

"You trying to be intriguing or something?" she asked me.

"God no," I said. "Intriguing is the last thing I want to be."

When Carmel melted back into the crowd inside the hall, I collapsed against the deck railing to catch my breath. I expected that within minutes she would take Brittany somewhere quiet – likely out front – and be pressing her for answers, ones that likely ensured she'd keep her distance. Brittany might naively believe Tom Opal fell to his death, but I doubted a stranger could hear the story without feeling enough suspicion to think maybe she was better off finding another drunken firefighter with a less complicated past. I had begun accepting I would never see her again, at least in my arms, when a drink was suddenly thrust into my hand.

"It's beer and tomato juice," Dr. Roberts said, taking a spot on the railing beside me, his own drink in hand. "Tastes good, still got a kick and you won't feel like shit in the morning."

"Thanks," I said, unsure what else to say.

"So I see you've landed on your feet," he said, his voice slightly slurred.

I struggled for words – was he talking about Carmel or my new career?

"Not a bad line of work. Serving the public. Of course, the pay sucks. That's the trouble with some of these so-called noble professions. They don't pay shit."

I started to respond, then he said, "I've been waiting to talk to you. Waiting for your girlfriend to leave."

Before I could tell him Carmel wasn't my girlfriend, he continued, "She's pretty. Anyway," he said, his voice rising uncomfortably loud, "you've done better than the rest of them. Especially that piece of shit whose very existence threatens my daughter."

I felt the need to say something positive about Sam, to come to his defense. But the best I could do was carelessly utter a lame, "Sam's harmless enough." Words I regretted the moment they'd spilled out. "I mean, he seems to care for Sarah, and…"

"C'mon, he likes fucking her. And having her pay all the bills."

He stood in silence as I debated walking away.

Then he muttered, "Harmless," still stuck on that word.

"Well, maybe that wasn't the best…"

"You know, a new mole can seem harmless, so you leave it because it becomes part of you, but over time you realize there's something wrong with it and then just like that" – he snapped his fingers – "you find out it's really a malignant melanoma, and this so-called harmless thing is suddenly a serious threat, but it's too fucking late."

He laughed a bitter laugh, and took a swig of his drink. "You don't know how right you are. He's like a mole, a cancerous sore on her body."

"You..."

"This won't surprise you," he interrupted, "but Sarah's done fuck-all the past two years. Her friend Brittany's graduated from dental school – well you know that – but Sarah's done nothing. Never will when she's got two leeches attached to her."

He took another swig.

"Had the three of them over last Thanksgiving. An olive branch, if you will. That Luke Newell kid. Fucking piece of work he is. Studied him all night, trying to figure out what the fuck is wrong with him. Fetal alcohol syndrome. Some other retardation. At the very least I see that he's ADHD."

"Yes, he was on medication as a kid. Attention Deficit Hyperactivity Disorder."

Dr. Roberts looked at me. "Very good, the way you spat that out. Maybe you're not as drunk as me yet."

"I..."

"Listen," he said. "Down to business. You know I had a lawyer draw up a wrongful arrest lawsuit against the police department? I took it to Sarah and told her I was about to file it, and she asked, 'Would there be a trial?' I said, 'Likely, unless they settle.' So she asked, 'Who will have to testify?' I thought, for fuck sakes, here we go. So I ask her, 'What happened in there? In the garage?' And she yelled, 'I already told you,' then turned and walked away." He took one more sip, one I could only describe as violent. "So the lawsuit is sitting in my dresser drawer with my socks and underwear."

He sighed, and continued. "You know what I'm saying? I can't file that thing unless I'm convinced Tom Opal fell. You care to convince me, Brady?"

"Sarah's already answered you," I said.

He studied me, then finished his drink and dropped the cup to the ground. "Well there's my answer."

I waited for him to leave, to sense the disappointing yet natural conclusion of our conversation, but he remained at my side, staring out toward the night.

In time, he said, "One night when I was filling in as the on-call doctor at the emergency, I asked this guy what it cost to get someone whacked."

He turned and studied my alarmed face, perhaps trying to decide if he should continue.

"He was some criminal type, who brought in a gunshot victim. Tough bastard. Straight shooter though. Told me this guy had been shot in the leg for a drug debt. Likely some kind of hit aimed at scaring him, because he'd be dead if the shooter had wanted him dead. So I asked him what it costs to get someone killed. He told me about $10,000 to $25,000, with Joe Average citizens coming in on the high end, anyone known to police on the low end. I asked how about two people at the same time. He looked at me, a huge grin across his face."

I wanted to tell Dr. Roberts how offensive, how absurd he sounded. But I also wanted him to finish.

"He pulled up outside my office about a week later as I got into my car. I had given him the names for, you know, a quote. Don't know what possessed me, maybe just curiosity that you could arrange such a thing, and for how much, but I'd given him the names. He said he could have the pair done for $25,000 total. Be easy because they're into drug dealing and half the town hates them for killing that grumpy bastard from Albertsons. His words, not mine."

"What…what…"

"'So what do you say?' he asked me. I told him no, that I wasn't really serious. But you know, the money was no problem. I'd gladly have paid it. You can't put a price on your daughter's life."

Dr. Roberts looked at me. "But could I really go that far – commit murder – to protect someone I love? I'd always thought so. I thought I could have done it with my own bare hands if the need ever arose."

I looked away from him, out into the night, and when I turned back he was walking away, weaving crookedly, without saying good-bye. He stopped suddenly and came back. "You know, remember our conversation at that fast food place after your failed camping trip. I told you stories of what a slut Sarah was. Terrible stories. Well, for the most part they weren't true. I made them up. We might have moved away from Seattle partly because I didn't like her friends, one kid in particular with a criminal record, but there was nothing even remotely like I told you. I thought it would drive you away, and with you, your friends."

He shook his head. "Guess I was mostly wrong about that too."

Carmel found me hanging out with some new colleagues, who'd tracked me down to join them for a round or two of vodka shooters. Never had something been so perfectly timed: Not Carmel's arrival, but that shot of nerve-calming, Dr.-Ian-Roberts-forgetting alcohol.

I noticed Carmel just outside the circle of firefighters, and stared for several seconds in surprise before finally stepping toward her.

"I don't want to bother you," she said. "Looks like a rite of passage, those shooters."

"Want to join us?" one of the men asked.

"No. Thanks, anyway," Carmel answered, turning back to me. "Brittany and I are going now."

"Oh…" I stuttered. "Good night."

She didn't leave.

"So you talked to her?" I finally asked.

She nodded.

"Well, goodnight," I repeated.

She smiled, then stepped forward, and in a whisper that tickled the hair in my ear, said, "Call me."

The log book at the Deception Pass Fire Department's No. 1 Hall shows my first call as a fully-paid firefighter came in at 9:57 a.m. Monday, nearly two hours after my first shift began.

It was a garbage truck fire.

I had barely met the guys and located the bathroom when the dispatch bell in the fire hall rang and my heart began pounding. The oldest of our four-man crew, Tom Marriott, just a couple of years from retirement, laughed when he saw my anxious expression. "C'mon, kid. You get to earn your keep."

As we slipped on our gear, Captain Len Boerne appeared and shouted, "Truck fire, Fifth and Main downtown. Let's move."

We scrambled into our truck, Boerne impatiently behind the wheel, me riding with Marriott and Carson Kilgore. Boerne looked at the three of us and shook his head.

"Unreal what they give me," he lamented out loud. "An old man, a high school student and a girl."

I looked at Marriott and Kilgore, who tried to conceal their grins.

Finally Marriott said, "Get used to it kid. He likes to go on about how hard done by he is. But I think he's really proud of this group. Right Captain."

"Whatever you say, Tom."

"What does he mean – a girl?" I asked. "I assume I'm the high school kid and..."

"That's right," Kilgore said. "And no, I'm not gay or haven't had a sex change, or any weird shit like that. I love to paint and sketch – you know, art. Works of art, though that's not what the captain calls them. I also like to read – literary novels usually, not *Maxim* magazine like the captain. So I've been stereotyped."

By the time we arrived downtown, a crowd had gathered around a city garbage truck, from which smoke poured out the back. It looked like the driver had left the truck in the middle of the road and leapt out to call for help.

"Shit," Boerne said as we climbed out of the fire truck. "I was expecting an engine fire, not a hot load."

I stood uselessly by as Boerne assessed the fire and Kilgore and Marriott went to work pouring foam on the flames in the hopper where the garbage was gathered before compacting.

After a minute or so they cut the flow of foam, and the heavy smoke turned to flames once more.

"I think the fire's further inside," the truck's driver yelled. "In the heavy compacted stuff. And just so you guys know, this truck's worth $240,000 to the city."

Kilgore and Marriott poured more foam on it, but the flames shot up again.

"Joseph," Boerne bellowed at me. I stepped forward.

"We're going to have to send you in there with a hose."

I stared panic-stricken at the flaming mess, and back at Boerne, who finally revealed a tiny grin.

"That's your first lesson. Keep your head about you.

And run into the hardware store across the street, get four steel rakes and tell them to put them on the city's account. Got it?"

I nodded. As I walked away, Boerne shouted, "Everyone back up. We're going to have to dump this baby."

When I returned with the rakes, Main Street had been transformed into a mess of burning and smoking debris. I couldn't believe how much garbage a single truck could hold. Kilgore poured foam on the flames, and Boerne grabbed a rake and told me and Marriott to help him break loose the compacted stuff, which spewed forth the foulest smelling air you could imagine.

That was how my career began – sifting through piles of garbage while hundreds of people watched and laughed in a twisted fascination and while a photographer from the local paper snapped away.

An hour later, when Boerne was satisfied the fire was out, a city works crew helped us load the truck back up. Then we hosed the street down. Boerne sniffed the air and said, "You guys smell like shit. Anyway, who wants a coffee before we head back to the hall? Starbucks is just a half block away."

He left, Marriott lit up a cigarette, and we waited. An opportunity, I thought.

"Be back in a minute, guys," I said.

I trudged up an office's front sidewalk, my boots pounding and my heavy pants scrapping together at the inseam. Though it felt like the smoke and damp garbage stuck to my skin, I realized my pants had soaked up most of the mess, and as I turned the doorknob I knew I should have changed them back at the truck. Too late now. I entered the crowded waiting room, and saw heads turn immediately.

The receptionist didn't even attempt to hide a wide smile when she looked up. "Let me guess," she grinned, "you're here to see Carmel."

15

Carmel laughed, her hands and arms wrapped tightly around my ribs as I swayed my motorcycle gently from side to side in a mock loss of control. I didn't so much hear the sounds of her delight – my helmet and the engine's roar saw to that. I felt it, a joyous shaking that resonated out from her chest, through her limbs and into my body. We left the downtown and built up speed on the highway as we neared the big bridge, and Carmel settled in with her chin resting against my shoulder, our bodies perfectly entwined.

Just before the bridge, I turned off into a seaside city park and killed the engine.

We climbed off the motorcycle and walked past the spot where Sarah cajoled me into asking her out, past the public restrooms and onto a small trail at the base of the channel that cut its way to the ocean.

"So you're wearing your swim suit under your clothes, right?" I asked.

"Yes, just like you ordered, and I have a change of clothes in my knapsack, plus a towel and hairbrush. You know, all the things I usually carry with me on a first date."

We laughed.

"And I see you have sturdy rubber flip-flops on?"

She looked down at her feet. "Yep. So you gonna tell me why?"

"You'll see."

She smiled. "That's what I'm afraid of."

"Hope you don't mind. We don't have a lot of nice nights like this left this year. Good to take advantage of it."

"Not at all." She looked at the water rolling slowly by between Whidbey and Fidalgo islands. "So is this where we're swimming?"

"Not exactly."

"Why are you grinning like that?"

"We're gonna follow this trail for a ways. Then jump in, and float back here with the current."

"Sounds like fun."

I slipped my shirt off. "We leave our clothes here."

"Okay," she said, pulling hers off to reveal the top of a blue two-piece swimsuit.

I sneaked peeks at her light brown skin and long limbs as she removed her jeans and tossed them onto her knapsack.

"So that's why you wanted me to wear these rubber sandals?" she asked as we set off along the trail. "The path's rocky."

"Well that's only part of it," I said.

"What's the other part?"

"They protect the soles of your feet from the force of hitting the water."

She stopped for a moment, and arched her eyebrows. "So how high did you say we jump in from?"

"I didn't. But it's about twenty-five feet."

"Twenty-five feet, huh," she said starting to walk again.

About a hundred yards along the trail, I led her down a side path to a rocky cliff jutting out over the water. Carmel walked to the precipice and looked down and back at me. "I don't know about this," she said, smiling nervously.

"It's okay," I told her.

She looked down again with apprehension. "I can't get my depth perception. How far did you say that is?"

"Only about twenty-five feet."

She glanced at the water once more, and I took her hand, caught her eye and asked, "Do you trust me?"

"You sure it's deep enough? The spot where we'd land."

"Pretty sure."

"What about the rocks on the way down? Are we going to hit the side?"

I kicked a few small stones off the ledge and they landed in the water six or seven feet from shore. "See. It's a natural overhang."

"So you've done this before?"

"Never with someone like you."

"But you've done this before?"

I smiled. "I've jumped hundreds of times in the last ten years or so, from this very spot. It's an outward tide tonight. Just perfect. And as long as we stick close to shore, we'll be fine."

She shook loose my hand and looked out past Friday Island, in the direction of two sailboats gliding along beneath a sun that still held about two hours light. I thought she was searching for a way to say no. After all, wasn't I asking too much? I looked down at the water, and wondered, just for a second, if we did jump together, her hand in mine, would I drag her too deep.

Carmel turned back to me and laughed, then wrapped her fingers around mine and we stepped off the ledge.

We took the plunge five times. After the third, Carmel admitted she'd kept her eyes closed during the first jump. Each time we hit the water I expected her to let go of my hand and surface on her own, a natural sink-or-swim reaction. But she kept her grip, and screamed and laughed when our heads finally popped up and we began bobbing down the channel.

"Not as scary as it looks," she said, hanging onto my shoulders as we floated back toward our knapsacks after our final jump.

We scrambled ashore and quickly changed back into our clothes in the public restrooms, and perched ourselves on a log and slowly began draining the sun of light and heat.

From my knapsack I pulled two roast beef sandwiches I'd bought at a deli near the fire hall right after work and two half-warm beer. I can't remember anything ever tasting as good.

We sat close, her bare arm often brushing mine, the sun inching down behind the San Juan Islands, a familiarity growing.

"Has anyone ever swum across the channel?" she asked. "You know, between here and the state park on the other side."

I laughed and leaned back. "With the nine-knot current and waves that sometimes hit six feet, it's not very wise."

She smiled. "But that doesn't mean no one's tried it."

In the fading light and the shelter of the big firs, I sensed we'd both found a comfort that surprised us. One that we were in no hurry to leave. So I told her about the Civilian Conservation Corps, the fearless men who built the bridge back in the 1930s. Stories abounded about how these men – when not breaking up thousands of yards of rock for the bridge's piers or building a cableway to ferry supplies across the water – would challenge each other to a Sunday afternoon swim from Whidbey Island to our side of the channel. Always one guy in a wooden rowboat accompanying a half-dozen or so swimmers in case someone wore out too soon. I regaled Carmel with tales about men who raced across the channel in their hurried, uneven strokes, smoked a cigarette on the rocky shore, and then swam back, barely drying off before disappearing together to their hidden stash of booze in the woods. Some men had to be pulled exhausted and freezing from the water when they underestimated the current's strength and were swept far off course. One swimmer, or so I had heard, had slipped silently under the water and was never seen again, a mystery that remained long after the bridge opened in 1934. Carmel laughed when I told her the special name bestowed upon the men not brave enough to make the foolish journey across the channel: Shore-chickens.

"Sounds like there's little you don't know about this channel and about the bridge," she said.

It would be another four months before I told her all I knew about the bridge. That no one had ever survived a jump off it. Not even my own father.

I would eventually discover that her mouth, which I would kiss that night, concealed its own secrets. As with mine, time would pass before they would slip free.

I unlocked the glass door to my new apartment and slid it open, and turned to Carmel. "This is the surprise," I told her.

She stepped past me and went inside, casting her eyes around the bare rooms, unable to hide her grin. "Well, it's a real bachelor pad."

"Okay, it needs a little work."

"Nah," she said looking around. "Just some decorating. You know, pictures on the wall, maybe some appliances, some furniture, that kind of thing. But that's it."

"Okay, enough. It's a start."

"Yes," she laughed, "It's a start…and maybe by the time you're finished you'll have some food in the fridge or cupboards."

"I told you. I'm going to treat you to some ice cream. I've got the world's biggest freezer downstairs. It's called Baskin-Robbins."

"Good thing you invited me for dessert and not dinner, or else I guess we'd be having one of those ice cream cakes as our main course and eating it with our bare hands."

Of course, she was right to be kidding me. I'd overlooked a few details. I'd only gone apartment hunting four days ago, one day after my first date with her. I'd stumbled by accident upon this place, which sat above a row of shops on Main Street. I had tried all four Suites-For-Rent ads in the local paper, and all had already been rented. But one apartment manager told me about this place, which had just become available. Mom, who had actually cried when I told her I'd be moving out, even if my new place was only a mile or so away, had given me a set of dishes and plates earlier in the day as a housewarming gift, but I still didn't own silverware. I had also picked up some beer, cola and chips from the convenience store, but I hadn't gone grocery shopping yet.

On the bright side, Mom and Amanda had taken me on a circuit through our town's garage sales in the morning, and that had netted me, among other things, a kitchen table and chairs and a La-Z-Boy recliner.

I had told Carmel about the apartment last night, on our more conventional second date – dinner at a little Italian restaurant after she got off work. She was puzzled.

"I thought you lived at home with your mom?"

"And the Lesbian chick?"

"Brady, that's not nice, but, yes, at home."

"Well I did. But I just took possession of the apartment, and I'm moving in."

She plunked herself down on the La-Z-Boy and reclined, and I sat on the arm next to her.

"And to think I almost wound up in San Antonio, Texas

rather than here in this luxury," she said. "San Antonio. That's where the other dental school was that I considered."

"That's right," I said, recalling our very first conversation. "You came up to Bellingham because you had an aunt and uncle there, right?"

She laughed. "So you weren't totally drunk the night we met? You do remember some things."

"They're all a little hazy, but I remember."

"Almost had to go to San Antonio, though. They had accepted me and Western Washington had turned me down, so I filled out all the papers and found a place to stay in San Antonio, and just about had sent my money in when I got this call from Western Washington. Right at the last minute. Someone had dropped out, so they had an opening and were shopping it around. They had a hard time filling it; most students had already committed elsewhere. Guess I must have been a ways down the list, but that's all right."

It took a few seconds for her words to register; they were like a punch in the gut.

"When did that happen? When did they accept you?"

"It was mid-July. Two years ago, of course. Why?"

I shook my head. "No reason. Just wondering."

"Why do you look so…I don't know how to describe it. Brittany reacted the same way when I told her a spot had opened up really late in the process. I did qualify, you know. I did earn it. My high school marks were really solid."

"Of course. Anyway, I'll go down and get the ice cream," I said, standing suddenly. "You wanted that strawberry thingy in a cup, right."

Carmel looked at me strangely. "Yes." She paused. "I can come down with you."

"No, stay here. I like to wait on my guests."

I rushed out the door, debating whether I should have told her. But how could she understand the sad irony that there was a good chance she had taken Sarah's spot at university, then had won my affections two years later.

Down the hall I walked, my mind screaming out different outcomes, all flying off in a series of random arcs. At the bottom of the long flight of stairs, I stopped at the door, and before I realized it my hands flew out towards imaginary doors, towards imaginary directions in life.

I groaned out loud.

What would have happened if Sarah hadn't got booted out of Western Washington before she even started? Would she have a career in another town, her life propelled forward by responsibility and happiness, instead of languishing in her home town with Sam and Luke?

Without the ultimatum to move to Seattle, would I have not done what I did? Would I have broken off our relationship without telling her why?

And what about Carmel? Where would she be now? Not in my apartment. Would I even have this apartment if I hadn't met her?

Would Sarah despise Carmel if she knew any of this?

Would Sarah's dad lie awake at night thinking about hiring a hit man to kill Carmel too?

Would…

"Brady."

I jumped, then turned around to see Carmel standing at the top of the stairs, staring down.

"What are you doing? Making sure you've got your key?"

"Yes," I told her.

"I could have buzzed you back in."

"Oh, wait, here it is, in my pocket," I said, holding it up.

"Okay. I was coming down to find you. I think I want something with chocolate in it instead."

She walked downstairs, took my arm, and touched my face, like her hand could elicit the reasons for its sudden tenseness.

"You okay?" she asked.

"I'm fine. Just really hungry. It's a guy thing."

She smiled. "Well I won't get in your way."

We got our ice cream, climbed the stairs and crammed together on the La-Z-Boy, where I soon relaxed enough for a friendly debate about the merits of my mint selection against her chocolate. She ran her tongue along my slightly green upper lip for a taste. I did the same back, reveling in a sweetness I knew had already hooked me.

"That wasn't so bad," Carmel told me as we drove through the evening rain three weeks later, in a mid-September summer-ending storm.

"No worse than a trip to the dentist," I agreed. "Or maybe a minor traffic accident."

"Stop it. I thought your mom was nice. She lent us her car so we didn't have to drive home in such yucky weather on your motorcycle."

"Which mom? The aging semi-reformed substance abuser or the younger fanatical lesbian."

"Your real mom," Carmel said. "You know, the one who pushed you out of her body after hours of labor and raised you for the next twenty years, just so you could go over to her house for dinner and be grumpy."

"I wasn't grumpy."

"You were to your mom. Bit insensitive too."

"Well, that's the only way to get through to her. Words have to be blunt and forceful just to penetrate her thick skull."

All in all though, the evening had gone as well as could be expected. Mom had exhibited a certain aloofness as she met Carmel for the first time, politely shaking her hand and embracing her with the same affection as she would an ex-husband. Amanda, meanwhile, bestowed her usual kindness, however questionably sincere, upon Carmel.

"I liked Amanda," Carmel now told me.

"Well I bet she really liked you too," I said grinning. "Really liked you."

"Brady…" Carmel scolded me.

"What?"

"You know what. You're far too critical of Amanda. Based on everything you said about her I envisioned this nasty radical guy-hating feminist. She was really sweet."

"And cunning."

"That's it, Brady. I'm serving notice. No more Amanda-bashing."

"You're what?" I said smiling. "Serving notice. What is that?"

"You heard me," she said. "Serving notice. I won't tolerate you bad-mouthing Amanda any more. And just because I'm grinning don't think I'm joking either."

We stopped at a traffic light, and turned to each other with amused smiles. "I've never had a girl serve notice on me before."

"Well get used to it," she said, the swirling wind outside whipping the rain against the car in waves.

I undid her seatbelt and pulled her close on the bench seat of my mom's old Pontiac. I slid my arm around her as we waited contentedly for the signal to change, the windshield wipers squeaking back and forth in a hypnotic rhythm, warm air blowing in from the car's aging heater.

"You know, I've fallen in with love you," she said, her voice smooth.

"I feel the same way," I told her, then drove on.

❧

My two worlds collided far sooner than I expected.

"Hello, Brady," Sarah said as I cruised the frozen meat section of Safeway with Carmel. I looked up to see her and Luke before us.

"Where you been, you prick?" Luke offered menacingly, before smiling.

"Hey," I said awkwardly. "Carmel, these are my friends, Sarah and Luke."

"Friends," laughed Luke, turning to Sarah. "He still calls us friends."

Sarah ignored Luke, and politely said, "Nice to meet you. Carmel is it?"

"Yes," Carmel said. "Nice to meet you too. I've heard Brittany mention you."

"That's right. You're Brittany's friend. From dental school."

"Yes," Carmel said, and I prayed Sarah didn't pursue the dental school conversation.

"So, is that how you met Brady – through Brittany?" Sarah asked, partly to my relief.

I watched them exchange pleasantries, Carmel taller and leaner, Sarah steadier, Carmel's facial features finer, subtler, Sarah's beauty more overpowering, tenacious, bewildering, Carmel slightly insidious in her determination, Sarah direct but often ineffective.

"So are you two, you know," Luke suddenly said, waving a finger back and forth between Carmel and me.

"Luke," Sarah said.

"Living together," he said.

"Oh, no," Carmel said, a little too quickly. "I live with Brittany, in a basement suite in her family's home. I'm just helping Brady shop, for his new place."

The awkward small talk continued until, I suspect, none of us could stand anymore. After we said our goodbyes, I sensed Carmel watching me as I pretended to study packages of raw hamburger meat.

"She's very pretty," she said.

I nodded.

"So she was your girlfriend when it happened? And that man died in *her* home?"

I nodded again.

"So did you break up with her, or she with you?"

"Why?"

"Just curious."

"I guess I sort of broke up with her. Look, that's a good buy on lean ground beef."

"I thought so," she said. "And, Luke," she continued. "He's the one that some people still suspect?"

I nodded.

When we unloaded the groceries back at my place, Carmel said in passing, "I think she still has feelings for you."

"What," I said, burying my face in the fridge.

"Sarah. I think she still has feelings for you."

"No."

"I can pick these things up. She does. I think she's even a little proud of you, you know, becoming a firefighter."

"Don't be silly, it's been two years," I said, throwing some canned corn into a cupboard.

"So what," Carmel said, grabbing me so I had to look at her.

"It's not always affection that keeps someone thinking about someone else years later. Sometimes it's something worse."

Once the groceries were away, I grimaced and asked the question I'd been dying to ask. "So do you hear much about it? Mr. Opal's death. From people who hear you're seeing me. You know, people who say, 'You're dating who?'"

Carmel considered her words carefully, and I immediately wished I hadn't brought it up.

"Sure, I hear about it sometimes."

"Do people tell you to steer clear of me?"

She weighed her words again. "I think Brittany's dad is a little concerned. A few others. But most give you the benefit of the doubt. Some seem to like you. Think you got treated unfairly by the police."

I knew I should have stopped.

"So," I persisted, unable to help myself. "When are you gonna ask me what happened that night? In Sarah's house."

"What's to ask? I understand he fell, and after the police cleared up the confusion, it was over. I certainly don't want to know all the sordid details of the accident."

She paused, and subtly pressed the issue by hanging six words in the air: "So really, what's there to ask?"

Six words. So gentle, so benign, so murderously eviscerating. Words innocently intended to hunt down and expose duplicity.

I stood in silence as Carmel studied me, and I turned back to the fridge and began stuffing it with cans of soda. I'd thought about offering a stock answer, like, "That's right. There's nothing to ask. Nothing to tell." But I'd seen it flicker to life in her eyes before I turned away. The knowledge of my deception. She saw it in my silence, in my every expression, in my every move, and if I'd spoken, she would have heard it in the feeble opaqueness of my words. Or so I thought.

I ran out of cans of soda, and had to close the fridge and turn and face her. She glanced down, then back at me. We stood, eyes connected, and I waited for her to nod, slowly, and then to walk out, her footsteps heavy.

She moved forward and slid her arms around me, and I pulled her head close. "So are you hungry?" she asked.

"You gotta see this," Sam told me, tossing me a beer. "An incredible money maker."

"Sam, I told you on the phone. I can't get mixed up with any of your shit. Not now."

He laughed. "This is legal shit. Even got a business license."

"I bet," I said skeptically.

"Believe him," Luke chipped in. "The man's a genius. Least this week anyway."

Sam led me to a computer in what I assumed was the bedroom he shared with Sarah, and brushed a cat off the warmth of the monitor.

"Why are there so many cats in here?" I asked.

"Well, that's not what I brought you here to see, but I might as well tell you. It's almost as amazing. We have six of them living with us right now."

"Six cats. Why?"

"One word," Sam said. "Sarah."

"Let me guess. She couldn't have a pet at home so now she's making up for lost time."

"Not exactly. You see, these aren't our cats. We're just borrowing them."

"You stole them? I don't get it?"

"No, you jerk," he said. "They're from the town's animal shelter. Part of a new program to see that fewer cats wind up in the big incinerator. Anytime they get more cats than cages, which usually means the extra cats get put down, you know, the ones that have been there the longest and no one wants, anyway, we volunteer to take them. So do a couple of other people. When room opens up or someone wants to adopt them they go back."

"Oh. Makes sense."

"To Sarah it does. Try fucken sleeping with these things fighting and meowing and pissing all over the place. Anyway," he said sitting down and booting up the Web. "'Enough about cats. I got something better. And you can't tell Sarah I showed you this, okay."

I nodded.

He went to his favorites and brought up a website that screamed, "Teen Slut Exposed on Hidden Camera." He clicked below the image of a woman wearing a tight blouse, and the so-called "Free Preview" came to life. The woman's face was pixilated, and words at the bottom of the screen said, "Image pixilated on order of New York State Court. This video resulted in the conviction of a fifty-five-year-old man for planting a hidden camera in a seventeen-year-old girl's bedroom." She brushed her hair and stared at the camera, as if she was looking into the mirror. The woman then removed her top and bra, in a seductive manner that belied the suggestion she was unaware of the camera, and ran her hand across her bare breasts. Then the video clip ended.

"Now watch," said Sam, who clicked on a members only button and typed in a password while he went on about buying some cheap servers and video equipment. Soon he restarted the video of the girl. This time she didn't stop once she took her bra off. She slipped off her pants, and slid one hand into her panties and one back over her breast, stroking and massaging.

"How do you like it so far?" Sam asked as I studied the screen.

"He must like it," Luke said, "he hasn't taken his eyes off it."

I admit I stood transfixed, though not for the reasons they thought. I watched the so-called teen slut until I could watch no more. I turned to Sam, disturbed, disgusted.

"That's Sarah."

He bristled, and abruptly shut the computer screen off. "Okay. I won't deny it. You've seen her naked before, so I guess you'd recognize her."

"Why are you doing this, Sam?"

"Don't be a jerk," he said, "to make money."

"But Sarah?"

"Don't believe everything you read on the screen," he said sarcastically. "She's not a teen anymore, and no the camera wasn't hidden. She's in on it."

"I know, but…"

"So don't make her out to be so innocent in this. She didn't take a lot of convincing. And she's hoping to be giving up her day job for this. We're filming a whole series of these alleged illegally taken videos that somehow made their way out of a police evidence locker."

"You know," Luke said, "you may not be fond of Sarah any more. Lot of other guys are though. And they don't mind paying to see her."

On a night when darkness came early, Carmel and I wound our way down to the beach, arm in arm, along a black path illuminated only by a half-moon occasionally cloaked by a drifting cloud. We walked in silence, our steps comfortably in stride, content with the night's quiet, and partway along she stopped, and I knew instantly to find her lips with mine. We embraced, and moved on.

"So you're sure you know where you're going?" she joked. "You're not going to take us over some cliff or something?"

"I ran these trails for years as a kid. Could walk this one in my sleep."

In the distance, the waves slammed onto the beach in a fierce, steady rhythm.

"You know," Carmel said, as the tall cedars gave way to smaller beach-side bushes, "you know so little about me."

I didn't respond at first, sensing she wished to be heard. We emerged on the beach, straining our eyes for a path between the logs to the shoreline.

When she didn't continue, I offered this: "I know you love good Italian food, tasty pasta, yummy salads, that sort of thing. And you hate television – specially sports and sitcoms – but you enjoy movies, not stupid action flicks, but dramas, ones with a good story. Books, you love the classic American authors, Steinbeck, Hemingway, and you hate cheesy romance novels. You like the fresh air, though not necessarily the great outdoors. You..."

"Okay, okay," she laughed. "I should be more specific. Those are good observations, but you know nothing about my past. Why I am the way I am."

"Does it matter?"

"You tell me."

I didn't wish to reflect on how the past shapes and marks someone.

"I don't know," I said.

After a short silence, she said, "You already know I'm not really a blonde. I'm a true brunette. But that's not all."

"Okay," I said.

Her grip tightened on my arm as we walked carefully over the stones scattered by an earlier high tide.

"You know this great California-girl tan I've got? You wonder why it hasn't begun to fade? Have you wondered that?"

We kept walking.

"It's because its roots lie much further to the south than California. Say El Salvador. That's where my mother was born. She met my dad there when he served as an advisor for the U.S. military. They got married and moved back to the States, and I came along. You know what I'm saying? I'm telling you my genetics. It's not the sun that makes my skin brown."

"Okay."

"Well it's not just okay," she said, her voice fast, hurriedly unloading a burden. "You've heard of racism, but do you know what it really is? Try growing up in Idaho, in Coeur d'Alene. That's where we lived when we came back to the States, where my dad had a wilderness guiding business, where I grew up. Do you know what it's like to grow up in an almost all-white town when you're not white? When your mother's of Spanish descent, or as other kids in school liked to say, Mexican, or Border-Jumper, or Just Not One Of Us? Can you understand what that's like?

"So my mom and dad felt the stress of living in Idaho, and my mom wanted to move. But my dad's guiding business was taking off, and he wanted to stay. So we stayed, and they fought, and it all fell apart. That's when my mom moved the two of us to Redding, where Hispanics abound. My mom had me keep my dad's surname though. She always looked ahead.

"So you see, I'm not exactly who you think I am."

We stopped walking, and she stood on her tip-toes, her eyes straining to look into mine, searching.

I laughed softly. "Do you think I changed how I feel about you in the last few moments, and that you'll see it in my eyes?"

"It happens with some people, you know. Just like that. And you *can* see it."

I smiled, and swore I loved her more than ever.

We walked in silence, the wind sweeping the cold mist from breaking waves into our faces.

"So nothing's changed?" she asked.

"Shut up," I said affectionately, and we laughed.

When we left the beach and plunged again into the darkness of a shorter trail back to the streets of Deception Pass, I took a deep breath and said, "So if this is honesty night, I've got something to tell you."

She said nothing at first, and we soon walked out of the bush and onto a paved street, lined with expensive homes.

"If we keep walking down this road, we'll pass it won't we?" she asked. "The house where it happened. Sarah's old house."

"Yes."

She stopped and slid her hands around the back of my neck, beneath my jacket's collar.

"You don't have to tell me. I already know."

"I want to tell you everything. So you'll know what you're getting into. Because you don't really know – not everything."

"Yes, I do."

"Not all of it."

"Yes, all of it. One has instincts for this sort of thing. Trust me. I know."

We stopped, and I studied her in silence. Her eyes, which so often revealed only what she chose, held nothing back. It really was all there. Everything.

"I wouldn't blame you, you know," I said. "If you…"

"Now you shut up," she said burying her face into mine.

As we neared the Roberts and Opal households, an unfortunate gauntlet, I asked her, "What should I do?"

"Just look ahead," she said. "Can you do that?"

I leveled with her once more. "I don't know."

16

I warmed my hands on a tall coffee as I waited for Carmel outside a small deli and espresso shop just off Main Street. When she had phoned me during her lunch break, she told me to meet her at an outside table at 5:30 sharp, exactly when her workday ended.

"It's too cold to sit outside," I had lamented, reminding her it was still mid-March, then asking her why we couldn't meet in my apartment.

"Just be there, okay," she said.

"What are you so anxious to talk about?"

"Just be there."

So I waited, huddled in my heavy coat, steam rising from our coffees. I saw her a half block away crossing the street, dressed lightly for her usual twenty-foot walk to her car, which she parked each morning behind the dentist's office.

She smiled when she saw me, and I wondered again why she insisted on a meeting in a public place. I thought people only did that when they were breaking up.

She kissed me and pulled her chair close, either for warmth or to speak quietly, then ran her hands over her coffee container. "Okay. It's not quite as warm out here as I thought. Sorry. But I wanted to catch you before you went to work."

"What is it?" I asked.

"Brady, don't look so worried," she said, her words reminding me of Sarah's usual refrain. "It's nothing bad..."

"So the outside table isn't so you can break up or anything like that?"

"No," she laughed. "God it's so ironic you'd say that, cause you may be the one who wants to break up." She stared down at her coffee, her forced grin quickly evaporating. "I'm pregnant. I took the test today at the doctor's."

I stifled a gasp.

"I know" she said, "it's a shock."

"When..."

"I'm about three months along. So the baby was conceived in late November."

"Oh."

"Doctor hasn't quite set my due date yet. Likely early August."

"August?"

"Yes. They'll pin it down better when I go for an ultrasound."

"Oh."

"Yes."

"So how could this happen?" I asked. "I mean, I always used a condom."

"Not always. You haven't always kept your condom jar fully stocked. Twice I recall we tried it without one, with you, you know, pulling out kinda just in time. Remember?"

"Well, yes, but that shouldn't be enough to get someone pregnant."

"It's not someone, Brady. It's me. And, apparently it was."

"I just don't see how."

Carmel sat up straight. "Are you doubting you're the father?"

The word father associated with my name sounded both disturbing and strangely beautiful. "No, I'm not doubting anything."

She leaned forward once more and placed her hands on mine. "Look into my eyes, Brady. You're the only guy I've been with in some time, and I think you know that."

"I do know it, it's just that..."

"We'll get any test you want done, no problem, but..."

"But what?"

"Well, before we go to that trouble, it may be a moot point. I mean, God, there are other options."

"Like what?"

She sighed. "Like putting the baby up for adoption, like aborting it." Tears began rolling down her face. "God, Brady. We're both twenty years old. Do you think I planned this? Do you think I wanted this now? I've always dreamed of having kids, but not now. I wanted to take a year or two off work, travel the world. With you. Enjoy being young, you know. Pretty impossible now."

I wanted to comfort her, but didn't know how.

"No one else knows," she said. "Not Brittany, not my mom or dad. I've suspected for the past week, if you wonder why I seemed so preoccupied."

I sat back, overwhelmed.

"You see what I'm saying," Carmel continued. "You've got a say in this too. I'm carrying it, but it's your baby too."

She lifted her coffee to her mouth, and before I could think to warn her, she took a sip and winced as she burned her lip. "I'll start showing soon, so we have to make up our minds."

I nodded.

She shivered, looking nowhere in particular. "I wanted

to meet you somewhere different, somewhere neutral, in case this goes wrong. In case this is the end of us. Didn't think you would want your apartment associated with something awful. In case it comes to that."

"Don't talk like that."

She looked at her watch, and rose. "So think about it, about everything."

I nearly told her that was all I suspected I would be doing.

That night I took the cordless phone out onto the fire hall's back deck and called Carmel. She sounded pleasantly surprised to hear from me.

"Hope I didn't wake you."

"No. Just a minute."

Silence.

"Okay," she said quietly. "Just going into the bedroom so Brittany doesn't hear."

"Okay."

"Quiet night at the fire hall? No garbage trucks spontaneously combusting?"

"I wish. Not a single call."

"Well, you still get paid."

"That I do. Hey, listen. I was thinking about what you told me today."

She laughed. "No shit."

"Well," I said. "I still don't quite know what to say, what to do, how to act, but, well, I wanted to suggest we rule one thing out."

"What's that?"

"An abortion."

For a moment she didn't answer, and I felt sure an abortion was exactly what she'd had in mind.

"Well," she finally said. "I'm kinda relieved to hear you

say that. I've never much thought before about whether abortion is right or wrong, never much even cared, but it's a strange thing. My brain tells me it would be okay in this case, the easy way out after all, but the rest of my body, every last cell, seems to be screaming for me to protect the baby. Maybe it's just hormones."

"Good."

"You know, I've said this is our decision, the two of us, right, but I had sort of made up my mind already. To have the baby. Of course, I don't know what do with it once I have it."

"That's our next step. Deciding that."

"Okay. So let's keep all other options open. You know, putting the baby up for adoption. Anything else we come up with. Giving it away to gypsies. Selling it on the black market."

"Sure."

"So this means I can start telling a few select people, before they notice? Like Brittany, who I think wonders why I'm acting so weird? And my mom, my dad?"

I hesitated. "I guess so. Are you gonna tell them I'm the father."

"Kind of obvious your name will come up, isn't it?"

"You're right. I'm not thinking straight."

"Brady," she said.

"Yes."

"Why are you against an abortion? It makes sense in so many ways for me to sneak away and get rid of our little secret."

I weighed my answer, and for a moment considered not answering honestly. Finally I did. "I don't know. It's the whole thing about death. You can't go back and undo it if you have regrets."

❧

When I got home the next morning, I climbed on my motorcycle, ignoring the warm call of my bed. Carmel was meeting me for lunch. My body cried out for sleep – something I didn't get much of that night at the fire hall, even though we never were called out. By 9 a.m. I sipped coffee outside a Mount Vernon jewelry store, waiting for it to open.

When I worked nights, Carmel often stopped by for lunch – it was the only time I'd see her during that four-day rotation. Sometimes, if a morning patient canceled without notice, she'd surprise me as I slept, sneaking into my bedroom and quietly slipping off her clothes while I lay oblivious with my earplugs firmly implanted. I'd suddenly feel her cold feet and hands on my body, burrowing in for warmth, searching relentlessly, hopefully, never settling until they'd found what they needed. She'd bury her face into my neck and giggle deeply as I jumped, at first resisting the coldness of her flesh, until finally I relented and let her draw freely from my warmth. She'd apologize for waking me, whisper for me to go back to sleep, though how could I do that? Then we'd talk, her words always forging ahead, always focused on something in the future, something sure to be perfect in our lives. She'd keep an eye on her watch, and slip away suddenly, leaving me with a small grin when she shut the bedroom door behind her.

Today no patients canceled, and she simply came for lunch. We ate corned beef sandwiches on some deliciously fresh white bread, as she playfully prodded me under the kitchen table with feet encased in white sneakers. The ring sat in my pocket, waiting to be unleashed at the right time.

We lingered at the table. Then she helped me do the

dishes and straighten up the kitchen. As I sat back down she looked at her watch. "Got my first afternoon appointment in six minutes." She kissed me on the cheek and as I started to stand she whispered, "Wait. Stay there."

She pulled up her shirt and pressed my ear to her smooth belly so I could listen. "Hard to believe – somewhere in there is another life." She laughed. "Growing furiously out of control. Cool, huh. And scary."

I just nodded, my hand in my pocket fingering the ring, spinning it absently, pointlessly.

At the door she slid her cold fingers under my shirt, and I jumped. She laughed and was gone, and I wondered how I could deny her something so essential.

In the coming days, I searched for the right time to propose, but never found it. I carried the ring with me everywhere I went with her, and started to become worried she'd find it. That she'd notice a bulge in my pants or jacket pocket.

In the meantime, word of the pregnancy spread. I had to tell Mom and Amanda before they heard it somewhere else.

"Carmel's pregnant?" Mom responded.

"Congratulations, Brady," Amanda said hugging me.

"Now don't get mad," Mom said. "But are you sure you're the father?"

Once my colleagues at the fire hall heard, I knew it was just a matter of time before the whole town knew.

"So when are you gonna make that lovely Carmel an honest woman?" Tom Marriott asked.

I shrugged.

"I see the way you look at her. C'mon, what are you waiting for, you dumb fuck," he cajoled.

Others weren't quite as forthcoming as Tom, but asked

in their own way. Brittany, for example, simply remarked to me one day, "I think Carmel's uncertain future is weighing on her."

For her part, Carmel did explore various adoption services, and sat down one evening to enlighten me about how our baby could have a good life with someone else, if that's what we wanted.

I sensed, though, she wasn't pushing me this way. I suspected she wanted to keep the baby.

About three weeks after she'd delivered the news, Carmel asked one night if I had reached a decision.

"I'll be showing pretty soon, you know," she said as we walked to a movie, the trees and shrubs around us budding to life, a brisk spring breeze blowing in off the ocean.

I said nothing, and after a short silence, she asked, "You ever felt trapped, Brady?"

"Sure," I told her, aware of the hurt my indecision had caused.

After a short time, I said, "What if I asked you to marry me?"

"Well, you haven't."

"I know. But what if I did? What would you say?"

"I guess I'd want to know if you're asking because you love me and want to spend your life with me or if you're asking me out of duty because I'm pregnant."

"Well, what if I told you it were both? I want to be with you, and I want our baby to have a father. Then what would you say?"

"I'd say 'Why haven't you asked, so you can find out?'"

"You know it's not that simple, because there's the whole other issue. And you'd suddenly be dragged into that, and everything that comes with it."

She looked down as we continued walking, and finally said: "I know, but with that, I'd only ask one thing. That you promise to put it behind us, and when I say us, it would be us, three of us, cause we'd all be affected if you couldn't."

We stopped walking.

"I'm still not sure I can do that. That I can just act like nothing wrong happened."

"You must. You must promise. It must be as strong as a wedding vow."

"It's not getting any easier. Not even as time passes. I thought it would, but it's not. I don't know if I can continue ignoring it."

"Yes you can." She squeezed my arm. "Promise me."

I laughed nervously.

"Promise me," she repeated.

"I can try."

"No," she said, her voice firm. "You have to promise me."

Carmel's smile belied the seriousness of what she'd just asked.

Before I realized it, my hand reached down and touched her tummy. "Sometimes I can't believe there is another life in there."

"I know," she said.

I looked away, at nowhere in particular, then back to her. "Okay," I finally said. "It's behind me."

"Is it?"

"Yes," I said, pointing behind my back. "Can't you see, it's back there?"

"C'mon, stop it. Are you certain?"

"Yes."

"Okay," she said breathless. "Okay."

I took her hand out of her jacket pocket, where she'd stuffed if for warmth, and led her across the street toward the high school grounds. She looked uncertain but pleased. Finally we were going somewhere. We cut across the football field, made soggy by spring rains.

"Where are you taking me?" she laughed as the ground grew softer and we tip-toed across muck, the edges of our shoes stained muddy brown.

"You'll see."

We reached an old pine tree, and stopped by a bench underneath. The rainwater had made the ground unstable, cracking and bulging the blacktop that the bench was set upon. On this shakiest of foundations I reached into my pocket and finally produced the engagement ring.

Carmel's eyes swirled with tears.

"Guess you'd kill me if I told you I've carried this around for three weeks."

"Uh-huh," she said.

We married on a Saturday in early June. Carmel's wedding dress bulged with life as she walked down the aisle of the town's small chapel, a wide smile on her face that easily outdid those of our fifty-five guests. Her mother sat in the front row next to her father and his new girlfriend. Mom and Amanda huddled together across the aisle.

We snuck glances at each other as the minister spoke well rehearsed words we would soon forget. When I took her hand and slid the ring on her finger, I thought how utterly perfect it was that our baby was present to share our love and the first stirrings of a new family.

That night we danced again at Mullins Hall, a place Carmel had months earlier suggested as the only possible venue for our reception. I didn't disagree. It did hold a certain magic for me too, though it also came with blurry and disturbing memories of Dr. Roberts and Brittany confessing more than I ever wanted to hear about how a single act could hurt so many.

Of course, almost everywhere lurked reminders of my teenage regret. I saw it etched all over Luke, who came to my wedding with a date who wore a skin-tight dress, prompting laughter and whispers of "slut" from Carmel's friends. Or on Sam, who came alone, explaining that Sarah didn't feel comfortable accepting our kind invitation but did sincerely wish us happiness and all that shit. Even on Carmel's dad, who the night before the wedding heard the tale of Tom Opal's demise from strangers while he and Susan, his fiancée for the last four years, went out for drinks at the Rusty Nail, on Mom's encouragement.

But reminders of my new, brighter adult life also pervaded the room. Tom Marriott and Captain Boerne brought their wives, and Carson Kilgore brought a girl whose wardrobe had its origins in the 1960s. I could almost hear Boerne, at the moment he laid eyes on her, muttering in his gentle way, something like, "Well at least he likes girls, even if they're damn hippies."

Then there were Carmel's various aunts, two high school friends from Redding, and two friends from her dental office. All of us ate together in the storied hall, toasted one another, traded stories, danced, and, for the most part, looked to the future, which for a rare moment in my life gleamed with insinuations of brightness.

I danced into the shadows only once that night, when I pressed Sam about Sarah, about what she did for a living now that she'd quit the restaurant. The conversation took place in the corner of the hall by the door, where our well-wrapped wedding gifts were neatly stacked on a fold-up table.

"Sarah picked out your wedding gift," Sam said. "Mostly baby stuff. She says you're gonna have a girl – says she can predict these things – so she got you a couple of girly type outfits in addition to the regular baby stuff. She's still got the receipt in case she's wrong."

"Great. So how is she doing?" I asked.

Sam studied me, and I suspected he thought back to the last time I asked about Sarah, a week or so after I spotted her on their website in the flesh in a new video, one titled, "NEW – Hidden Camera Catches Teen Slut Seduce the Boy Next Door."

He had looked stunned when I brought it up back then, like he had expected I'd never return to the website after his short tour of it.

"Okay," he had said. "So you memorized the URL. Big deal. We had to change up the site. Take it up a notch. Found a kid who would work for free. For the pleasure of being with Sarah. Turned into a big money-maker."

"How can you do that to her?" I had demanded. "Use her like that?"

"Don't give me that shit. It was her idea."

Now he shifted uneasily. "What have you heard?" he asked.

"Why?"

He sighed. "Well, what would you say if I told you Sarah's now an actress? Been in two adult films. You know, pornos."

I grimaced.

"That she saw an ad in the classifieds. Someone looking for adult movie actors. She called, and they asked if she had any experience. She directed them to our website, and they were interested. Did some shooting in Seattle one day. She had a small part."

"God."

He sighed. "You seem to think it's easy on me to see that happen."

"I never said that."

"I can see it on your face. But that's not the way it was. Not easy on me. Driving home, she was quiet and everything. You know, not herself. I suggested it went well. She nodded. I suggested she didn't seem to mind it, you know, she didn't look uncomfortable or anything. She started to get mad. Say stuff like, 'You think I enjoyed that.' Well, I made the mistake of saying something like, 'Kinda looked like you enjoyed it. Yes.' Anyway I stopped for gas, and I'm filling up and all of a sudden a pail of water comes flying over the car, bounces off the roof, and nails me. Followed by the squeegee. Sarah starts screaming. 'How could you say that? How could you say that I enjoyed that.' She went nuts. I go in to pay and dry off in the washroom, and she drives away, so I'm, like, stranded out near I-5 in Burlington. So I say screw this. I'll walk. I'll fucken walk home."

"So what happened?"

He shrugged. "She came back and got me. I only got a couple of blocks. Saw the car approaching, and I just kept walking. She did a u-turn and pulled up ahead of me. She stopped and slid over to the passenger seat. Didn't look at me. Just waited. I thought of walking right past, but I got in and drove off. We didn't speak about it. Didn't say another word. She just took my hand, and we drove." He sipped his beer. "So what do you say to that?"

He went on to tell me few others knew Sarah's secret. Luke, his date, a couple more. And that Sarah's father knew only the sanitized half of the story. That Sarah joined an acting group, The Deception Pass Players, where she won a role in their summer play. That she was taking acting lessons and had started playing the piano again and writing songs.

"Got a creative side, you know?" Luke told me. "Anyway, she wants to be an actress, and she won't get there by being a waitress."

"Sure, but getting there by being a porn actress – that probably won't work either," I said. "And it's just not right."

Sam's face grew hard. "That's right, Brady. And it wouldn't be right to sell crystal meth to kids to finance a new career as a firefighter, would it?"

❧

"So where are you going for your honeymoon?" the technician asked two days later as she massaged Carmel's stomach with a strange gel and readied an instrument that seemed like a hand-held mirror.

"Southern California," Carmel said. "The car's all packed up and ready to go. We're dropping my Mom off in Redding. Hope to get there late tonight. Then stay the night and sleep in and continue."

"Sounds like fun," she said as she began flipping switches on the monitor. "Going to Disneyland?"

"That and every other tourist trap," I said. "Don't know how many rides the three of us will be able to go on."

"Probably most of them," she said. "Okay. Let's see what we've got here," she said, her eyes on the screen.

In time, she said, "This machine uses high frequency sound waves. They're emitted from this probe device in my hand, called a transducer. Look there's a spine, and a leg. I think it's a leg. Part of the skull right there."

Carmel smiled widely at the x-ray-like images which came and went on the screen as the probe moved across her skin.

"That's…" the technician's voice fell silent. "Just a minute," she said after a short silence, carefully studying the screen.

My heart fell at this hint of trouble, and a look of pain engulfed Carmel.

After what seemed like forever, the technician smiled, and quickly said, "Everything's fine, don't worry. It's just that…"

"What?" we both asked.

"It's just that it looks like you're carrying twins."

⁂

Tom Marriott swears you can see death in the eyes of the worst junkies weeks in advance of their final overdose. See it in their vacant stares. The resignation. The unhappy ending they flash as they stagger blindly in front of cars, or weave along the sidewalk headed nowhere in particular. He'd call them the walking doomed.

What would he see, I wondered, if he laid eyes on Sarah's face today, just two weeks after she overdosed on cocaine and spent two days in the hospital with horrendously high blood pressure and stroke-like symptoms?

The night after her OD, Sarah said she hadn't felt a brush with death, she told Sam, but she had experienced an epiphany, a moment of enlightenment in which she knew the two of them, if they were to have a future, needed to get the hell out of Deception Pass. So after she regained her strength and registered a normal heartbeat, after she assured her family and friends she would never again indulge in any drug, Luke drove them to Bellingham Airport and they flew to Los Angeles, where they would nurture Sarah's talent. With determination and meager savings, they were prepared to risk it all.

The night before they left, I stopped by after work to wish them well. Their suitcases stood in the hallway by the front door. Luke ambled anxiously through the house, like a kid who wondered if his parents would ever return from the trip they were about to take. I wondered too if we'd ever see them again.

"Just look after our web business, Luke, and you'll have no trouble paying the rent," Sam told him. "We'll send you some more content from LA."

Sarah glanced at me when Sam spoke those words, and I could see she knew Sam had told me everything. Her eyes, dark and sunken in her pale face, seemed to be challenging me to openly pass judgment. I looked away, unable to meet her stare.

"Look after the cats too, Luke," she said. "They're good company, you know that."

When I said I had to go, Sam laughed and shook my hand, then said, "Looks like you won't be the only one seeing Disneyland this year."

Sarah gave him a dismissive look. "Look after your girls, Brady," she said.

"What if I have a boy," I countered. "Or two boys."

"You won't." She surprised me by stepping forward and hugging me tightly. Her grip felt stronger than ever – infinitely more solid than the last time we touched, back when we were teenagers. Her touch caused an ache to swell inside me. I searched her eyes for death, but instead found someone carelessly clinging to the vestiges of her own imperfect life, holding it absently like a once-precious photo.

Our two children, with their wonderfully typical sense of timing began their descent into the outside world at the very moment I was playing the most important basketball game of my adult life.

Carmel's call came in the third-quarter of a tight game between our fire department and the volunteer one from Langley. She had wanted to see the game – it was the final of the firefighters' outdoor basketball league – but above all she needed sleep, after tossing and turning in the August heat the night before. I encouraged her to stay home, and she immediately took me up on my offer, sprawling out on the bed in our stuffy apartment.

Carmel had agreed to call Carson Kilgore on his cell if she needed me. So when I went to the sidelines during a time-out, my heart skipped when he handed me his cell phone.

"Catch your breath, Brady, and talk to your wife."

My hands shook. "Carmel?"

"I've tried to hold out so you could finish the game, but the contractions are two minutes apart. Sorry."

"Don't be sorry. I'm coming home."

"I'm starting to walk to the hospital. It feels better when I walk. I'll be going down Roper Street, very slowly."

"No. Wait for me. Be there in two minutes."

"Well in two minutes I'll barely be out the door, so I'll meet you."

"Okay."

I apologized to my teammates, grabbed my bag and fled, down the hill toward the downtown, my legs suddenly re-energized. When Carmel saw the speed of my approach, she laughed so hard she had to lean on a streetlamp for support.

"Don't worry," she said placing her arms around my sweaty body, "I won't have our babies out here in the street. Lots of time still, I think."

She was right, of course – she had hours of hand-squeezing, sweat-inducing, gut-wrenching labor left in her, before finally pushing out two baby girls in an exhausting rush of blood and guts.

While the doctor stitched up Carmel's torn body, two nurses placed the babies in what looked like heated glass baking pans and ran them through a quick series of observations under harsh light. They then expertly bundled the crying pair in tiny blankets and placed one on Carmel's chest and the other in my arms.

Bewildered and amazed, I stared down at the tiny life I held.

The older nurse stroked my daughter's matted hair with strong, soft hands, and laughed at my overwhelmed expression. "It's not so hard," she said simply. "Just support her head. And give her lots of love."

I sat on the floor, my back against a chair, Leanne's tiny face on my shoulder, my fingers gently tapping her back, my ears listening for the relief of a burp. On the floor beside me lay Jennifer, in rare peace, her belly full of her mother's milk.

Carmel had dragged herself out the door, joking, without a smile, that she had never looked forward so much to running errands, to being by herself for a precious hour or so, to be unneeded, unwanted, unfettered. I had looked forward to tonight, my first night-shift rotation since the babies' arrival, and my best bet for any kind of sleep. Yes, I was confident that somewhere someone I had wronged in my life now laughed at my misery. I had not one, but two helpless creatures who could not find sleep if they were lying on top of it. Those first ten or so days were a blur of appeasing the unappeasable, of watching Carmel rise in the middle of the night to feed the insatiable, of pretending I slept soundly when she called me in the darkness to burp one or comfort the other.

How could you love something you so badly wanted to escape? How could a mixed-up twenty-year-old be a decent father when he struggled to be a decent person?

"Call me on the cell if it turns bad," Carmel had said grumpily before closing the door. She opened the door a crack and called back, "Or better yet, just deal with it."

"Funny girl, your mom, isn't she," I said gently to our babies.

After Leanne let go a small belch, I rubbed her back and closed my eyes for a moment, and began to drift off. Jennifer's wail brought me back, and I lay Leanne down on the floor and picked Jen up. Then Leanne began crying, and

I soon wandered the apartment, bouncing on my tiptoes, two wailing girls awkwardly in my arms. I looked at the clock in the kitchen. Carmel had been gone for only eight minutes. Oh, God.

Two full bellies, two gas-free stomachs, two dry diapers. Now what? I bounced them some more as I walked, but they only cried louder. I lay them down in their cribs, at opposite ends of our tiny living room. "You two need sleep...just like me." I went into the bedroom and shut the door, thinking wishfully they would cry themselves to sleep. They cried themselves into a frenzy.

When I could stand it no longer, I retrieved the pair, and sat back down on the floor, taking turns resting one on my chest while I twirled my fingers before the other's still-developing eyes. Slowly, their cries diminished to a few sad bursts. In time, Leanne stared at my finger, and then my face as my eyes crinkled up into a twisted caricature of myself. Jennifer, with a little extra coaxing, also found comfort in the same silly game, the same strange expressions, and maybe in my soothing voice.

I smiled, pleased with myself, though only for a moment. My thoughts, as they often had in the past few days, slipped back to Carmel's swollen pre-delivery stomach, which had seemed to grow visibly each time I studied it. She often told me it terrified her, this expanding force determined to fight its way dangerously out into the light. I, of course, kept my own thoughts secret, never sharing that I too felt a terrifying stirring inside, one that grew by the hour, one not to be denied. It was something I had craved for so long, for years, but seemingly struggled to find. It took clear form when Carmel reached for my hand on a rocky ledge, and now swelled with every tug of a tiny hand on my fingers, with every squeal of delight, of need, from two small girls.

And like Carmel, when I embraced what grew inside

me, I nearly shook with fear. Because, I knew, with love comes at least a trace of morality. With it comes a tiny aching to do what is right.

I lay Jennifer next to Leanne on my chest, my arms and hands clamped gently around each of them, and slid down until I lay on the floor. On my warm body, rising and falling, they found enough contentment to finally drift asleep. Now what? They had me hopelessly pinned to the hard floor, unable to move for fear of waking them. I relaxed my grip, closed my eyes, and drew from their warmth, their touch. Soon I joined them, my slumber less intense but still heavenly.

17

Leanne rushed to the window and scanned the rain-soaked street, which glistened in a cascade of colors from Christmas lights. "I wonder when Aunty Sarah will be here," she said, bouncing away from the window.

"Any minute," Carmel said, wiping dust off the living room coffee table.

"She's not really your aunt," I reminded her. "And why are you so excited, you can't even remember the last time you met her?"

"You think she's bringing a present?" Jennifer said as she spun into the room, before whirling back out, her question still unanswered.

Carmel smiled at me. "They're allowed to be a little excited, aren't they? All part of being three."

I nodded. "I guess."

"You sure Luke's not coming?" Carmel asked.

"I'm sure," I said. "Unless he shows up."

Carmel considered this apparent contradiction before moving on to dust around the gas fireplace.

I watched her work, in the minutes before our guests' arrival, wondering what had possessed her to invite Sarah and Sam to dinner after hearing me casually mention the two of them had returned to town for Christmas. I had looked at her puzzled, especially because we'd seen them only twice – almost in passing – since they'd gone south over three years ago, and each of those times I detected a certain discomfort emanating from both Sarah and Carmel.

Luke's rejection of our dinner invitation was the only thing that didn't surprise me. He was more at ease on the margins of society than in the comforts of someone's dining room. Sometimes I wondered if Luke would scream if he caught a glimpse of my life. Work, spend time with kids, sleep if possible, and eke out a few spare minutes with Carmel. It carried the rhythm of someone older, not in his early twenties.

"They're here," Jennifer screamed, and ran past a disappointed Leanne, who had wanted to spot them first.

Jennifer opened the front door, and in time I heard Sarah's voice and then her footsteps on the outside stairs. "Which one are you: Leanne?"

Jennifer shook her head.

"Hello, Jennifer," Sarah said. "Do you remember me?"

"Yes," Jennifer lied skillfully, like it was in her blood.

Carmel greeted Sarah and Sam, introducing them once more to the kids, while I slowly made my way to the door.

Sam stepped forward and shook my hand. He looked tanned, relaxed, like everything was going his way. Always a master illusionist.

Sarah slowly smiled when she saw me. "Merry Christmas, Brady."

A diamond stud glistened from a piercing in her nose, another one from a piercing in her eyebrow. Her lipstick, a slightly disturbing shade of purple, helped give her lips a fullness I'd never noticed before. Her breasts, though I tried not to stare, pressed forth with a roundness, an aggressiveness I didn't recall.

There were other changes I couldn't describe though, even as the night went on. They ran deeper, seemingly down to her core, which had been encased in some thick, hard substance, like a crust or scab left by time. She still existed, only somehow further out of reach.

And there were changes I wouldn't find out about until later; her lungs, for instance, so damaged from smoking heroin – she hated needles – that walking a flight of stairs left her in great pain. And her uterus, removed after a persistent and nasty infection, had left her unable to have children.

I fixed everyone a drink – God knows we all needed one – and we politely tried to catch up on each others' lives, focusing mostly on the good, shunning all else.

"Come here, girls," Sarah said reaching into a large bag she brought. "Got something for you."

"Presents," they screeched.

"You didn't have to," Carmel said.

"It's so much fun buying for kids." She looked at Sam. "We don't get to do it. Maybe my brother will get married one day and have some."

"Any kids in the plans for you two," Carmel grinned.

Sarah quickly shook her head, and asked, "Can they open them now?"

She had spoiled them each with a dress, a stuffed animal and two movie DVDs. One at a time, they plunked themselves on her lap. She cuddled one in each arm, tenderly, her voice sweetly regressing to her own childhood, her smile projecting a delight I couldn't recall ever seeing. I felt strangely moved — and saddened – and quickly retreated to the kitchen on the pretense of opening another bottle of wine.

We ate steaks and buttery vegetables, and laughed as our girls quickly left the table, Sam remarking that their attention spans were still more developed than Luke's. He sipped on his large glass of cheap red wine and talked of the screenplays he'd pitched, making me wonder how a guy who could barely compose a proper sentence could be taken seriously in Hollywood, if he really was. He did have a knack for storytelling though, and spoke of parties they attended at B-grade celebrities' homes, of lunches at Venice beach, and of Sarah's television commercial and small part in a soap opera, all with hardly a mention of the porn industry I suspected existed at the heart of their lives.

"That sounds exciting," Carmel said after soaking in every detail of their visit to a star-studded restaurant in Santa Monica.

"Not really," Sarah said. "The exciting bits can be told in a few moments." She looked at Sam. "Unless someone's dragging them out, making them sound like more than they are."

"So are you still pushing for the big role in a movie?" Carmel asked.

"You mean a non-adult movie," Sarah said shrugging. "I'm not holding my breath."

"Oh, c'mon," Sam said. "Just a matter of time."

"Well, so is death," Sarah replied. "Just a matter of which comes first."

While Carmel and Sarah finished the dishes, Sam slipped out front for a smoke and I took the garbage out back. I lingered on our small back deck, gazing up at the moon, which had temporarily emerged from the dark clouds.

"Think it will snow?" a voice behind me said, startling me.

I turned to face Sarah.

"No. We've barely had a trace of it in the last few years.

It gets cold, but warms up when a moist front comes in, so we just get rain."

"Ah," she said, joining me by the railing, then nervously tapping against its wooden top with her fingernails. "I nearly forgot how much it rains here."

"So things are going well in Los Angeles, with the movie business?" I asked awkwardly, slightly daunted to be talking to her alone.

"L.A.'s a shithole. But the adult movie business? Yes, going well. Guess I've found something I'm good at, though you remember that."

I didn't know how to respond.

She looked up at the moon for a moment, and said in a not quite accusing voice, "You seem to have settled into a nice life here."

"Yes," I agreed.

She studied me, and said, "So what's wrong?"

I sighed and thought of going back inside. "Do you always have to be so damn direct? Nothing's wrong."

"You're a fucking liar."

"You're still a sweet-talker," I said.

She laughed, a short, almost-scripted sound. "I see it, you know. Something's not right. Here's my guess – you're still carrying it, you know what I'm talking about, almost like nothing's changed."

I shuffled my feet, and said, "I'm fine."

"Bullshit. I hope your lovely wife can see something's wrong, cause I sure as hell can and I'm practically a stranger now."

I looked away.

"So what exactly is it?" she asked.

When I didn't answer, she pressed, "C'mon. Don't make me answer for you."

"It's just that..."

"By the way," she interrupted. "If you say everything doesn't *feel* right, I think I'll rip your vocal cords out and trample on them."

I paused, thinking back to my clumsiest of sentences during our breakup. "No, I won't use those words," I said with a sad grin. "It's…well…do you know I haven't talked about it in God knows how long? Years. No one mentions it, at least not in front of me. And I promised Carmel I'd drop it, put it behind me forever, so…"

"So…"

"Some things just can't be tossed aside."

She forced a small smile. "But there's no other way, you know that. You're way past the point of no return."

"I know. But I feel like…like I'm just waiting for something to happen, for it to leak out somehow."

Sarah brushed her hair away from her eyes, a subtle move that conveyed both a weariness and a sureness. "We are all waiting for something to happen, Brady. Something good, something bad. Just something."

I said nothing, and she offered, "Sometimes you just got to learn to accept things the way they are. You know why I started seeing Sam?"

"No."

"To make you jealous. To piss off my dad. For all the wrong reasons. How fucked up is that? Still, here we are, still together; it's just the way it is."

"Why did you want to make me jealous?"

"Why do you think, stupid?"

I shivered in the cold, and turned to her. "You must be freezing." She shrugged, a gentle movement defining her life. I shivered again.

"You know, people seem to think the worst day of my life was when Opal fell in my garage," she said. "But it wasn't."

to me the details of their visit to Sarah's old house. Why her parents hadn't sold that place after Tom Opal died I'll never know. If it wasn't cursed before his fall, it soon became so, at least in my opinion.

Sam disagreed. "A house can't be cursed. Just the people in it."

His account of that night was part of a larger story, told over two pitchers of beer and plenty of downward glances. He began it in typical Sam fashion.

"Okay. Picture this. We'd just left your place, slightly buzzed from the wine, when Sarah yells, Stop. Pull over.

"'What, you forget something,' I asked her. 'No', she says. 'I just need to mellow out.' So like, twist my arm, you know, we smoked heroin. We get to the Roberts place, a bit wasted, in our jeans and shit, and there's women in dresses, kinda like evening gowns, like some fucken Oscar night, some guys even wearing suits and ties, and us in jeans. But you know this was okay cause Mr. Roberts was alright. So was Mrs. Roberts. 'Glad you could make it.' They got us a drink and introduced us to all these people, you know, their friends, and he'd say, 'This is my daughter Sarah, who lives in Los Angeles, with Sam.' Some would say, like, what do you do down there, go to university or work, you know, do you want to be a doctor like your old man, Sarah, and Sarah would smile and say she was an actress, or trying to be, and I'm her agent and a part-time scriptwriter. A few asked what she had appeared in, and I'll give her credit, she didn't care if people knew she did porn. She's not ashamed of it. But you know, she sensed they didn't know, so she did something untypically Sarah, she cloaked her answer and told them about the commercial and her bit parts, and how she studied acting here in Deception Pass and acted with the local players group. A few people even recognized her from her commercial.

"So, it started out pretty well. She played the part of the perfect daughter like you wouldn't believe. I swore, Brady, and I'm not shitting, not one damn bit, I swear her dad was almost proud of her. Only she didn't see it. She would never see it.

"And you know, he knew everything about her. Her struggles to get off cocaine, then heroin. Her time in detox, in a methadone program. Hell, he paid to get her in treatment programs twice. He knew about the movies, might have even watched a few for all I know, and he even tried to pull some strings with a friend of a friend and get her a decent part in a prime-time television series, filmed up in Vancouver. Guess he thought it would be her salvation, or something. Couldn't quite pull it off though.

"He musta been scared to shit when she accepted his invitation to his party. All his friends there, his colleagues, and his daughter, the junkie porn actress who hung around with losers who might have, or might not have, killed some poor fucker in his garage. Can you imagine it? The moment we walked through that front door, and he wondered, what the fuck is going to happen tonight? What will happen next? And the people there, who mostly knew about Tom Opal but not the drugs and the films. All closely watching. Wondering if it would all go wrong.

"So when Sarah held it together, it's like, Hell yeah, the Roberts must have been amazed. Relieved. Like for one fucken moment, life is just the way they planned it, just the way.

"I wished the story ended there, Brady, I really wish it did.

"You know Dr. Roberts had hired a bartender. That's where I hung out. Eventually Sarah gravitated there too. Drank some wine, did a couple of shooters. I could see it, the change in her. The hostility and aggression rising, like the water in your basement during a flood. Seen a look like that in her eyes when she used to do crack, and it was like, everyone get the fuck out of the way. I can't explain it, 'cept to say she wouldn't be herself. Not at all.

"So I took her arm, and said, Sarah, listen, let's just walk out that door, right now, no good-byes. Just phone your parents from our motel and say we had to rush out, not feeling well, but will visit them in the morning. Let's just get the fuck out of here right this second, I told her. Quit while we're ahead, while everything's fine.

"She looks at me, and asks what I'm scared of. I say let's just go. She laughs and plants a big sloppy kiss on my face, tells me not to be a chickenshit. I watched her, and listened as her conversations with people got more and more outrageous. Only every word she said, it was the truth. She started telling people what she really did for a living, just to watch their faces, to see what it took to make them excuse themselves and walk away. Told them the names of the movies, how many times she got fucked, and where. I took her arm once, and she grabbed my face and snarled, fuck off. At first she was careful to do all this when her mom and dad were out of the room or out of earshot. After a while she no longer cared, and when I took her hand the last time, when I thought, it's better, you know, if she slaps my face and I carry her out of there than watch her self-destruct like this, she turned to me like she'd rip me apart, and when she saw I wasn't backing down, she whispered, come with me. She led me to the nearest bathroom and closed the door behind us.

"So, she slides down her pants and panties, and leans over the sink and says, I want you to screw me. Then we'll go. That's the deal. C'mon, Sarah, I ordered her. Cut the shit and let's go. She turned and kissed me and undid my pants and whispered, just a quickie, then we go. So, okay, I'm not thinking straight either, but there she is leaning over the sink again, in front of me, and my pants are down, and she lifts her shirt and undoes her bra, so I can see in the mirror, and anyway, how can I resist, she is so beautiful, and it was the only way we were going to get out of there, and I'm already, you know, aroused, and I thought, this wouldn't take too long. So I do what she told me, and she starts moaning, louder and louder, and I say Sarah, not so loud, and she ignores me, and I say, Sarah, I'm gonna pull out unless you stop fucken screaming, but how can I stop, so I place my hand over her mouth, and she knocks it loose, so I cover her mouth with both hands, and she sees she can't get them away, she's not strong enough, so she bites me hard and lets out a scream, and then, fuck, there's a knock on the door, more like a pounding, and it's her dad, and he screams, what the hell's going on in there, but I can't stop now and I'm so close, and he starts pounding really hard, like he's going to break the door down, and I'm just seconds away, I'm almost there, then the door squeaks and he knocks it in with his shoulder, and I jump so much I slide out. And he's right there, and fucken horrified and I'm trying to get my pants back on, and Sarah's making almost no move, like she's ready for her close-up, and she starts to say something like this is what I do for a living, but she only gets the words, This is what, and then he slaps her across the face, hard, and I take a swing at him, but he's ready for me, and he blocks it and knocks me over into the bathtub on my back, then he screams 'get out.' Then I'm struggling out of that fucken bathtub and Sarah's mom is suddenly in there in her silver cocktail dress and high heels, and now she's screaming, why, why would we purposely try to ruin her father's life? Why? And I've barely got my pants back on and Sarah's putting hers on, and I take both of Sarah's arms and I drag her out, past this fucken crowd of people that's gathered in the hall, and everyone's so shocked, and so righteous and silent as we come out, Merry fucken Christmas, and her dad is gone I notice, and I think that fucker, why did he have to slap her like that. So we race through the living room, and she tries to shake loose, and I almost rip her arm off, and we get outside, and Sarah's yelling, let me go, I'm not a dog, not a fucken dog, and I said, well I just screwed you like you were a dog, and she tries to kick me in the nuts and falls, so I'm now draggin' her down the driveway, and I get blindsided by her dad, he's outside waiting for us. He knocks me to the ground and starts kicking me in the head, and Sarah gets up and screams, you're hurting him, and grabs at his face and tries to gouge his eyes, and he bats her aside, and by this time, I'm up, and I've had enough, enough of the whole night and their screwy family, and he sees he's going to get the shit kicked out of him, and I see all his friends have followed him outside, but no one is stepping in, they're just staring with their mouths wide open and I feel so fucken sorry for him, but I hit him anyway, and he's trying to fight back, but he's in his fifties and smaller – he just seems big – and he goes down, and Sarah stands over him and spits and screams, you were always ashamed of me. Admit it, you prick. He's on the ground, and he's stunned, and says, do you think I would have invited you if I was ashamed. And she screams, you are ashamed. And he tells her, look, all my friends are here, and I'm not ashamed to say you're my daughter, and you need help, and you'll never get it with that parasite feasting off you. So he starts getting to his feet, and I was ready to put him back down, but I heard what he said, and he's right of course, he's a prick but he's mostly right, and I grab Sarah's hand and this time I don't pull, I say we have to go, and she sees he's right too, I know she did, so she comes with me. We get in the car and she starts sobbing, and I want to comfort her, but at that moment I could slap her too, hard."

Sam, his voice slightly slurred by warm beer, told me that was the night their lives turned ugly. Funny, I thought it had been years earlier.

18

Is it possible to pinpoint the exact moment a body's drug receptors, in their siren song, get the upper hand? The precise instance of addiction. Sarah's dad would tell me years later it came when she was in her mother's womb, when she fell victim to a rogue set of genes from the mother's side, genes that had destroyed Sarah's uncle, who drank himself out of the army, then into the grave. Sam maintained Sarah had never fallen to addiction, that she'd always maintained control. And me? What did I think? What did it matter, cause I was no longer there, no longer in her life.

Sam was there, at least in body, though one seriously wondered if he could pick up the nuances in someone else's behavior. Could he detect the malaise in Sarah's movements as she dressed in the morning, or the longing in her touch that remained even after making love? How about a single indifferent shrug while they talked quietly over take-out dinner: Was it tiredness, or was it boredom, emptiness, or even something far worse?

Sam only knew what was palpable, what was so obvious that even he could see it and touch it. This is what he told me: Sarah had rejected the crystal meth produced in Luke and Sam's garage, and encouraged them to do the same. If you want to rot out your teeth, your brain, your life, she told them one day in the kitchen, why not produce the same result much quicker. For effect, she pulled a large carving knife out of a kitchen drawer. Why not let me just slit your throat and get it over with. Luke and Sam laughed. Nervously.

She tried cocaine, both powder and crack, before renouncing it after her hospital visit with the wonky heart.

She injected heroin for the first time in Los Angeles, at a party. She had watched the eastern European girls from her first adult film shoot up before, intrigued by their meticulous approach, how they would mix the powder with water and citric acid on a spoon, then heat it until it bubbled, no more. Sometimes they'd add more citric acid if the liquid didn't turn clear. Then they'd use cotton wool to filter out the grit as they drew the liquid into a syringe, checking carefully for air bubbles. She was impressed by their knack for finding a vein, the way they'd pull the plunger back and produce a small amount of blood, confirming their target.

Now they were asking her to try – "It'll keep you skinny," one said – and in time, and reluctantly, she did try. They helped shoot her up the first time, and she turned to Sam after the rush of well-being and nodded calmly, before slouching back in a chair at their friends' home. After the second time she became dismayed by the way the drug's impurities and poisons raced through her blood, a bird trapped indoors, finally settling around the only exit available, a small cut in her knee, which soon became sore. She swore her heart beat had turned irregular again.

Sarah didn't like the way Sam refused to shoot up. "I don't want to become an addict," he told her. "One of us has got to think straight."

The next time, on the advice of a friend, she smoked it instead, rolling it into a joint of marijuana. This was much better. No needles. Less stigma. Less chance of addiction, or so she thought. Sometimes she'd inhale the burning drug from a piece of heated foil, pulling the rising cloud of smoke through a small tube.

On her worst days, she'd need three hits to avert the sickness of withdrawal. On her best she could survive with two.

She auditioned for movie and television roles, snapped up parts as a movie extra when their money got low, swam in the ocean that lay an inviting four miles from their apartment in El Segundo, wrote songs and played them on a neighbor's piano, wasted hours playing games on their Xbox, and hours more with various friends who drifted in and out of their lives. And acted in three adult movies, all in her first year.

She hated being dependent on anything or anyone. She also hated that she needed more and more heroin to get high, then more to keep from getting sick. Her period went off, her throat dried, her breathing labored. She put herself on the waiting list for a state-sponsored drug rehabilitation program, but saw she'd never get in. She confessed to her parents her problem, and borrowed money for private treatment.

Afterwards, she compared going clean to what she assumed giving birth would be like. It was a bitch at the time, the vomiting and convulsions, but later, when it was over and you were looking ahead, it didn't seem so bad.

Months later she started drinking — drawn by the temporary hope it provided, I suspect — then realized she missed the heroin. Besides, she now knew she could quit any time.

Her second detox wasn't the breeze she remembered. This time she stayed away from heroin's call for only three weeks.

But she functioned. And like me, she could lie when someone asked how are you doing.

Here is what Sam failed to see: Sarah sitting alone by their open kitchen window where she'd inhale the sticky, poisonous tar. A hint of traffic noise from the street below, footsteps from the apartment above, the drone of the television in the next room. And Sam talking on the phone about some movie part that would never be. She'd close her eyes, shut them so tight her lids wrinkled like an old lady's, and for at least a moment, everything would be right, or at least bearable.

Sam claims he clearly recalled the hours, the moments, before it all went wrong. Maybe he searched them, over and over, in his mind, looking for meaning, trying to determine how he could have changed the way it turned out. I suspect his thoughts first circled back to the night Sarah returned home from a foray to the bank machine and the corner store, and, in one of the rare moments their apartment didn't seem to be teeming with other people who didn't belong, she abruptly turned off the television.

"I'm watching that," he protested.

She sat next to him, on their dust-seeped sofa, and shook her head. "We need to leave. This is going nowhere, living here. The whole acting thing, it's not working. Same with the screenplays you write. We need to cut our losses and start again somewhere else."

Sam searched for the best approach to reason with her, and said, "What's wrong?"

"Did you not hear a word I just said? Everything's wrong. We need to go."

"What happened? Something happened?"

"I'm just tired of it. No one thing happened. It's everything."

"Something had to happen. You were fine earlier today."

She shook her head. "Nothing's fine. Don't you get it?"

He shook his head.

"You really don't see it, do you?" she asked.

"See what?"

Sarah got up and went to the window.

"You know that little room with the ATM at the bank?"

"See," Sam said, "I knew something happened."

"Will you shut up. I was getting my money and at the next machine was this middle-aged man. Balding, thick glasses, chubby, tired eyes, looked like he'd been run into the ground by his job, his family. He got his cash and was putting it in his wallet, but there was a voice all of a sudden. A teenage girl. I didn't see her come in. She said, 'Hey, want to have a little fun with a hundred of that? Out back in your car, quick as all that.' He looked at her as he tucked his wallet into his jacket, like she was some kind of thief or pickpocket. But she was like fourteen. Pretty figure. Matted hair. Bulky clothes that looked like she had slept in them. Probably had. Must have been a runaway or something.

"So this guy looked at her, then glanced quickly at me, and shook his head like he wasn't interested. 'You should be at home,' he told her. Good, I thought as the machine started spitting out my money. Then I heard him whisper. 'Forty. I'll give you forty dollars,' he told the girl. 'No, fifty,' she said. He frowned, then said, 'Okay, in my van, right now.' So I watched them go outside and head around back to the parking lot, he much bigger, older. They looked like a father and his daughter. So I got my money, and I thought, like I'd give her fifty bucks not to screw him, to come home with me and to have a warm bath and a hot meal. So I went out back, and this guy was removing two child seats from the back bench seat in his van, and throwing them into the very back. And the girl climbed in and he slid shut the door behind them, and the windows were tinted, and I couldn't see them, and I got ready to pound on the door and tear into that fucker. But then I thought, this is Los Angeles, and who knew how long that girl had being doing it, and who the fuck was I to judge people, and what business was it of mine anyway. So I stood at the edge of the parking lot, torn, watching the van start to gently rock, and I turned and left."

Sam shrugged. "You did the right thing. It's not your business. She probably had a pimp hanging around the corner who would have kicked the shit out of you."

"You don't get it?" Sarah said.

"Get what?"

"You really have no idea what I'm saying, do you."

"You're talking about this city, I know, about what a cold..."

"No. I'm not talking about this city at all."

"What then?" Sam asked.

Sarah stared at him for only a moment, before grabbing the remote, flicking the television back to life and leaving the room.

Two days later they stood in the morning sunlight outside a Culver City nightclub, waiting for someone to open the door.

"You're sure about this?" she asked.

"Yes," he said, "if you are?"

"I'm sure we can use the money to pay some bills so we can start to make a move out of this fucken city."

"Whatever you say," Sam said somewhat reluctantly as he pounded on the door again.

A pale-skinned man, tall and slightly overweight, finally yanked the door open. "What," he said impatiently.

"Sarah Roberts here for the shoot," Sam said.

"And you are?" the man said to Sam.

"Her agent. Sam Simpson. I talked to Johnny."

He laughed: "Agent, huh."

Inside, a half-dozen men and three women loitered around the bar with drinks in their hands. One of them, a small Asian man, turned to Sarah then ran his eyes down her body, then nodded his approval. "I am Johnny. And you are ten minutes late," he said.

"Sorry," Sarah shrugged.

"We run on schedule." He turned to Sam. "You staying?"

"Yes," Sam answered.

"Then get a drink and stay the hell out of the way." He paused, his eyes locked on Sam. "You've watched this before, right. You know what to expect, cause this is supposed to be rape, it's supposed to look disturbing."

"I know the routine," Sam said, slipping behind the bar.

The shoot's simple premise would see Sarah dance with one of the guys, get him hot, and then be raped in a corner of the club. Simple work, fifteen-hundred dollars for a few hours' effort.

The day before she had protested to Sam that if she was to do porn, she would rather work with people she knew and trusted, even if it ate up weeks of her time and kept her away from finding more mainstream work.

"Trust me on this one," Sam had told her. "These guys are well known. Own plenty of nightclubs, run a huge Internet business, among other things."

So Sam sipped rum and Cokes as Sarah and some punk danced and groped under the dance floor's lights, three other couples adding to the illusion of a nightclub winding down in the early morning. In time, the three other women left, a few hundred dollars cash in their purses.

That's when he should have figured it out, Sam told me. Instead, he poured another drink.

There was one detail Sam left out in his retelling. One

revealed in the $8.95 web version of the video and made clear in the $30 DVD you could have shipped to your home so you could watch it again and again, along with a dozen or so other episodes of violent sex. It was this: Sam had a small, likely impromptu part, leaning up against the bar when Sarah and her imminent attacker strolled past on the way to the washroom. I suspect he'd been asked to stare at his drink as they walked by, because that's exactly what he did.

When Sarah exited the washroom, her new boyfriend pulled her into a nearby private room and slid his hand under her shirt and grabbed her breast. She shook loose and slapped him, all as planned. He then wrestled her to the soiled carpet, far too easily, turned her on her stomach and began ripping her tight skirt off.

Anyone who knew Sarah could pinpoint the exact moment the script changed. One single person could not overpower Sarah so easily, and not without paying a price.

The second man appeared out of the shadows, and started ripping her top off over her head. For a split second you could sense her surprise, see it in her hesitation. Then the fight was on, arms and legs flailing, body wriggling, jaw snapping, fingernails digging. A third man entered the scene and pulled her arms over the head so her shirt and bra could be fully removed, and a fourth man held her legs down.

When she was naked, they flipped her over onto her back, all four of them struggling to hold her down, and a fifth man appeared, dropped his pants and descended on her. She was spitting and swearing, and one of the men holding her arms slapped her face and pushed her head to one side.

You could hear her voice screaming, calling for Sam, demanding they stop, because this wasn't the deal. Over the next eleven minutes, each of them took a turn. Each of them went at her in a different position, one of them with her folded over like a large doll, another with her slammed against the beige and gold wall.

At first she called them fuckers. Then later, as she implored them to let her go, it was c'mon guys, stop, that's enough, like she held some fragment of control. Finally, when she knew she couldn't stop them, when she knew Sam wouldn't be helping her, she hissed with eerily calm resignation, "I'll kill each one of you. I'll hunt you down like dogs. I swear I will. I'll find your families, your children, and kill them too."

You didn't see Sam on-screen during the gang-rape, though I was convinced myself that if you listened carefully you heard him once, just once, screaming her name, before, he later said, the large bouncer and a second man dragged him to the opposite corner of the nightclub and held him down, a gun at his head, until it was over. In my mind I could see him struggling, getting punched, silenced, restrained and, much like Sarah, waiting in horror for it to end.

Whether Sarah ever believed he put up a fight, I didn't know. When the men had finished with her, after the last man stumbled to his feet and the man filming the episode threw her a towel and laughed, "That's a wrap," she wanted no part of anyone. They all sickened her. When Sam finally appeared at her side, she swore and punched him on the side of his head.

She had dressed on her own, awkwardly, back into her own clothes, not the ones torn off her body. Her wrists and ankles ached from being held down, her groin was raw, and her back and knees burned from the dirt-caked carpet. Sam screamed back toward the bar, you motherfuckers.

"Take me to the hospital," she told him. "We'll call the police from there."

He tried to take her hand as they walked out toward the bar, but she slapped it away, and he fell in behind her.

Johnny and the bouncer waited alone for them. "Here's

your money," Johnny grinned, holding out a wad of bills. "You're good. Very believable."

Sarah batted the cash from his hand and spat in his face. The bouncer grabbed her – she was half his size – and pushed her toward the door.

"What's wrong?" Johnny said. "You agreed to a simulated rape and that's what we did. Then I paid you. So fuck off."

"Just wait 'til you're in jail. You're gonna get gang-raped yourself until you can't walk, you little prick. Only I bet you'll enjoy it."

Then she was gone, leaving Sam standing before Johnny, staring at the money on the floor.

When Sam walked out in the blinding afternoon sunlight, he could barely remember where he'd parked the pickup truck loaned to them by their friend, Ted, who painted houses. Everything looked different, like he'd exited through the wrong door.

He stood in the empty lot for a moment, lost, before remembering he'd parked across the street. Sarah sat perfectly still in the passenger seat, her arms and legs pulled to her chest, a discarded hunk of foil paper at her side.

Sam drove for a few blocks, and turned to her. "You sure you really need the hospital. I mean, I'll take you where you want, but I can…I can help look after you at home."

"Fuck off."

"Okay."

They drove in silence, a warm, dusty breeze wafting in.

"It's because the hospital's fine, but they will definitely involve the police, and I don't think…I think we should think twice about that."

She turned to him, her eyes bulging, and yelled, "Just drive. Don't say another fucken word."

They stopped at a traffic light before an on-ramp to the freeway. "It's just that this guy's connected. They don't just do porn. They control a lot of the drug trade in the clubs. They're into some serious shit. People who turn against them. Well, they don't live very long."

He waited for her to explode. He'd braced himself. Instead she got out of the car and walked around to the driver's side. "Move over. I'll drive myself to the hospital. You can come or not, you useless piece of shit."

Sam didn't budge. "The last thing you should be doing is driving. I'll take you to the hospital if...."

"Move over," she screamed, and he did.

When the light changed she pushed the small pickup onto the 405.

"We're gonna have a tough time convincing the police, you know," he said. "It was porn, it was supposed to be a rape scene. Granted, not by five guys, not like that, but..."

"You took the money, didn't you?" she asked suddenly.

"What?"

"After I left. You got down on the floor, on your knees, at that fucker's feet, and picked up the money. Didn't you?"

"Don't even say that. I..."

"They acted like I was nothing, not even human, just some animal. But you know something, you're a bigger humiliation than what they did to me."

"I didn't take the money," Sam pleaded.

With one eye on the road, she reached for his jacket, where he kept his wallet, and he grabbed her hand. "I didn't take the money. I told you," he yelled.

The truck swerved, her left hand losing control as her right ripped at Sam's jacket. "Prove it," she screamed, "take your wallet out and show me."

"Listen, just drive the truck before we're in an accident."

She lunged again, and this time the truck swerved with her, clipping the front fender of the car in the next lane, spinning out of control. Sarah's foot pounded on the brake, but the thick cement beam propping up an overpass suddenly filled her vision. In the split second it took to strike it at almost fifty miles an hour, Sam had just enough time to squeak out the words, "Oh, God."

The call from Sam came while I was working, going door-to-door in the downtown inspecting shops for expired fire extinguishers and other violations of the town's fire code. On a typical day, Carmel would have been at work too, but she had taken the morning off to take Jennifer, who had a persistent cough, to the doctor. What would Sam have done if he found no one at home? Leave all the details in a message on our answering machine?

I suspect Carmel cried when Sam told her, and did her best to comfort him as the reality began to sink in. She then punched in the phone number for the fire hall and found out from Captain Boerne exactly where I was in the downtown.

I imagine she looked at Jennifer, pale and hacking, before deciding to make one more call, to Brittany's younger sister Jane, a cashier in the drugstore whose wide front window commanded a broad view of Main Street. "Have you seen Brady?" Carmel had asked. "He's somewhere downtown making inspections."

"No, why?"

"There's been an emergency."

"Oh, no. What happened?"

Carmel paused, and answered, telling Jane to make me wait if I showed up but not to tell me what happened.

In the next ten to fifteen minutes, Carmel wandered by the drugstore, Jennifer in tow, and Jane shrugged, to say she hadn't seen me. Carmel gave her the thumbs up, a sign meant to say, thanks for trying, but interpreted as, it's okay, I've found him.

A couple minutes later I entered the store. Jane

always made me smile, her oversized earrings, her eager and toothy grin. I started to speak, to say something like, "Okay, this is a raid. Everyone up against the wall." But she spoke first, her face heavy. "Oh, Brady, I'm so sorry to hear about Sarah. About her death in that terrible accident."

"What?" I said, wondering how I could mishear so badly.

She gasped, cupping both hands over her mouth, leaving only bulging eyes.

Carmel found me sitting on a bench a half block away, my hands resting on a clipboard teeming with meaningless tick marks.

"Sorry, Brady," she said, sitting next to me. "I hadn't meant for you to hear like that."

I couldn't look up, even as Jennifer hugged me with her tiny arms and climbed onto Carmel's lap.

Finally I looked up at the sky, grey and hinting at a storm. "Do you think it will snow?"

"What?" Carmel asked, almost startled by the question.

"Do you think it will snow?

"I…uh…I don't know."

"Seems like we never get snow. Just the grey. But never the snow. God I wish it would start to fall. Lots of it. Covering up everything, all the dog crap and…"

Carmel shivered and put her arm around me.

"When I was a kid, the weather wasn't like this," I told her. "It would change, first…"

"Let's go home," Carmel interrupted. "I cleared it with the captain. He said it's okay for you to take the rest of the day off. He's lined someone up to come in early."

I stood up. "No. I want to work. I want to stay busy."

Carmel paused. "C'mon with me. We'll have a drink, we'll talk."

"No, I'm gonna keep working."
"Are you sure?"
I shrugged. "I'm sure."

19

Over pitchers of beer at a local bar, we talked, Sam's words coming at first in a trickle before releasing in a violent gush.

"Okay, picture this," he said. "We'd just left your place, slightly buzzed from the wine, when Sarah yells, Stop. Pull over."

He recounted the Christmas party gone wrong at the Roberts' house, then moved on to the lazy Los Angeles days before the crash, the gang-rape in the nightclub, then finally Sarah's last moments. The tires screeching as the aging pick-up veered off the highway and struck an eighteen-inch-wide concrete beam. The sad cacophony of the vehicle's steering wheel, windshield, engine and hood exploding into Sarah, followed by the final sound, a single gasp, like a lover sighing at climax. Sam thought the sound had come from Sarah, but now he wondered how that was possible – how could she have lived for even a fraction of a second after the crash.

Sam had been thrown into the windshield, and he remembered regaining his wits, looking left to where Sarah had sat and seeing only grey concrete. He climbed back into the wreckage reeking of gasoline and death, and found her spread-eagled, her throat and chest bloody, her face crushed,

On our fourth pitcher, his voice strained and weak,

Sam reached deep inside and said, "I really did love her, you know. Most people wouldn't believe that. But I did."

I nodded, trying to look convinced.

He leaned back in his chair. "Time to move on," he finally said. "Got a good plan. I've watched enough of these clowns make adult movies. Figure I can make one myself. You know Sarah had some life insurance? Not much, but I'm the beneficiary. So wouldn't it be good to make a movie in her memory?"

I didn't know how to answer.

"Anyway, I'll get to hire the girls, the actors I mean, write the script myself, and choose the director."

I didn't want to hear any more, but he continued serving up details, almost like he'd flown into town on business, nothing more.

In time, his words slowed, as if his focus had waned. "So, Brady," he finally said. "You know, I've kind of kept, like a record, or a transcript, of everything, that's happened to us. You know, like the detailed outline for a screenplay?"

I felt my eyes narrow. "You mean your years in LA with Sarah?"

He paused, so unlike him. "That, and more. Starting from when all of us, you know, the four of us, met in high school."

"Sam," I said, my voice thin.

"Relax," he said. "I've written it, but that's as far as it goes. Just needed to get it down in words, to make sense of it all. That's what writers do. No one else will see it. That's a promise."

I stared out the window, and when I looked back, he'd moved on to something else, and pretty soon so did I.

When our words had run dry, when my watch told me I was expected home for dinner, we rose and I offered to pick him up for tomorrow's funeral.

"I appreciate that," he said. "But I'll go with Luke."

"How's he doing, anyway?"

"He's doing fine. Still got all those damn cats. I could barely find a place to sleep last night."

I laughed for the first time since I'd entered the bar.

At the door, he paused. "Brady. You know what's missing?"

"What?"

"You didn't ask me if I picked up the money. The fifteen hundred dollars."

"No. I didn't ask," I said. "C'mon, I'll drop you off at Luke's."

"Thanks, but I want to walk."

"Sure."

As I fumbled to unlock my car's door, he called over from the sidewalk. "I took it, Brady. I picked it up, every last dollar, and put it in my wallet, just like she said."

"I know you did," I yelled back. What I didn't tell him was I also suspected that he'd secretly negotiated in advance a higher price for the extra guys to join in the rape scene; that he'd betrayed Sarah once too often.

When we pulled into the funeral home's parking lot, I immediately spotted Dr. Roberts positioned at the door, like a failed sentinel, squinting into the May sunlight. He'd always appeared so robust, the kind of man you'd want to lead you into battle. Now he simply looked old, his hair grey, his body thin and slightly hunched.

"Hello, Mr. and Mrs. Roberts," I said as we reached the door. "This is my wife Carmel and our daughters Leanne and Jennifer."

Mrs. Roberts gushed stoically over the girls, and hugged me with a seemingly huge weight. I wanted to tell them both how much I'd loved their daughter; I thought they deserved to know.

"I'm so sorry," was all I could say.

Dr. Roberts surveyed my new family and shook my hand and Carmel's in a business-like fashion. "Glad you could make it," he said before turning back toward the parking lot.

In a large foyer just inside the door stood Mom and Amanda, a happy couple in summery-colored dresses.

"You okay, Brady?" Amanda asked.

"Sure," I said. "You two gonna come sit with us?"

"In a moment," Mom said. "Save us a seat next to you."

"Why don't you come now?"

As she looked out at the Roberts, Mom's pained expression suggested she thought of not answering. Then she said, "I'm waiting for Luke and Sam to get here. To make sure everything is okay. To make sure they feel welcome."

"Okay," I said, stunned by my mother's rare instinct to do the right thing.

Inside the dim room more than one hundred people had taken seats before Sarah's closed casket: Friends from school, distant relatives, people who'd watched Sarah slip in and out of their lives, like those in the actors' group, the animal shelter, the restaurant where she worked on and off.

We sat down and I warned the girls to behave. Then I stared silently at the worn linoleum floor that had seen so much death.

More people filed in. Brittany, Cynthia and more friends from school. Finally, when I didn't think they would make it, Luke and Sam suddenly stood before me, Mom and Amanda at their sides.

Luke wore faded jeans, sneakers and a buttoned-shirt I suspect was the dressiest garment he owned. He took a seat near us and cast his dark eyes on his lap as he worked his hands nervously.

Sam slapped Luke on the back and smiled too brightly at Carmel and the girls. I had to look away.

A minute or so later Mr. and Mrs. Roberts passed us and took a front-row seat with Sarah's brother and some other relatives I barely recalled meeting years ago. Mrs. Roberts delivered the eulogy, with a strength that surprised me. People sobbed at her stories of Sarah's youth, of her determination, her kindness, all those good qualities that were so easily forgotten, so easily eclipsed by other things. I crossed my arms, stared at the coffin, which Sarah's family had decided to keep closed, and waited patiently for it all to end.

When it did, everyone shuffled quietly out into the foyer for coffee. As Carmel chatted with Brittany I watched the funeral director close the doors to the chapel, the doors to Sarah's life.

Just like that.

When I thought no one was watching, I crept back inside, into the room where Sarah lay encased in wood and satin. I walked up to the casket, felt its heaviness.

My fingers ran across a seam, and I forced them into the gap, lifting the lid a few inches. Then a few more. Finally I swung it open and gasped at what I saw.

Sarah had never looked more beautiful, her face perfectly reconstructed. I reached forward with my fingers and touched her smooth bare neck, unable to tell where it had been ripped open. I ran my eyes up past her cheek and stroked her wonderful straw-colored hair, neatly tied back, the way she liked it.

"Forgive me," I whispered, wondering what she would say to me if she could talk.

I closed my eyes, searched inside me and felt deserted. Stranded. Then a small surge of panic rose.

Before I'd realized what I'd done, I slipped one hand

beneath Sarah's back and the other behind her head. Then I lifted, carefully, like you would a baby whose fragile neck needed supporting. I pulled her body into mine, feeling a coldness I didn't remember.

A scuffing sound behind me made me jump, and I jerked my head around to see Dr. Roberts. I expected him to scream or to throw me to the ground over this final violation of his daughter. Instead he nodded, like it was okay, like he didn't realize I was selfishly trying to take something away because I had nothing inside me left to give.

I laid Sarah back down gently, carefully readjusting her hands, her head, her hair – back to the way I had found her.

"They did a nice job," Dr. Roberts said moving beside me. "The mortician, fixing all the damage."

"God, I'm so sorry I did that," I said, starting to close the casket.

He stopped me and looked down at her sweet, hardened face.

"...wanted an open casket service, but even though they filled in all the holes, pushed her face back out, I just don't think...I just don't think it looks exactly like her. She looks a little bit like someone else. Don't you think?"

I studied her face. "No. This is exactly how I remember her."

He reached into his suit jacket and pulled out a small bottle of Baileys Irish Cream and poured it into his half-empty coffee cup. "Well," he said, "maybe you remember her differently than I do."

When we arrived back home, I longed to climb into bed, pull the sheets over my head and descend into a long, deep sleep, finding the same peace as Sarah. But I knew there would be none.

"I'm gonna drop you three off and go for a little drive," I told them.

Carmel pressed her lips tightly together. "Why not come in and we'll put the kids down for a nap and have a bath together, with a glass of wine."

"No," I said, "I just feel like going for a drive."

"I can see if I can get a sitter and we can go out, you know, get our minds off things."

"I want to be alone."

"Okay." She didn't look at me again – keeping the hurt in her face hidden – as she helped the girls out of the car and into the house.

I drove past the stores downtown, where people shopped like nothing had happened, past the beach where we first felt the touch of each other's skin, across the big bridge that always towered over us, like a cruel reminder that something could be accomplished. On the road outside of Oak Harbor, I saw them, a stand of black cottonwood trees, their bark ashy-gray and deeply furrowed. They looked like they had stood there forever, for the most part unnoticed and forgotten.

I parked at the side of the road and hopped the short wire fence that separated the grove of trees from the highway. Falling cotton-covered seeds swirled and drifted down like snowflakes. They blanketed the hardened dirt in a glistening white. Soft, clean, angelic. I stared up past the treetops, to the sky, and let them rain down upon me.

20

A few nights later a siren woke me from a heavy sleep. My colleagues staggered to their feet and promptly dressed in the dark. I lingered in bed, just for a moment, my stomach bloated and churning, my energy depleted.

Boerne, or was it Marriott, bellowed something like, "You gonna lay there all night feeling sorry for yourself?"

I responded, "Maybe," before swinging my feet out of bed and dressing.

In the truck, Boerne read the address, 1845 Edison Road. Shooting. Possibly one dead, one injured. Good chance we'll beat the paramedics.

All of us looked at each other. Fatal shooting? In our town?

Carson muttered, "Shit."

I mumbled, "Edison?"

Boerne looked back. "What is it, Joseph?"

"Nothing…well, some friends live on that road."

The truck bounced along F Street, the most pot-holed road in the county. Four of us rode in silence.

We pulled onto the street in no time, and Boerne turned back to me as I squinted out the window.

He saw it in my eyes, and confirmed, "Is that it, Brady? Is that your friends' house?"

I muttered, "Fuck," and struggled to my feet. Boerne pushed me back down. "You stay in here till we know what we've got. That's a direct order."

Doors opened, men with gear exited. A small crowd of people huddled together on the street. I climbed down from the truck, slamming the door twice because it didn't close properly the first time, and drifted toward the house, one bare bulb above the open door, the welcome mat facing the wrong way. Inside, Carson hovered over a body, checking for a long-gone pulse. A tabby cat with a crooked tail, Luke's favorite, sniffed the body, and was batted away by Carson.

I climbed up the front steps, brushed past a cop who issued orders about preserving the 'crime scene'. I pushed closer, confused as I looked at the body, because the person on the hall floor didn't look like Luke or Sam, or anyone, because faces weren't meant to have one eye obscured by a gunshot.

Carson reached out as I passed, half-heartedly trying to stop me but looking instead like he needed help. Blood stained the hall wall. Another cop stood in the kitchen, his face wearing a helpless calm. A second siren grew loud behind me. Puddles of blood blotted the kitchen floor, streaked by boot prints. Failing fluorescent lights hummed. Boerne and Marriott huddled over someone, trying to plug him up, trying to keep him from bleeding to death.

I leaned forward, catching the victim's defeated eyes, Luke's eyes, as they fought to focus. Boerne looked up at me and swore.

Paramedics arrived and dropped their gear. Marriott pushed me back, away, my hand brushing the fridge door, knocking off a photo of Sarah that had been improperly affixed by three small magnets.

I whispered, "What have I done now?" and Marriott, puzzled, whisked the photo off the floor with a flick of his wrist, and reattached it to the fridge, like this would make everything right.

Back at the fire hall, I downed four aspirins with a cup of coffee and told Boerne I was running up to the hospital.

"I just got off the phone with them," he said. "Your friend's stable. The shot in the gut wasn't as bad as it looked. The bullet in his knee looks like it shattered the bone. They're prepping him for a few hours surgery. So you might want to go home first, talk to your wife."

"I don't want to wake Carmel," I told him. "We haven't been sleeping. Maybe I'll hang in here a few more hours, then go to the hospital and then home."

About 3 a.m., Marriott led in Detective Morrison, his thin hair half erect and bent by sleep, like a dog-eared book.

"Christ," he said when he saw me. "I heard you were called out. I'm sorry you had to find out that way."

I just nodded.

"You called home?" he asked.

"No, I'll tell my wife in the morning. I want..."

He pulled his cell phone from his pocket. "What's your number?"

"I'm not calling."

"Humor me. I've got a squad car in front of your house. I wanted to make sure they were all right and I'm sure they'd rather you phoned than an officer knocked on the door."

"They're in no danger," I told him, irritated. "It's not about that."

His eyes narrowed. "How do you know what it's about?"

Boerne shouted out my home phone number and Morrison started dialing. I snapped the phone from his hand. "Sorry to wake you," I said when I heard Carmel's groggy voice.

❧

Morrison followed me to the back deck, into a half-darkness evoking memories of our midnight meeting in the park.

"Look, I know you're partly estranged from your old friends, with your new life and all. I susp…"

"How would you know that?" I asked him.

He looked out across the alley. "I just do. But as I was saying. I suspect the attack was drug-related, but you never know if it's something else, like friends of Opal's settling an old score."

"There's no score to settle," I responded, my head aching.

"Whatever you say, but with some a perception exists that there is, and it's my job to look at all possibilities. That's why I wanted to check on your family."

I sighed, and rubbed my forehead, not even thinking I should be grateful.

"Back inside," Morrison said "you said something like, 'It's not about that.' What exactly did you mean? Why do you think they were shot?"

I shrugged. "I don't know. They were into a lot of things…"

"They were," he said, "but anything you think might help. I'd like to hear it, any theories, no matter how ridiculous. Okay?"

"I'll let you know if I think of something," I said annoyed, dismissive.

He looked like he would press me, but didn't. He lingered, saying something about sitting down with me later in the day, and when he was finally gone, I steadied myself against the railing, thinking of how we were all closely spaced dominoes, all living in each other's shadow. Was I really ready to give another one a push?

❧

I changed and ran eight mindless blocks to the hospital, where Luke's dad sat outside intensive care, half asleep. I felt bad for not being the one to call him.

"Mr. Newell." He looked up blankly, his face sagging.

"It's Brady. You remember me?"

He nodded, his face sad, his face always sad. "They say someone shot him," he said, shaking his head. "Got one son dead from cancer, now this."

"How is he?" I said sitting next to him, smelling the sharpness of whisky in his breath. "Is he still in surgery?"

"He's out."

"Good," I said.

He nodded after a slight hesitation.

I returned to the fire hall, picked up my motorcycle and rode to Sam's house in the day's first light. Morrison said he'd broken the news to the Simpson family himself.

Sam's mother answered the door.

"Brady, you've heard?" No surprise or sadness in her voice.

"Yes, I'm here to offer my condolences."

She folded her arms in front of her chest, and sighed, "Oh, Brady. There was no cleanliness in Sam's ways, neither spiritual nor moral. That's why he's dead."

I wanted to tell her he was dead because some fucker had shot him in the head.

"He was tempted by the Devil, the unseen ruler, whose voice is everywhere."

I leaned back, scared she'd try to pull me in. And she did try, "Come on, Brady. We've got so much to talk about."

"My wife's waiting at home. I'm sorry."

❧

I circled the police station three times that afternoon, unsure whether I was trying to see justice done or simply assuage my pathetic guilt. When I finally went in, part of me hoped Morrison had gone home to sleep. He hadn't.

We sat in an interview room, and he asked, "How's your wife holding up?"

"Fine. A little shaken though."

"Nice lady. You know she cleans my wife's teeth? Kim says she's thorough but gentle. Friendly too."

I nodded. "No. I didn't know that."

"Guess it's upsetting for her," he said. "You know, when things come out of the past all of a sudden like this."

"I guess it is," I said.

We studied each other awkwardly, and he finally asked, "So…"

I took a deep breath and leaned forward, wondering if I was wasting everyone's time, if I was heaping more heartache on the innocent.

"Sarah's dad. Dr. Roberts. He once revealed something kind of strange."

Morrison's face divulged no expression. "Dr. Roberts?"

"On the night I became a firefighter, we had this conversation. When he told me he had inquired about a hit man to take out Sam and Luke. Even got a quote on the price. Said he didn't know what possessed him. That he was never serious. Still, he got a quote."

"Okay. Hold on. Let's go back to the beginning. But one second." Morrison went to a desk in the corner and took out a tape recorder. "Do you mind?"

He had me go over the story three or four times, with him asking all sorts of questions. Getting me to repeat Dr. Roberts' words over and over again, to the best of my memory.

"Do you feel you're in any danger," he asked me.

"No. This probably means nothing. Probably not related. But even if it was, I don't think he meant me any harm. Didn't blame me for Sarah."

Finally, he shut off the tape and said, "I'll look into it."

"Can you do it discreetly?"

"Don't worry. Just leave it to me."

When the hospital finally allowed me to visit Luke, he squirmed in his bed, his right leg stretched out in a cast, and talked in a drug-slurred voice of only two things: revenge and his cats. Revenge would be difficult – he had no idea who did this, only a short man wearing a black ski mask. The cats would be a little easier – he asked me to look after the two that were his and return the other five to the shelter.

I promised to do whatever he needed. I knew it wouldn't be enough.

Carmel and I gathered up a bucket of cleaning supplies, dropped the girls off with Mom, and went to Luke's house. It was locked, his keys and wallet still inside, the landlord still in Hong Kong waiting for the right time to redevelop the entire block. I managed to force open a back bedroom window – Sarah and Sam's old room – and let Carmel in the front door.

She stared at the blood stains on the carpeted front hallway and kitchen linoleum, and tears welled in her eyes.

"You sure the police are finished here?" she said.

"Yeah. I checked with Morrison."

With a mop and bucket she went after the large patches in the kitchen, before getting on her knees to scrub the hallway walls and carpet with her hands. I opened windows to air out the house and tackled the cat shit and piss that had accumulated in the days since the shooting. I found only three cats inside, and carried them out to our car. While we cleaned, three more returned, one by one. The seventh never came back.

We left the garbage out on the curb in a rusty can. Then I found a hammer and a couple of nails and secured the wooden frame of the window I'd busted through. We hid a key underneath a planter by the back door. Then we gathered up Luke's wallet and some clothes, which I planned to take to the hospital after I dropped the cats off, four at the shelter, two at our house.

Finally I began collecting Sam's possessions – well actually carefully sorting through what he'd left behind. Carmel watched me, puzzled, as I flipped a button to boot up his laptop, then began, one-by-one, examining his notebooks full of ideas and stories. Suddenly she understood what I was doing. She nodded and leaned forward, suddenly eager. "How can I help?" she offered.

I sighed. "Why don't you keep going through the papers, every last one. And I'll delete whatever's necessary from his laptop."

She nodded once more, and began sorting.

I wondered how the police had missed this material but then I thought that to them the papers would have looked like drafts of scripts or plays, poorly written ones at that. They wouldn't expect to find anything remarkable in Sam's jottings. And what criminal saved a history of his crimes on his computer.

"It's important we be thorough," I told her, not revealing what Sam had told me about his screenplay detailing our lives, our transgressions.

It took nearly an hour, in which time I'd deleted two folders, one of them a backup, before finally deciding to wipe clean the entire hard drive. Why take any chances.

On paper, Carmel found an outline in red pen, written slightly out of order like he thought some of the events weren't really connected. It was just shit that happened, for no reason. It was all there, though, except the ending.

"He's written it all down, Brady. Everything."

She made two piles of paper, and the second one she folded up and carefully placed in her jacket pocket, until she could get it to our shredder.

We placed the rest of Sam's belongings back in the suitcase he'd used when he returned to town. I would drop this off at his parents' home, and get the hell out of there.

Our dirty work done, we washed our hands, locked the front door behind us and drove away in a car full of nervous cats.

That night I read *The Lookout's* article about the shooting, four hundred or so words which had the effect of a shovel unearthing a long-forgotten grave. It detailed the crime and quoted police as having no suspects. Then the story pointed out Luke and Sam had both been temporarily charged in the death of Tom Opal. The reporter simply asked Detective Morrison if police were investigating whether Opal's death could be a motive in this shooting. The detective's answer: "At this time we are not ruling anything out."

Carmel and I sat the girls down side-by-side on the living room sofa. We looked at each other, and when I didn't speak, Carmel sighed, and said, "Girls, your daddy and I have something to tell you about. Something you may start hearing about from other people."

I had always expected them to hang on every word when we told them the story of Tom Opal's unfortunate fall and the suspicion that temporarily fell on the four people who witnessed it, including their dad. Instead they shifted restlessly in their seats, just like, well, just like two kids not quite four years old.

Carmel repeated the story twice, and we answered all

their questions, the first one being Leanne's excited, "So Daddy really got to see a dead person?"

"No, he didn't die right away. He died later in the hospital."

"Oh," she said, looking somewhat disappointed.

"Have you two heard any of this before?" Carmel asked. "Have you heard anyone mention it in any way?"

They both shook their heads.

"Not in any way at all," she asked again. "Like anyone saying anything bad about your daddy?"

Jennifer giggled. "Just grandma."

Both girls laughed, and began bouncing on the sofa, screaming wildly, even though they knew better. Carmel forced a small smile, then left the room saying, "They're all yours."

I sat on the floor and watched them bounce, not anxious to discuss the matter further.

For the next week, Carmel thrashed in bed each night, getting up several times to check on the girls and make sure the house was tightly locked. A distant barking dog would set her off. Or even our cat visitors fighting in their temporary home in the garage. Had I been sleeping soundly myself I might not have known just how little rest she was getting.

Two of the girls' scheduled play days with friends were canceled, with one of the parents at least honest enough to say she didn't feel comfortable letting her daughter visit while a killer roamed free and our family remained a potential target.

The girls started hearing whispers about Sam's death as well. One of their friends told them I would be killed next, precipitating a late-morning trip to school by Carmel to pick up a crying Jennifer.

Brittany told Carmel we could come and stay in her small, anonymous suite. We declined. We also kicked around the idea of leaving on an impromptu vacation, but decided not to draw more attention to ourselves. So we tried to live like nothing was wrong, something I was adept at.

The fire department gave me the rest of my four-day shift off – more time if I needed it. People I knew looked at me differently or fell silent as I approached. I felt myself uncomfortably slipping slowly out of the shadows, targeted not by Sam's killer but by everyone else.

"I don't think there's any danger, you know, to us," I told Carmel one night as she brushed her teeth before bed.

"What do you base that on?" she said, just like Morrison, so analytical. "And if you suspect something why haven't you gone to the police?"

"I did. Two days ago."

She looked up, angry.

"Why didn't you tell me this?"

"I don't know. I just wanted to see first if anything came of it. I mean it's more of a gut feeling."

"What is? What did you tell them?"

"That I heard something once. That could be connected."

"What?" she demanded, her voice touching upon hysterical.

"Well, like I said, it's a gut feeling."

She threw her toothbrush in the sink.

When I told her what I'd divulged to the police she worked the information around in her mind. Finally she shook her head. "No. I don't believe Dr. Roberts would do that. Not even after Sarah's death. He keeps people alive and well for a living."

I shrugged. "I'm never surprised by what people are capable of."

❧

While Carmel struggled most after going to bed, the worst moments for me came in the tender minutes right after I awoke, when the old wounds that had been encased in sleep suddenly became exposed once more. If I had been dreaming, I'd fight to continue reveling in whatever escapism I'd found – whatever wish-fulfillment blotted out the truth – before reality quickly crashed in and death pervaded my thoughts. Most mornings I saw Sam's bloodied one-eyed head and Sarah's perfectly reconstructed face before my feet hit the floor beside my bed. I carried these images throughout a litany of mundane tasks – brushing my teeth, opening the blinds, or calmly smiling at my wife and kids.

On a good day, and if I was working, someone's terrible crisis would serve as an adequate diversion, a shift in focus. On a bad day, like any four I'd have off in a row, I'd be left to ponder what went wrong, and how thinking about it had become an obsession.

Once I grabbed a sheet of paper and wrote at the top, Tom Opal dies. At the bottom, Sam shot to death, Luke debilitated by same shooting. In between, lay nineteen entries, all in chronological order, each and every one linked in some way, many screaming for me to go back and change just one thing, so everything below would change too. Before ripping this sheet apart, piece by piece, until the individual scraps of white were too small to tear further, my eyes moved to the eighth entry from the bottom, the source of my latest fixation: The one immediately below the entry, Met Carmel. It read: Heard Dr. Roberts confess he'd inquired about having Luke and Sam killed; Did nothing.

The next domino fell two weeks after the shooting. I didn't hear the echoing crash or feel the silent horror of those scrambling to get the hell out of the way. In a strange way, I never saw it coming, even though I'd made it tumble with a single belated push.

When I had told Morrison my theory about the shooting, he never mentioned one thing that had been troubling his linear mind: How the shooting ended, with the killer leaving Luke on the ground but clearly alive. A true professional, if he was targeting both Sam and Luke, would have finished Luke off. So when I had thrown out the name Dr. Ian Roberts as a suspect, another scenario quickly emerged: Could the shooter only have been after Sam, and Luke simply got in the way, a mere inconvenience to be neutralized? Could the shooter have been working for a distraught man who'd just lost his daughter and held only one man responsible?

With the few details I'd provided, Morrison had little trouble tracing back through police records the name of the man who had brought a gunshot victim to the hospital on a night Dr. Roberts was working. The man, one Robert Hayes, had been known to police, and when Morrison brought him in and said he wanted to talk about Sam Simpson's murder, Hayes gave him a how-the-fuck-did-you-figure-this-out look. Under interrogation, he rolled on the gunman, someone brought up from Seattle to do the job. He also rolled on Dr. Roberts, who'd hired him to arrange everything. It all happened so quickly that even Morrison was amazed.

Morrison said he managed to keep my name out of it, and that suited me just fine. Not because I feared what a pissed off Dr. Roberts could tell Morrison about Tom Opal's death – the doctor knew nothing other than what he suspected. It was really more a case of not leaving a score to be settled with a person who had already employed a contracted killer.

Morrison told me in person about Dr. Roberts' arrest. How they went to his office, handcuffed him and led him out past several stunned patients. How he can always tell when he arrests someone whether that person is guilty, just by his expression, by a feeling in his gut. Only the psychopaths can fool him, not Joe Average.

He told me this, and I nearly laughed hysterically.

21

For the next three years, we moved in our own way, me like the cliff jumpers that bobbed and floated silently under the Deception Pass Bridge, pushed and pulled by the prevailing current, and Carmel more like the kayakers who fought against the shifting tide, always with a purpose, body and mind engaged in a struggle to get ahead – determined, stubborn and sometimes dangerously misguided.

I kept the promise I'd made on the day I proposed to her, locking my teenaged transgressions away like a forgotten prisoner. And people did forget. The news of Sam's death and Dr. Roberts' arrest and conviction slowly fading with time. But they were never gone forever, or at least completely. I could try to hide things, but I couldn't make them vanish entirely.

Sometimes the name Tom Opal would arise above the clatter of beer pulled from chests of ice or other summer barbecue sounds – forced on a friendly outing by someone new to town, someone who'd heard the story and wanted to know more about the alleged code of silence, unaware of my role.

One time the awkward moment came in our own home when Carmel had hosted a ladies night out, a drink-filled gab session involving a dozen or so friends. I fled with Leanne and Jennifer to a movie, returning only when the girls were too tired to carry on. They kissed Carmel goodnight and hovered long enough to revel in the drunken attention of a room mostly full of mothers. After tucking them in, I hid out in our upstairs bedroom reading, waiting for peace to return.

In some ways it was no surprise to hear Luke's name drift up the stairs. After all, he attracted conversation just like any blight on the town would. Most found his sad, pathetic story engaging, though they didn't know the half of it.

Most had heard that six months after the shooting – and after his failed rehab left him walking with a cane and a limp – he was arrested selling weed outside the high school. Only a small amount, just enough for a few joints, but enough to put him behind bars for more than a year. Luke alone knew what happened to him inside prison; it was something he wouldn't even share with me.

When he was released, he had changed in ways only those few close to him understood: he emerged hating blacks, Hispanics and Native Indians and swearing he'd never deal drugs again or even jaywalk, because he'd never go back to jail. Within six weeks he'd chosen crack cocaine over living in a small rental suite and eating. He made most of his money by panhandling and collecting bottles and anything of value tossed away in downtown trash bins. Sometimes I'm sure people gave him money to get him out of their sight. He slept in a small tent in various public places in town, often moving before police could track him down and run him off like a wild dog.

So why should I be surprised to hear Luke's name rising up from a drink-fueled conversation in my own living room?

"You know what that homeless guy did?" a woman asked.

"What homeless guy?" a voice responded.

"You know, Luke Newell. Brady's high school friend, the one who got shot, the one the police suspect attacked Tom Opal."

I could sense Carmel's anger rising.

"I was breastfeeding Maria in the playground near the school and he walked by. You won't believe this. He grinned and asked, 'Can I be next in line?'"

A chorus of laughter and disbelief rose up the stairs.

"It's true," the woman said. "It really happened."

I strained my ears to hear Carmel's calm voice, not loud like the others, but measured, thoughtful, like a high school counselor advising testosterone charged Grade 12s. She told them to show some pity, that Luke's life had been difficult since the shooting, which wasn't his fault. That's when I heard another woman, her voice resonating in an outraged tone.

"I don't buy that," she said. "'You know what he said to me. You've heard about it, right?"

Another woman said, "You've got to hear this."

"Before the shooting, maybe by six months, I was in the bar on H street, waiting to meet some girls after work. He came up, looked like he'd been drinking all day. Hit on me a couple of times. I told him to leave. Then he takes one last stab at it. He leans in close and says, 'How would you like to get next to a cold-blooded killer?'"

They shrieked and laughed so loud I thought our girls would wake up.

What these so-called friends didn't know was how much Carmel had tried to help Luke get off the street. At first she pushed unsuccessfully to find him space in a detox program. But when that failed and Luke expressed reluctance anyway, she made weekly visits with food and other provisions. She'd often buy him new clothes at the Value Village in

Mount Vernon, soon learning his pant size and shoe size. Sometimes she spent hours just trying to find him, to bring him blankets in the winter, to see if he had survived a cold snap. Other times she'd look out the window of her office and see him groping through a dumpster, then slip out and give him whatever cash she had in her purse, even though he never asked for anything, not a single thing.

No one else other than Luke and I knew of her acts of kindness.

No one else other than Luke and I understood exactly what drove her to carry them out.

I had first laid eyes on Luke on his first day of Grade 8 about one week after he moved to Deception Pass. My eyes down, I glanced up from my locker and somehow picked him out of the chaotic pre-bell masses, the same way you would a lone deformed apple in a neat supermarket display. His home room teacher had shown him to his locker across from mine, and he carefully hung up his coat, which looked two sizes too large. His body was small, his hair unkempt, his eyes unfocused, and his pants far too short, the hems hovering well above his ankles.

Only a week earlier he'd moved into a decaying house near the downtown, and one day earlier he'd ventured in alone to register himself for the final eight and one-half months of Grade 8.

None of us knew what I later came to suspect. That Luke was eager for a fresh start in our little town. And nobody knew what would become painfully clear later that afternoon as his first day of school stumbled to a close: That I would play an immense role in making sure he never got a fair chance.

As I hung up my coat and gathered my books, I found my eyes again drawn to his hands and fingers, which ran over his combination lock with relentless precision.

"You want something?"

His voice startled me.

"I said, 'You want something?'" he repeated, staring at me from across the hall, his gaze broken only by the throng of students passing between us, like long blinks of the eye.

I half-heartedly shook my head and turned back to my locker.

"Motherfucker," came his voice through the crowd.

I thought nothing else of him until two hours later, when I crept into math class and he looked up from the once-vacant desk beside me.

Our teacher, Mr. Matthews, walked to the front of the class, introduced Luke and gave us a lengthy in-class assignment.

I looked over at Luke. "Do you know what you're supposed to do?" I asked him.

"Sure. But do you?"

I buried my face back in my textbook, my face stern, already wishing that the day everything turned on him would soon arrive, and he'd suddenly find himself sneaking through school stoop-shouldered and shallow-breathed, slipping silently in and out of class mostly unnoticed by the suddenly sexy Grade 8 girls who would laugh and look right through him, if they looked his way at all.

Mr. Matthews excused himself and left the room, and I swore under my breath, because I knew what that meant, what it always meant.

"Hey, Brady," said Tom Stewart, a dim-witted monster who'd just as soon kick you in the balls as look at you. "Where's the teacher going? Home for a little quickie with that tramp mother of yours?"

A few classmates laughed. I sensed Luke staring at me, puzzled, waiting for me to respond. He hadn't yet learned that my mother was dating our math teacher, which led to no end of abuse from loudmouths like Tom Stewart.

He also didn't know I would quietly amuse myself with my own thoughts when the taunting began, mundane things like taking the X-acto knife from my locker and plunging it into Tom's upper thigh, just below the hip-bone, and severing the large artery running down his leg. Watching him bleed to death.

"Might have to take a number outside her bedroom," Tom continued. "Probably a couple of other guys in there screwing her already. Might want to hose her down first."

My classmates roared, a few in disgust, others snickering. All of them stared at me as my mind filled with images of the blood spurting out, like it does from arteries, and Tom's panicked face wondering why he bled so profusely, too stupid to know he'd be dead soon.

"You must have her confused with your own mother," I mumbled, picturing myself spitting those words defiantly over his lifeless blood-stained body.

"Ouuuu…" The sound of surprised groans emanated from those who had heard me.

"Shit," I whispered to myself, suddenly terrified I'd blurred the line between fantasy and reality.

Tom hesitated, gazing at the door and back at me. Finally he strutted to my desk and without a word, popped me in the mouth. Not a hard punch, just enough to silence the class and swell my bottom lip.

As he returned to his seat, I stood up, trembling. "You vacuous…" The words slipped out before I could stop. I held my breath.

Tom turned around, creases on his large forehead, his mouth twisted by a grimace. "What the fuck did you say? Vack-u-is… What is that?"

He walked back to my desk. I sat down.

He roared, "I said 'what is that shit?' Vack-u-is?"

He looked around. "Anyone know?"

"Yeah," giggled Sophie Hayes, a pothead who loved large earrings and big talk. "It's from the Latin word vacuum. It means 'you suck.'"

The class exploded with laughter, none louder than Sophie, whose face beamed with pride at her own rare cleverness.

Tom turned to me. "What the fuck does it mean?"

It was the one time in my life I'd curse my Grade 7 teacher for the theory he'd put to practice the year before: That a large vocabulary meant a better education and better job. He always found fun ways to insert new words into our everyday conversations and lives, and more than a few stuck with me, like vacuous.

"What does it mean," Tom demanded, clenching his fists.

"It means boisterous, you know, in a scrappy sort of way."

He hovered over me, and glanced around the class, possibly seeking confirmation, before ambling back to his seat and cramming his six foot frame into a desk designed for a much smaller body. He turned back to me one last time. "Fucking right I'm vacuous. Don't you forget it."

A few minutes later Mr. Matthews returned, and I tried to concentrate on my work, my lip stinging and tightening.

I ate my lunch alone at my homeroom desk, avoiding the cafeteria or anywhere else large groups converged. Before the bell rang, I dug out the social studies books from my locker and wove down the crowded hall toward my next class.

I didn't see him coming.

Tom Stewart reached out of the crush of bodies, grabbed my neck and threw me against a closed classroom door. He jammed one forearm against my chest and locked one hand around my throat. "You think you're so smart," he snarled.

"You think I can't read? Huh? I looked it up. Dull, vacant, lacking ideas or intelligence."

I looked into his wild eyes and surprised myself by seeing something I didn't expect, something that shifted my thoughts away from him and the gathering crowd.

"You and me, after school. We'll settle this once and for all."

He slammed me into the door one final time, turned and announced to anyone in earshot. "Me and Brady at Rotary Park after school. Gonna be an old-school shit-kicking."

Word of my imminent date with Tom Stewart quickly spread. Students passed it on in whispers, in impromptu conversations and in loud taunts thrown at me between classes, until any thought I had of quietly slipping away after the day's final bell quickly vanished in a way that I couldn't.

When the bell rang, I returned to my locker to gather my homework. Already, several of Tom's friends stood waiting to escort me across the street. I caught a glimpse of Luke at his locker, his fingers spinning the dial of his combination lock, the rest of his body frozen. Your turn will come, believe me, I thought.

We walked out the front door and across the street, passing the three-man city parks crew that lit cigarettes and abandoned their mowers for a break. Far too quickly I arrived in the midst of one hundred or so students, the curious, the bored, the blood-thirsty.

I looked for comforting faces, and found none. Surprisingly, Tom hadn't arrived. I stood waiting, not knowing where to look or place my hands.

Seconds later he appeared, shaking his wrists and hands, loosening up his knuckles and the various small bones that he would let fly.

"Hurry up," yelled a lanky Grade 11 student, a member of the school basketball team. "We don't have all day."

"Let's see some blood," another student shouted.

Tom turned to me, and tried to harden his face. "I'm gonna hit you so hard you'll get ticketed for speeding on Interstate 5."

He raised his fists.

"I don't want to fight you," I said, words greeted with laughter and derision by our audience. "I want to apologize. Say I'm sorry."

Tom frowned, and cast his puzzled face upon the crowd, which shifted uneasily at the prospect of a blood-free afternoon.

"C'mon," shouted one of Tom's friends, "don't let him get away with that."

"Fuck him up," snarled a Grade 10 girl with diamond piercings in her flared nostrils.

Tom looked back at me confused, like I somehow knew what he should do. More impatient shouts filled the air. More vile encouragement.

Eyes huge and wild, he moved forward, hesitated, and threw a haymaker at my head, no doubt hoping to silence his critics with one punch. I barely managed to duck and back out of his way.

Our audience exploded with cheers, a dull roar that both sickened and terrified me, like a lightning storm I couldn't escape.

Tom stepped forward, this time with a flurry of jabs, two or three striking my head, but most glancing off my arms, which I had raised in self-defense. His large fists made violent thuds as they struck, though the blows felt strangely restrained. I staggered back, and again thought of running, or just falling to the ground and cowering.

He came at me again with another flurry, and I bent over and covered up the best I could, absorbing the blows mostly with my arms and back, except for one that bruised my right cheek. I felt his arms grab my coat, felt my world tip on its side and the ground rise up and slam me. I lay still, face down, and he kicked me once in the ribs, leaving me gasping for air.

Tears streamed down my face, and I hated myself for so wrongly thinking my apology would be enough. Back in the hallway, as he had wrapped his large hand around my throat, Tom's eyes had revealed something startling, just beneath the anger: hurt, which I had inflicted upon him with a single word. It was an emotion I thought he could never feel, a sensitivity that I hadn't realized could exist in him. So as we faced off in the park, I had sensed he simply ached for my public servility, not the squirting of blood, the snapping of bone. And maybe I had been right. But I'd forgotten about the ultimate peer pressure – our frenzied audience, which sought something I'd never understand.

So now I was fucked.

"I give," I groaned. "I've had enough."

Tom looked out at the sea of faces, anxious for the slightest indication we were done, but saw no confirmation, heard only screams like, "Finish him," or "You've hardly touched him."

That's when I decided my only chance was to tear away from this mob while I still could. I selected a gap in the crowd, stumbled to my feet, froze for a second or two like always, and exploded forward. I broke through the line of bodies, saw the deserted street emerge large and bright and then sorrowfully felt two arms close around my hips, a heavy weight bringing me down. Hands clutched at my shoulders and back, four or five people, dragging me back, pushing me toward Tom.

I fell at his feet, and when I looked up I could see the disappointment in his eyes, the why-didn't-you-run-faster expression. He sighed and raised his fist once more.

I didn't even see Luke at first, though looking back, I suspect he stepped quietly through the crowd, his eyes fixed on Tom like Tom was the sole cause of this mess.

"You're not so tough," Luke shouted at Tom. "Without all your friends helping you you'd be nothing."

I looked up to see Luke standing defiantly, a soda container in his hand. Tom, mindful of appearance, stuttered some tough words. "You just wait there, new kid. I'll give a two-fer you'll never forget."

The crowd cheered, eager for more. Luke didn't move. I couldn't take my eyes off his hands – they were perfectly still, a kind of hysterical calm falling over them.

Then suddenly one reached up, revealing the words "Big Gulp," and flipped the lid off the container. Before anyone knew what had happened, Luke flung the large cup's contents at Tom, drenching his shirt and neck.

Tom stood stunned, staring down at the soaked mess. He looked at Luke. "You're dead," he whispered.

Tom stepped forward, and Luke's hands quickly dropped the cup and moved into his jacket pocket. In the second it took Luke to light a match, Tom stopped dead in his tracks. We knew what our sense of smell finally told us: He'd drenched Tom with gasoline.

Suddenly everything changed: gone were the careless expressions on everyone's face, the shouts of violence.

Tom and Luke stood frozen, six feet apart, the match burning down. Luke dropped it, and in no time had extracted another from the book and lit it.

I waited for Tom, or anyone else, to dare Luke to actually do it, to set Tom on fire, for a single person to set the crowd in motion with a shout of, "Burn that prick." But no one spoke. Something told us Luke would push this to the end.

In the next half minute Luke lit three more matches, the tiny flames transfixing almost everyone, before Tom, his face pale, finally stepped back. He glanced at the crowd, and back at Luke. He turned and slipped away silently.

A wave of voices rose from the audience, words like "weirdo" and "psycho" wafting up in disbelief. Their fun spoiled, the crowd dispersed, many of them still unable to take their eyes off Luke as they walked away.

One of Tom's friends – the same one who'd escorted me out here – stepped up to Luke. I could see Luke's hands start to raise the book of matches, in defense.

"I'm not scared of those matches, you little shit. Case you hadn't noticed, I'm not all covered in gasoline."

For as long as I would know Luke, he would struggle for the right words, the right reaction. Not that day.

"No. You're not covered in gasoline. Least not right now."

Tom's friend hovered over Luke for another few seconds, and he too retreated.

I stood silently, my head aching, my face swollen, my clothes covered in grass and dirt stains, uncertainty sweeping over me once again. I wanted to tell him that he'd made everything worse, for both of us, by not letting the fight come to its natural end, by upping the stakes. More than all that, I simply wanted to ask him if he really would have done it.

"Shit," was all I said, exhaling the word in amazement.

He smiled. "Fucken intense, huh?"

I knew Luke waited for the slightest offer of friendship, for me to repay the debt I had just incurred, even though I didn't yet fathom how much he'd given up to help me. I thought of turning away from him; no, of taking a deep breath and running away.

"Let's walk," I finally said, and as we did I could see hatred and misunderstanding in the faces of those who had witnessed Luke's misguided attack. The easy characterizations had already started, way back then, and would never stop. They were already forming their opinions of him, already convincing themselves of the darkness poorly concealed in his inner reaches, of his infinite capacity for inflicting suffering. I was just beginning to learn that they, all of his judges, didn't know shit.

22

In July, Carmel found what she described as a perfect home, a three-bedroom place on a tree-shaded street dead-ending on a bluff overlooking the channel. She called me at work and told me about its large, private backyard, its bright and spacious family room, its immaculate condition, the peek-a-boo ocean view from the master bedroom, descriptions evoking the overblown wording of almost every real estate advertisement I'd ever read. She asked me to meet her and the girls there immediately after my shift ended. When I arrived, they were waiting in the driveway like hungry children, with our realtor, an overweight woman who always seemed out of breath, hovering officiously nearby. We toured the house, Carmel seeing her dream home, me a place that needed too much updating, the kids their own bedrooms, and our realtor a commission.

"Let's make an offer," Carmel whispered after returning to the island counter in the center of the large kitchen.

"Let's walk to the end of the street," I told her. "I want to see how loud the traffic from the bridge is."

We rounded up the girls and walked the three houses to the bluff as our realtor leaned against her car and phoned her office for messages.

"See," Carmel said, plunking herself down on a bench the city had placed in the scenic roadside gap between houses. "You can hardly hear the bridge. And what a view. Look, there's the state park across the channel, and you can see the San Juans in the distance."

Trees obscured the bridge, but you could hear the hum of traffic crossing the structure and continuing along the highway, three or so blocks away.

"Can we get down to the water from here," Jennifer asked, trying to peek over the small chain link fence.

"No," I told them. "There's no trail, it's too steep."

"What do you think?" Carmel asked me. "Great house, beautiful neighborhood."

I placed my elbows on the top of the fence and looked down.

In time, Carmel whispered, "Is it too close? To where your father…"

"It's not that," I said. "But I do worry about the girls, the drop off."

"The city's got this fence," she countered.

"It's only four feet high. What if they climbed it?"

"We would never do that, Daddy," Leanne chipped in.

"We want this house, Daddy," Jennifer pressured.

"See," laughed Carmel. "And, you know girls, look down the channel a little way. See that point there. That's where your dad took me on our first date. We went cliff jumping there."

"You mean you jumped off this cliff?" Leanne asked, her eyes wide.

"No, no," Carmel said. "Not this one. Way down there. That one."

"Only twenty-five feet or so high," I said.

Leanne tried to pull herself on top of the fence so she could see better. I gave Carmel a told-you-so look, and she picked Leanne up in her arms.

"Why didn't you jump from up here?" Leanne asked.

I wanted to give them an answer they'd never forget. Something like, "You're grandfather tried it, and he's dead. Body shattered by the fall. Then washed out to sea." But this was my history, my fear speaking.

"A fall from this high would kill you," I told them. "You'd be moving so fast when you hit the water, it would be like striking the road."

"So put up your hand if you promise never to climb this fence or jump from up high," Carmel said.

The girls threw their arms into the air.

"And put up your hands if you want to buy this house," she continued, pushing both hands in the air with the girls.

They all looked at me.

"It's a further walk to school, girls."

"We don't care," Jennifer said.

"You may not have any friends living nearby."

"Carla lives right around the corner," Leanne said.

I looked out across the channel, and felt Carmel brush up beside me.

"We can afford this – the mortgage wouldn't be that much more than what we now pay in rent," she said.

Behind us, the girls fidgeted, the realtor paced by her car.

"So…" Carmel said.

"Do you really want to do it? Put roots down in this town?"

"Yes, I do," Carmel said firmly. "We've got good jobs here, friends, family, and this area's like paradise, a great place to raise two girls."

"You know what I'm talking about," I said. "Do you really want to put roots down here?"

Her face grew serious for a second before her smile returned. "Yes."

I stared down over the cliff, and wished I could see a profile of where we stood, because I sensed we were on an overhang, with nothing between us and the water but a few feet of rock and earth and a whole lot of air. What would it take for the ground to fall away and send us tumbling down?

"What does dis-cep-shun mean?" Jennifer asked as we packed her books into a heavy cardboard box a week before the move.

"Deception?" I responded as I placed some light but bulky stuffed animals on top to prevent the box from getting too heavy. I sighed. "Why do you ask?"

"Why is our town called that? Deception Pass?"

"Oh," I said. "You sure you want to know – it's a long explanation?"

She nodded.

"Okay." I took a deep breath. "About two hundred years ago an explorer named Captain Vancouver sailed through the small channel, the one under the big bridge."

"The bridge is that old? Is it safe?"

"No," I said. "The bridge didn't exist back then, and there were few people, mainly natives who settled this country first. Now Captain Vancouver was British, but they were using maps or charts that were made by the Spanish, who'd explored this area first. The Spanish charts said the channel was an inlet or a bay, kind of a dead end."

"Like the street we're moving onto."

"Exactly. And the Spanish thought that the island on the south side of the bridge – we now call it Whidbey Island – was really a peninsula, you know, something connected to the mainland by land. So Captain Vancouver sailed in, and managed to keep sailing around the so-called peninsula until his ship emerged back into open waters down the coast a little ways, proving the inlet was not really a small bay but a channel that encircled an island."

"Okay, but…"

"I'm getting there. So Captain Vancouver named the island Whidbey Island, in honor of his chief navigator, Joseph Whidbey. And he named the channel, what the Spanish had thought was a bay, Deception Pass, because it had fooled the Spanish."

"Oh," she said.

"So, to make a long story short, deception means to trick or fool someone, to make them believe something that's not true, just like the Spanish had been tricked into thinking Whidbey Island was really connected to the mainland and Deception Pass was really a bay."

"I thought only people can trick someone. How can water trick someone?"

"Well, I guess rock and water and land can't, like, you know, deliberately deceive someone, but it can still happen."

She still looked puzzled, but I pressed on. "Now, as you know, Deception Pass isn't just the name of the narrow body of water, but of our town too."

"So why do they call the town Deception Pass? Is it because lots of tricksters live here?"

I shifted my weight uneasily, my knees sore. "No. I think the first settlers just took the name of the channel and applied it to the town. Nice and simple."

"I don't understand. Why would they do that?"

"They just did. That's all."

"But why?"

"I don't know. It's just what they did," I blurted, my voice crackling unevenly.

"You sure it's got nothing to do with the people who live here?"

"What are you getting at, Jennifer?"

"I'm just asking a question."

"But what are you getting at?"

"Don't yell at me."

"I'm not yelling. I just want to know what you're saying. What you've heard."

She turned and left her room, mumbling, "Someone's grumpy," and for a moment I wanted to chase after her, to squeeze the tender skin encasing the brittle bones of her arm, to stop her until she answered, until she really answered.

I picked up the box and carried it down to our garage, dumping it beside the fifty or so others. We'd amassed an amazing amount of stuff in six years together. Funny how possessions clung to you and gathered, like barnacles on a boat's bottom, secretly transforming the very shape and mass of your life, until you suddenly realized you'd become dangerously heavy, slightly uneven, and moving or turning or trying to stay afloat became difficult. Funny, too, how things would gain some strange sentimental value, a photograph from a family vacation, or an article of clothing worn for some milestone, like Jennifer's first step, or Leanne's first day in kindergarten, and you couldn't get rid of them. You were pinned under all this weight, or, at the very least, hobbled, and there you languished.

The girls seemed to understand that somehow we had become more sensitized to their every action, thought, or statement in the years that followed their arrival. That we winced at their emotional pain, or bruised in sympathy to their physical follies. And they could use it against us as well, brandishing a single question like a sharp object, forcing us to wonder what wounds our very existence inflicted upon them.

I found Carmel wrapping cups and dishes in old newspaper and packing them with towels in the most durable boxes we'd found at the recycling depot.

"Getting there," she said, pleased.

"This was a good place," I said, staring out the window.

"Sure was. The next one will be even better."

I couldn't look at her. Her satisfied smile, her light, thin fingers working toward something better, her instincts always moving toward building, never destroying.

"Lots of great memories here," she continued, "but the good thing is we take them all with us."

I took her words and twisted them in my head until they became something ugly.

"Really? So we carry our pasts with us wherever we go?"

She looked up, a fallen strand of hair curved across her eyes, an upside down question mark.

"So based on that, you're saying a person is made up of everything he's done and experienced in the past, rather than being an always changing entity, you know, someone who each day reinvents himself?"

"What's wrong?" she implored.

I wanted to strangle her. "How can you ask what's wrong? You know what's wrong. So answer my question, and remember this: If I'm not someone made up by the past, someone anchored by what I've said and done and what I feel inside, what does it say about the last six years? Everything good we've shared together – does it all mean nothing, like the rest of my past?"

"Stop it, Brady," she whispered. "Stop talking in riddles. Moving's stressful, but don't do this. Don't ruin everything."

"How can I ruin something that's already rotten in the middle?"

Tears slid down her face, and I felt surprised by how fragile she looked, a neglected cardboard cutout dampened by time and the elements. I sensed she desperately needed a few words of reassurance, but I needed the damn question answered. "So tell me, what's the answer?" I demanded.

She sobbed, and abruptly inhaled, a gasping sound constrained by her tears.

"Why are you doing this?"

"Okay, if you won't answer that question, how about this one? Why have you never let me say what happened that night? Never let me utter those words, like speaking them would somehow make them more real?"

"Don't...the kids could hear. They worship you."

"I want them to hear, because maybe they shouldn't worship me."

"Don't say that."

"You've always known what happened that night. You quickly sensed it, put it all together. You've made that no secret. You've known for seven years. So why don't you want me to say the words?"

"It's seven years I've given you to put this behind you," she said, her voice losing its softness. "Like you promised when you proposed to me, or have you forgotten?"

"Just let me say the words."

"What would it accomplish?"

"I need to."

"No."

I forced my lips together hard. "Yes."

"Don't you see, everyone makes mistakes, especially..." She stopped trying to reason with me and sat down at the kitchen table, the color drained from her face.

I took a seat across from her.

"Everything would have been different, you know, if he hadn't barged into the party, hadn't pressed so hard. The music was loud, lots of noise. Everyone was so drunk. Especially me. I was more than drunk, though. I was angry, with a jealous rage I'd felt building all night. Over Sarah. Over how I felt she was slipping away from me. I'd watch her dance with some guy, talk with her girlfriends about her future like I didn't exist, and I'd start to think, someone has to pay for this. Someone."

"Anyway, Sarah could have just told him to go home. To get lost. Instead they went across to the garage to talk, because he said he wasn't leaving until he'd restored order. Restored order. Those were his words, that stupid prick."

I caught my breath. Carmel buried her face in her hands. She wouldn't look at me.

"Me and Sam and Luke followed. Tom Opal was yelling at Sarah when we got there. Saying her dad would be disappointed when he heard about the party. Then when we walked in, and Luke started to get in his face, Opal said to Sarah, all the while staring at Luke, something like, 'He'd be most disappointed to see the types you're keeping company with.' I don't know what he expected. I guess he thought Luke wouldn't go after him. I don't know. He was angry – and ready for Luke. Luke threw a punch and Tom Opal dodged it and grabbed Luke like he weighed nothing and tossed him toward the freezer."

Carmel still hadn't looked up, and I wondered if she was trying to tune me out, to make the words go away.

"Then it happened. In a second, just like that. Before I even knew it. I grabbed Tom Opal from behind, caught him off guard, off balance, and threw him to the ground. I never saw him hit his head. I didn't realize he wasn't even struggling to his feet..."

Tears stung my eyes.

"Then I kicked him, twice. In the ribs. Hard. Even though he was all but dead, freakishly dead. But still dead."

Carmel was staring at me now, her eyes round and sad. I hadn't noticed her look up.

"Sarah. She was the one who stopped me. Pushed me aside. She tried to revive Tom Opal. Me and Sam and Luke, we looked on stunned. Couldn't believe he wasn't moving. I started to leave to call an ambulance but Sarah screamed for me to stop. She said he might be knocked out but she had a shitty feeling about it so we better get our stories straight, right now, just in case. Then she said something like, 'Our story is this. He fell.' She looked around. 'On the stairs, coming down here. Okay.' I couldn't get my eyes off his motionless body. Sarah yelled. 'Okay, Brady.' I nodded to her. So did Luke and Sam. She repeated, 'Fell on the stairs coming down here.' Finally she was gone, to call the ambulance."

Carmel and I sat in silence, the only sounds our breathing and the girls waging some mundane argument upstairs.

"Does it feel better to have told me?" Carmel asked, her words gentle, careful.

"I suppose." I wondered if she'd get up and come around the table to me. To embrace me like she would one of the kids when they were hurt.

"Good," she said. "I sincerely hope it feels better to get it off your chest, to indulge yourself in the past like that. But I don't want you to ever speak those words again. Ever. Do you understand?"

When I didn't answer immediately, she added this, each word more hostile than the one before: "Nothing's changed. You've still got a wife and two girls and a career and a new house waiting down the road. And I'm not going to let you screw it up in a moment of weakness."

She got up and finished wrapping a glass in newspaper, and placed it not-so-carefully in a box that was still half empty. She folded the box shut and taped its top and bottom with masking tape, before lifting it into her arms and disappearing into the garage.

23

I always expected Luke would break our code of silence, not necessarily intentionally, but in a machine-gun-like slip of the tongue into the ear of a doomed lover or a stranger at a bar. He'd fire the words out before he realized what he'd said, and then in a hysterical and futile struggle try to take them back. In the days before his drug trafficking conviction, I'd envisioned him cutting a deal with the police. Me for him. A killer in exchange for a petty drug trafficker. Whenever the phone rang I expected to pick it up and hear Detective Morrison inviting me down to the station, just for a friendly talk. Each time I saw a police car cruise close I waited for it to pull up beside me. I jumped whenever I heard a knock at the door, ate nervously, and lived in a troubled past and damned future, not the nearly beautiful present I'd built with Carmel and the kids.

To my knowledge, Luke had never slipped up, never cut a deal. The one who couldn't seemingly hold anything inside somehow had done so for the past eight years.

Sam was second on my list of those who would betray me. I suspected the truth would eventually spill out through a crack in his character, possibly in a drunken boast, or more likely in a deal to get him where he wanted to go, wherever that was. Maybe to sell a screenplay, if given the chance.

He, too, held it together, long enough to die with the secret.

And Sarah. I knew she'd take our pact to her grave, not because she was complicit, but because, well, she was Sarah.

What about me? I'd carried the secret for nearly eight years, too. Eight years. I never expected it to continue this long, this monstrous thing that refused to die, refused to starve and shrivel from neglect. Days, weeks, maybe even months. But not years. And not so many of them. If I'd confessed immediately after it happened, I could very well be out of jail, my debt paid, and I could be starting a new life.

Of course, Carmel loved to point this out. In the rare instances we'd talk about it, she would end the conversation with the same hushed words, always making the same point. That I would never have met her if I had confessed and gone straight to prison, and the girls would not have been born. And of course, what kind of life would an ex-con face? Carmel would lean in close and ask, "What would you be doing right this moment, assuming you were even out of prison? What?"

While she tried to engage my mind with that question, I focused on another. What would I do now if the truth did somehow leak out? How would I respond if the police accused me of killing Tom Opal?

In the months after Opal's death I had slowly embraced Sarah's philosophy that the whole thing had been nothing more than a freak accident. With that in mind, I had even selected the defense lawyer I'd hire if the police ever did catch on. I followed his career in the pages of *The Lookout*: He often lost but always put up a great fight, usually tarnishing the prosecution's case. All he had to do was conjure up enough reasonable doubt – just a small sliver, in other words – and I'd be exonerated, if I chose to contest the charges against me.

Of course I didn't realize at the time that I had already crammed myself into that sliver, into its dark and tight space. I'd been there so long that I would look at my wife and kids, their bright hope, their always expanding larger-than-life presence, and wonder if I even belonged in their world.

I would wonder, too, that if my guilt became public, whether Carmel could endure the shame, whether my daughters could survive without me until I returned from whatever sentence the court imposed. I would stare at the girls, sweet mouths revealing toothy gaps, thin fingers as breakable as match sticks, and their tender hearts that could be so easily trampled to pieces by others, if left exposed. I would stare at them, and feel trapped.

In our first few months of marriage, I'd sometimes study Carmel as she energetically performed an insignificant household task and I'd feel deeply fortunate she chose to spend her life with me. With me. A man she knew had committed one of the most horrendous crimes imaginable. What an amazing person, I would think, to give herself to someone so flawed. She'd sometimes catch me watching her, and, with her face consumed by a satisfied grin, ask, "What?" I would deploy a lustful smile, too embarrassed to share the deeper feeling surging through me.

As the months turned to years though, this ritual slowly changed. I still studied her – watched her move so comfortably through a house build upon lies – but if she noticed I would quickly lower my eyes before she could see that I was searching her for flaws, perhaps ones worse than my own. Horrible imperfections that could make someone fall in love with a person like me.

Over time, I also found myself slowly sickened by the way she embraced our wedding day as something it wasn't, as if she forgot why we hurried to the altar, as if she no longer recalled the promise she elicited from me before accepting my proposal. At least this is how I rationalized my behavior. So when Carmel plunked a small, crinkled poster down in front of me after dinner one night, I knew, as soon as I recognized what it was, that I needed to control the anger I felt rising.

"Tonight," I told her. "I planned to tell you tonight that Tom Marriott is retiring in two weeks and the guys are planning a big drunken party at Mullins Hall. Want to get a babysitter and go?"

She sat next to me at the table. "Of course I do. Specially with everything that's been going on – the stress of the move, you know – we both can use a break. I just wondered if you planned to tell me about it. I had to take that poster from the board outside Albertsons."

"It's just another wild booze up. I wasn't even sure you'd be interested."

"Brady, how can you say that? We met at such a dance, at the very same hall. The hall where we held our wedding reception."

"You forget," I told her, "I'm not allowed to hang on to the past. You've ordered me to only look forward."

She grimaced, and said, "Don't get like that, Brady. I just thought…it would be nice to get out, on a date, to dance and laugh. But if you're gonna…"

"I'll pick the tickets up tomorrow. You find a sitter."

She nodded. I stood and began clearing the dishes from the table as a satisfied smile stretched across her face.

One week before Tom's final shift after thirty-four years of service, Captain Boerne called me and Carson Kilgore aside, his face serious.

"You boys might as well know now, sooner than later, cause you'll find out anyway."

"What?" Carson asked, a tinge of alarm in his voice.

"It's about Tom's replacement." Boerne sighed like a B-Grade actor. "They're sending a woman to do a man's job."

"A woman," Carson laughed.

"Wipe that smile off your face, son. Because when your life's on the line one day, remember it could be her backing you up. With her scrawny arms and long fingernails prone to breaking."

"Have you seen her, you know, met her yet?" I asked.

Boerne gave me a stern look. "No, but I can just imagine. Anyway, the city's gonna send a crew in next week and build a wall in our sleeping quarters. The girl will get her own room while the three of us will discover we're suddenly in close quarters. You bastards snoring and farting all night. Bloody hell. I'm the captain. I should have my own room. Not the princess."

Boerne shook his head. "And one other thing you should know. The girl didn't necessarily earn her job like you two. Her father's a chief in some crappy little town, and that went a long way with our chief, who's got three boys. None of them wanted to be a firefighter. He has a soft spot for kids who want to follow in dad's footsteps, even if they're a girl."

When we returned to work four days after Tom's final shift, the new wall was in place, though still unpainted, and Sophia Russell sat in my seat at the kitchen table, sipping on black coffee brewed by the departing night shift.

We shook hands. I squeezed hers gently and she nearly crushed mine. She stood tall, almost six feet, meaning she looked down on Boerne from almost four inches.

"So where's home?" Carson Kilgore asked.

"Aberdeen."

"Aberdeen. You must know Kurt Cobain?" he joked.

"Everyone knew him. From time to time I used to party with him and Courtney, before he became a big star."

"Really?"

"No," she said.

"Got me," Carson shrugged.

"Who the hell is Curt Cobain?" Boerne demanded.

The rest of us looked at each other and grinned. He shook his head and stormed off muttering, "I'm gonna miss you, Tom."

Later, when we returned hot and sweaty from a small grass fire set by a motorist's cigarette, Sophia changed into shorts and a T-shirt, and I marveled at her smooth legs, lean and muscular, her quads rising from her bones like padding.

I found my eyes drawn to the space between her shoulder blades, wide and healthy, and to her well-defined upper arms and shoulders. She looked unstoppable, a fully-grown tomboy. She noticed me sizing her up, and returned a stare, long and direct, not harsh yet not soft, until I looked away absently.

"So," she said. "You trying to decide if I'm strong enough to do the job, or are you wondering if you'd sleep with me if given the chance?"

I dug deep into a box of outgrown clothes tucked in a corner of our garage and pulled out a thick envelope addressed to Brady Joseph, care of Fire hall #1, Deception Pass, Wash. With a knife from my tool kit I cut through the packaging and removed the DVD I'd purchased over the phone from a distributor in Phoenix. Dorm Nights was its title, starring, among others, Sarah Roberts, no assumed name, no craving for anonymity, no secrets, at least when it came to this.

I pulled the blinds in the family room, even though it faced our well-treed back yard. Then I went straight to the DVD player, inserted my movie and plunked myself down on the loveseat, right next to the end table that held the sandwich I'd assembled for lunch.

The DVD had sat in my locker at work for almost a week, not because I hadn't been itching to see it, but because Carmel usually chose to meet me at home for lunch on my days off work. Not today though – she planned to terrorize shoe stores with Brittany.

I anxiously hit the Play button on the remote, and for the next thirty or so minutes sat transfixed, twice turning up the volume, more than once almost leaving my seat for a closer look at Sarah, who removed her clothes before so much as uttering her first line.

I forgot about my sandwich, swept up in a confusing mix of emotions that started with a stark sadness but built alarmingly into arousal. My fingers grappled for the remote's rewind button at least four times, playing back Sarah's longest sex scene over and over. Then my hand reached for my pant zipper, only to create a little room, only for the sake of comfort I told myself.

But it didn't end there, and I hated myself as much for that as for not hearing the front door opening and footsteps making their way inside.

"You bringing a little entertainment home from the fire hall?"

I nearly jumped from my chair at the sound of Carmel's voice behind me, and began quickly stuffing myself back inside my zipper, though not nearly fast enough.

"Brittany cancelled, but don't let me disturb…" Her grin vanished as she entered the room and her eyes moved from the television set to my hands and the failing bulge I was still forcing awkwardly away.

I did my zipper back up and grappled for the remote while fumbling in my head for an explanation. I shut the television off, but Carmel yelled, "Wait."

She approached the TV and flicked it back to life while I watched helplessly.

She stared at the set and looked like she would cry. "Is that Sarah?" she demanded turning to me.

I shrugged.

She raised her hand, and it shook, just like her voice when she began to speak. "This is sick. It's so sick. You at home by yourself masturbating to one of your dead ex-girlfriend's pornos."

I stood lost before her, not even able to muster a simple apology.

"Why?" Carmel screamed.

"I don't know."

She moved to the DVD player and angrily punched the In/Out button, struggled to remove the DVD and flung it against the wall.

She faced me once more, still waiting for some kind of explanation, for some kind of answer I didn't have.

I turned, no longer able to meet her stare, and picked up the pieces of the broken DVD.

"She had a good heart," I told her, unsure of why.

"Tell me that this fucked up obsession of yours ends right here, right now."

I couldn't though. I just couldn't say yes and stomach another illusion. I shook my head.

"Get out," Carmel whispered.

I dumped my shattered DVD back into the envelope and walked past her out the door. I tore away on my motorcycle, realizing I had tucked the envelope into my jacket, next to my heart, like the broken movie remained something dear to me, some part of me. Contrived lives. Faked moans of satisfaction. Wooden, unreal promises whispered softly. So many damn lies. The movie wasn't just part of me. It was me.

❧

I waited around the corner from Carmel's office, and secretly watched her arrive back at work. I looked away for a moment when I saw her, fighting back tears, trying to look composed, in control. She was a worse actor than me.

Then I raced back home, unsure if self-destruction or self-preservation now called the shots. What a fine line.

I packed up several days' clothes, my toothbrush and deodorant, and stuffed them into two plastic bags. I called Monica, a friend with kids the same age as ours, and asked if she could pick the girls up from school and look after them until Carmel got home. At the door I hesitated, just for a moment, while I grasped my hands together, tightly, so they wouldn't flail out, so they wouldn't try to tell me there were other choices.

24

When I told Luke I wanted to crash with him, his reaction was instant, like always: "I'd almost think you were the one that fried his brain on drugs."

"Just for a few days," I told him. "Until I work some things out."

"You really looked at this place. It's a dump. The old man's dying, you know. Not exactly a lot of fun to be around, not that he ever was."

"That's okay."

"He pays the rent through his pension," Luke continued. "$550 a month. That's all. That's all this dump is worth. He pays for booze too. I scrounge up enough money to buy food. Pretty simple arrangement."

"Beats the hell out of the tent you were living in." And it did. For the first time in years, you could argue some aspect of Luke's life had actually improved, instead of slipping further into the abyss.

"I'll buy food too and whatever else is needed," I added. "And help clean."

"Suit yourself. But I think you're nuts. Tell Carmel sorry for whatever you did. Put your tail between your legs and go home."

"It's not that simple."

Lines formed on his forehead and only partially retreated. I stared at him, amazed my old high school buddy had wrinkles. "You're not telling yourself this is connected to…you know, to that?" he asked.

I shrugged.

"You are crazy," he muttered, staring off somewhere. "One crazy motherfucker."

Luke took me into his father's bedroom, a dim depository of sadness barely big enough for the double bed and badly chipped dresser. The stale smell of sweat and vomit nearly triggered my gag reflex.

"Hey, old man. You remember Brady. My friend from school. He's going to stay with us for a few days. He's not getting along with his wife."

Luke's father didn't look at me – his eyes stared straight ahead, like he was deep in thought. "You know how to make a Bloody Mary?" he asked.

"I think so," I told him.

He nodded, almost to himself.

That night I phoned home.

"Where are you, Brady?" Carmel asked, in a tone revealing nothing.

"You told me to get out," I told her.

"And then return home when we'd both cooled down. But you took some clothes, your toothbrush," she said.

"Yes."

I heard her take a deep breath, like she was trying to calm herself. "Okay," she finally replied, neutrally.

Neither of us spoke, each one waiting for the other to concede something.

Finally she blinked.

"I forgive you, Brady. I realize you've been through a lot, and I understand, sort of," she whispered, her business-like words belied by a hollowness. "So please come home."

"I can't."

"The girls are sick with worry. What do I tell them? What do I tell our friends?"

"I'll tell the girls."

"Tell them what?"

I paused. "I don't know."

"Why are you doing this, Brady? Why?"

"I don't know."

I could almost see her tears. "What, Brady?" she said, her voice starting to break. "What do you want me to do? Tell me."

"I don't know," I repeated. "Why am I expected to have all the answers?"

I listened for her response, afraid to speak, and was startled to eventually hear a small voice.

"Where are you, Daddy?" Jennifer asked

"Not far away. I'll visit you soon, don't worry."

"I'm too frightened to sleep. We need you here."

I sighed. "Did your Mom ask you to tell me that?"

"Yes."

She worked on me for a full five minutes – why aren't you coming home, are you mad at us, don't you love us, how can you do this to us, what do we tell our friends at school, does grandma know – then Leanne did the same. After I finally said goodnight and snapped my cell phone shut, I collapsed on a ratty old chair in the living room. Luke immediately handed me a drink – a rum and Coke – and I downed it like water.

"You mix the next round," he said, nodding to the various booze bottles, mixes and glasses scattered bar-like on a stained coffee table in the center of the room. "And make that old prick a Bloody Mary while you're up."

I did, my efforts only eliciting a sharp grunt from Luke's dad. "You put any vodka in here," he barked as I retreated back to the living room.

"He likes 'em strong," Luke said when I handed him his drink. "I should have told you that."

"I don't even know your dad's name, you know."

Luke shrugged. "Call him whatever you want. I just call him 'old man.'"

The three of us drank, terribly alone together, until the sound of restless snoring replaced the shouts for another round from Mr. Newell's bedroom and the tortured syntax of Luke's drunken musings wound down to the occasional grunt. In time, Luke got up and pissed, then mumbled something incomprehensible as he staggered to his room and collapsed on his bed, without turning off the light or closing the door behind him.

That first night I naively thought I witnessed some special celebration, a drunken toast to the arrival of another lost soul. Soon I discovered what I should have instantly surmised: The two of them drank themselves to sleep every night.

The following night I learned something even more disturbing: Each night Luke did his level best to kill the old man.

In the coming days I found the time I needed to think, only I didn't much like the questions that kept popping into my head, to say nothing of the answers. So I eventually sought ways to curb my mind.

I studied my temporary home, a place collapsing upon a rotting and decaying inside.

"Those front stairs are a hazard," I told Luke. "The woods all rotted, and someone's going to fall through and break a leg."

"The landlord doesn't give a shit," Luke said. "Won't spend a penny."

So I phoned him – Oscar Miller, the man whose company managed dozens of homes and apartment buildings owned by faceless overseas or out-of-state land owners – and told him we had some health and safety problems. I'd come in contact with him several times over various fire code violations, and found he usually responded to problems, as long as you stayed on him.

"Don't bust my balls," he told me. "The owner won't spend a penny on that place. He's waiting for the city to rezone it as commercial property."

"That's fine," I said. "But he shouldn't be renting it out if he's not going to make it inhabitable."

"Careful what you wish for. Your friend will be out on the street then," Miller said.

"He's lived there before. But if you're renting this place out, and you are, there are health and safety considerations."

"God, Brady. You know how uncomfortable I am arguing with someone who works side by side with the fire inspector. You're putting me in an awkward spot."

"So what do you say?"

"Two months' rent," he told me. "That's all I can afford to re-invest back in this place, or else the owner really will let the house go vacant."

I purchased the wood and cement that afternoon, and got immediately reimbursed by Miller, then went to work. Luke helped me tear down the old stairs and haul them to the dump, then lay the concrete footings for the new ones, using the limited construction knowledge I'd gleaned doing the occasional paid job for a moonlighting firefighter at Hall #1.

"Tomorrow we'll finish up," I told Luke that night as we sucked back cold beer.

"If you say so," he said, trying to conceal a hint of satisfaction in what we accomplished.

"So he's happy here, instead of in a hospital?" I asked, nodding at his father's room.

"No," he said. "But happier. A nurse comes to see him once a week, shakes her head, nags the pair of us, then leaves. He gets personal care once a week – a sponge bath. Thank God someone's trying to clean him. It stinks enough in here."

"So what's wrong with him?"

Luke shrugged. "Where do I begin? He's exhausted, so much so he can't get out of bed. He's lost weight, got no appetite, but still explodes with diarrhea, sometimes bloody. Throws up almost every day too. Bruises when you try to lift him. His feet and hands are swollen like a fat man's. Confused about many things, but not whether there's booze in his glass. Hair's falling out, always itching like he's got fleas. Turning yellow too."

"So what's the cause," I pressed.

Luke began pouring two drinks, one for him, one for the old man. "Want one?" he asked.

"I'll stick with beer," I told him.

He grunted.

"So what is it; the cause?"

Luke stirred his father's Bloody Mary."

"He's got cirrhosis."

"What's the treatment?" I asked, staring at the drink in his hand.

Luke stood up and gazed absently into the corner of this room awash in the odor of spilled booze.

"He's too far gone, you know, though there's one thing he can do to prolong his life a little. Stop drinking. Let the liver repair itself best it can. The more he drinks, the more scar tissue from the disease replaces the healthy tissue.

Or that's what those fuckers tell me over and over again. The scar tissue blocks the flow of blood and stops his liver from working. Simple. The more he drinks, the closer he gets to death. Doctors won't even consider him for a liver transplant, cause they know he drinks like a fish. So they're just waiting for him to lapse into a coma or die from an infection."

"So, shouldn't you, shouldn't you be…"

"Trying to get him to stop drinking?"

"Yes."

"Hell, no. He's a drunk, Brady."

"Well, there's programs, there's…"

"And there's already way too much scar tissue. You know what I'm saying?"

I did know.

"There's no hope for him, Brady. He knew that, and he knew he could only find one person who wouldn't mind helping kill him. So here we are."

The next day we built the stairs, starting slowly and finishing in a whirl of fast saw strokes and confident hammer strikes. The day after we stained them.

Every hour or so Luke would disappear into the house and check on the old man, sometimes mixing another drink, or emptying the bedpan with a string of obscenities or sometimes just yelling at him to shut the fuck up and go to sleep.

Once, we heard a thump, and both raced inside to find his father in a heap on the floor, struggling to lift himself up.

"Help me get him, Brady," Luke asked.

"Wait. We may want to change the sheets first," I said pointing at the brown streaks on the yellow sheets. "I think he had an accident."

"Christ," Luke said. "Look at that. Not the first time though. Stay there old man."

Luke quietly stripped the bed while I threw open the bedroom window. "You know, the only good thing about this shithole is that it has a washer and dryer. Cause this happens a lot."

He looked down at his dad, "A lot, old man. You got a bed pan, so use the fucken thing."

Luke started the washer and brought fresh sheets and quickly remade the bed. Then he stripped off his father's underwear and cleaned him up with baby wipes.

We lifted his father carefully. Luke stared at him for a moment, watching him wince in pain under the covers. He kicked aside the empty ice cream bucket beside the bed and pulled a bottle of lotion from the bedside nightstand. He dumped a gob of the cream into his hand and pulled the sheets back to expose his father's swollen and cracked hands.

"I'll be back out there in a few minutes," Luke said to me, his hands now going to work, fast as ever, but gently.

Two hours later, Luke gazed at what we'd done, inhaling the fresh scent of cedar and paint, and shook his head. I too viewed the stairs in near-amazement. With a Bloody Mary in my newly-callused hand, drops of dark brown stain splashed across the old shorts and T-shirt I'd picked up from home earlier that day.

"Still on the fast-track to becoming a hell-hole," Luke said nodding at the house.

"Yep, but it's a slightly more bearable hell-hole."

He grinned, and I drank quickly, right to the chipped glass's bottom, the alcohol going straight to my head, fomenting feelings, stirring thoughts. In more than one hundred hours apart from my family, I'd determined this: I could build a perfectly adequate set of wooden stairs, but I couldn't figure how to tell my family they were better off without me.

❧

Carmel had talked of Tom Marriott's retirement party in such romantic terms, and I knew she envisioned us dancing again out onto Mullins Hall's back deck like the night we met. Alone on an endless expanse of floor, under a night sky bright with promise, the two of us gliding smoothly and unfettered on the uneven decking.

But, I wondered, doesn't she know our dances haven't been like that for some time? That we've danced back inside, into the lights. That the floor's crowded, the air heavy, the eyes of everyone in the room upon us. Our every move watched, judged. That it's like a dance competition only worse, maybe more like those dance marathons decades ago, when the contestants knew they were being examined for the smallest sign they were fading – an arm not raised high enough, a foot dragging ever so slightly, a dullness in the eyes, a weakness in the touch. We couldn't dance back outside, out of the spotlight, because that door had been closed long ago, and we couldn't hide from the stares, so we moved self-consciously, clinging to the appearance of being perfectly in synch and in control.

Hours before Marriott's party, I readied three cans of clam chowder soup and one loaf of sourdough bread for a light fire hall dinner. "Don't make too much," Boerne had ordered. "We all need lots of room in our bellies for beer tonight."

As I struggled with the antiquated can opener, Sophia worked next to me, slicing the bread and carefully spreading it with a mixture of butter and garlic.

The two of us didn't talk as much as one would expect, given the long hours we spent together, rushing headlong into potentially-dangerous-but-usually-mundane calls, killing time with card games, eating side-by-side and sleeping about fifteen feet apart, albeit separated by a partition.

"Not a great night for Marriott's goodbye bash," she said. "I've never seen a storm like this in the summer. Gusts of up to sixty miles per hour."

I nodded. "You see those rain clouds. I get the feeling when it starts, it won't stop until Mother Nature's seriously drenched everything."

She grinned. "Just make it all the more cozy inside that little hall. What's it called?"

"Mullins."

"Mullins," she repeated. "You bringing your wife?" she asked suddenly.

The question startled me. "Yes. Yes, I am."

Sophia nodded.

"But you're still separated?"

"Not exactly separated. We just need some time apart."

She nodded again, and began assembling four glasses of ice water.

"I'm sure it will all work out," she said.

I forced a small smile. "You don't sound very convincing when you say that."

Sophia placed her hands on the table and leaned across toward me, her shoulder muscles bulging slightly beneath her shirt. "Well, what I meant was it will work out, one way or another."

I didn't really take in what she'd said. Instead I ventured, "You ever wonder if this is what we're meant to do?"

She looked at me puzzled.

"You know, all of this. Us working as firefighters. Living in this town."

"No," she said. "I always planned on being a firefighter. This is exactly what I expected I'd be doing."

"But how would you know?" I continued. "How would

you know if your life was all wrong? If maybe the thing that would make you the happiest, bring you the biggest sense of fulfillment, the biggest sense of your destiny, was really something else. Maybe it's something you pass by every day, or something just up a road you've never traveled. I dunno, like being a tour guide in Arizona, or maybe a doctor in some war-torn African hell hole."

"Guess you don't know," she said.

"Did you ever think about how one small change in your life could affect everything else? You know, it could lead you to meeting someone and kissing that person and spending the rest of your life with her. How..."

Sophia leaned forward and grabbed my chin with her cold hand. "I know exactly what you mean," she said. She kissed my mouth firmly. Her lips were thin, her weakest feature, but seemed to carry the same punch as her heavy hands.

We both heard Carson's heavy footsteps coming up the stairs from the garage, and she stepped back, eyes shining anxiously at me, before I could tell her she misunderstood, that she didn't know at all what I was talking about.

When my shift ended I showered and changed at the fire hall, and stepped out into the heaviest August rain I could recall. The brown lawns and shriveling trees soaked some of it up, but much of the water tore down gutters and into the storm sewers, where it was swept down to the ocean.

Carmel and a girlfriend had dropped off the car for me earlier in the day, while our crew was out tending to a traffic accident precipitated by a power outage that knocked the signals out at the busiest intersection in town. I suspect Carmel saw the weather forecast and the dark clouds massing over the San Juans, and didn't want me riding my motorcycle home in a heavy rainstorm. Who could blame her? She didn't want her special night, our reunion, to be spoiled by something as simple as the weather.

I swung by Luke's house, and saw him nursing a drink in the sanctuary of the newly-built front stairs, the wind howling, the rain pounding, and Luke just barely under cover, for once untouched by the fury around him. I ran across the front lawn and sat down beside him.

"You sure you don't want to come tonight?" I asked.

"Naaa," Luke said, watching the tall evergreen across the street sway from side to side. "Don't feel much like partying these days."

"You could stop by for an hour or so. Say hi to Carmel."

"If you see me, you see me. But probably not."

"Sure. Suit yourself."

I stood, and he stopped me. "Sometimes I think about that day the three of us drove up to the garbage dump in Sedro Woolley," he said.

I laughed. "Hard to forget. Nearly being some black bear's dinner."

He grinned. "Boy you guys were pissed at me."

"Yeah," I said, "we were."

"I couldn't quite understand it at the time, you know, why you were so upset. Never figured one of those bears could even catch a person, and if it did, never figured it would do more than smack you a couple of times, like you guys deserved for tormenting him." He paused to stare out at the rain. "Couldn't really see the danger."

I nodded, unsure of what to say.

"You're gonna be late," he said finally.

As I ran across the grass, Luke shouted, "Hey. By the way, I was talking to the old man. We don't really want to see your sorry ass 'round here no more."

❧

In the car, I listened to a news station that told of the storm's impact: the power was out in part of Deception Pass and Anacortes; the ferries to the San Juans and Port Townsend had stopped sailing; and there was some flooding in low-lying areas near La Conner. A Korean freighter so rocked by heavy winds had spilled dozens of containers and one crew member had gone overboard in the Strait of Juan de Fuca. Coast Guard crews had been dispatched from Anacortes and Bellingham, as well as a Canadian crew from Victoria on Vancouver Island.

I nearly shivered when I thought about a man alone, tossed about in the big waves, fighting to hang on until someone found him, his screams for help unheard, maybe hopeless.

At the door to my house I paused, like I should knock, like I no longer possessed the right to walk right in. I turned the door knob and pushed, and they were on top of me, two tiny masses of arms and legs and short bursts of breath, grabbing, climbing, giggling.

I lifted them both up, and smiled at Carmel, who stood in the hall looking like she'd waited for this moment all her life.

"Hi," she said sweetly as I carried the girls past her into the living room, where they remained attached to my lap as I sat on the sofa's soft center.

They told me how much they missed me, clinging tightly like they feared I'd get up and leave any moment. They had me trapped once again, under the weight of their sixty-pound bodies, the pressure of their tiny hands, the stare of their clear eyes. I had fought so hard to get away, maybe for their own good, but now questioned my decision; all of my decisions.

"The sitter will be here in twenty minutes," Carmel told them, "so re-acquaint yourselves, girls."

I laughed. "They already seem to be doing just that."

They told me about their week in sharp bursts of cryptic insight, followed by wide-eyed questions about how I'd spent my time. They felt just right in my arms.

I waited for Jennifer, the least cuddly of the supposedly-identical pair, to move away, but she stayed in my arms until a knock at the door signaled the arrival of their teenaged baby-sitter.

"Are you staying tonight, Daddy?" Leanne asked, at the precise moment Carmel wandered into the living room.

"I don't think so," I said sadly.

"Why not?"

I pulled her head to my chest so I wouldn't have to see her face – or she mine – and softly stroked her hair. Carmel slipped out of the room quietly.

Once we'd finally said goodnight to the girls and were outside the front door, Carmel took my hand and smiled. "I was really hoping we could walk there tonight, but I see the rain hasn't let up."

"It seems to be getting worse," I told her.

When we were two blocks from home, she asked, "So how have you been?"

"Okay," I told her.

"I've missed you."

I sighed, then conceded, "I've missed you too."

She nodded, and it occurred to me that she hung on my every word, my every gesture, like I controlled how she felt.

Just before we reached the hall, I pulled over, and said, "We don't have to go here tonight. We can go somewhere else, alone…"

She thought about this for a moment, and then countered,

"So many of our friends are going to be there tonight. Your mom and Amanda too. And there's old Tom's goodbye. So let's hang out there for awhile, then maybe sneak away early."

"Okay," I said, realizing she shared none of my uneasiness about our marriage or the public perception of it.

Inside, people packed every corner of the hall, mingling, talking. The west-facing doors to the patio were shut tight, to keep the wind from blowing drinks over, to keep the driving rain from soaking the floor. Only a few dozen hardy souls huddled outside, smoking in a small covered area.

Amanda and my mom spotted us almost immediately, their faces filling with delight at the sight of Carmel clinging to my arm.

"You two made it," Mom yelled, squeezing past me to hug Carmel, her gradual acceptance of my wife not lost on me. "And you look especially stunning."

"Thanks," Carmel smiled. Mom was right. It was like Carmel summoned forth all of her internal beauty. Part of me couldn't keep my eyes off her. Another part couldn't look at her.

Mom moved back to me, waving an empty cup through the air as she spoke. "So, I guess you've finally come to your senses."

"Don't start, Mom."

"I'm not starting anything, just stating facts."

"You're drunk. So why not zip it up."

Carmel gave my arm a short squeeze. I turned to her. "Don't worry, Carmel. When she's drinking she's got no feelings. I can't offend her."

"She's had one drink, Brady," Amanda said.

"Sure. And the sun's about to come out."

The four of us stood in silence for a moment, everyone scared to utter the next word.

Then my mother laughed. "God, I've missed you, Brady, you miserable prick."

I had to smile, just for a moment, just long enough to see a look of relief wash over Carmel.

"There's Brittany," Carmel said suddenly. "Do you mind, Kathy, we're gonna say hi."

"Go," Mom smiled.

When we reached Brittany, she had been joined by Cynthia and Chantel. They hugged Carmel, and they smiled at me while voicing the usual polite comments. I looked away, unnerved by the way Carmel had taken Sarah's spot in this tight circle of friends.

While Carmel talked, I drifted, as far away as she'd allow, popping in and out of various nearby conversations, gleaning a tumble of news: Increasing fear about the fate of the missing sailor, word that Tom Marriott's roast would begin in forty-five minutes and, finally, that no dancing, thank God, would take place until after the final speech, when maybe the storm had abated and people could move outside. If all went well, Carmel would allow us to leave before the first song, before she pulled me onto the dance floor and bestowed upon me a look of absolute love; before she held her breath while she waited for me to return the same expression, something resembling the warmth I'd shown the night we met. I didn't dread such a moment because I doubted my feelings for her – far from it, my love for her was unquestionable – but because I couldn't understand how anyone could convey such an emotion when they were consumed by fear and panic?

Ten minutes before the speeches began, Carmel joined Brittany in a foray to the restroom and I made my break.

"I need some air," I told her, slipping out into the cool night, relieved to be alone, off display.

I drank my beer oblivious to a handful of smokers, my only thought centering on how they managed to even light their cigarettes in such a vicious wind.

"Hi, Brady," Sophia said suddenly.

I nodded to her cautiously.

She ambled up, harmlessly it seemed, then ran her one hand across my belly while the other stroked my face. She leaned in far too close, until her lips tickled my ear, and whispered, "Maybe once this place starts to clear we can get a dance together."

I searched for a response, but then she moved away, her arm outstretched, her fingers clinging one last second to my cheek, hungry, unable to let go.

I looked down at my drink as she faded away, and glanced up at the hall to see Carmel standing at the base of the stairs, her eyes frozen on me, her body deflated, as if somehow shrunken by the powerful storm that rolled overhead, shaking everything below.

She closed her eyes, maybe trying to conceal her emotions, maybe wondering if I'd betrayed her twice in the same week, though this time at least with someone alive. I waited for her to turn and run.

Instead she stepped slowly forward, weaving around the smokers. When she drew close I could see the tears building in her eyes, the raw hurt elicited by what she thought she had seen, what she thought she knew.

She took my hand, firmly, without saying a word, and led me out onto the rain-soaked ground, into the downpour and the wet sting of the wind, toward the darkness and the angry sea beyond. I didn't yelp out an explanation, didn't protest how we'd soon be drenched. I followed, strangely taken in by her leadership.

We reached the end of the grassy back expanse, where the property fell sharply to a road below, then to a group of houses, and finally to the ocean itself. Carmel stopped in an inch of water under a small maple tree, one that offered no shelter from the storm, which whipped unimpeded off the ocean, pushing rain sideways at our bodies.

Before she even spoke, her dress was soaked, her mascara running down her water-swept face. She placed her hands on my shoulders and squinted through the storm.

"Are you sleeping with her?" she cried over the howl of the wind, her words so brittle they almost broke apart in the heavy air. "Are you having an affair?"

"No."

"Do you have feelings for her?"

"I don't think so," I told her. "But, God Carmel…I just don't know what to say anymore. About anything."

"Is it me? Do you not…" She stopped and leaned forward, placing her hands around my back, and I felt sobs rising from inside her ribs and breasts, a heaving that almost broke my heart.

I forced my hands up and placed them carefully around Carmel's back, holding her, not in a protective embrace, but in one I feared that in some way threatened her. I was a doomed man clinging desperately to someone else. I was perfectly aware that if I didn't let go soon I would drag her down with me.

25

When we reached the car I quickly started the engine, cranked up the heat and pulled away from Mullins Hall, our departure sudden. We didn't speak at first, the only sounds being Carmel's labored breathing and the small heater churning out not-quite-warm air. So much rain water dripped across her face from her soaked hair that I couldn't tell if tears still flowed; I just assumed they did.

I knew I had to tell her why I had chosen to remain estranged from her and the kids, even if the effect would add more weight to our strained relationship.

I reached over and felt her dress, dripping-wet. She shivered, then pulled herself close to me, resting her head on my damp shoulder.

"I feel like I've been swimming with my clothes on," I said.

She ran her hand across my shirt and forced a small smile. "We almost were."

We drove the dark residential streets above the ocean, the wind and rain lashing the car. I pulled off into a small tree-surrounded parking area that gave way to a short trail to the beach. I cut the headlights, but left the engine and heater running.

Carmel looked out into the blackness, then reached down and began pulling off her dress, its damp fabric clinging to her skin. When she finally held it crumpled in her hands, she whispered, "Watch." She twisted it violently with her hands, and we saw, in the light from the dashboard a stream of water dripping onto the floor.

We laughed quietly, almost sadly, and she smoothed and folded the dress the best she could, and lay it on the dashboard where it flapped, rising and falling against the heater vent.

I dimmed the dashboard lights, unbuttoned my shirt and peeled it off my back and arms. Carmel wrung it out, placing it next to her dress over another heat vent. Next I slid off my shoes, socks and pants, and she tucked them down by a vent at our feet.

She pulled me close, and we stayed that way, our bodies slowly growing warm as we stared off into the storm, afraid to speak, terrified to venture away from what comfort we had found.

In time we noticed lights a mile or two out in the ocean.

"You see that, right?" Carmel asked.

"Yes. Search and rescue helicopters I bet. A pair of them."

We watched them moving back and forth, in some strange pattern we couldn't quite detect. Carmel turned to me and said, "Let's go down to the beach and see what's happening."

"It's the sailor," I suggested. "They must be searching for him. Guess they figure the west wind and tide would have taken him along the strait to here."

"Let's go see."

"I'm just getting warm. Besides, we can see from here."

"C'mon, Brady."

"You are persistent," I said, smiling, reaching for my shirt.

"No. Our clothes will just get soaked. Grab your keys and we'll go like this, in our underwear."

I looked at her, wondering if she was kidding.

"C'mon. It's pitch black. Besides, there's lots of places to hide if we see someone, though I doubt anyone else is crazy enough to be out here."

She followed me out my door into the whipping wind and rain, and we tip-toed briskly to the sandy trail we'd taken so many times when we first started dating. Sand and leaves blasted our bodies, forcing us to cover our eyes as we moved through the darkness. The waves pounded and roared as we approached, spewing wet foam and spray into the air, licking our bodies with sea salt.

Carmel held my arm tightly. "You ever seen waves so big?" she yelled.

"Not here."

We huddled together, fighting to keep our balance. Between waves we heard the undulating sound of the helicopters, their search lights trained on the rising and falling ocean.

Carmel tugged my arm then pointed. "What's that? There."

My eyes strained in the darkness at an object that washed ashore near our feet. "It looks like a shoe."

I snatched up the shoe and brought it back to her.

"You don't think…?" she asked.

"That it comes from the sailor. No. It looks pretty small, like a woman's running shoe. And new."

Carmel looked around for a source of light, and finding none placed the shoe in front of her face. "Brand-new Nike. Looks like a woman's size six or seven."

"Wonder if it came from the container ship?" I offered.

We both scanned the beach, and began working our way along the water's edge. We hadn't gone one hundred feet before spotting two more shoes along the high-tide mark. I grabbed them, then saw two more.

"They all look new," I said dumping them at Carmel's feet. "They must be from the ship."

Carmel had already slipped one onto her foot. "Size seven and a half. Perfect fit. We just need to find the mate."

I laughed. "It's probably in Bellingham by now."

We ventured another short distance along the beach, and this time Carmel helped me scoop up another half-dozen shoes. We laughed and shivered, our eyes stinging, our hands and feet growing numb, and I motioned toward the thick brush at the beach's edge.

The storm had intensified, the pelting rain striking wickedly with the force of pieces of hail. We bundled the shoes in our arms and ran, thrashing carelessly across the driftwood, before collapsing into the meager shelter offered by squat trees and a tangle of driftwood.

Carmel pored over the pile of shoes, fumbling with her hands, forcing the occasional one onto her foot, until she gasped, "I don't believe it. I've got a pair that fits."

I studied the two shoes, side-by-side, and laughed. "They don't exactly match; slightly different design on each one. They're different models."

She shrugged, and returned them to her feet. "I'll take 'em anyway," she said, and I knew she would.

She kissed me on the lips, hard and breathless, and we looked out at the storm's chaos, like it was magic. "Have you ever seen anything so beautiful?"

I could only think about the lost sailor, who for all we knew bobbed in the surf somewhere near shore, fighting for his life. But who was I to stop her from embracing the beauty she'd inadvertently found, from savoring a rare carefree moment with me?

All night I had waited for her to ask why I stayed away,

to turn her gaze back to our struggling, mundane lives. Now I could see she didn't care what kept me away. She just wanted me back.

We huddled once more, the rain easing off but the wind picking up, until I couldn't stand her shaking. "Time to go back, before you get pneumonia."

"This is kind of cool."

"How about freezing cold. Besides, I should call the coast guard and tell them part of the ship's cargo is washing ashore here. Might help them in their search."

"Always the practical one," she said.

We left the shoes, except for the two mismatched ones she now wore, and hustled back onto the beach, the wind blasting us with sand. We struggled to keep our backs to the wind, running sideways, stumbling, overshooting the trail and finally doubling back. The storm lashed at us relentlessly as we made our way in the dark. Sand attached itself to our backs, caked itself in our hair, chased us into the parking lot and, after we'd piled inside and slammed the car's door, threw itself against the car's windows, chrome and light gray metal. I swore it searched the car's seams for a way in.

Our chests rapidly rose and fell, and we sprawled together on the front seat, waiting for our hearts to slow. I took my cell phone from the glove compartment, and got the 911 operator to patch me through to the coast guard. "They know about the cargo," I told Carmel after hanging up. "First reports came from Whidbey Island. They've got volunteer search and rescue teams checking the beaches for the sailor. Gonna redirect some of them up here."

"Good," she said, leaning back into me.

I squeezed her in my arms: "Better get you home. Bet you'd love a hot bath."

She sat up at these words, and turned toward me, her face hopeful. "I would, but only with you."

I knew what I had to say, for her sake, for the kids' sake. I started to speak, to snuff out her naïve optimism, but I found myself hesitating. I turned away from her and stared out my side window at the wind-swept darkness, where I wouldn't have to see the heartbreak that would instantly sweep across her face when I finally opened my damn mouth, or more likely, when she finally figured out my answer. My sudden silence, I knew, had already reinforced the thoughts that had hounded her the past few days: That everything we shared was slipping through her fingers. Another night apart would turn into another week, then a month. Then we'd start surviving without one another, and then…

"Brady," she said, her voice tiny, like she could draw no air.

"Brady." Again, as though I were choking her.

My words spilled out before I realized I had spoken them, before I could curse my weakness, my propensity for the most expedient choice. "Yes I'm coming home."

26

We awoke to the girls piling onto our bed, laughing and giggling like it was Christmas Day. They bounced over us, all elbows and knees, squishing themselves between us under the sheets. Leanne peaked out, "Are you home to stay, Daddy?' she asked.

"I hope so," I told her, and they laughed and screamed, and Carmel grinned, sleepy-eyed, her face pillow-creased, beautiful.

All so perfectly wrong, the three of them seemingly unaware of the fact that the one thing they missed so badly threatened them the most.

I stretched out my hands, revealing both love and loss, and hugged them all.

The girls squirmed loose from the covers, and as I watched them wrestle together I wondered if they'd be like their mom, able to survive anything, or if they would simply, obliviously, inherit their dad's curse.

My fear of endangering another generation did come to life, and quickly, though not in a way I had imagined. I hated myself for not seeing it develop.

This time the call came, late one afternoon, not from

dispatch, but from Captain Boerne to my house, four days after my reunion with my family, three days after a dead Korean sailor washed up on one of the San Juan islands.

"Joseph," he said briskly, though not without compassion. "That friend of yours, Luke Newell. You've heard, right?"

"Heard what?"

"Shit. Okay. Listen. He was hit by a car. Hit and run. The night before last. Up on Eighth Street. At least that's what they suspect happened, because he was found on the side of the road unconscious. Still is unconscious, but the doctors think he's beginning to come round. His brain's swollen."

"He's in the hospital?"

"Yes. Glad I called you. Bill Williams from C-shift mentioned it to me when I ran into him at the hardware store. Your friend didn't have his wallet, and was only finally identified today. Find that hard to believe; thought the whole town knew him."

In a small corner in intensive care, Luke lay in bed, his forehead stitched and black, his mouth forcing out small, disturbing groans.

"He's not suffering horribly; not as bad as it looks," a nurse told me. "He's struggling to pull himself from the coma. Like someone trying to wake from sleep."

"Will he recover? Fully?"

She looked at him carefully while composing her answer. "I suspect he'll be okay. But you can never completely tell. Head injuries are funny things, you know."

I stayed with Luke for twenty minutes or so, until the same nurse came by with a clipboard tucked under her thick arm and said she needed my help. "Can you help me fill out the blanks in his chart? We had him on file, but I wonder about his current address."

It hit me suddenly. "His address?" I said. "He looks after his father, who is very sick and has probably been alone now for a couple of days."

The nurse's forehead wrinkled. "Does anyone else check on him, the father?"

"Once a week," I said, already moving toward the stairs. "But I better go and see."

"How sick is he?"

"Pretty sick. He's bed-ridden. I don't think he has much time left."

"Give me the address. I'll get an ambulance dispatched."

I beat the ambulance to Luke's by nearly five minutes. The front door was unlocked. I called out to Mr. Newell as I walked back to the stale-smelling bedroom. The bed sat stained and empty, and I rushed to the far side, where his father lay in a heap on the floor in a puddle of urine, sheets knotted around his legs. His body jerked when I touched his arm, and I almost jumped. He tried to lift his head, but was too weak. He strained his eyes in recognition, and closed them. I half expected him to whisper, "Where's my Bloody Mary?"

Later that night, in another corner of the intensive care ward, about the same time Luke fully regained consciousness, his dad died of complications from dehydration.

The doctor examined Luke, and allowed me to spend some time attempting to re-orient him, trying to straighten out the twisted timeline of his life leading up to the hit-and-run.

We went over events from the last few weeks, especially my short stay at his house. In time he remembered walking to the store for cigarettes, turning up onto Eighth Street. That was all.

"What about the old man?" he finally asked.

I sighed. "I got there as soon as I heard. But he was dehydrated. He died an hour ago."

Luke narrowed his eyes for a moment, and asked. "The driver. Caught him yet?"

"No. But I hear Morrison's on the case."

Luke smiled, and whispered, "Good." Then he fell asleep.

Luke spent most of the next day sleeping and performing mobility tests for the doctors, who were worried about a lingering numbness in his lower body. I stayed out of the way, but waited to bump into Detective Morrison somewhere in my travels. He had a way of tracking you down and engaging in seemingly inconsequential conversations, which were always so much more. I felt a tinge of disappointment when I hadn't encountered him by dinner time. That night, while the girls played in the back yard, I cut the lawn and Carmel pulled weeds, the four of us wringing the last few pleasant evening hours from a slowly fading summer.

When Morrison pulled up about seven in his unmarked police sedan, I nearly laughed. He got out and didn't hesitate to shake my hand.

We leaned against his car, and he said, "Sorry about your friend."

"He seems to be bouncing back."

Morrison puckered his lips slightly. "More or less. Takes time to tell."

"Any suspects yet?"

The detective reached into his car and pulled out an orange and a pocketknife. "You mind if I have a snack. I haven't eaten all day and I'm dying of thirst."

"Go ahead. You want a glass of water, or a beer, or something?"

"Beer sounds good, but I'll have to take a rain check. My wife's expecting me soon for dinner."

"Sure."

"I am making some good progress in the investigation," he said as he opened his knife and began peeling the orange effortlessly, in long narrow strips.

I watched him, fascinated by the care he took with such a simple task.

"Guess you've never seen someone peel an orange like this," he laughed. "Learned it from my dad. He'd always peel me oranges, with a knife, when I was little. Not necessarily the fastest way to do it, but you know, just one of those things I picked up from him. He's sort of responsible as well for me becoming a cop. He always said the secret to happiness is to find something you like doing, and find someone crazy enough to pay you for doing it. I always liked problem solving, so I became a cop, a detective. So you see, I got more than my good looks from my father."

We laughed, and I realized he'd aged noticeably in the eight years since I'd first met him. He was nearly bald, except for a little hair above his ears and around the back of his head. His forehead was creased by frowns and his arms had thinned out and seemed to be almost devoid of muscles.

"Nice home you've got," he said, waving at Carmel who had moved around front to tackle the bed alongside the garage. She came over and I introduced them.

She returned to her weeding and Morrison studied her absently.

"Definitely a better place to talk than that deserted clearing in the park where we met once at midnight," Morrison remarked.

Or Sarah's parents' bedroom right after Tom Opal's accident, I thought. "Haven't been in that clearing for years. I'd be curious to see if the picnic table's still there."

Morrison laughed. "It's not. I phoned the parks department shortly after our meeting and had them reclaim it. Took them a few weeks to actually find it though."

"You're not kidding about that, are you?"

"No, I'm not."

"I didn't think so."

I would never admit this to Luke – who spat confrontationally on the ground each time he bumped into Morrison – but I admired the detective. He always knew what was right, and worked tirelessly toward that goal, never wavering, never second-guessing. Always at peace with himself. There was so much to like about him, even though he was the one man who could take away everything I had, assuming he could figure it out or someone helped him put it all together.

"So you're close to an arrest you said?" I asked.

He sighed. "Hope so. I got it figured out. Mulling it over with the prosecutor. Even got some physical evidence, but as you know, there's a huge difference between thinking you got it solved and getting that person convicted."

"You ever arrest an innocent man?" I asked.

"No. Not that I know of. It's a danger of this profession, always. It's bad enough sending a guilty man to jail. Hate to send an innocent one."

"The suspect in Luke's hit-and-run. Is it someone I know?"

"Can't tell you that, but I know it will be of interest to you. Call me tomorrow afternoon. I may have something for you then."

He waved goodbye, walking around to the car's driver side.

Was that it? Was this why Morrison had come by the house? To tell me he had an interesting lead. As usual, he was planting a seed.

"Is the arrest going to...?" I paused, searching for the right words. "Will the person..."

He seemed to know what I was trying to ask.

"This whole incident will touch more than the Newell family, what's left of it. Others will feel pain too when I make the arrest. I've always said, Brady, when someone does something horrible to someone else, at least two people get hurt. Always."

I didn't have to phone Morrison the next day to find out who he'd charged. Shortly after ten, Carmel called from her office, a hotbed of town gossip.

"Did you hear, Brady?" she said. "They charged someone in Luke's hit-and-run. It's Mrs. Opal's son. I think his name is Josh."

I felt pieces inside my head shifting, like they were clumsily falling in place, something they should have done days ago. "Oh, God. That's terrible."

"No," Carmel said. "What's terrible is what he did to Luke, mowing him down and leaving him for dead."

From two stories in *The Lookout* I learned that Josh Opal had turned sixteen three months ago and had earned his driver's license only six weeks earlier. Both stories suggested he turned himself in one day after first being questioned by police and was promptly charged with vehicular assault and hit-and-run, as well as dangerous driving – as a juvenile, not an adult.

"He should be charged with attempted murder," Carmel said one night as we got ready for bed. "And as an adult, where he'd get more serious jail time."

"Give the kid a break," I told her.

"Sure," she said brushing her teeth vigorously. "I'll give him the same break he gave Luke."

❧

Two days later, I found myself in Mount Vernon inside the county's juvenile court, a cramped wood-frame building that protruded from the historic brick courthouse. Luke remained in hospital, struggling through severe back pain and persistent numbness in his legs. I had expected him to ask me to attend the hearing. He didn't, but I went anyway.

Morrison had told me they worked the juvenile cases each day in alphabetical order, all scheduled at 9 a.m. Sixteen names sat above J. Opal on the paper tacked outside the courtroom's door, so I took a seat in the corner of the hallway outside and watched the stream of passing lawyers, parents and teens, trying to guess what crime brought them there.

When Eunice Opal passed by quickly with her son and lawyer, I assumed she didn't see me, and if she did I wondered if she'd still recognize me. Josh, athletic body pressed into a grey suit, shot an anxious look at his mother as they approached the court's wide wooden door, then went inside without speaking a word.

I glanced at my watch. It would be five minutes before proceedings began and God knows how long before they got to Opal. I wished I'd noticed which direction Eunice Opal turned when she entered the court. I'd make sure I went the other way.

I didn't see her leave the court a few minutes later, and her presence didn't register until she lowered herself into the chair next to me, carefully, like her body was one large wound that ached with movement and touch.

"Fuck," I whispered to myself.

She drew a deep breath and looked straight ahead, then suddenly asked, almost to no one in particular, "You here to support your friend, Luke Newell?" Each word she spoke came slowly, each a sentence unto itself.

"Yes," I said.

"Good," she said, and remained focused on the wall across from us. "I'm here to support my son, Josh."

I nodded uncomfortably.

"We've arranged a plea bargain with the prosecutor. You'll hear about it soon. Josh will plead guilty to reckless driving and get a suspended sentence. He'll lose his driver's license for one year, pay a $500 fine and spend one year on probation. If he meets those conditions, he won't get a criminal record."

"Oh," I said, turning the numbers over in my mind.

"I know it sounds like he's getting off easy, but he's really not…" Finally, she turned to me, and I got my closest look ever into her blue eyes, each one stained with a splash of gold. "Josh has a good heart, and he'll have a difficult time living with what he did. Mr. Newell's head injury. And what happened to Mr. Newell's father. Living with that will be Josh's real punishment."

Her eyes swelled, and she looked down.

"I know it will," I said, my mind still stumbling over her use of the word 'mister.'

Mrs. Opal looked back at me, like she was sizing up the sincerity of my answer.

We sat in silence for a moment, the only sound in the small room the departing shuffling of those who had faced justice.

"You have two girls, right?" Mrs. Opal asked, squeezing her purse like it gave her strength.

"Yes," I said.

"I've kept track of you. Since it happened. Clippings from the paper. The city's announcement that you'd been hired as a firefighter. The wedding announcement your mom took out. Your daughters' birth announcement. I've followed your friends too. Sarah Roberts' obituary. Then all the articles around Sam Simpson's murder, and Mr. Roberts' conviction. I've tried to piece it all together, how it's all connected, if it's all connected, all these clippings, little pieces of paper, all representing lives spun off in this direction or that, for some reason I may or may not understand."

Now her words were spiraling out, thoughts she couldn't suppress taking life. "I've seen Luke Newell around town lots, and was sure he'd freeze when he was living in that orange tent. Swore I felt sorry for him, especially when people would say he was getting what he deserved. Swore I felt sorry for all your friends and their families, especially Mrs. Roberts, who knows what it's like to lose a husband, because even though he's not dead, nothing will be the same when he comes back, and Mrs. Roberts never saw this coming, never saw any of this coming, just like me."

I looked at my watch, perhaps trying to suggest to her it was time to return to court. But I didn't move, and it suddenly came to me that this may be why I was really here, not to support Luke, or some pretend shit like that. Maybe I had hoped to meet Eunice Opal, and perhaps discover that she was a bitch, someone that any reasonable person would hate. Then I could take some comfort in knowing that maybe it was justice that crappy things happen to crappy people.

"But what I'm getting at, Brady, well…" she paused, unsure, "it's why I asked you about your kids, because I suspect you understand the one thing that worries me the most."

"No."

"It's what happens next. With Luke Newell. Does he seek revenge? Does he go after my son? Or my daughter, who's two years younger? Tom used to say, 'Never get involved with people who have nothing to lose.' But, you know, we are all involved, like it or not, and your friend has very little to lose, and I'm worried for my family, about losing even more."

I wanted to erase her fears. To tell her Luke wouldn't do anything. But who knew.

"Luke doesn't always listen to me," I told her.

"I believe that," she said. "If you can…"

"I'll talk to him," I said.

"Thanks. And I'll keep talking to my son too. So nothing like this happens again. But he scares me, Josh does, what he might do. It's like Jenga."

I didn't want to ask. "Jenga?"

"Yes. J-E-N-G-A. It's a game you play with wooden blocks."

I shrugged, confused.

"You start with a tall tower built out of blocks. Three per floor, laid down at right angles. Two people play, each one taking turns removing a block and placing it on top. The tower gets taller and taller, but more unstable each turn, as you remove blocks from the base and place them on top. Sometimes an entire floor is made of one block in the center. The game goes on until one person finally topples the tower and loses."

I nodded cautiously. "I think I've played that."

"My son was born strong," she continued. "But with, well, you know, he's become more and more unbalanced with rage. He's wobbling, and I can't help him, because each time he sees Mr. Newell somewhere in town, spots his face on a street downtown or something, it's like he's getting transformed into something less stable. And I can only watch."

She leaned forward, awkwardly squaring her body to mine. "You should know this, Brady. My son is a lot like me. He doesn't hate Luke Newell for what he was accused of doing to Tom. He hates him for what he didn't do afterwards.

If it really was an accident, I'm sorry, I really am, for being so terribly wrong. But I don't believe it was an accident, and I hate Luke Newell for being able to live with what he did."

She slid down in her chair, just enough for me to notice, and I hoped to God that meant she was finished, because I hadn't expected this.

We sat in silence, with me realizing that like that day at the cemetery, she'd trapped me once more. Finally her lawyer reappeared and took her into the courtroom, where the judge released Josh Opal back into the fishbowl that was our town.

27

I had hoped our lives would slip back into some form of normality, even with Josh Opal back on the streets and Luke soon to be released from hospital. Morrison told me he had met with Josh twice, in a mentor role, and would continue doing so as needed. I occasionally talked with Luke, espousing restraint and forgiveness while he blurted out things like, "That fucker's gonna pay." In spite of Luke's usual stream of hostility, I felt a trace of optimism that he had at least heard my message, maybe even grasped why I said it.

What did I know.

Carmel helped Luke write an obituary for his father. It took her two hours to dig out enough content to write four short sentences. Then she told Luke she'd arrange a funeral service. He laughed, and told her not to bother. His father died without friends and family, other than him. Then Carmel asked Luke if he knew whether his father had wanted to be buried or cremated.

"What's cheaper," Luke asked.

"Cremation, I think," Carmel told him.

"Yeah, that's what he wanted," Luke replied.

On the afternoon Carmel dropped the obituary off at

the newspaper, Leanne and Jennifer both pressed me about Luke's accident, wanting to know how a driver could be so careless. I decided they should know the truth – they would hear it sooner or later anyway – and told them Josh Opal had hit Luke on purpose.

"Why, why," they asked, "why would someone hurt Luke on purpose?"

I reminded them of our earlier conversations – one we'd revisited various times over the years. That some people didn't believe Tom Opal fell. They carried around bitterness toward the four people who were present, especially Luke, who they figured had hurt him.

"Will Josh Opal come after you, Daddy," they asked. "Will he come after us?"

The questions poured forth, and I found myself unable to guarantee our safety. Although I felt I should keep my mouth shut, I spoke, partly I suppose to assuage my own guilt. I qualified everything in the subtlest of ways. We should be okay. It's unlikely Josh Opal or anyone else would try to hurt us. Odds were nothing would happen. I rambled on. When Carmel arrived home they ran to her at the door, telling her we could all be in danger. She looked at me, wide-eyed and in disbelief. Why had I done this?

That night a series of haunting screams from Leanne and Jennifer's room interrupted my sleep. First one voice – which one I couldn't tell – followed by the other. By the time Carmel and I reached their room, Jennifer was standing on her bed, still screaming, her hands moving her head from side to side as if to shake something unwanted out. Leanne shrieked from her bed, her eyes locked in horror on her sister.

"What is it?" Carmel screamed, herself caught in the hysteria.

"My window," Jennifer yelped. "A man's face in my window."

I pulled the curtains aside and saw nothing but the view: the living room's shake roof immediately below, the streetlight illuminating the bench that looked out over the channel from across the street, and in the distance, the darkness of treetops and the ocean beyond.

"I don't see anything," I told them, somewhat annoyed, "but I'll go out and look."

I crept out in my boxers, no shirt, and tip-toed down the driveway. Not a sound except the occasional car on the highway in the distance. I circled the house, my feet soaked by the dew, and saw nothing out of place, both gates and all windows securely shut. I even took our step-ladder out of the shed and checked the roof underneath the window for signs of an intruder. The roof was slippery from the dew, though it was still possible someone had pulled himself up from the top of the side gate. I had tried it once myself, and it was possible – when the roof was dry.

Back inside, all three girls anxiously awaited my pronouncement.

"Did you catch him, Daddy?" Jennifer asked from her spot on Carmel's knee, right next to Leanne.

I sat on her bed. "There was no one out there, but I think I know what happened."

"What?" she asked.

"It could be one of three things," I said, trying to sound convincing. "A bad dream, your own reflection on the window, or the tricky glare of the streetlight on the window pane. But I don't think there was anyone on the roof."

"I saw him," she said, her small voice steeped in annoyance. "Why don't you believe me?"

For the remainder of the night, I slept in Jennifer's bed, waking often as she thrashed about. It took four nights of taking turns sleeping with the girls before Carmel and I both returned to our own room, and even that first night apart from them was interrupted by a series of visits from the two of them over the first couple of hours.

The morning after what became known as "that night," Carmel asked me over a groggy breakfast, before the kids awoke, "Do you sometimes notice something, I dunno, different about Jennifer?"

"What, like she sees faces at her window in the middle of the night?"

"No, not that. You know, that she's not exactly the same as her sister?"

I shrugged. "They're twins, not the same person."

"I know, but, well, she's a lot more serious, intense, than her sister. She takes things harder. She seems a little darker about things, don't you think?"

"I hadn't noticed."

She leaned forward. "C'mon. I've noticed it more and more. She can kind of get wrapped up in things, maybe fixate on something a little, yet hold it all inside, kinda like an adult would."

I shook my head again and shrugged.

Carmel stared at me, almost like she thought I was joking, like I'd soon laugh out loud and say something like, "Yeah, I know what you mean." Only I wouldn't give her that, so I looked away like someone too distracted to detect a single nuance in my own child's behavior, or like someone who fails to understand that sometimes you dislike your own child, want to shake and scream at her, because she so perfectly exhibits all the qualities you hate about yourself. Jennifer showed a propensity to brood over the smallest failure and she had an unnerving ability to fear what's not there, even though I'd done everything I could to show her otherwise, to teach her to learn from her mistakes.

"Anyway," Carmel finally said, "do you think someone could have been at Jennifer's window? Someone like Josh Opal?"

I had lain awake for hours tossing that around for myself.

"I don't think so," I told her.

"But you're not sure."

"I'm sure of very little," I told her.

"What does he look like?" she asked.

"Athletic kid. About six feet, muscular. Blonde hair like his mom. Rectangular face. Why?"

"Just good to know."

As she cleared her plate from the table, she leaned close. "I was so pissed at you yesterday for telling the girls they could be in danger. But now I'm glad you did. They should know there are people out there who may mean them harm. They should know not to trust everyone."

A week or so later I could have easily pointed Josh Opal out to Carmel, although I was glad she wasn't with me. I'd left an ATM machine outside my bank when we passed each other on the street. I tried to pretend I didn't recognize him, but he stopped before me and I paused as he tried to give me a menacing smirk, one that said something like, I got away with running over your friend, and maybe more. He didn't play a convincing role as a dangerous ex-con or a rogue high school student; his sad eyes belied his forced swagger.

When the kids were in bed that night, Carmel asked me, "Does Josh Opal have short hair or long hair?"

"What…why?"

"I'm curious."

"Short. Like his whole head was cut with a number two or three clipper."

"Oh," she nodded. "I've seen this guy who I think is him around a little. Specially when I'm running the girls around after school. He sometimes looks at me and doesn't say anything."

"Do you think it's him?"

"I don't know. Might not even be the same person each time."

I thought for a moment, and said, "I'll talk to Morrison and get his picture. Then we'll know."

"It could be paranoia, so hold off. Unless I see him again."

The next four days I worked the night shift, something that now frightened the twins and, though she wouldn't admit it, Carmel too. Before I left for work the first night, Carmel showed me what she'd stashed underneath our bed. The girls' T-ball bat. "Just in case," she said, businesslike. "And, by the way, if I hear anything suspicious outside, I'm calling you first, then 911. I like your response time better than the cops."

The first night everyone slept peacefully, something Carmel attributed to the girls getting plenty of fresh air at soccer practice hours before.

So the next night, when Carmel had the choice of getting a ride home from a friend's house or walking home through Whiteside Park with the girls, she chose to walk.

"Why," Leanne protested. "There's coyotes in the park, you know. It's been all over the TV news."

"The walk will do us some good," Carmel said, not admitting she'd seen the television and newspaper reports that speculated about what had gone awry in the food-chain to force dozens of coyotes into the area around Deception Pass, with ground zero being Whiteside Park.

It had rained again, and the maze of gravel trails through the kidney-shaped park were riddled with puddles and the trees were heavy and dripping with water. They waved at an older woman jogging as they entered the park in fading daylight, and soon found a comfortable rhythm.

"See girls. Nothing to be afraid of. Remember, the coyotes are scared of people, though these particular ones are a little curious."

Minutes later an undulating howl broke the evening's serenity, and a thin-trunked cedar tree a hundred feet or so away began to rock back and forth.

Both girls gasped, grabbing one of Carmel's arms. Carmel studied the tree and listened again to the howl, then grew angry. "That's not very funny at all," she screamed, then muttered, "Asshole."

"Don't yell at them, Mom, or they'll get mad," Jennifer implored.

"It's not a coyote, sweetie. It's just a person, playing a practical joke. No coyote could move a tree like that, and no coyote sounds like that."

She pulled the girls forward along the trail, struggling to move as they clung to her hips and legs. "Let's run," Leanne pleaded. "'Cause it sure sounds like a coyote."

"We're not running," Carmel said sternly. "We won't give whoever it is the satisfaction."

The howling continued, and Carmel knew the park well enough to estimate the two-legged coyote traveled along a parallel trail and they would soon all emerge in a large clearing that held a picnic area, small duck pond and playground. She would straighten out whoever had so carelessly scared the girls.

When they emerged into the clearing, Carmel felt a tinge of disappointment and anxiousness that it was empty of other park-goers, who were likely driven home by the earlier rain and failing light. That didn't stop her from swinging around to the parallel trail to lay into whomever she found. But it was empty.

"Told you it was coyotes," Jennifer said. "Now will you run?"

"It's not a coyote," she told the girls. "Just a big human chicken. C'mon."

They selected the main trail out of the park over two smaller ones on either side, and continued on. Carmel took a final glance back into the empty clearing. They walked in silence, the girls' breathing shallow, until the howl cut through the dusk again, and the girls screamed. Carmel swore, more than annoyed, now alarmed by the assailant's persistence.

"Don't panic girls. It's just someone trying to be scary. Like on Halloween."

Up ahead the brush moved as someone crashed through, howling and grunting. Carmel stopped, and for the first time did think about running, only back into the clearing and out the other side. Instead she picked up a large rock and tucked it partly up her sleeve.

The girls stood frozen, and Carmel tugged at their coats.

"It's in front of us," Jennifer whispered.

"Don't worry," Carmel cajoled. "It's one person being silly."

Whoever it was made short forays closer to their trail, close enough to reveal a lone person in dark pants and a dark hooded sweatshirt, pulled over his head.

The girls screamed but Carmel pushed on, anger and fear wrestling in her chest for control. When they were less than one hundred yards from where the trail spilled out onto a busy residential street, the hooded figure dashed across their trail about fifty feet away from them, this time screaming like a lunatic. He stopped, waved a knife across his throat in a cutting motion and disappeared back into the woods, but not completely out of sight. He kept himself between them and the park exit.

Even without clearly seeing his face, Carmel knew who it was, and for the first time was terrified, really terrified. She grabbed the girls, and said, "Okay. I want you to run back through the park to Mrs. Hutchins house, and have her call the police. You understand."

"What about you?" Jennifer cried.

"Just go. I'll make sure he doesn't follow. Run as fast as you can and stay together."

They nodded, but held on tighter, their small fingers and sharp nails digging into Carmel's flesh. She tore their hands loose and gave them a push, and finally they took each other's hand and ran back into the park, not looking back.

At the trail opening about fifty feet ahead, Carmel saw the hooded person emerge from the trees and drop himself onto a large boulder designed to keep cars from driving down the path. His head was down like he was studying the ground, maybe searching for something. She approached him, rock in hand, watching for the slightest movement, watching for any sign of the knife, waiting for him to leap up and attack. Suddenly she was out of the darkness of the trees and on the sidewalk. He still didn't move, and she felt the urge to run across the street to one of the houses to get help.

Only she stopped and approached the stooped figure, the rock clutched in her hand, prepared to strike at his head with all her force, more than ready to spill his blood and brains.

"Why?" she snarled. "Why?"

Josh Opal raised his head slowly, revealing tears streaming down his young face. He sobbed gently. Then he cried, "I can't even hate you properly."

Morrison met us at our house. He wore a wrinkled suit, and I could imagine him hurriedly changing back out of his jeans or sweatpants and kissing his wife goodbye for the second time that day.

He sat down with Carmel and the girls, and said, "Tell me what happened."

After hearing the story, he pulled six photos of six different people from an envelope and showed them to Carmel one at a time. She identified Josh Opal.

"You sure?" he asked.

Carmel nodded. "He even spoke to me, before finally getting up and running off."

"And you're sure what he brandished was a knife?" Morrison asked.

"We all saw the knife," Jennifer said.

Later we sent the girls out of the room, and Morrison took a deep breath. Did he still love his job tonight, I wondered.

Carmel sighed, and said, "We don't want to press charges."

Morrison looked surprised. "Sorry, Mrs. Joseph, but it's not up to you. The police press charges, the prosecutor approves the charges. In this case, there's little choice. Without the knife you could write it off as mischief, harassment. But with the knife a much more serious threat is implied. I suspect at the very least his parole for the incident with Mr. Newell will be revoked."

She sighed. "He's so lost."

Carmel knew lost. She had lived with me for more than eight years.

Jennifer approached when Morrison went to leave.

"Are you the man who arrested my Daddy a long time ago?" she asked.

Morrison gave off a startled smile. He turned to me then back to Jennifer.

"Yes," he said softly.

"My Daddy wouldn't hurt anyone, you know. He doesn't believe in hitting. We don't even get spankings when we're really, really bad."

He smiled at her. “Yes, I know. Your dad was in the room at the time, but we never suspected that he hurt anyone.”

She flashed me a look of uncertainty, as if asking if she could continue, before turning back to Morrison and saying, “Well, he didn’t.”

Morrison asked Josh and Eunice Opal to meet him at the police station. He shared a few details with me about their meeting. Josh Opal quickly admitted to several disturbing weeks of trailing Carmel and the girls after school, at first from a distance, then slowly revealing himself, the whole thing culminating in the bizarre incident in the park. He denied ever climbing on the roof outside the girls’ window. I think Morrison believed him.

Eunice Opal cried as her son recounted his fixation with my family, how this twisted need for revenge consumed so much of his time after school. Like all parents, I’m sure she felt shaken by his capacity to do something other than good.

I suspect Morrison wished he could have simply warned Josh Opal. He made it clear to him that he was never to see our family again. That if he happened upon us on the street, he was to turn and run, as fast as he could. If he somehow found himself driving by the girls’ school at 3 p.m. or our house at anytime of the day, he better be prepared to sacrifice his freedom.

Josh Opal returned to jail that night, and appeared before a judge the next morning, not to face new charges – the state prosecutor hadn’t yet decided what to do – but to revisit whether he should remain free while awaiting trial for running down Luke. With a sad assortment of people watching silently, the judge threatened to revoke Josh’s bail, but in the end did not. Instead he issued a stern warning and a restraining order meant to keep Josh Opal from my family.

We filed out of the courtroom, Morrison signaling to

me that he planned to talk to Josh yet again. Before I reached my car, Eunice Opal appeared, her body covered in a dark blue skirt and brilliant white blouse, her hair neatly styled back, her moist lips forcing a small smile, her right hand oddly placed across her stomach as if to hold in her insides.

I heard her say, "Brady," and wanted to run from the sight of her before the pain on her face became further etched in my memory.

I stopped, and she caught her breath and offered this: "He won't bother your family ever again, Brady. Please tell your wife and girls. Tell them he's sorry. That he stopped there at the end of the trail to turn himself in. To end this. You won't see him again, except by accident. Will you tell them? Those sweet girls should never have to experience fear."

"Yes," I told her, creeping away.

And I did, and Carmel, more than the girls, took comfort from her words.

Then Luke was released from hospital, struggling to stand or walk, popping pain killers like breath mints, laughing when the nurse reminded him how much physiotherapy he still needed, how much some state-funded counseling would help him.

That night, someone threw a large rock through the Opal family's front window.

Morrison, playing an unfamiliar role of peacekeeper, visited Luke the next morning at his house.

"Let it pass," he warned.

"Don't know what you're talking about," Luke told him, then spat on the floor before he realized he was in his own living room.

Late that night, someone set Josh Opal's car on fire, and the flames spread up the carport and nearly engulfed the house, sending Eunice, Josh and Kerry running for their lives. Huddled in blankets, the three of them watched from the street as firefighters put the blaze out before everything was lost.

Morrison and another cop arrived at Luke's house within the hour. He wasn't home, and I'm sure it crossed their minds that they had beaten him there, as he didn't own a car and could barely walk. Morrison waited an hour – time enough to call the local gas stations and discover that someone fitting Luke's description had come in and filled a jerry can. The detective pinned a note to Luke's door ordering Luke to contact him, and left, though not before deploying two plainclothes officers to watch the house from an unmarked car up the street.

Morrison told me all this the next morning. What I didn't know was that he'd phoned Luke's parole officer and asked him to detain Luke if he showed up the following day for his monthly appointment. Nor did I know where Luke was and how desperate he'd become.

28

I spent much of the next day unsuccessfully scouting out Luke's old haunts, while Carmel vainly worked the phones in between patients, checking with Morrison and a street worker who helped the homeless in both Deception Pass and Anacortes.

Luke had simply vanished.

The Opals had vanished too, abandoning their house to insurance adjusters and contractors who would need weeks to repair the fire, smoke and water damage. Of course, even if the Opals could move back in tonight, they wouldn't, not with Luke on the loose.

"I wonder where he is?" Carmel said, the base of her spine resting against the fridge. She glanced at her watch. "Hey, you better get to work."

"I know," I said, lingering. "If you hear from him, call. I'll keep the cell phone nearby."

As I grabbed my keys off the table, I noticed a piece of paper with a large heart carefully drawn in the center in red crayon. In behind it lay another two dozen or so sheets full of hearts of slightly varying shapes and sizes.

"What's all this?" I asked.

"Oh, the girls are studying the human body at school,

and they started talking about the heart and how to draw a perfect one. They were quite horrified to hear a person's heart isn't shaped like...well, like a heart. That a heart is really a symbol of love, not a true representation of what's ticking away in your body. Anyway, in the end it didn't stop them from their pursuit of the perfect heart. It's the top one there. Drawn by Leanne."

I looked at it one more time, but only saw the flaws: how it was slightly less than symmetrical; the small overlap where the two sides joined; even the way it tilted to the right.

An hour into our shift, just as the sun dipped beyond the trees south of town and the damp air filled the void, we were called to a fire in an abandoned house.

"Your friend still missing?" Sophia asked me, above the whine of the siren.

I nodded.

"I hear they scrambled out a back window. The family in the house. Could have been deadly."

"Could have, but wasn't," I told her.

Two blocks from our destination, I asked Captain Boerne for the address. When he answered, everything clicked into place. Seconds later we stopped in front of an abandoned two-storey home, the one where Luke spent much of his school-aged years. I had wasted the day searching the places he chose to go; it should have dawned on me to check the ones he chose not to revisit.

An elderly man with hunched shoulders and an Eastern European accent greeted us on the street. "Smoke's pouring out of the basement. The back door's been forced open. S'posed to be an empty house. No one's lived here for years."

Boerne kicked in two basement windows – the only two not boarded up – and watched billows of grey smoke tumble out. The four of us entered the house through the back door, and I went straight to the front door and pried it open – it had been nailed shut – trying to create a breeze to dissipate the smoke. Flashlight in hand, I led the way to the basement, down the rickety stairs I'd often climbed as a kid, to where a pile of newspapers smoldered on the floor. Carson blasted away with a fire extinguisher, and we retreated upstairs, quickly searched the house for occupants and went outside to let the smoke clear.

"Looks like maybe a squatter got a little careless," Boerne said. "Might have started the fire for some warmth last night."

More like tried to burn the place down this morning, I thought. Someone good at setting fires, at using flames to black out everything.

Boerne lit a cigarette. "Five minutes, guys. Let's give it five before we go back in."

He returned to the truck, and I slipped back inside the house without my airpack, the air stinging my lungs, the empty rooms echoing with neglect. I moved down a dim hallway into Luke's old room.

The windows had been boarded shut, and my flashlight cut an eerie swath through the darkness, falling onto the corner where Luke had kept his bed. I cringed when I saw the crude black felt tip drawing, still ominously present, a stain that would exist until the walls crashed down. The poorly-printed words, "This Way Out of Hell," and an arrow pointing to a large black circle that had been colored in to resemble the mouth of a tunnel.

The words looked like they'd been printed by a right-handed person using his left hand, and in fact they had. I knew the circumstances behind them and could almost feel the pain behind each letter. If my colleagues had been in the room right then, they would have looked at the drawing and surmised some teenager drew it sometime after the house became abandoned, not during the years this dump was inhabited. They would see it as a lame joke, not as a hopeless scream never intended to be noticed, one precipitated by shattered bone and spilled blood.

I suspect I was the only one who saw Luke's desperation on that day near the end of our Grade 8 school year – the year he brought a Big Gulp cup full of gasoline to a fight. In the days that followed, we had aimlessly stalked our town together.

On that night, like he often did, Luke shoplifted his dinner from a local market, tucking some junk food under his jacket before paying for a soda to avoid suspicion. He ate the package of mini-donuts quickly, and threw the box and its crumbs into the back seat of an open Mustang convertible. At the town's public tennis courts, he plucked seven glass beer bottles from a garbage can and lobbed them one by one over the fence, listening with only faint interest to the popping sound they made as they shattered on the empty courts. At the Little League diamond, he pulled a small can of orange spray paint from his pocket and scrawled the words, Get a Life Fuckers, on the fence near centerfield. On Kensington Avenue, he grabbed newly-emptied garbage cans from in front of homes and placed them in the middle of the busy road, creating an obstacle course for traffic. He tried to pick a fight with a group of older teens, who lost their nerve and walked away.

Almost everything he did that day elicited both fear and pathos from me. Everything but his final act – shoplifting a crowbar from the local hardware store. That act evoked only fear.

"What's that for?" I asked him as we walked home, on a route that would take us past his house first.

"Rodent control," he said, his pre-Ritalin eyes lit up.

"What rodents?"

"What rodents do you think, stupid?"

As we neared his house, I quickly considered – and rejected – inviting Luke over to my place. Instead I said, "Maybe you shouldn't take that crowbar inside."

"Maybe I should bust it over your head," he said.

"Someone could get hurt."

"No shit."

A block from his house he whipped the crowbar from his jacket and slammed it down on a tin mailbox, caving it in. I jumped. He looked at me and grinned, not losing his step.

In that last block to his house, Luke's swagger slowly evaporated. He tucked the crowbar back inside his jacket. His mouth twitched rapidly. At his front sidewalk, he hesitated. Just for a second. His hand rose in a waving motion and he walked slowly up the stairs, without looking back. He froze at the door, just for a second, just long enough for me to notice.

Once inside, he pulled open the small curtain by the door and peered out at me, his pale face suddenly transformed into an incongruous mask, one with calm, hollow eyes and a terrified mouth that seemed to stifle a scream. The curtain closed and he was gone.

What happened next was conveyed to me in dribs and drabs over the following two years. A tiny piece of the story here, another there, some overlapping, separated by gaps he left for me to fill in. After that Luke never mentioned any of it again.

"Where you been, you little shit?" Paul snarled from the kitchen, drink in hand. "We've been getting hungry. Nearly 7 o'clock."

"Then make yourself some dinner," Luke told him, noticing the vodka bottle on the kitchen table, the old man sitting across from Paul a half-dozen or so glasses into it.

"I don't cook crap all day at the base to come home and make dinner for you two lazy fucks," Paul shot back. "Neither of you works, and I'm not even convinced you go to school."

"Later, losers," Luke said leaving the kitchen, slamming his bedroom door shut, knowing it would not be that easy.

The door flew open less than a minute later – it didn't have a lock – and Luke's dad leaned against the frame, and slurred: "Your stepbrother wants to see you. In the kitchen."

"Surprised you can stand old man."

His father staggered forward and grabbed Luke's arm, pulled him toward the door, his physical strength always surprising. Luke grappled for the crowbar, and stopped, thinking it wouldn't be right to strike an obedient old dog.

"I can walk, old man," Luke hollered in the hallway, then marched ahead of his father into the kitchen, where Paul waited.

"You think you can walk away from me," Paul said, before nodding approval at Luke's dad and pouring him another drink. "I'm the only one in this house who earns a fucken penny, and no one will treat me like that. I buy the food we eat, the booze the old man needs. All of it."

"Got anything new to say?" Luke asked.

Paul nodded again at the old man, who clumsily reached over and tried to slap Luke's face. Luke drew back and the old man missed, knocking his own drink flying with his arm. Luke stood up.

I don't imagine a look of regret even had time to wash over Luke's face before he eased the crowbar into his fingers and slammed it down hard at Paul's head. Paul raised his arm quickly across his face and his hand caught the brunt of the blow, which broke two fingers cleanly and tore tendon and flesh.

Even with his damaged hand, Paul grabbed the crowbar

and threw Luke to the ground. Then his stepbrother was on him.

Luke cowered on the floor as feet and fists pummeled him from above. He started to get up but felt a jolt, a surge of electricity through his body, before his nerves and muscles failed and he collapsed back down, face-first onto the kitchen floor. He had no idea how many times Paul zapped him with his hand-held stun gun? Did he see the spark, smell 50,000 volts of electricity in the air? I never pressed him for these details.

What I did know was that when Paul finished he dragged Luke back to his room and dumped him inside. "I'll shoot you if you try to leave," he told him calmly, "and you know I've got a .45, not just a stun gun."

Luke lay on a scratched hardwood floor, his nose bleeding, his ribs bruised, his collar-bone broken, his shoulder separated, and his back seared with reddish-purple welts that would remain for months, though you could argue the marks never faded.

Luke glanced at the window nailed shut by Paul a month or so earlier after Luke had snuck out one night. He thought about breaking it and fleeing, only he pictured Paul shooting him in the back as he ran across the uncut grass.

So he lay crying for a half-hour or so, listening to Paul cursing and swearing, pouring more drinks, opening another bottle while the old man mumbled in compliance. Luke heard the sound of a bag of potato chips being opened, like at a party, before he felt strong enough to crawl to his feet. His right arm hung at his side unresponsively. He swore revenge, death. He pulled the bed out from the wall with his good arm, his left arm, and got his thickest and blackest felt-tip pen. Trembling and faint from pain, he wrote the five words on the moldy light blue background, and drew the arrow and tunnel. He tried to will it to life, wishing he could crawl into the wall and disappear forever.

Luke heard Paul leave early the next morning, and suspected he planned to see a doctor at the naval air force base to get his hand repaired. He heard his father rise, then piss, before coming down the hallway, where his footsteps paused by Luke's door. Luke waited for the door to open, then heard the footsteps retreat.

Luke struggled to get dressed, grimacing at the pain that shot through his entire body. He cried about his arm, and feared it couldn't be fixed, that it would never work again, that it had gone dead.

He crept out to the kitchen, where his father already sat with a vodka bottle in front of him. The old man studied Luke for a moment, started to say something, then looked away. Luke waited until finally his father, his face twisted in a familiar family trait, raised his hand to signal he couldn't bare the sight of him anymore, and Luke left.

His home room teacher looked at his swollen face and twisted body. She sent him to the nurse's office, where the nurse gasped and called over the school counselor, the crew-cutted Mr. Rose, who drove him to the hospital.

They treated his injuries, and brought in a cop, who, like Mr. Rose, asked Luke how it happened. When Luke refused to answer, the cop took a social worker to visit Luke's father, who claimed he didn't see Luke return home last night, before launching into a story about Luke's uncontrollable behavior.

"Anyone own a stun gun here," the cop asked.

"No," Luke's father lied.

The cop returned to the hospital and pressed Luke one more time for an answer, before giving up. Where was Morrison when you needed him? The social worker, with no proof Luke sustained the injuries at home and with Luke's reputation for pissing others off, simply referred Luke to another doctor who within minutes prescribed Ritalin, which placed Luke in his first drug-induced stupor. Some credited the drug with finally reigning Luke in. I knew otherwise.

When I heard about Luke's injuries, I felt sick. Physically sick. My stomach churned as I recalled two images: Luke's face peering through the curtain, pale and frozen. And me walking away.

Now it came to me in that rotting smoke-filled bedroom, that Luke's early life, and mine and Sarah's and Sam's, were defined more by my weakness than anything else. Not just the one notorious thing I did, but the many others I failed to do. We all paid immensely for that weakness, the others much more than me.

I thought about the so-called shore-chickens who helped build the big bridge eighty years ago but were too fearful to plunge into the channel's cold water and race for the other side. What held them back? I thought about how much like them I was.

"Hey," Sophia said, her voice startling me. "Your wife called on your cell phone. Says it's an emergency. Wants you to call her right away."

I swore under my breath, and struggled to remove my gloves as Sophia held the phone. "Don't worry," she said, "your family's fine. That much she told me."

The drive to Mount Vernon usually took twenty to twenty-five minutes, depending on traffic. I did it on my motorcycle in fifteen, with little recollection of speeding. I crossed a small bridge into the downtown, where squat one hundred-year-old buildings bragged of a successful revitalization and renewal project. Traffic slowed on the narrow streets, and up ahead a cop waved vehicles towards a detour, the street behind him roped off by yellow tape. I parked on the sidewalk, wound my way past an assembled crowd and a pack of television cameramen and reporters, and approached a lone cop.

"I'm Brady Joseph. I've been asked to see the lead officer, Friedman is his name I think."

The cop studied me, checked my ID, and summoned another. "Take this guy to the captain."

The next block sat ghostly quiet: Empty stores with OPEN signs still in their front windows, parked cars packed into every available spot, but not a single person, except a handful of cops huddled around a large van.

I noticed Detective Morrison about the same time he saw me. He tapped one cop on the shoulder and pointed to me. The other cop, well-dressed in a grey suit, looked toward me blankly, his eyes dark and deep-set.

Morrison introduced me to Captain Friedman and we shook hands.

"You've known this Newell guy for a long time, right?" the Captain said.

"Yes."

"So he pistol-whipped a 63-year-old security guard. Before today would you have believed he was capable of that?"

"Ahh…" I struggled to answer.

"He let the guard go. Let one person help him out. But he's got a half dozen or so hostages still. So tell me, what do you think he's capable of?"

I looked across the street at Luke's parole office, the cops' focal point, the target of a half-dozen large spotlights. "I really don't know," I said.

Friedman glared at me hard. "I'm gonna get you on the phone with him. Try to convey to him that the guard he struck will be fine. That everyone can walk away from this in one piece, if we all relax. Understand. Soothing voice. Positive thoughts. Remind him of how much everyone has to lose."

"So you've talked to him?" I asked.

Friedman nodded.

"Once," Morrison added. "Newell hung up, and now he's not picking up."

For the next ten minutes, I stood on the street in a misty rain, my breath shallow, my head nodding as I professed to understand the instructions relayed by Friedman.

On the roofs of neighboring buildings sharpshooters lay in wait. Another five cops sat in the back of the van, covered in vests and helmets with shields, their rifles ready. In the distance, the small crowd behind the police line buzzed in idle conversation, like the noise in a busy restaurant. In the brick office building across the street, I could only imagine what was going on.

"He'll pick up in time," Friedman told me after consulting with another cop who repeatedly pushed the redial button on a cell phone. "He may get hungry or something. So don't go anywhere."

I nearly laughed. Don't go anywhere. Didn't Friedman know that wouldn't be possible? Even if I had wanted to leave, Luke and I were fettered by my failures, intertwined by whispers, by pain and loss. For Luke, there was no escaping the misfortune I spawned.

"There," one cop exclaimed, and everyone focused on the window across the street, where I saw the face of a terrified boy peer out, mouth twitching before it disappeared behind a curtain, back inside.

"You see him?" Friedman asked. "Keep dialing. Looks like Newell wants to talk."

I stood frozen, useless, like always. Like always. Then my body swayed, and my hands rocked back and forth, pointing across the street and back to the sidewalk where I stood. Finally my feet moved forward, toward the road, indicating a decision I didn't recall making.

"Mr. Joseph, where are you going?" Friedman called as I left the protection of the police van and began venturing across the street.

Two other cops hustled toward me, but stopped when I began to run.

"Joseph, get back here," Friedman yelled. "What are you doing?"

I neared the door, and Friedman's voice blasted over a loudspeaker, "Luke Newell. Your friend is at the door. It's your friend."

I pushed the door, surprised to find it unlocked. I peered inside to an empty waiting room, then at a gun in my face.

"I'm alone, Luke," I told him, stepping inside, locking the door behind me.

He threw me back against the door, pinning me with bare arms I swore still stunk of gasoline. "You idiot," he said. "Why did you come?" His head bobbed violently forward as he spoke, and he lowered his gun and wrapped his arms around his chest, twisting from side to side.

I reached forward, hoping to temper his desperation with my touch. He instantly jumped back, hair falling over glassy eyes.

"What the fuck is wrong with you, Brady?" he shrieked, throwing his hands in the air.

I stepped toward him again, arms open and unquestioning, and he retreated, his eyes for a moment losing their rage, settling on some other emotion only he understood. Then he turned angry again.

"Stay away from the windows," I muttered. "They have sharpshooters out there."

"No shit."

"Where are they?" I asked. "The hostages."

"They're not fucken hostages," Luke screamed. "I told the cops that. I didn't take any hostages. They all work here; this is their office. They chose to stay. They just haven't gone home yet, alright?"

"It's eight o'clock, Luke. They should be with their families now."

I ventured behind the counter, and almost choked at the sight of five men and one woman, cowering on the floor, backs to the wall, stinking of sweat. The woman clung to an MP3 player, tiny headphones protruding from her ears, and stared straight ahead, her lips slowly repeating some distant tune. The men looked up, imploring me to help, pleading for sanity, without uttering a single word.

"Oh, Luke," I groaned as I returned to the waiting room. "Let me call that cop, Friedman. Let's end this all right now."

Luke languished in a chair facing the door, his eyes closed. I wondered if he was sleeping. "Luke," I repeated, and he exploded to his feet, his hands trembling. I had never seen his hands tremble before; they always moved with such precision.

"Just get out, Brady. Get out and let me think."

"The guard's gonna be okay," I told him.

"I beat the shit out of him, Brady," he said, pacing urgently. "He's an old man, but I had to do that. Tried to keep me from leaving. He was waiting for me, in case I showed up to see my parole officer. I had to come, though. Couldn't violate my parole. Two more visits and I'd be free. Just two fucken visits. But they know. They know I did it; set the Opal house on fire."

"No one was hurt. They all got out."

"Then this," he said pointing to the hostages. "These fuckers who should have been smart enough or fast enough to get out. But they stayed, and now they're my problem. Add it all up, Brady. Add it all up, and I'm so fucken screwed."

I closed my eyes and fought an urge to find a black felt pen and begin furiously coloring the wall, producing a tunnel wide enough to fit the two of us. "It's not that bad," I lied.

"Serious fucken jail time," he groaned, hands hugging his chest. "I can't do that. No way."

"I can help."

"No one can help me."

"I can."

"Get out."

"I can tell them. What really happened. That night. It will change their perception of you. Start to set things right."

Luke stared at me blankly, like when I'd asked to move in with him and his father. He glanced back toward the room where the hostages were huddled, out of sight, possibly out of earshot, and leaned forward, and spat. "Shut your mouth about that and get the fuck out?"

How could he not understand?

"Time I came clean," I told him.

Luke shook his head and closed his eyes. Then he raised his gun to my face.

"Luke," I whispered.

His fingers clenched around the weapon, and tears streamed down his face. His mouth twisted like he wanted to speak but couldn't. I knew what he wanted to scream at me. I knew it like he'd spoken the words. That all these years of taking the heat for me – the seemingly one decent thing he did in his life – it would all be wasted if I confessed, especially now when so many people had put Tom Opal's sorry tale behind them.

His hand shook violently – like he was fighting for

control – and the gun's nozzle bounced up and down, its target shifting in between my eyes and throat. I started to speak, to tell him to put the gun down before it went off, but he opened his eyes suddenly, almost making me jump, and I saw his confusion. I saw someone who believed nothing made sense. Nothing had ever made sense.

"You're wrong," I started to say.

Then a gunshot exploded. I didn't jump, or scream or wail, or even think of Carmel and the girls and what was suddenly lost. For a moment, everything was right. An agonizing ordeal ended, justice finally served.

But I didn't collapse to the floor. Luke did, dropping in an awkward heap of twisted arms and legs, his head revealing a bloody hole. I tried to scream, could only gasp, my brain telling me sharpshooters had killed my friend.

That's when I heard her, the woman hostage, the one with the music and headphones. She stood behind the counter, a gun still raised in both hands. "You should never have made me do this," she screamed in Luke's direction.

I looked at her in disbelief, and all I could think about was how she should turn down her MP3 player's volume, because she was yelling over the music, her voice too loud, bordering on offensive.

The front window exploded, and the emergency response team crashed in. Soon Friedman hovered beside me. "Shit," he moaned "Shit."

I couldn't pull my eyes away from Luke's body, the way his legs had folded when he fell, like a bridge collapsing. I saw little of what was going around me. Hostages being rushed out the front door, one cop carefully picking up Luke's gun from the floor and examining it like precious jewelry, another cop checking him for a pulse, Morrison's presence in the room, strangely unimposing.

"Stupid fucker," Friedman muttered, and I couldn't tell if he meant me or Luke.

They led me to a police car, and drove me through the crowd assembled at the police line to the police station four blocks away. They left me alone in a tiny room with a table and two chairs and a water-heated radiator that ticked.

In time, Friedman and another cop came in and took my statement. Friedman chastised me once more. Told me I could be criminally charged for disobeying his command, told me the woman who shot Luke – a 35-year-old probation officer who packed a gun because of a series of threats against her – was a wreck, told me they could have brought Luke out alive if given the chance.

"That's not all," Friedman said. "The gun your friend brandished. It wasn't real. Just a pellet gun. Just a fucken pellet gun."

Before they sent Carmel in to take me home, a young woman from victim services breezed in, and spoke far too quickly about post-traumatic disorder and how she could arrange counseling for me back in Deception Pass.

I stared at her smooth skin and her clear eyes, and all I would let myself think was that she was younger than me, and pretty.

I told Carmel I would drive, and she argued, like I knew she would. We stood there in the police station's back parking lot, 11:30 at night, another standoff, until she acquiesced, grumbling as she walked around to the car's passenger side.

I drove less than a half-mile before I missed a traffic light, flung my door open and puked on the road. Then I got out quietly and walked around to the passenger side.

At home Jennifer and Leanne were awake, watching a movie with my mother and Amanda. The girls rushed to my side, saying comforting words about Luke. I pushed them away and went upstairs without an acknowledgment, ran a bath and climbed in the warm water with the light off.

I had always thought I knew the exact moment everything had gone wrong. Now I wondered if anything had ever been right.

I found a rhythm I could bear in the days that followed. Rise after hearing Carmel leave with the girls for school and work. Shower, then eat, then walk to the liquor store for its 10 a.m. opening. Buy one liter of vodka, take it home and drink it with orange juice, with 7-Up, on the rocks, whatever. Move through the house pausing at each door to free my hands in an explosion of options. What if I went to the phone and called the fire hall and told them I'd be back at work tomorrow? What if I called that psychologist I'd been referred to? What if I raced down to the liquor store and got a second bottle? What if I could replicate the soothing feeling I had when I thought Luke had shot me, when I thought I was dead?

I started spending time sitting at the computer, drinking, pursuing whatever thoughts came to mind. How large a hole does a 9mm handgun leave in someone's head when fired from eight feet away? Does the skull, or the brain, stop the bullet? I found a morbid and frivolous fascination with certain answers. Like how long does it take a body to decay to bone?

At 3 p.m., I would walk to school and pick up the girls, if I remembered. If I forgot, the school phoned, and I would go and get them. On the trip home, I moved at a breathless pace, careful not to indulge their small hands grappling for mine.

At 5 p.m., Carmel would return home, often groaning something like, "Oh, Brady," when she saw me. She would smell my breath, stare into my eyes and swear, and search the house for booze bottles, not knowing I threw them in the trash can outside the school before I picked up the girls. She would stand or sit far too close, try too earnestly to engage me in conversation, speak too frequently about the girls and their mundane lives and try much too naively to instill hope where there was none.

For a while, I would get visitors. Friends and colleagues handled me carefully, like overripe fruit. Morrison dropped by one day and sat down at the kitchen table to talk. I got him a knife and an orange, so I could watch him peel it, watch him lay bare its fragile insides. He looked at the orange, large in his small hand, then at me, puzzled, before mentioning something about how I could now clear my conscience, for the good of the Opal family, and how I'd be immune from all charges.

Mom and Amanda started dropping by, cutting into my drinking time, until I told them I needed to be alone. They still intruded, though not as often, especially after I began ignoring their incessant knocking.

Then came the visits from friends that at first left me trembling. I would jam my eyes shut, until I remembered my friends were never vindictive, never carried a grudge. Well, maybe not never, but hardly ever.

As I sat by the computer one afternoon, I felt a familiar presence, close, in my space, as always, though my space no longer belonged to her to occupy. I shook it off, this abstract feeling, because anything so indirect was unlike Sarah. I tapped the desk beside the keyboard, nervous, the way I first acted around her, and slowly became engulfed in her scent, the sweet, acerbic odor of her body after making love. I ran from the room, out to the back yard's fresh air. She followed, determined, never afraid to reveal herself.

"What do you want?" I whispered, shaking, until I

shivered alone in the November mist, and knew she was gone, for now.

Sam came later that night, as I sat outside the bathroom while the girls splashed in the tub. I caught the skunky smell of the cheap cannabis he enjoyed, felt him linger beside me, uncertain, directionless, ineffective, harmless. I said nothing, just waited for him to drift off.

I waited the next two days for Luke, expecting to round a corner in the house and see him, always at the worst time, always unexpected and out of synch. Unlike the others, he didn't manifest himself in scent or in an unseen yet still invasive presence. He simply flashed past me in the hall one afternoon, like an unexplained breeze, a lost rush of energy. Each day he brushed past me again and again, like a child on a swing, gliding back and forth, here and gone, screaming with joy and pain, both emotions separated by the finest of lines, by a single push. I never asked him what he wanted. I feared I already knew.

With them, my not-quite departed friends, I languished in my dark home, lost in my thoughts, desperate to suppress a scream.

One day on the Internet I Googled a series of words on what I considered my most pressing question. Cursed, harmful, fate. I didn't have to search long. Hundreds, maybe even thousands of web sites pushed forth the answer. Karma, simply, emphatically. Sins from the past brought forward. I nodded. To use Luke's words, I was fucked.

29

I counted out the dollar bills carefully, and with some difficulty, and handed them to the clerk, who counted them for himself and appeared to shake his head, perhaps in a thought he could not contain, before tucking the cash in the till and slapping some change on the counter. He slipped the bottle into a long paper bag and held it out in his beefy arms, his icy demeanor almost daring me to take it. I wondered if liquor store clerks could spot the ones who paid with dollar bills stolen from their daughters' piggy banks.

Outside in the rain, I cut through the side parking lot, my intent never to repeat my route or exhibit any type of pattern in my daily movements. One hitch, of course, was the clerks. Only two worked mornings, and they'd both already tucked my face away in their memory.

I pulled my jacket's hood over my face, pleased by the extra stealth it offered, and squeezed past a Mazda SUV parked facing the store. My eyes glanced inside at a woman talking on a cell phone, and a jolt of recognition slapped me. Amanda didn't blink, didn't really react. I suspected she'd seen me coming and realized she had nowhere to hide.

"Brady," she said leaning out the open window, her mouth still pressed against the phone.

"It's Carmel," she said. "She wants to talk to you."

I stared at the phone in disbelief that I could literally stumble into such shit, and then remembered who I was. "Get in," Amanda said, pushing the passenger door open.

I walked around and slid out of the rain, placing my bottle on the seat between my legs and taking the cell phone from Amanda.

I held it cautiously to my face. "Carmel?" I asked.

"I'll be home at lunch, Brady," she said. "Don't touch that bottle. Understand?"

"Yes," I told her.

I searched for the correct button to disconnect, and when I couldn't find it I simply handed the phone back to Amanda, who shut it off.

"Don't hate me," she said after a short silence. "I'm only trying to help you."

"I don't need help." I searched for a convincing lie, and only came up with, "I just need some time."

"What's in the bag?"

"Vodka."

"We thought that's what you were drinking. What size?"

"750 ml."

"So how long will that last?"

I looked past her, and said absently, "You followed me."

"Just came here and waited. Kathy's at the other liquor store. The one downtown."

"Oh."

"Don't hate me," she repeated.

"I don't hate you."

"It's always been…difficult between us. I don't want to make it worse."

I reached for the door's handle, but paused and stared out at the rain. "It's not your fault, you know, the way you and me are. It's got nothing to do with you."

Amanda nodded, almost as if to offer encouragement.

I laughed out loud and she looked startled. "Sorry," I said, "it's just that you possess one of the skills Mom doesn't have. You listen."

She smiled now, wrinkles forming around her eyes and above her nose, reminding me I'd known her now for a considerable time.

"I never thought it would last very long, you know. You and my mother."

"Why?"

"Nothing ever did last with her. She'd start one thing and move on. Relationships, housework, dinner, you name it."

Amanda laughed softly. "She's not so much like that anymore. People change."

I took my hand off the doorknob. "I used to think that everything she did was to embarrass me. Getting high with my classmates, dating my teachers, getting arrested for drunk driving."

"So what made you change your thinking?"

I shrugged. "No one thing. I dunno, it was just an attitude, a belief, that slowly slipped away."

"She does care about you. That's why she's parked outside a liquor store right now. We all want to help you."

She reached over and squeezed my hand, and even at a time when everything lacked clarity, when my most lucid thoughts centered around quickly getting drunk, I realized the risk she was taking. The risk she felt she needed to take. She had often reached out to me – unsuccessfully. I wondered if she thought my aloofness, my coolness toward her, had been about her being a lesbian. Now I wanted her to know the real reason.

I squeezed her back, and reached over with my other hand and engulfed her short icy fingers with mine.

"I've always wanted to hug you, you know," I told her. "To let you know I'm okay with you and Mom. That I'm happy for you both."

Amanda let go a soft gasp, and her eyes grew moist, like her plump lips. "You can hug me anytime you want," she told me.

I reached up to her face, its welcoming expression, and leaned in and kissed her softly on the mouth. I sensed surprise, maybe shock, but felt the muscles in her face relax, and she kissed me back, her eyes closed.

When I finally pulled away, she opened her eyes slowly, like a confused person in the morning, and nodded her head. We stared at each other in a warm silence and then she said, "I'll give you a ride home."

"No," I told her. "I want to walk."

"It's really raining."

"That's okay. It'll help clear my head."

She nodded, and took another chance. "Did you want to give me the bottle?"

I thought about this for a moment, about how it would all play out, and handed it to her. She smiled, and tucked it under her seat, satisfied. "You gonna be okay, Brady?" she asked.

"Yes," I told her, and she smiled, pleased.

Still thinking about the touch of her lips, I said goodbye and got out of the car. I watched her drive away, and then turned and went back into the liquor store and used the remaining money in my pocket to buy another bottle of vodka, the cheapest brand, the largest size.

On the way home I cut through the familiar trails of Whiteside Park, felt the grasp of a haunting thirst, and twisted open the bottle. I poured back two or three ounces, its contents spilling down my throat and seemingly falling soothingly into the pit of my stomach, like foam on fire.

Carmel arrived home at six minutes after twelve, greeting me with a hopeful smile, one that faded quickly. She drew close, her eyes searching mine for clues before closing, like she summoned up some brilliant thought. "Help me make some toasted sandwiches," was all she said. She moved surely through the kitchen, watching me carefully as I awkwardly counted six slices of bread. When I clumsily took out the cutting board, one tomato and a sharp knife, her movements slowed, and I sensed she held her breath, like a mother hovering over a small child trying to execute the simplest of tasks. I felt a strange pressure, one that extended down to my hands, and I struggled to cut uniformly thin slices, the knife slipping with a thud onto the cutting board, the tomato buckling under the weight of my fingers.

Carmel took the knife from my hand and motioned for me to sit down. I watched her slice away, tears falling down her face.

"After I heard from Amanda this morning, I inquired about some time off work," she told me. "I'm going to follow through and take some vacation time. Using next summer's vacation, and taking it now. Starting tomorrow. I'm going to stay home and help you get better."

"That's not necessary," I told her.

She threw the knife into the sink with such force we both jumped. "Yes, it is," she told me in an angry, even tone.

We ate, in a way that seemed almost formal, Carmel's back slightly hunched, like a great weight had been foisted upon her.

She did up the lunch dishes and returned to work, with a curt, "Don't forget to get the girls from school." I nodded and closed my eyes, though only for a second. Then I raced to the computer.

I used my remaining time alone wisely, scouring the

Internet's vast wisdom in a flurry of Google searches, offering up a longer series of words individually or in different combinations: Life, death, loss, lies, failure, mistakes, family, doomed, silent, love, guilt, overwhelmed, muddled, cursed, capitulate, lies, alone, desperate, exhausted, lost, hopeless, screwed. The results provided nothing to take away and use. Nothing to collapse into. In time I felt Sarah's presence at my side, her sharp hip digging almost palpably into my shoulder as she peeked down at the screen. I knew she understood what I searched for, and maybe ached to help me find it. My fingers paused over the keyboard, and then began typing, pulling forth one word, one new word, from my subconscious. The possibilities suddenly exploded before me on the screen.

My heartbeat quickened as I narrowed my search and immersed myself in excerpts from books, in summaries from various groups, in first-person accounts. How had I missed something as old as life and death, something all around me? I drank and read, intoxicated and excited by the words. Then came the one account I would read repeatedly and attempt to memorize over the coming hours, haunting words that fell with great importance, rain on a scorched ground.

The snow came swift and deep like the old men in Lewiston had foretold, first in tiny specks that one wondered if she really saw, then in large, wondrous flakes that stuck like sap from the trees, enshrouding everything. In one hour it had covered the dirt road into town; in another hour it obscured all signs of the cold yet beautiful limestone rocks on Scott and Melissa's graves. Obscured but not erased, and that's where the problem lay: You could bury someone or something away, but how do you forget? How do you push on?

I lit one lantern absentmindedly, then blew it out. From

the chair, I took my winter coat, the one Scott had ordered from the Sears catalogue three Christmases ago, before his own body turned against him. I slipped into its warmth, ignoring the draft running across the wooden floor and rippling over my bare feet. I checked the windows, making sure each was tightly fastened, then pulled my boots from under the bed. They were worn, both on the sole and at the toe. I tied the laces tight and double-knotted them.

I paused, wondering if I should eat something, a piece of dried beef perhaps, but I liked my body better light, empty. I surveyed the house's cramped insides. For a moment, I thought a tear may come, and then I shook off such an indulgence. Crying was never me. I sobbed only twice after Scott's death; not even once after Melissa's. I did cry once before she died, just once, at the moment I knew the brain damage she suffered at birth far eclipsed what the doctor had predicted. Three years old and she still couldn't walk, or stand, or sit up, or talk, or even eat on her own. How would she survive when I was gone, because everyone goes, sometimes sooner than they think? What would become of her then?

The phone rang and I looked at the clock and cursed. 3:30 p.m. I let it continue ringing while I printed the story, all of it, then folded it neatly and tucked it into my jeans' pocket. I ran out the door and down the street toward the school, where Jennifer and Leanne would be sitting outside the principal's office, looking alone and abandoned. Halfway there, I slowed and pulled out the story and read it again as I walked, once slightly twisting my ankle as I stepped into a road-side rut. Never had I seen words so beautiful, so perfect, so hopeful.

"I'm telling Mom," Jennifer said coolly when I walked into the school breathless, past the long stare from Mr. Rourke, the principal.

"You do that," I told her, knowing she would.

"We were scared, Daddy," Leanne said, trying a different approach.

"I know," I told her, certain that time would show this to be among the smallest of disappointments I'd inflicted upon them.

When we got home I fixed them a snack and turned on the television for them, before sequestering myself to the bathroom, where, drink in hand, I read on, over and over.

Out into the sharp cold I went, pleased to have shed the small house, all its reminders, its familiar scents, its not yet abandoned pains. Only November, and already a second heavy snowfall. A cold winter upon us in Idaho. A long winter.

I knew the trail well enough to find my way in the snow; we had carried Melissa along it often as a baby, our eyes even wider than hers at the amazement. The bluffs falling magically into the Snake River, golden eagles in languid flight, milky boulders strewn by God in a display of His power.

I turned back and looked at the spot where I knew the graves lay, protected by a cover of white. When the moment came, how would I recall Melissa? The beautiful baby born half strangled by her own cord, fighting, crying, gagging, never so alive? Or the toddler who remained that baby, her crippled mind locked in time, trapped forever in a heartbeat, freed only by my loving hands wrapped so gently, so brutally, around her tiny neck?

Carmel arrived home to a flurry of tattle-tailing. She looked at me sternly. "How could you forget?" I didn't answer, because words always led to more words. And the only words I wanted swirling around me lay neatly in my pant pocket.

At dinner, Carmel told the girls she was taking some time off while I recovered. The girls cheered and laughed.

Then Carmel told them she was using up next summer's vacation time. They shrugged, and told her the summer was a long way off. They were so right.

After dinner I told Carmel I felt sick and excused myself to the bathroom, where earlier I had filled an old shampoo bottle with vodka. I sat on the edge of the bathtub and drank and read.

I walked and climbed slowly, careful not to slip, buoyed by each step, by my deepening resolve. In the distance I could hear a hum of commerce from the sawmill just outside Lewiston, but I expunged such earthly creepings from my mind. I ignored too the snow spilling over the tops of my boots and numbing my feet, and the little voice of doubt, whose nagging words would bristle in others, yet not in me. Instead I pushed forward, toward atonement.

I thought of stumbling into the bedroom and lying down, but felt strangely energized, like I'd suddenly shaken loose what had hopelessly mired me. Downstairs Carmel studied me closely as I fell into a chair, my vision blurred, my ears registering a vague crackling. She tore upstairs to the bathroom, where I heard cupboards slamming, and returned minutes later, looking puzzled.

We spent the early evening together in the living room. The girls watched television while Carmel attempted to pull us all into a conversation, into her perfect little world. I moved carefully inside my head toward a visible point in the distance, toward a way of making it all right.

"Are you okay?" Carmel asked.

"Yes," I told her.

She shook her head, as if to call me a liar.

"What are you thinking about? Right now. What are you thinking about?"

"Nothing," I said, knowing the truth would make her scream; would hurt her.

She sighed. I waited for her to tell me she couldn't live this way. Instead she rose and began to wander the house aimlessly, like she was looking for something.

As I sat, my chest suddenly tightened, much like I suspected a heart attack would feel, and I began panting in short, forced breaths. Far inside, I realized, I had just made a decision, one provoking a quick response from my body and which would defy me if given a chance. I stood straight up and quickly asserted control, feeling a dead calm coolly suffocate the last few stirrings of emotion.

Up I climbed, over rocks made slippery by the wet snow, over ground once traveled by the Blackfoot before we shoved them cruelly aside to the reserves, by the grizzly bear and the caribou before them. My breath grew short, and I rested, my eyes falling to the east, across a canopy of cedars dabbed with white, toward Mount Rainier in the distance, cloaked in fog. In time I reached the bluff, the very spot on which I'd sit with Scott and Melissa and stare ahead into all the beauty. This was in the days before his sickness was even a whisper, in the days before I wrongly put my own uncertainties ahead of my daughter's life. Time seemed abundant back then, when the three of us would drop rocks and watch them fall gracefully, almost eternally, into the rocky valley carved over centuries by the unyielding Snake River.

About eight, Carmel wandered in and placed her hand on my arm. "I'm running down to Albertsons. We need a few things. Can you make sure the girls have a bath and put them to bed?"

I nodded slowly at the opportunity.

"Can you do that, Brady?"

"Yes."

"Are you sure? Look at me. Are you sure?"

"Yes," I told her coldly. "I'm sure."

She paused, and said, "Girls. Daddy's going to put you to bed while I run down to the grocery store."

They stood and kissed her goodnight, then obliviously turned their attention back to the television.

Carmel paused once more, seemingly taking in everything in the room, unable to recognize what was out of place, and left. I followed her to the window, watched her climb into the car and disappear into the blackness.

For a moment, I thought a tear may come, and then shook off such an indulgence.

I shut off the television. The girls protested as I ordered them upstairs to get their pajamas on and get into bed.

"But we're supposed to have a bath," Jennifer whined. "Mom said."

"Do what I say," I told them.

In their room, they grasped for the soft comfort of stuffed toy animals as they slipped beneath the warmth of their silky sheets. Methodically I kissed each one on the top of her head, only vaguely aware I now drew my strength, my moral direction, from elsewhere: Sarah's wispy presence and the insights of a stranger who lived a hundred years ago.

Over Leanne I hovered, my fingers slipping down her white cheek and across her jaw, which for once rested. I reached down to her neck, barely noticing her skin had lost its familiarity; she felt like just another stranger.

"Goodnight," I said, turning and leaving their room, not looking back, certain it was long ago I had first failed them.

I pulled the last vodka bottle, half-full, from where I'd

placed it at the bottom of the blue recycling box, the last place I suspected Carmel would look. I poured it down in great gulps, so much so that I had to lean against the wall, and sit for a moment. I staggered up to the kitchen where I found a piece of paper and a red pen, one that gave me a moment's inspiration when words failed to come, when no explanation conveyed what I was about to do and why.

I drew a large heart, terribly misshapen.

Suddenly I found myself standing at the front door, my hands lifeless at my sides, confirming everything. A moment later I moved across the cold driveway in my sock feet, onto the road, toward the bench and the small, barren lookout over Deception Pass. The night felt dead quiet, as though all sounds, all distant voices, had been brutally smothered.

I crept out to the precipice, as close as I dared go, then knelt down, hugging my knees, searching myself for something that would stop me. But this was right, I knew it; the only way to end the regret and self-hatred, the only way to finally push forward.

For a brief second, I told myself I'd miss this pristine view, the fresh breeze from the west that had called us from Boston, but I regained control and pushed my thoughts ahead, toward the drop, away from fantasy. I stood up and stepped out over the ledge, all in one certain motion, and gasped as my feet left the ground and I plunged, falling, falling.

I closed my eyes, forcing darkness on the sea of white enveloping me, and felt the air ripping at my clothes, felt my body accelerating, endlessly, faster.

For a moment, I blacked out, and came to with a start, still falling. I opened my eyes and saw my battered body below, twisted on the snowy rocks at the riverside. Above it I floated and bobbed in the wind, hovering above the earth, then thought of rising up and did, transcending my long-doomed human form, that mass of flesh and bone and blood weighed heavy by such sorrow.

Up I drifted over the river valley, into the snowflakes, freed, ready to begin anew.

My name was Anna Reid, and that is how my 11th life ended. Today I am Sylvia Bruholland, living a 13th time, in Boston once more, fully, and at times painfully, aware of all my past ventures, each of them a lesson, each of them an opportunity to bring something new and valued to our world.

I reached the chain-link fence before I realized it, and scaled it without stopping, without even so much as wondering how I got there, my body flying up and over, my feet awkwardly landing on the narrow ledge on the other side, my hands grappling behind me for the thick wire mesh to regain my imperiled balance. I hooked my outstretched fingers into the fence and stared down into the blackness, and knew my plunging body would strike the stone sides before hitting the channel's water, before drifting out to sea, abandoned, unfettered.

I crept out to the precipice, as close as I dared go, then knelt down, hugging my knees, searching myself for something that would stop me. But this was right, I knew it; the only way to end the regret and self-hatred, the only way to finally push forward.

I closed my eyes and waited for the hidden force that put me here to push me finally from my purgatory. The wind whipped and swirled. A dull ache resonated through my fingers, those small pieces of flesh and bone that kept me suspended, that separated me from the salvation of everyone around me.

I called out for Sarah's encouraging presence, searched

for her confirmation in the darkness, but found only the roar of the wind. Then before me a shape emerged and quickly leapt into focus, and Carmel stood an arm's length away, on the beach the night of the storm, the night of our reunion, a pile of soaked sneakers at her feet, the lights of a hovering coast guard helicopter circling in the distance.

"I have to go," I told her, my voice deep and raw with certainty.

She smiled, her dark body thicker than I remembered, and she whispered something I couldn't hear. In the distance, one of our girls struggled to shout over the wind.

"You can't stop me," I told her.

I eased my grip on the fence, coaxing my feet forward to where the dirt and rock fell away.

I regained control and pushed my thoughts ahead, toward the drop, away from fantasy.

Carmel leaned in and spoke into my ear once more, her words strong although barely audible.

I let go of the fence and leaned forward. Again she pressed close, her face revealing nothing, and she spoke once more, earnest though still incomprehensible. I paused, confused, but only for a moment.

"Nothing you say matters," I told her. "It's too late."

On my arm a sudden tug. A small voice screamed "Daddy."

I waited to tip forward, for gravity to prevail.

Another tug on my arm. A voice, Jennifer's maybe, pulling hard, pulling me back, "Daddy. What are you doing?"

I opened my eyes, looked down into the darkness, swaying forward before tipping back against the fence.

Jennifer's hands, cold, alive, touched my neck, and I screamed in frustration.

"Back inside," I ordered her, without turning around.

"What are you doing on that side of the fence?" she demanded, using words I could barely understand.

"Inside," I spat.

"I'm not going in until you do," she announced.

I let go of the fence with my left hand and swung around, over the peaceful darkness below, until I faced my daughter, saw her bare feet standing on the small bench, her tiny pajamas rippling in the cool breeze, her posture familiarly straight and defiant.

"Go to bed, you little bitch," I screamed, lunging for her over the fence.

Jennifer backed away.

I pounded the fence with both hands and tried to tear it loose. I rested my head on top of it, closed my eyes and silently implored my daughter to give up on me, to turn and walk inside. I waited, how long I don't know, until only the sound of my breathing remained, until I felt sure she'd left, way past that. Until I wondered where I rested, until I questioned how I got there. And when I looked up she hadn't moved from her place on the bench. She shook her head, just like her mother sometimes would, and jumped down, reaching up and grabbing my face with her tempering touch.

"I know you're sad about your friends going to heaven. We all know."

Her words still sounded distant, foreign. "Go to bed," I whispered.

"I know what you're trying to do."

"Shut up and go to bed."

"You're trying to fly. Fly to heaven to be with them."

I looked at her, really looked at her. "What did you say?"

"I said 'you're trying to fly to heaven, aren't you?'"

"Yes," I told her.

She leaned in closer, and whispered, her voice painfully heavy, no longer child-like, "Take me with you."

I turned away once more, unable to face her. "Go inside."

"I'll follow you," she said.

I grappled to push aside her words, but when I closed my eyes all I could see was her tiny body plunging swiftly under the weight of my death, a weight that even surpassed the heaviness that my life, my very existence, had placed upon her. It was all too familiar. Suddenly I knew she told the truth. She would follow, if not now, later, a third successive generation doomed to the same fate. It was all I felt certain about, knowledge only the size of the tiny outcropping of crumbling ground I stood on, but enough.

The blackness below made a final pull, one only slightly less appealing than my twisted world on a dead-end street where the wrong people kept dying and the one person who could stop it was afraid. I struggled back over the fence, falling in a heap, safely, trembling and then shaking violently, still lost.

"It was you, wasn't it dad?" Jennifer asked suddenly, looking down at me.

"What was me?"

"That hurt that man? That Mr. Opal?"

Her question should have surprised me – even if I understood she possessed an eerie insight into peoples' emotions – but it didn't. "Yes, it was me," I told her, finally uttering those ineffable words, strangely warmed by their sound.

But this was right, I knew it; the only way to end the regret and self-hatred, the only way to finally push forward.

I staggered to my feet, dizzy and sick, and Jennifer

climbed onto my back, this time literally. She slipped her hands around my chin, and I piggybacked her across the street and into the house. I looked up at the stairs to her room, breathless, and she slid down and took my hand and led me up to the security of their room.

Leanne bounced on her bed wide-awake, the curtains pulled to reveal the view of the lookout across the street.

"What were you doing out there, Daddy?" she asked.

I reached out my arms and pulled them into my embrace, hanging on for life, and only let go when a flash of light splashed across their bedroom and I knew Carmel had pulled into the driveway.

"Your mom's home girls. Into bed before she realizes you've been up late."

They protested, and I left them, this time knowing I'd return. I stumbled down the stairs and heard Carmel's footsteps resonating up the front walk toward the door, which I suddenly locked. She tried the handle, and as she searched for her keys I found the presence of mind to run into the kitchen and grab mine, as well as my cell phone, and to tear out the back.

30

Rain dotted the windshield as I put blocks between me and my wife, between me and our fragile home, which sat incongruously close to the Deception Pass Bridge, a marvel of human determination to span any treacherous channel that obstructs us. The bridge that, at least until tonight, was everything that I was not.

The car responded sluggishly to my moves. I slowed, remembering the great mouthfuls of vodka I'd consumed, and gripped the wheel tightly, making sure I reached my destination. Up I drove into the winding streets above the beach, past Sarah's old house, the lights in the garage eerily on, like a reminder. I pulled into the Opals' driveway, and almost couldn't bear to look at the house so badly damaged by tragedy. A blue tarp still covered burned-out sections of roof that had only been partially repaired – a single tarp flung out in the hope of keeping out everything that inadvertently rained down.

The rain-puddled driveway felt solid under my sock-covered feet, a small island of stability for someone who had let himself be tossed dizzily around for so long.

I rang the doorbell, and only the tiniest part of me

wished to be greeted by silence. Footsteps, loud and angry, responded, and I felt my chest and throat tighten.

The door flew open and Josh Opal stared out, his eyes at first wide, then squinting with suspicion.

"What do you want?" he asked. "You know I'm not supposed to be anywhere near you."

I searched for the words to begin, and he waited for me to speak. He had always waited.

"I've come to talk to you and your mother."

His mouth flew open. Then his face flushed with rage, so much he spat out the words instead of speaking them. "Bit late now to turn your friend in, you prick."

I thought of cursing his stupidity, of once more indulging my weakness by simply turning away. Instead I summoned a large gasp of air – and something more – and finally said it.

"Luke didn't kill your father. I did."

Josh Opal didn't react at first. He studied me, at first like he suspected I was playing some sick joke. Then he simply nodded for me to come in.

I circled the brick building three times, scanning its front waiting area, its wide steps and the empty street for a sign of Carmel, fearful she would again materialize ghostlike from the darkness, from nowhere, her long arms and thin fingers restraining me. Nothing stirred, and I laughed to myself because for the first time I could finally admit that only one person had kept me silent all this time. I parked across the street and ran through the rain.

The door was locked, and I knocked impatiently. Morrison appeared, his jacket still on, and motioned me inside.

"On the way, I called your wife and told her you're okay," he said.

"Did you tell her you're meeting me here?" I asked.

"Yes, though I didn't say why, just as you asked."

"Is she on her way?"

He shrugged. "Didn't say she was. Sounded relieved you're okay. And a little distracted."

"Don't let her in until after I'm done."

Morrison's eyes narrowed, and he grinned slightly and said, "I've waited a long time for this. You think I'd allow an interruption."

In his office he asked, "You okay? You look a little under the weather."

I forced a smile, wondering if my body conveyed signs of its brush with death, or if people simply looked unsettled when they move an immense affliction into the light?

"Did you want to have a lawyer present?" he asked. "As I said before, we've got a standing deal that you won't be charged if you talk, and it's been okayed by the state prosecutor."

I alone knew the irony of his words – how such a deal would be nullified, because it didn't take into account the simple fact that I committed the crime. I would instead be at the mercy of the court. "No, no lawyer necessary," I told him.

"Okay," he said business-like. "Do you want to record your statement with a video recorder or write it down on paper?"

I grappled in my head with which would be clearer. "Write it down, I guess."

He handed me a pen and large pad of unlined paper. "Write your full name and address at the top. And today's date."

He moved to the door. "I'll give you some space to think."

I closed my eyes to gather my thoughts, and I studied

the expanse of white, wondering where to start. I wrote my name, and address, and the date, and the rest of the words began falling quickly – heavy objects suspended for too long.

When I was finished I read my statement just once, correcting two misspelled words but changing nothing else. I had kept my admission to a single page of concisely-written sentences, an indelible mix of printed words containing just five names: Mine, Sarah's, Sam's, Luke's and Tom Opal's. Just five, though so many more names were engulfed by what I did that night and didn't do in the years to follow. Eunice Opal, so desperate for what the misguided professionals would call closure, so desperate to move on. Josh Opal who battled daily with a forgivable need for revenge. Josh's sister, whom I imagined often found their house empty, preoccupied. And Mrs. Roberts, her daughter dead, her husband imprisoned for a wicked act of anger, his career and life a wasted memory. There would be others too, more than I knew, who would live quietly with the loss of those doomed by my mess. I sometimes felt relieved that Luke had no family left to notice the void where he once existed; and that Sam's parents were too screwed up to know what they'd lost.

Morrison hovered in the hallway, another case almost cleared, another piece of justice nearly dispensed. I caught his eye and signaled I was done. He came in quickly and took the pad from me. He took his seat behind the desk, ready to read the words confirming everything he knew.

"Okay," he said, casting his eyes on the paper, his encouraging tone of voice more like a high school teacher than a cop.

He leaned back in his chair, and read, his cheeks and facial skin slowly falling like gravity's pull had suddenly spiked. He looked at me just once, eyes sad, before continuing on.

When he was done, he turned my confession face down, like he was hiding it, and looked into a corner with loathing, as if he saw some disturbing act taking place there.

I couldn't tell if he slipped deep into thought, playing back in his mind several years of scenarios with me replacing Luke as the villain, or if he simply struggled to comprehend in some way what he'd just read.

Minutes went by in silence. Finally he turned my statement over and read it quickly once more, then looked up at me, his eyes blinking.

He started to speak, hesitated, then said, "So why now?"

I sighed. "Ask me anything but that."

He stared off again and said to no one, "So does anyone else know what happened, what you did, besides your wife I assume?"

"I just stopped by the Opals and told them everything."

Morrison turned to me, surprised. He nodded, flipped my confession face down once more and looked into another corner, like he was searching. "When Tom Opal approached you that night, did you feel at all threatened?" he asked. "I mean, was there anything in his manner that scared you, made you fear for your own safety, because if there is something like that, even in the slightest, you should take your statement and rewrite it, and add that element, because that context would be important, it could go to cause, and to sentencing."

"No," I told him.

"Think back. Are you sure? Because it could make a difference, a big difference."

"It wasn't self defense," I said. "It was a stupid mistake on my part."

Morrison nodded, and tapped his fingers nervously on the desk. "Okay, then. So you know all deals are off. I'm going to have to arrest you?"

❧

I sat quietly inside a small boardroom, my world contracting to small spaces and long waits. My knees pushed up against a short, bare table as I studied the door and wondered if it was locked. Footsteps came and went twice, before a third set stopped on the other side. The door didn't open at first, and finally Morrison peeked in and flashed a forced smile, before stepping aside and saying, "You have a visitor."

Carmel crept past Morrison, thanking him with a polite nod, turning to me with uncertainty. I stood, but didn't immediately move from behind the table. She walked around it and took hold of my arms with her icy hands, as if she were checking to see if I was real. Her dark hair dripped rain, and I thought of how she'd allowed it to return to its natural color over the years; how she'd slowly shunned the blonde California girl look; how she'd slowly shed her disguise. All I wanted was to do the same.

She took a deep breath, and I waited for her to scold me for the near-fatal moments the girls had no doubt so vividly described. To explain to me that she never knew I'd been driven that far, to scream at me for ruining my family's life with my confession, for publicly exposing her as a liar.

"I'm sorry," she said. "I was so wrong."

My mind slipped back several hours to the inaudible words she had whispered when I conjured her on the ledge, to what she'd needed to tell me so urgently, to what she could never bring herself to say in the months before. Those were the words.

I realized now that a subtle change had taken hold inside her over the last few years, perhaps as the gap between existing and really living grew too large, too dangerous for us all. She'd never explicitly told me her position had shifted or at least been softened by doubt. In the weeks before tonight, her change of heart had not taken the shape of words, only in her sometimes silent lingering presence, or her sad smiles.

When the judge called her name, Eunice Opal stood slowly, squeezed her son and daughter's hands and came forward to the witness stand holding a black loose-leaf binder, one that seemed to match her neat black blazer and skirt. Her body trembled as she walked past me, and when our eyes met I knew nerves – and not anger – caused the shaking that seemed to flow from her hands and rise up to her face. Something inside me said she needed encouragement, and that such a courtesy would be right, and I smiled at her gently and nodded as she passed. Eunice Opal smiled back, and took her seat.

She stared out at the courtroom, packed with strangers and media, as well as her friends and family and others. Carmel and the girls sat with Brittany, Amanda and my mother, right behind my place at the defendant's table, and a few of our friends gathered around them, as did my former colleagues from the fire hall, even Capt. Boerne.

Eunice Opal opened her victim impact statement and stared at it blankly. Her voice broke when she started reading, but in time she found her strength and moved with sincerity into a less tortured rhythm.

While *The Lookout* newspaper would call her seven-minute statement "a heart-wrenching story of loss and devastation," I focused less on her words and more on her voice. Time and tragedy had laden it with a sadness which I'm sure everyone in the courtroom felt.

I felt a brief urge to close my eyes and drown out her sound, to repel her pain. Then instead I embraced it. Took it into my body, let it rattle around and remind me how right I was finally to come forward, to accept my punishment and allow us all to move on, no matter how difficult it would be.

Beside me my lawyer tensed, her fingers tightly folded together, and I knew what she was thinking. That Eunice Opal's statement packed so much power the judge might decide to reject the carefully crafted plea bargain that was to see me serve the minimum sentence for second-degree manslaughter – three years, out on probation in less than two, more than one.

But what my lawyer didn't know was that Eunice understood more than all of us the need for forgiveness, for reconciliation. That's why her statement ended with words that would kindly prevent my girls from losing for too long the one thing I had taken away from her children.

"I forgive Brady Joseph for what he did, for what he took away from my family," she said, her eyes leaving her binder and turning to me. "I know he never intended to harm my husband. I know that he never intended to keep his actions a secret for so long. I know he feels remorse. I ask the court not to prolong this tragedy."

But while her compassion amazed many in the courtroom that day, few knew how deep it really went or how much it transcended. They did not know that on the night she heard my confession in her fire-damaged home, at the very second her face filled with horror at my guilt, her thoughts did not move toward what she and her family had lost, or how her husband's killer had lived a seemingly idyllic life just blocks away. Instead this is what Eunice did that night at that moment: She looked at Josh and Kerry, searching their eyes for certain values she hoped she had instilled in them, and turned back to me. She placed her hands on my shoulder, and then whispered softly, "Don't go to the police. Do you understand? This is enough. This is enough."

While she knew about reconciliation, about forgiveness, it was me who understood about secrets, about their insidious nature, about the way they can slowly eat away at you until nothing is left, until you're just a shell.

So when the judge approved the plea bargain, when he assigned me to a minimum security prison just an hour away, I simply nodded at him, accepting this punishment as the price to live again, to stop from sliding backwards.

I heard the girls crying softly behind me, Jennifer lamenting how it wasn't fair I would be going to jail, and I felt a sudden surge of regret our lives would never be the same, before forcing myself to remember those who had lost so much more.

As the court emptied out, as people filed out into the hallway and then out through the thick double doors into the morning's damp air, I could almost hear Luke's exasperated voice, yelling and laughing, raging about how I must be an idiot to come clean after so long, after moving unequivocally into the clear. But I knew he would understand what it was like when your life was not right, when it was not the one you ever imagined climbing into.

I could see Sam leaning against a parked car outside the courthouse, ready to dispense all sorts of misguided advice about how I should approach my incarceration, how he knew someone who knew someone who knew a sure way to make my time easy, if I would just listen, if I just had a little faith.

And Sarah. Oh, Sarah. She would be reclining inside the parked car, her bare arm resting outside the open window, her eyes not quite shielded by some flashy but cheap sunglasses, her smile calling out for me to race off down the coast with her, to see what we would find around the next curve.

I liked to think all three forgave me, even if I would

never forgive myself. That said, I could finally start to live with myself.

Now Carmel and the girls leaned into the wooden railing that separated the public seating from the defendant's table. The bailiff – Tom Marriott's best friend, a man who often dropped by the fire hall for a coffee with the guys – appeared at my side and nodded to my family. "Take a moment," he said quietly. My lawyer hovered behind me, the only other person left in the room. I stepped toward the railing, but stopped.

For the past three nights, I had told Leanne and Jennifer this story, omitting few details, trying to prepare them not just for my departure but for the confusing years ahead. I tried to tell them how they must face up to their mistakes when they happened, and get on with things. More than that, I tried to leave them with memories to draw on when they needed strength to do the right thing.

Now I wondered if this was enough for our girls – enough to cling to in my absence. So I asked my lawyer to pull a pen and piece of paper from her briefcase.

And I drew a single heart, misshapen, crooked, but always strong if given a chance.

Acknowledgements:

My profound thanks to the following people: Doug Berg, for his expertise in the field of firefighting; my editor, Ron Smith; and my publisher, Randal Macnair.

Jeff Beamish works as newspaper editor and reporter in Metro Vancouver, where he lives with his family. He has been fortunate to find inspiration in the strange and moving stories that present themselves each day in the newsroom, as well as in the stunningly beautiful scenery in the Pacific Northwest. *Sneaker Wave* is his first novel.